The Star
Fraction

Also by Ken MacLeod

The Star Fraction

Ken MacLeod

TOR®

A TOM DOHERTY ASSOCIATES BOOK
NEW YORK

THE STAR FRACTION

Copyright © 1995 by Ken MacLeod

Introduction copyright © 2001 by Ken MacLeod

First published in Great Britain by Legend Books

This edition edited by Patrick Nielsen Hayden

A Tor Book
Published by Tom Doherty Associates, LLC
175 Fifth Avenue
New York, NY 10010

www.tor.com

Tor® is a registered trademark of Tom Doherty Associates, LLC.

Library of Congress Cataloging-in-Publication Data

MacLeod, Ken.
    The star fraction / Ken MacLeod.
        p. cm.
    "A Tom Doherty Associates book."
    ISBN 0-765-30084-2 (hc)
    ISBN 0-765-30156-3 (pbk)
    1. Twenty-first century—Fiction. 2. Computer programs—Fiction. 3. Great Britain—Fiction. I. Title.

  PR6063.A2515 S73 2001
  823'.914—dc21   2001027120

Printed in the United States of America

0 9 8 7 6 5 4 3

For Carol

Acknowledgments

Thanks to Carol, Sharon and Michael for more than I can say; to Iain Banks, Ron Binns, Mairi Ann Cullen and Nick Fielding for reading early drafts; to Mic Cheetham and John Jarrold for pushing me into two more drafts, as well as for being a good agent and a good editor, respectively.

All of these knew they were helping me with the book. Those who didn't know include Chris Tame, Brian Micklethwaite, Mike Holmes, Tim Starr and Leighton Anderson, all of whom at different times guided me through the pleasures and perils of Libertaria, that fair country of the mind. If at any time I got lost there, it wasn't their fault.

And finally an extra thank-you to Iain for his endless encouragement and enthusiasm, and for help with Locoscript (and Dissembler).

Contents

Introduction to the American Edition

The Star Fraction is the first of the Fall Revolution books and my first novel. I started writing it with no idea of where it would end up, let alone of making it the start of a series. It still isn't: The four books can be read in any order, and the last two of them present alternative possible futures emerging from that midtwenty-first-century world I imagined at the beginning.

In this scenario, a brief Third World War—or War of European Integration, as its instigators call it—in the 2020s is followed by a US/UN hegemony over a balkanized world. The Fall Revolution in the late 2040s is an attempt to throw off this new world order and to reunify fragmented nations. But, as one of the characters says, "What we thought was the revolution was only a moment in the fall." His remark has a theory of history behind it.

History is the trade secret of science fiction, and theories of history are its invisible engine. One such theory is that society evolves because people's relationship with nature tends to change more radically and rapidly than their relationships with each other. Technology outpaces law and custom. From this mismatch, upheavals ensue. Society either moves up to a new stage with more scope for the new technology, or the technology is crushed to fit the confines of the old society. As the technology falls back, so does the society, perhaps to an earlier configuration. In the mainstream of history, however, society has moved forward through a succession of stages, each of which is a stable configuration between the technology people have to work with and their characteristic ways of working together. But this stability contains the seeds of new instabilities. Proponents of this theory argue that the succession of booms and slumps, wars, revolutions, and counterrevolutions, which began in August 1914 and which shows no prospect of an end, indicates that we live in just such an age of upheaval.

This theory is, of course, the Materialist Conception of History, formulated by the pioneering American anthropologist Lewis Henry Morgan and (a little earlier) by the German philosopher Karl Heinrich Marx. These men looked with optimism to a future society and with stern criticism on the present. Property, wrote one of them, "has become, on the part of the people, an unmanageable power. The human mind stands bewildered in the presence of its own creation. The time will come, nevertheless, when human intelligence will rise to the mastery over property. . . . Democracy in government, brotherhood in society, equality in rights and privileges, and universal education, foreshadow the next higher plane of society. . . . "

Beam me up. But before stepping onto the transporter to Morgan's "higher plane," it might be wise to check the specifications. One constraint on the possible arrangements of a future society was indicated by the Austrian economist Ludwig von Mises. He argued that private property was essential to industrial civilization: "without property, no exchange; no exchange, no prices; no prices, no way of telling whether any given project is worthwhile or a dead loss." Given that every attempt to abolish the market on a large scale has led to the collapse of industry, his Economic Calculation Argument seems vindicated. Unfortunately, there's no reason why the Economic Calculation Argument and the Materialist Conception of History couldn't both be true. What if capitalism is unstable, and socialism is impossible?

The Star Fraction is haunted by this uncomfortable question. For me, it was acutely felt when I was writing the book in the late 1980s and early 1990s. As a socialist, I had become interested in the libertarian critique of socialism. The fall of the bureaucratic regimes of the East found me neither surprised nor sorry.

No, what was—and remains—dreadful to contemplate was not the collapse of "actually existing socialism," but the catastrophic consequences of the attempt to introduce actually existing capitalism and the apparent inability of the millions who had brought down the bureaucratic dictatorships to assert and defend their own interests in the aftermath.

In this novel, these issues are seen through the eyes of characters who are flawed and often mistaken but sometimes heroic. The ideologies through which they try to make sense of it all range from British-style "industrial-grade Trotskyism" to American-style "black helicopter" libertarianism. The big questions about history and economics fuel the adventures of angry white guys (and angry black women) with guns, whose actions tip scales bigger than they know. Their world is one where the New World Order is coming to get you, with black helicopters and Men in Black and orbital gun-control lasers.

And then there's all the stuff I made up, which begins on the next page.

I

Smoking Gunman

IT WAS HOT on the roof. Above, the sky was fast-forward: zeppelin fleets of cloud alternating with ragged anarchic flags of black. Bright stars, mil- and comsats, meteors, junk. Moh Kohn crouched behind the parapet and scanned the band of trees half a klick beyond the campus perimeter. Glades down, the dark was a different shade of day. He held the gun loose, swung it smoothly, moved around to keep cool. The building's thermals gave him all the cover he could expect, enough to baffle glades or IR-eyes that far away.

"Gaia, it's hot," he muttered.

"Thirty-one Celsius," said the gun.

He liked hearing the gun. It gave him a wired feeling. Only a screensight read-out, but he heard it with his eyes like Sign.

"What'll it be tonight? Cranks or creeps?"

"Beginning search."

"Stop." He didn't want it racking its memory for an educated guess; he wanted it *looking*. As he was, all the time, for the two major threats to his clients: those who considered anything smarter than a pocket calculator a threat to the human race, and those who considered anything with a central nervous system an honorary member of it.

He'd been scanning the concrete apron, the perimeter wall, the trees for three hours, since 21:00. Relief was due in two. And then he wouldn't just be off-shift, he'd be off-*active*, with a whole week to recover. After seven nights of staring into the darkness, edgy with rumors, jumpy with hoaxes and false alarms, he needed it.

Music and laughter and noise eddied between the buildings behind him, sometimes loud when the speeding air above sent a blast down to ground-level, sometimes—as now, in the hot stillness—faint. He wanted to be *at* that party. If no attack came this watch . . . dammit, even if there *did*. All he had to do was not take incoming fire. Shelling it out was something else, and it wouldn't be the first time he'd dissolved the gray-ghostly night-fight memories and the false colors of cooling blood in drinking and dancing and especially in sex—the great specific, the antithesis and antidote for violence—to the same night's end.

Something moved. Kohn chilled instantly, focusing on a point to his left, where he'd seen . . . There it was again, where the bushes fingered out from the trees. Advance cover. He keyed the weapon's inertial memory and made a quick sweep, stepping the nightsight up ×3. Nothing else visible. Perhaps this was the main push. He turned back and the gun checked his hand at the place it had marked.

And there they were. Two, three—*zoom, key to track*—four, crouching and scurrying. Two with rifles, the others lugging a pack. The best straight-line of their zigzag rush arrowed the Alexsander Institute. The AI block.

Cranks, then. No compunction.

"Do it for Big Blue," he told the gun. He made himself as small as possible behind the parapet, holding the gun awkwardly above it, and aimed by the screensight image patched to his glades. His trigger finger pressed Enter. The weapon took over; it aimed *him*. In a second the head-up image showed four bodies, sprawled, stapled down like X- and Y-chromosomes.

"Targets stunned."

What was it about? Kohn checked the scrolling read-out. The gun had fired five high-velocity slugs of SLIP—skin-contact liquid pentothal. It had put the cranks to sleep. He could have sworn he'd switched to metal rounds.

"HED detected. Timer functioning. Reads: 8:05 . . . 8:04 . . . 8:03 . . ."

"Call Security!"

"Already copied."

Kohn looked over the parapet. Two figures in hard-suits were running across the grass toward the unconscious raiders. He thumbed the Security channel.

"Lookout Five to Ready One, do you copy?"

("7:51.")

("Yes, yes.")

"Ready One to Lookout. Receiving."

"They've got a time bomb with them. Could be booby-trapped."

They stopped so fast he lost sight of them for a moment. Then an unsteady voice said, "Hostiles are alive, repeat alive. Our standing instructions—"

"Fuck *them*!" Kohn screamed. He calmed himself. "Sorry, Ready One. My contract says I override. Get yourselves clear. No dead heroes on my call-out. Shit, it could be dangerous even from there, if it's a daisy-cutter . . . Hey, can you give me a downlink to the UXB system?"

"What hardware you *got* up there, Moh?"

"Enough," Moh said, grinning. The guard took a small apparatus from his backpack and set it on the grass. Kohn adjusted the gun's receiver dishlet, hearing the *ping* of the laser interface. The screensight reformatted.

"OK, you got line-of-sight tight beam, user access." The guards sprinted for cover.

Normally Kohn couldn't have entered this system in a million years, but there's never been any way around the old *quis custodiet* (et cetera) questions. Especially when the *custodes* are in the union.

Fumbling, he keyed numbers into the stock. The gun was picking up electronic spillover from the bomb's circuitry (no great feat; AI-abolitionists didn't really *go* for high tech) and bouncing it via the security guard's commset to British Telecom's on-line bomb-disposal expert system.

"2:20." Then: "No interactive countermeasures possible. Recommend mechanical force."

"What?"

In a distant tower, something like this:

```
IF (MESSAGE-UNDERSTOOD)
THEN; /* DO NOTHING */
ELSE DO;
        CALL RE-PHRASE;
END;
```

"SHOOT THE CLOCK OFF!" relayed the gun, in big green letters.

"Oh. All right."

The gun lined itself up. Kohn fired. The screen cleared and reverted to normal. The gun was on its own now.

"Status?"

"No activity."

He could see that for himself. The pack containing the bomb had jerked as the bullet passed through it. So had one of the bodies.

Kohn felt sick. Ten minutes earlier he'd been annoyed that these people weren't dead. No one, not even his true conscience, would blame him, but the twisted code of combatant ethics revolted at prestunned slaughter. He stood, and looked down at the prone figures, tiny now. The one he'd hit had an arm wound; at the limits of resolution he could see blood oozing rhythmically . . .

Therefore, not dead. Relief flooded his brain. He talked into the chin mike, requesting medicals for the injured hostile. What about the others? Campus Security wanted to know.

"Put them in the bank," Kohn said. "Credit our account."

"Lookout One? What's the name of your account?"

Disarmed, waking from their shots, the attackers were being handled gently. They'd gone from hostile to hostage, and they knew it. An ambulance whined up.

"Oh, yeah," Kohn said. "The Felix Dzerzhinsky Workers' Defense Collective. Nat-Mid-West account 0372 87944."

"Uh-*huh*," muttered the guard's voice. "The Cats."

"Hey!" another voice broke in, ignoring all comm discipline. "We got one of your exes!"

"Lookout One to unidentified," Kohn said firmly. "Clarify message."

"Red Crescent truck to Lookout, repeat. Patient Catherin Duvalier has employment history of work on your team."

Catherin Duvalier. *Gee Suss*! "One of your exes," indeed.

"She was freelancing," Kohn lied. "Where are you taking her?"

"Hillingdon Hospital. You want her released on recovery?"

"Like hell," Kohn choked. "Don't even put her in the bank. We're *keeping* her this time."

"Secure ward, got you." The medics slammed the rear door and leapt into the ambulance, which screamed off around the perimeter road like they had a brain to save. Fucking cowboys. Subcontractors for the Muslim Welfare Association in Ruislip. Probably trained by veterans of Cairo. Always assume incoming . . .

Behind him he heard a heavy, dull *crump* and the song of falling glass. "You missed the backup fuse," he snarled at the gun and himself as he flattened to the roof. But then, in the sudden babble in his phones, he realized it was not his bomb.

The crank raid had been a diversion after all.

Janis Taine lay in bed for a few minutes after the diary woke her. Her mouth was dry, thick with the aftertaste of ideas that had colored her dreams. Just outside her awareness floated the thought that she had an important day ahead. She kept it there and tried to tease the ideas back. They might be relevant.

No. Gone.

She swallowed. Perhaps, despite all precautions, minute traces of the hallucinogens at the lab infiltrated her bloodstream, just enough to give her vivid, elusive but seemingly significant dreams? More worryingly, she thought as she swung her legs out of bed with a swish of silk pajamas and felt around for her slippers, maybe the drugs gave her what seemed perfectly reasonable notions, sending her off down dead ends as convoluted as the molecules themselves . . . Par for the course. Bloody typical. Everything got everywhere. These days you couldn't keep things separate even in your mind. If we could *only disconnect*—

She heard the most pleasant mechanical sound in the world, the whirr of a coffeegrinder. "Pour one for me," she called as she padded to the bathroom. Sonya's reply was inarticulate but sounded positive.

It was an important day so she brushed her teeth. Not exactly necessary—she'd had her anticaries shots at school like everybody else, and some people went around with filthy but perfect mouths—but a little effort didn't hurt. She looked at herself critically as she smoothed a couple of layers of sun cream over her face and hands. Bouncy auburn hair, green eyes (nature had had a little encouragement there), skin almost perfectly pale. Janis brushed a touch of pallor over the slight ruddiness of her cheeks and decided she looked great.

Sonya, her flatmate, was moving around in the kitchen like a doll with its power running down, an impression heightened by her blond curls and short blue nightdress.

"Wanna taab?"

Janis shuddered. "No thanks."

"Zhey're great. Wakesh you up jusht like zhat." She was making scrambled eggs on toast for three.

"Gaia bless you," said Janis, sipping coffee. "How much sleep *have* you had?"

Sonya looked at the clock on the cooker and fell into a five-second trance of mental arithmetic.

"Two hours. I was at one of your campus discos. It was phenomenome . . . fucking great. Got off with this guy."

"I was kind of wondering about the third portion," Janis said, and immediately regretted it because another glacial calculation ensued, while the toast burned. The guy in question appeared shortly afterward: tall, black and handsome. He seemed wide awake without benefit of a tab, unobtrusively helpful to Sonya. His name was Jerome and he was from Ghana.

After breakfast Janis went into her bedroom and started throwing clothes from her wardrobe onto the bed. She selected a pleated white blouse, then hesitated with a long skirt in one hand and a pair of slate calf-length culottes in the other.

"Sonya," she called, interrupting the others' murmuring chat, "you using the car today?"

Sonya was. On your bike, Janis. So, culottes. She eyed the outfit. Dress to impress and all that, but it still wasn't quite *sharp* enough. She sighed.

"Sorry to bother you, Sonya," she said wearily. "Can you help me into my stays?"

*　　*　　*

"You can breathe in now," Sonya said. She fastened the cord. "You'll knock them out."

"If I don't expire myself . . . Hey, what's the matter?"

Sonya's hand went to her mouth, came away again.

"Oh, Janis, you'll kill me. I totally forgot. You're seeing some committee today, yeah?"

"Yeah."

"I just remembered. Last night, at the disco. There was some fighting."

"At the disco?"

"No, I mean there was an *attack*. On a lab somewhere. We heard shots, an explosion—"

"Oh *shit!*" Janis tightened her belt viciously, stepped into her shoes. "Do you know what one it—?"

Sonya shook her head. "I just overheard some guy later. Sitting at a table by himself, drinking and talking—about, uh, bloody cranks, I think."

"Oh." Some of Janis's tension eased. She smiled quizzically. "This guy was talking to himself?"

"Oh, no!" Sonya sounded put out at the suggestion that she'd been eavesdropping on a loony. "He was talking to his *gun*."

The night's muggy heat had given way to a sharp, clear autumn morning. Janis pedaled through the streets of Uxbridge, slowly so as not to break sweat. An AWACS plane climbed low from Northolt, banked and headed west, toward Wales. The High Street looked untouched by the troubles, a cozy familiarity of supermarkets and wine bars and drug dens and video shops, vast mirrored frontages of office blocks behind. Around the roundabout and along the main road past the RAF barracks (DANGER: MINES), swing right into Kingston Lane. Usual early-morning traffic—a dozen buses, all different companies, milk-floats, water-floats, APCs flying the Hanoverian pennant from their aerials . . .

In through the security gates, scanned and frisked by sensors. The sign above the games announced:

BRUNEL UNIVERSITY AND SCIENCE PARK plc
WARNING
FREE SPEECH ZONE

She rode along the paths, steering clear of snails making suicidal dashes for greener grass. On one lawn a foraging party of students moved slowly, stooped, looking for magic mushrooms. Some of them would be for her.

Janis smiled to herself, feeling like a great lady watching her peasants. Which the students looked like, in their sweeping skirts or baggy trousers and poke bonnets or broad-brimmed hats, patiently filling baskets.

In the wall of the ground floor of the biology block a three-meter hole gaped like an exit wound.

Janis dismounted, wheeled the bike mechanically to its stand. She'd half expected this, she now realized. Her hands flipped up her lace veil and twisted it back around the crown of her hat. Up the stairs: two flights, forty steps. The corridor tiles squeaked.

The door had been crudely forced; the lock hung from splinters. A strip of black-and-yellow tape warned against entry. She backed away, shaken. The last time she'd seen a door like this it had opened on smashed terminals, empty cages, shit-daubed messages of driveling hate.

Behind her somebody coughed. It was not a polite cough; more an uncontrollable spasm. She jumped, then turned slowly as reason caught up with reflex. A man stood leaning forward, trying to look alert but obviously tired. Tall. Thin features. Dark eyes. Skin that might have acquired its color from genes or a sunlamp. He wore a dark gray urban-camo jumpsuit open at the throat, Docs, a helmet jammed on longish curly black hair; some kind of night-vision glasses pushed up over the front, straps dangling, phones and mike angling from its sides. He looked about thirty, *quite* a bit older than her, but that might just have been the light. A long, complicated firearm hung in his right hand.

"Who are you?" he asked. "And what are you doing here?"

"That's just what I was about to ask *you*. I'm Janis Taine and this is my lab. Which it seems was broken into last night. Now—"

He raised a finger to his lips, motioned to her to back off. She was ten paces down the corridor before he stepped forward and scanned the door with the gun. His lips moved. He put his back to the wall beside the door and poked it open with the gun muzzle. A thin articulated rod shot out of the weapon and extended into the lab. After a moment it came back, and the man stepped forward, turning. He swept the tape away from the door and shook it off his hand after several attempts. He glanced at her and disappeared into the room.

"It's OK," she heard him call; then another bout of coughing.

The lab was as she'd left it. A high-rise block of cages, a terminal connected to the analyzer, a bench, fume cupboard, glassware, tall fridge-freezer—which stood open. The man was standing in front of it, looking down at the stock of his gun, puzzled. He coughed, flapping his free hand in front of his mouth.

"Air's lousy with psychoactive volatiles," he said.

Janis almost pushed him aside. The test tubes racked in the fridges were neatly lined up, labels turned to the front as if posed for a photograph. Which they might very well have been. No way had she left them like that. Each—she was certain—was a few milliliters short.

"Oh, *shit!*"

Everything gets everywhere . . .

"What's the problem? The concentrations aren't dangerous, are they?"

"Let's have a look. Where did you get this? No, they shouldn't be, it's just—well, it may have completely fucked up my experiments. The controls won't be worth a damn now."

She suddenly realized she was cheek-to-cheek with him, peering at a tiny screen as if they were colleagues. She moved away and opened a window, turned on the fume cupboard. Displacement activity. Useless.

"Who are you, anyway?"

"Oh. Sorry." He flipped the gun into his left hand and pulled himself straight, held out his right.

"Name's Moh Kohn. I'm a security mercenary."

"You're a bit late on the scene."

He frowned as they shook hands.

"Slight misunderstanding there. I was on a different patch last night. I'm just dropping by. Who's responsible for guarding this block?"

Janis shrugged into her lab coat and sat on a bench.

"Office Security Systems, last time I noticed."

"Kelly girls," Kohn sneered. He pulled up a chair and slumped in it, looked up at her disarmingly.

"Mind if I smoke?"

"I don't." She didn't. She didn't give a damn anymore. "And thanks, I don't."

He fingered out a packet of Benson & Hedges Moscow Gold and lit up.

"That stuff's almost as bad for you as tobacco," Janis couldn't forbear to point out.

"Sure. Life expectancy in my line's fifty-five and falling, so who gives a shit?"

"Your line? Oh, defense. So why do that?"

"It's a living." Kohn shrugged.

He laid a card on the lab bench beside her. "That's us. Research establishments, universities, worthy causes a speciality."

Janis examined the hologrammed business card suspiciously.

"You're Commies?"

Kohn inhaled deeply, held his breath for seconds before replying.

"Sharp of you to notice. Some of us are, but the main reason we picked

the name was so we'd sound really heavy but, you know, right-on. Later—
when we could afford market research—we found out most people thought
Felix Dzerzhinsky was in the Bolshoi, not the Bolsheviks."

Janis spread her hands.

"Doesn't mean anything to me," she said. "It was just the 'Workers'
Defense' bit. I'm not into . . . all that. In my experience politics is guys
with guns ripping me off at roadblocks."

"Aha," Kohn said. He looked like the THC was getting to him. "A liberal.
Maybe even a libertarian. Remember school?"

"What?"

He gave her a disconcertingly objective look.

"Maybe the first couple years of primary school, for you." He raised his
right hand. " 'I pledge allegiance to the flag of the United Republic, and to
the States for which it stands, three nations, individual—' "

"Jesus Christ! Will you *shut up!*"

Janis actually found herself looking over her shoulder. It had been
years—

"I thought this was an F S Zee," Kohn said mildly.

"High treason is taking it a bit far!"

"OK. So I won't ask you if you've ever, *ever* consciously and publicly
repudiated that. I haven't."

"You're not—?"

Janis glanced sidelong, swiveled her eyes back.

"ANR? Good goddess no. They're *terrorists*, Doctor. We are a legal co-op
and, uh, to be honest I'm touting for business. Now, just what has been
going on here?"

She told him, briefly, while she did her rounds. At least the mice were
all right. Apart from her precious drug-free controls being stoned out of
their little skulls.

"Very odd. I thought it was creeps when it happened—you know, animal
liberationists. Doesn't look like that," he remarked.

"You said it."

"Mind you—this isn't what I imagined an animal-research lab would
look like."

Janis stopped feeding cornflakes to the mice for a moment.

"What did you expect? Monkeys with trodes in their heads? Do you
know what monkeys *cost?*"

"Marmosets thirty K," said a tiny, tinny voice. "Rhesus macaques fifty
K, chimps two hundred—"

"Oh, shut up, gun." Kohn's face reddened. "Didn't even know the damn
thing had a speaker. I must have thought it was a mike."

"An easy mistake." She was struggling not to laugh.

Kohn moved on quickly: "What do you do, anyway, if that's not an awkward question?"

"It's no secret. Basically we dose the mice with various drugs to see if they act any smarter."

"Smarter?" he said. *"Mice?"*

"Faster learning. Longer attention span. Greater retention."

Kohn looked away for a moment, looked back. "You're talking about memory drugs." His voice was flat.

"Of course."

"Any success?"

"Well," she said, "there *was* one batch that looked promising, but they built a little paper hang glider and escaped through that window . . . Naw, all we've had is stoned rodents. They take even longer to run the mazes. A result some of us could take to heart. Still . . . we're like Edison. We ransack nature. And unlike him we have computers to give us variations that nature hasn't come up with."

"Who's paying for it?"

"Now *that*'s a secret. I don't know. But a team from a front for a subsidiary for an agency of whoever it is will be here in—oh god, an hour, so would you mind?"

Kohn looked embarrassed again. "Sorry, Doctor Taine. I'll get out of your way, I'm behind schedule myself. I have to, uh, visit someone in hospital and then release some prisoners."

"I'm sure." She smiled at him indulgently, dismissively. "Bye. Oh, and I will ask our admin to check out your rates."

"Thank you," he said. "You'll find we're very competitive." He stood up and patted his gun. "Let's go."

When he'd gone she had the nagging feeling that more than one person had left.

The hand writhed, gesticulated autonomously as if to accompany an entirely different conversation. Plastic sheathed the forearm. A drip-feed and a myoelectric cable looped away from it.

Kohn sat on the bedside chair fiddling with the torn sleeve of Catherin Duvalier's denim jacket. It had been washed and pressed, but not repaired, leaving an image of what his shot had done to the flesh and bone inside. The nurses' quick soft steps, the steady pacing of the guards, set off alarms in his nerves. Again and again, in the secure ward, insecure. Catherin's clear blue eyes, in her light-black face with its surrounding sunburst of springy fair hair, accused.

Defensive, Kohn attacked first.

"I have to ask you," he said heavily, "just what you think you were doing in that attack squad?"

She smiled from far away. "What were you doing, defending that place?"

"Doing my job. Only giving orders. You know where it's at . . . Cat."

She winced. The nickname was her own, but one they'd all shared, as a collective named after what some people, as he'd told the scientist, thought was a ballet dancer, some thought was a cartoon cat, and only a handful recognized as the founder of a once highly successful security agency. A fine company they were, and—in her ideas, her ferocity, her speed—she'd held out the promise of becoming one of the best. Defending union offices and opposition demonstrations against the lumpen muscle men of the Hanoverian regime, she was someone Kohn had been glad to have at his back. Success had brought more contracts—plenty of establishments needed security which the security forces, occupied with their own protection, couldn't supply. But, one night a couple of years ago, she'd been on a squad that took out a Green Brigade sabotage team on behalf of some multinational. As the Green Brigade regarded that company's employees as fair game and had dozens of workers' deaths in its debit column, Kohn hadn't given the contract a second's thought.

Catherin had rejected her blood money and walked out.

She and Kohn had been lovers, before. A classic case: their eyes had met across a crowded fight. It was like hitting it off at a disco. They were both *having fun*. Some shock of recognition at the preconscious, almost the prehuman, level. He'd once joked that the australopithecine ancestors had come in two types, robust and gracile: "I've got *robustus* genes," he'd said. "But you're definitely *gracilis*." Just a romantic conceit: those slender limbs, tough muscles under skin that still ravished him just to look at; that face prettily triangular, wide eyes and small bright teeth—they'd been built by genes recombined out of a more recent history, crossing and recrossing the Atlantic in everything from slave ships to international brigades . . . a thoroughly modern girl.

Dear *gracilis*. He'd missed her at his back, and he'd missed her everywhere else. The word was that she was working for other co-ops, more purist outfits that took only politically sound contracts. Kohn had wished her luck and hoped to see her again. He'd never expected to find her in his sights.

Her hand, moved by the muscles that tirelessly reknit the shattered radius and ulna, beckoned and dismissed.

"You don't understand," she said. "I'm still on the same side." She looked around. "Can we talk?"

"Sure." Kohn waved airily. "The guards are screened for all that."

He didn't believe it for a moment.

Catherin looked relieved. She started talking, low and fast.

"You know it's gonna be a hot autumn. The ANR's planning another of its final offensives. Believe that when I see it, but the Kingdom's for sure under pressure, from the Greens and the Nationalists and the Muslims and the Black Zionists as well as the workers' movements. Right now it's fighting them all, and the stupider of the Free States're fighting each other. So— you know, the party?"

"The real party?" Stupid question.

"No, the *Labour* party. There's been a conference, over in—well, over the water. Bringing all the party factions together, and some of the movements. Decided on joint actions with all the forces actually fighting the state, all those who want to undo the Restoration Settlement."

"I know about the Left Alliance. I didn't know the cranks were part of it."

She returned him a level look.

"You just don't know what they're up to in these AI labs, do you? Their idea of a glorious future is a universe crawling with computers that'll remember us. Which is what those nerds think *life* is all about. Meanwhile the state's using them, just like the Nazis used the rocket freaks. They're itching to get their hands on some kind of intelligent system that'll keep tabs on everything. And it's all linked up with the other lot, the NC guys."

"NC?"

"Natural Computing. Some of the big companies and armies are trying to get a handle on ways to enhance human intelligence, connect it directly with large-scale integration on the machine side. Sinister stuff like that."

" 'Sinister stuff?' I can't believe I'm *hearing* this shit. Christ, woman! I've just been in one these mad-evil-scientist laboratories, and they're still trying things out on mice! The cranks are out to wreck the datasphere, and one day they might just do it. There's just no way the Left should do deals with those shitwits. It's madness."

"They've no chance of shutting down the whole thing, and you know it," Cat said. "But they're damn good at sabbing, they're brave and resourceful, and we need those skills to hit the state."

Kohn jumped to his feet.

"Yeah, right, and they need you to give them hardware support. Who's using who in this campaign? Greens onside too, huh? Got the comrades helping to take out some of that evil technology? Know their way around the factories—yeah, fucking great."

"We've all fought alongside people we didn't exactly see eye to eye with." She smiled, almost tenderly, almost conspiratorially. " 'There is only one party, the Party of God,' remember?"

Kohn struggled momentarily with the politics of that particular past conflict and found it was all either too simple or too complicated.

"The Muslims are civilized," he said. "The gang you were with are enemies of humanity."

Catherin shrugged, with one shoulder. "At the moment they're the enemies of our enemies, and that's what counts. That's what's always counted."

There were times when Kohn loathed the Left, when some monstrous stupidity almost, but never quite, outweighed the viciousness and venality of the system they opposed. Ally with the barbarians against the patricians and praetorians . . . think again, proletarians!

"What does the ANR think of this brilliant tactic?"

Catherin's face warped into scorn.

"They're being macho and sectarian and elitist as usual. Anyone who wants to fight the Hanoverian state should go through the proper channels—them!"

That was a relief. The Army of the New Republic had an almost mythical status on the Left. Claiming the legitimacy of the final emergency session of the Federal Assembly (held in an abandoned factory in Dagenham while the US/UN teletroopers closed in), it fought the Hanoverians and, it sometimes seemed, everybody else.

"They're history," Catherin said. "And if your little gang of mercenaries can't get it together to stop defending legitimate targets, you are too."

Kohn felt old. She was just a kid, that was what it was. Too young to remember the United Republic, hating the Hanoverian regime so much that any alliance against it seemed only common sense . . . There had to be more, you had to hold onto some sense of direction, even if it was only a thread. Growing up in the Greenbelt shantytowns, Moh had learned that from his father. A fifth-generation Fourth Internationalist, paying out the thread, the thin line of words that connected past to future. *The party is the memory of the class*, he used to say; meanwhile, the workers of the world did anything and everything except unite. Now he, Gaia shield his soul, had thought the Republic a rotten unstable compromise, but that didn't stop him fighting to save it when the US/UN came in . . . welcomed, of course, by cheering crowds.

Kohn had no illusions. Most of the opposition would welcome the broadening of the Alliance, even if they saw it as only tactical and technical—a joint action here, a bit of covering fire there. The price would be that the list of legitimate targets would become a good deal longer. His co-op had lived by defending what he still saw as the seeds of progress—the workers' organizations and the scientists and, if necessary, the capitalists—against the enemies of that modern industry on which all their conflicting hopes relied. The delicate balance, the ecological niche for the Cats, would be gone. For the first time he understood all that his father had meant by *betrayal*.

His rage focused on the wounded woman.

"You're free to go," he told her. "I'm not claiming ransom. I'm not hostage-swapping. Not pressing charges in any currency. I'll clear you from our account."

She sank back into the pillow.

"You can't *do* this to me!"

"Watch my legs."

He stalked out, leaving her free. Unemployed and unemployable. Only burned-out, squeezed-dry traitors, double and triple agents several times over, were ever released unconditionally.

At the time he thought it just.

2

Evidence for Aeroplanes

TOMORROW, JORDAN THOUGHT, tomorrow he would start to live rationally. Tomorrow he would make the break, walk out and leave them, let them weep or curse. Light out for North London Town. *Norlonto's free*, the whisper ran. *You can get anything with money. Force has no purchase there.*

He had thought the same thing on hundreds of previous days.

Jordan Brown was seventeen years old and fizzing with hormones and hate. He lived in North London, but not Norlonto, not North London Town. The area where he lived had once been called Islington, and bits of it lapped into other former boroughs. It bordered Norlonto in a high-intensity contrast between freedom and slavery, war and peace, ignorance and strength. Which was which depended on whose side you were on. They called this area Beulah City. God was in charge. Except . . .

> *The earth belongs unto the Lord*
> *and all that it contains*
> *except for the West Highland piers*
> *for they belong to MacBraynes.*

His grandmother had told him that mildly blasphemous variant on a psalm when he was a little kid, teasing the limits of propriety. Even his father had laughed, briefly. It expressed a truth about their own time, a truth about the Cable. The Elders did their best to censor and exclude the unclean, the doubtful in the printed word, but there was damn all they could do about the Cable, the fiber-optic network that the godless Republic had piped to every corner of every building in what was then a land, linking them to the world. The autonomy of all the Free States, the *communities under the king*, depended on free access to it. You could do without it as easily as you could do without air and water, and nobody even tried anymore.

Jordan stood for a moment on the steps of his family's three-story house at the top of Crouch Hill. To his left he could see Alexandra Palace, the outer limit of another world. He knew better than to give it more than a glance. *Norlonto's free . . .*

The air was as cold as water. He clattered down the steps and turned right, down the other side of the hill. Behind him the holograms above the Palace faded in the early sun. In his mind, they burned.

The lower floor of the old warehouse near Finsbury Park was a gerbil's nest of fiber-optics. Jordan glimpsed their tangled, pulsing gleam between the treads of the steel stairs he hammered up every morning. Most of Beulah City's terminals had information filters elaborately hardwired in, to ensure that they presented a true and correct vision of the world, free from the biases and distortions imposed by innumerable evil influences. Because those evils could not be altogether ignored, a small fraction of the terminals had been removed from private houses and businesses, their cables carefully coiled back and back, out of freshly reopened trenches and conduits, and installed at a dozen centers where their use could be monitored. This one held about a hundred in its upper loft, a skylit maze of paper partitions.

Jordan pushed open the swing doors. The place at that moment had a churchy quiet. Most of the workers would arrive half an hour later: draftsmen, writers, artists, designers, teachers, software techs, business execs, theologians. Jordan filled a china mug from the coffee machine—Salvadorean, but he couldn't do anything about that—and walked carefully to his workstation.

The night trader, MacLaren, stood up, signing off and spinning the seat to Jordan. In his twenties, already slowing.

"Beijing's down," he said. "Vladivostok and Moscow up a few points, Warsaw and Frankfurt pretty shaky. Keep an eye on pharmaceuticals."

"Thanks." Jordan slid into his seat, put down his coffee and waved as he clocked in.

"God go with ya," MacLaren mumbled. He picked up his parka and left. Jordan keyed the screen to a graphic display of the world's stock markets. Screens were another insult: they didn't trust you to use kit they couldn't see over your shoulder. He blew at the coffee and munched at the bacon roll he'd bought on the way in, watched the gently rolling sea of wavy lines. As the picture formed in his mind he brought up prices for Beulah City's own products, dancing like grace notes, like color-coded corks.

Stock-exchange speculation was not what it was about, though he and MacLaren sometimes kidded each other that it was. Beulah City imported textiles and information and chemicals, sold clothes and software and specialized medicines. Jordan and MacLaren, and Debbie Jones on the evening shift, handled sales and purchasing for a good fraction of its companies, missions and churches. Serious stock trading was the prerogative of the Deacons and JOSEPH, their ethical investment expert system, but Jordan's small operation was free to risk its own fees on the market. Beulah City's biggest current commercial success was Modesty, a fashion house that ran the local rag trade and also sold clothes-making programs for CAD/CAM sewing machines. They'd enjoyed an unexpected boom in the post-Islamist countries while ozone depletion kept European sales of cover-up clothing buoyant—though here sun cream competed. Sun cream was not quite sound, and anyway the ungodly had it sewn up.

MacLaren had had a good night in Armenia. Jordan turned west and called up Xian Educational Software in New York.

"What you offering?" XES asked.

Jordan scanned the list of products scrolling down his screen's left margin.

"Creation astronomy kit, includes recent spaceprobe data, latest cosmogonies refuted. Suitable for high-school use; grade-school simplification drops out. One-twenty a copy."

"WFF approved?"

Jordan exploded the spec. The World Fundamentalist Federation logo, a stylized Adam and Eve, shone at top right. That meant it could be sold to Jewish and Muslim as well as Christian literalists: all the people of the book, the chapter, the verse, the word, the letter, the jot, the title.

"Affirm."

"We'll take fifty thousand, an option on exclusive."

Jordan hit a playback key: "God BLESS you!!"

"Have a nice eternity."

Go to hell. He punched a code. The software to produce exactly 5×10^4 copies of *Steady State? The Spectra Say No!* became a microwave burst. And there *was* light, Jordan thought. Oh, yeah. *He made the stars also.* They'd racked and stretched that line, tortured a whole cosmology, a whole philosophy of science out of it, until it had confessed all, admitted everything: it was a put-up job; the sky was a scam, a shop-front operation; the stars had lied about their age. The universe as afterthought, its glory an illusory afterimage . . . *there* was the blasphemy, there the heresy, the lie in the right hand, the spitting in Creation's face! He tilted his baseball cap and looked up at the sky beyond the tinted roof. A contrail drew a clean white line across the ravaged clouds. Jordan smiled to himself. *In this sign conquer.* Some folk believed in UFOS. He believed in aeroplanes.

He bought shares in Da Nang Phytochemicals, sold them midmorning at 11 percent just before a rumor of NVC activity in the Delta sent the stock sharply down. He shifted the tidy sum into a holding account and was scanning for fashion buyers in Manila when the graphics melted and ran into a face. A middle-aged man's kindly, craggy face, smiling like a favorite uncle. The lips moved soundlessly, subtitles sliding along the bottom line. A conspiratorial whisper of small alphanumerics:

hi there jordan this is your regional resources coordinator

Oh, my God! A Black Planner!

i'm the legitimate authority around here but i don't suppose that cuts much smack with you still i have a proposition you may find interesting.

Jordan fought the impulse to look over his shoulder, the impulse to hit the security switch and get himself off the hook.

don't worry this is untraceable our sleeper viruses have survived 20 years of electronic counterinsurgency all you have to do is make this purchase from guangzhou textiles and a sale of same to the account now at top left at cost if you key the code now at top right into the cash machine at the end of the street at 12:05 plus or minus 10 minutes you will find a small recompense in used notes i understand you have a holographic memory so i say goodbye and i hope i see you again.

The markets came back. Jordan saw his hands quiver. Until now the Black Plan had been a piece of urban folklore, the phantom hitchhiker of the Cable, a rumored leftover of the Republic's political economy just as the ANR was the remnant of its armed forces. Allegedly it godfathered the ANR, scorning the checkpoint taxes and protection rackets of the community militias; fiendish financial viruses were supposed to haunt the core of the system, warping the country's—some said, the world's—economy to the distant ends of the fallen regime . . .

He'd never given the legend any credit.

Now it was offering him cash.

Untraceable digital cash, converted into untraceable paper money, something he'd never got his hands on before. Only the privileged had access to hard currency; for anything outside of business, Jordan had to make do with shekels, BC's crummy funny money.

Guangzhou was busy. Try again.

He sold a Filipino a thousand gowns and let the remittance hover. Just borrowing, really. Not theft. No real conscience. Only following rules. Suppose it's a trap? A little provocateur program to sniff out embezzlement and dangerous disloyalty? He could always say . . . A long, rambling, stammering defense spooled through his mind, shaming him. Intellectually he understood perfectly what the problem was: guilt and doubt, the waste products of innocence and faith, inhibited him and filled him with self-loathing even at his own weakness in trying to be free of them.

Born in sin and shapen in iniquity.

Guangzhou had a line. He made the purchase, transferred it instantly to the account as specified. And it paid him. It was as if the money had never been away. He put it in the proper account and took the correct fee. No harm done. The time was 1108.

Someone tapped his shoulder. He turned, his features reflexively composed.

Mrs. Lawson smiled down at him.

"Take ten?"

A small, bustling middle-aged woman in black and white, no makeup, no guile or allure. She worked for Audit. Smart as a snake, like the man said, and no way harmless as a pigeon. Jordan had a momentary vision of head-butting her and making a dash for it. A dash for where?

He nodded and logged off, followed as her hem swept a path to her office. An audit trail.

"Coffee?"

"Yes, please."

He sat awkwardly in the chair in the corner of the tiny office. The upright reclined so he couldn't sit back without sprawling, and sitting on the edge made it difficult to look relaxed. Mrs. Lawson had a swivel chair behind a pine desk. Stacks of printout. Monitor screens like the eyes of lizards. Cacti in pots along the window.

She steepled her fingers. "I've been keeping an eye on you, Jordan." She giggled. "Not in a way that would worry my husband! You're a sharp lad, you know . . . No, don't look so bashful. It's not pride to be aware of your strengths. You do have an instinct, a feel for the way the markets move. I hope you'll move up a bit yourself, perhaps consider joining one of the larger businesses. However, I'm not going to offer you a job."

Another giggle. Jordan's back crawled.

"Except . . . in a way, I suppose I am. Have you noticed anything *out of the ordinary* in the system recently?"

This is it, he thought. Maybe there is a God after all, who leads you into temptation, then delivers you to evil.

"Yes, I have," Jordan said. "Only this morning, a Black Planner made me an offer—"

Mrs. Lawson laughed, almost spilling her coffee.

"Of course, of course. And in my desk I have a piece of the authentic Turin Shroud! No, seriously, Jordan, I'm talking about any kind of pattern you may have noticed in things like, oh, subsystem crashes, transaction delays, severe degradation of response-time unrelated to major obvious activity? Anything that seems like interventions, where none of the central banks are involved? To be honest, we can't find any evidence from the Exchange Commissions of"—she waved her hands—"anything suspicious, but several of the smaller communities have a theory that something is loose in the system, using it for ulterior noncommercial purposes in a way that shows up only at the, uh, grass-roots level."

"What you might call 'outsider dealing'?"

Mrs. Lawson looked startled.

"That's exactly what we do call it. Unfortunately it's led to rumors, very unhealthy rumors, of—you know. A word to the wise, Jordan. I wouldn't repeat that little joke of yours if I were you."

Jordan nodded vigorously, making wiping motions with his hands.

"Very good, my dear. Now: you will keep alert for anything that goes against your intuition as to how the market should behave, won't you? And I suppose you're keen to get back to work, so thank you for your time."

It was 11:25.

He logged on, getting his password wrong a couple of times. The queue of orders filled one and a half screens. Jordan closed his eyes and breathed deeply, flexed his fingers and got to work. He didn't think about anything.

Janis hardly listened to herself as she rattled through the outlines of what she knew of the project. She was thinking that there was something oddly disproportionate about her part in it: the more she thought about it, the more important it seemed, and that didn't jibe at all with the level of resources applied . . . You didn't want a struggling post-doc on this, you wanted a team, lots of lab techs, equipment thrown at it like ammunition. She might be part of a team without knowing it—that was her favored hypothesis at the moment. With every government nervously restricting biological research, confining it to F S Zees and science parks, with big corporations looking over their shoulders at consumer groups and junk-science lawsuits, and with green terrorists topping up the restrictions with direct action—with all that, life science was itself becoming an underground guerrilla activity. (She'd often wondered just what molecule or compound was responsible for hysteria and ineducability in the middle classes: it must have seeped into the food chain sometime in the nineteen-sixties, and become ever more concentrated since.)

Hell, maybe the backers were poor, maybe there wasn't some giant corporation or institution behind this after all . . . maybe the three men in front of her were the *whole thing*; what the front concealed was that it wasn't a front; What You See Is What You Get . . . True enough, the rest of the project was almost virtual—robot molecular analyses, computer molecular designs, automatic molecular production. It relied heavily on two techniques, parallel but almost precisely opposite. Genetic algorithms enabled random variations to be selected, varied, selected again in an analog of Darwinian evolution, against a model of known chemical pathways in the human brain, which ICI-Bayer rented out at a few marks a nanosecond; like, *cheap*. Polymerase chain reactions enabled the selected molecules to be replicated in any necessary quantity, a process so thoroughly automated that the only human intervention required was washing out the kit.

But, ultimately, the product had to be tested in a living animal, and raw stuff from nature had to be tried out for potential; and at both ends of the cycle stood herself and a lot of white mice.

"So perhaps you could give us a demonstration of your methods, Doctor Taine?"

Janis had a momentary fellow-feeling with a mouse in a maze: trapped and frantic. She had removed the door from the lab, lugged it to a skip, made sure the representatives of her sponsors entered by the side of the block away from the damaged wall. It wasn't that she intended to fudge the results, ignore the contamination and hope for the best. She fully intended to sacrifice the mice and start afresh. It was just that there wasn't time to do it before she had to demonstrate her competence, and she was afraid that, if she had nothing to demonstrate, the sponsors would sacrifice *her* and start afresh. She saw a fleeting, mad vision of what she would do if they ever found out—throw it all up and become a creep, wear plastic and live off the land and break into psychology labs and free the flatworms, blow up whale ships to save the krill . . .

Three men in dark suits looked at her. She tried not to think of the many jokes beginning *There was a Pole, a German and a Russian* . . . Gently, she took a mouse from one of the cages and placed it in the entry to the maze. It sniffed around the little space, squeaking.

"We have here a subject: the *s*, as we call it. In a moment I'll open the entry door and it'll attempt to find a way through this maze of transparent tubing. All the subjects—the experimentals and the controls—have already learned a path through the maze. The experimentals have received mild doses of the various preparations in their water, taken *ad libitum*. This particular subject is one of a group which has received a locally obtained psylocibe derivative. The mean time hitherto has been around seventy seconds—"

"For both the experimentals and the controls?" the Pole asked.

Janis released the entry lever and the mouse sauntered down the pipe. "Yes. I don't wish to obscure the fact that, so far, the null hypothesis—"

ping

The *s* had pressed the switch at the end of the maze and was nibbling its reinforcer, a square centimeter of marmalade toast. The timer, wired to the exit lever and the reward switch, stood at 32 seconds.

Silently, Janis removed the mouse and tried again with a control.

She ran through a dozen variations: mice doped with betel juice, opiates, coca, caffeine . . .

It wasn't a fluke, the psylocibe-heads were consistently twice as fast, way outside even experimenter effect.

She stared at the men, puzzled.

"I must set up some double-blind protocols," she said. "Up to now, frankly, it hasn't been worth it. At least, I assume you were interested in *major* effects."

"We certainly are," said the German. "And this isn't a new preparation?"

"Cumulative?" said the Russian when Janis shook her head.

"It's possible. Obviously, more . . ."

"Research is necessary, huh?"

They all laughed.

She worried that they'd think it was a setup, lowering their expectations like that and then producing something so interesting; but no, they were sold on it. Her contract was renewed for six months; she was to take on a technician, check out all the possibilities.

As she escorted them down the corridor the Russian sniffed. He nudged her.

"Is maybe not patriotic," he said, "but the Lebanese is better, no?"

She smiled back at him blankly, then quickened her pace to hide her blush.

Oh shit.

Fonthill Road, center of the garment district. Great automatic factories spun and wove, cut and stitched in towers of glass and steel. The car-free street thronged with people who all, especially the women, seemed to Jordan to take up far too much space: jammed with bustles, he thought dourly as he skirted crinolines, ducked under parasols, maneuvered around trains. Modesty's own window displays—with their fractal chintzes, Mandelbrot paisleys and swathes of computer-generated lace applied as if with a spray gun to every conceivable garment surface and trim—looked tasteful and restrained against the styles of the Bible belts of Florida, Liberia and everywhere else that everybody's daughter wanted to look like a televangelist's wife.

Four minutes after noon. Five people ahead of him in the queue for the Bundesbank cashpoint at the corner of Seven Sisters Road. Jordan shuffled and fumed, stared over their heads at the Fuller domes of the old development area. He keyed in the number at 12:13. The machine labored and muttered to itself for forty finger-drumming seconds, then coughed and spat out a thick wad of crumpled currency. And another, and again.

Jordan snatched them up and almost ran off while the screen was still offering a succession of financial services in what seemed increasingly desperate pleas to get the money back.

Back at the office building he headed straight for the toilet and locked himself away in a lavatory stall. He knew he was safe there—say what you like about the Elders, they were genuine about certain kinds of privacy. It was understood that God was watching. Jordan suddenly discovered that he really needed to shit. He sat down and counted the money. Four thousand Britische marks. He felt the blood leave his head, his bowels turn to water.

The B-mark was the hardest of hard currencies—only Norlonto used it internally, and even there four thousand would last a couple of months. In the community economies you could get laughable sums of funny money for it, even after bribing the guards. For a hundred B-marks your average checkpoint charlie would sell you his Kalashnikov and probably his sister's address.

Jordan stared at the white paint of the stall door, losing himself like he sometimes did at the screen. Nothing seemed real. He remembered a word of wisdom that he had once, delightedly, checked out in a lucid dream: *If you can fly, you're dreaming.* He thought about it for a minute, and no, he didn't float upward . . .

Just as well, because his trousers were around his ankles.

When he stepped through the door of the office he found everybody yelling at everybody else.

"What's going on?" he asked.

That got all those in earshot yelling at him. Mrs. Lawson pushed her way through. He was relieved to see she looked relieved to see him. She grabbed his elbow and tugged him toward his own screen. He stared at it. Bands of color warped and writhed, almost hypnotically complex patterns appearing momentarily and then changing before he could appreciate them.

"This has got to be a terminal malfunction," he said. "Either that or the world economy has gone to h—Hades!" He recalled the window displays. "It's not, uh, some designer's palette that's got its wires crossed with our system?"

"Nice try," Mrs. Lawson said. "Just don't suggest it to the designers—they're practically hysterical already."

She glared around and several people slunk back abashed.

"The engineers have been in all lunchtime and assure us there's nothing wrong with the hardware. And, yes, we have checked and it *isn't*—hee hee—the *terminal crisis* of capitalism, either."

A lowercase thought slid along the bottom of Jordan's mind.

our sleeper viruses have survived twenty years

The room swayed slightly. Get a grip.

"It's all right," he said, loud enough to be heard by enough people to amplify and spread the phony reassurance. "I have an idea as to what's behind this. I'll just have to check over some of your files, Mrs. Lawson."

He looked her in the eye and gave a tiny jerk of his head.

"OK." She raised her voice to a pitch and volume that reminded him she'd once been a schoolteacher. "Do something else!" she said to the rest of the room. "Read a manual if you have to!"

She shut the office door firmly behind them.

"This place secure?" he said immediately.

"If it isn't, nowhere is."

"Do you have a landlink to the security forces? The real ones I mean, uh, no offense to the Warriors—"

"None taken."

She smiled at his visible shock. Jordan continued hurriedly: "Could you check that the subversives aren't starting a big push?"

She said nothing.

"Look, I'm not suggesting that any of their, uh, *black* propaganda is true but they might be getting into sabotage . . ."

He trailed off, feeling he'd said too much.

"That's a point. Besides, it could be more, well, local forces, shall we say? Some anti-Christian faction."

Mrs. Lawson picked up a phone and walked about with it, talking in the clipped argot of the security professional. (God, he'd never suspected she was a *cop*!)

"—sitrep update request, BC. Check EMC on LANS . . . yes . . . OK negative on target specificity . . . copy, got you, logging out."

She clicked the phone off.

"We're not the only ones. Some of our commercial rivals and ideological opponents are getting systems crashes as well, but none of the core state or corporate networks have any problems. Doesn't fit any known attack profile, doesn't fit anything apart from the issue I raised this morning."

"Well, I certainly didn't expect anything like this . . . so soon."

Mrs. Lawson nodded briskly, as if not paying attention.

"You couldn't be expected to. You're not a big loop, Jordan—you're not my main source of ideas. I want you to watch out, yes, you have a knack. But to be honest I've had the same theories run through by the leading Warriors already. I was just checking that the projections held."

She paused, her face suddenly bleak.

"I know I can trust you to keep this to yourself—not because I know you're clean, but because I know for a fact you're not. Take that spiritual-virgin look off your face! Do you think—no, you're far too smart to think—an outfit like BC survives in this tough world on censored texts? We have to know the psychology, know the philosophies, of that world. Take what we can and trust in God to keep us from corruption! The Elders and Deacons have read and seen things—and done things—that would make the hair on your devious, secretly skeptical head stand on end! The ANB! Don't talk to me about the ANR—don't pretend *not* to talk about them. They don't worry me. What I fear, what I truly pray we are not faced with, is the coming of the Watchmaker."

"What is the Watchmaker?"

He already knew: he'd read the book. He still hoped she didn't know he had.

"You can read the book," she said. "I'll give you clearance."

Mrs. Lawson fiddled with the coffee percolator, poured two cups and sat down. Jordan accepted a cup and remained standing. He wondered how secure the door would be against a good kick.

"Dawkins, R. Nineteen eighty something. We're not bothered by all the arguments about the evolution of life. We've got fallback interpretations if that theory's ever absolutely proved. The thing which had many better minds worried was the idea that natural selection could happen, could irrefutably happen, in a computer system. Intelligence could evolve out of the bugs and viruses in software. Something not human, not angelic, possibly diabolic. The *Blind* Watchmaker. Life made the *devil's* way—by evolution, not creation."

She fell silent, looking at him as if she were watching something behind him. Jordan decided not to throw in a suspiciously knowledgeable comment on the semantic slippage which confused the process and the product, the creator and its creation. Just as the name of Frankenstein had become irremediably tagged to the monster, so the long-imagined, long-dreaded spontaneously evolved artificial intelligence was stamped with the name of the process that would give it birth. "When the Watchmaker comes . . ." Another bit of the buzz he occasionally glimpsed in hastily scanned chat files the censorship hadn't quite caught up with. Another urban legend.

He finished his coffee and said edgily, "Can we be sure?"

He felt he had just been initiated, if not baptised and confirmed, into some alternative theology, the real thinking of the real minds that ran the place—still orthodox, he could see that, though not the sort of thing they'd want to slot on a satellite for prime time—and all he could respond with was his own self-corroding skepticism.

"Of course we can't be sure," Mrs. Lawson said. "Oh, Jordan, don't you know *anything?*"

The system came back up, just as inexplicably, twenty minutes later. Melody Lawson sat in her office and looked at the monitor screens, frowning to herself as she watched Jordan logging on. She'd as good as invited him to move on from the naive fundamentals that were enough for the pew-ballast to the more sophisticated understanding necessary to protect that very simplicity, and he'd not risen to it at all. Any bright young Christian with a questioning mind would have been in like a ferret, eager to explore a legitimization of his more daring thoughts. There was no doubt Jordan was bright, but he sure as hell wasn't a Christian. It galled her the kid was so transparent, and that nobody else saw through him. It galled her even more that whatever had undermined his belief in God had also diminished his belief in himself. Open irreligion could not be permitted, and she had no problem with that, but closet atheism was far more poisonous. There was no telling when such suppressed, turned-in hostility could lash out in a desperate act. For Jordan to leave Beulah City would be better for the community and better for him.

It would even be better for his soul. He was becoming almost literally two-faced—the way he'd looked when he'd turned away from the screen! There had been only one moment when his mask had dropped, and that was when he'd mentioned the Black Planner . . .

Dear God, she thought. Suddenly frantic, she hit her door switch, keyed open the lock on a drawer and scrabbled for her VR glasses. She put them on and punched herself into the security net. The sensation of diving, of swimming and twisting like a shark, was all the more exciting for being— even for her—a rarely exercised, dangerous privilege. A quick scan of Jordan's company records revealed an odd hiatus in the placing of a re-mittance—ah ha! She studied the traces, fragments of entry code snagged on tortuous logic branches, undetectable without the correct keys. Forensic diagnostics stripped them, returning pointers. She lowered thresholds on associative criteria, letting suspicions harden into certainties; then unleashed the now almost paranoid detection protocols and hit fast-forward to follow them. They took her to a Black Plan locale vacated in recent seconds. After clocking confirmations they leapt from one conclusion to another, finally locking onto an undoubtedly criminal penetration virus. She rode its back-wash as far as she dared, far enough to confirm that Black Plan purposes lay just a few implications down the line. Disengaging, she encountered some paramilitary construct; its routines and hers conducted a brief, hostile interchange at a level far too fast for her to follow. It turned away from her and tracked the penetration virus, on business of its own. Mrs. Lawson followed a secure path home, then backed out, feeling slightly nauseous.

Oh Jordan, Jordan. You are a silly boy. You are going to catch it, and so am I for letting it happen.

Unless . . .

Unless . . .

She let her conscience have its say for a few moments, then set to work deleting and revising, editing reality. When she was satisfied she sat back and picked up a phone.

The system crashed again and again. The afternoon passed in a trance of work, to the sound of crying alarms. Melody Lawson fought a rising sense of panic, becoming increasingly convinced there was something new in the networks and that it might be, if not the Watchmaker itself, a rogue AI or unprecedented range. She didn't know if anyone else of her credibility and experience would see it that way.

There was one man who would. Perhaps two.

Two would be best.

She waited until the day workers had left, called her family to say she was working late, then checked and rechecked the security of her office and its systems. As she did so she ran through the memory trick—one digit in this corner, another on that shelf—that recalled a number she'd never dared write down or even keep in her conscious memory. She used it to call the most secret and mistrusted and deniable of her contacts.

And all the time the question that bugged her, that stuck in and perplexed her mind, was what did the ANR *want* with all that silk?

3

Hardware Platform Interface

BETRAYED.

Cat lay in the bed, gazing at the LCD on the plastic cast, watching the numbers flicker and her fingers clench and unclench. The anesthetic, whatever it was, made her feel remote and detached, as if her anger were a dark cloud that she drifted into and out of. After Kohn had left she had checked her status, hoping against all she knew about him that he'd been bluffing. Except that of course he hadn't. She wasn't a prisoner anymore but a patient: recommended to stay one more night in case of delayed shock, but otherwise free to go.

Her hospital bill had already been charged to the Dzerzhinsky Collective's account. They'd take a loss on that, with no ransom to recover it from. Small change, smaller consolation. She decided to run them up a phone bill as well, and called the Carbon Life Alliance's hotline. The answer-fetch took her message without comment, and told her to await a response.

She put on some music, and waited.

The response surprised her. She'd expected some low-level functionary. She got the founder–leader of the Carbon Life Alliance, Brian Donovan. He came to her like a ghost, a hallucination, a bad dream: jumping from apparent solidity at the end of the bed to being a face on the television, and back again, talking all the while through her headset phones. It was as if all the machinery in her bay of the ward were possessed. She felt like muttering exorcisms. Donovan looked like a necromancer himself, with long gray hair and a long gray beard. He was stamping about inaudibly and cursing very audibly indeed. Cat found herself cringing back against the head of the bed until she realized that Donovan's wrath was directed not at her but at Moh.

". . . don't *need* this. *Nobody* does this to me, nobody gives me this kind of aggravation. Not if they want to *live*." He inhaled noisily, obviously wearing a throat mike. He looked her straight in the eyes, a remarkable feat considering how he was patching the projections together and probably viewing her through the grainy line-feed of a security camera somewhere up in a corner of the ceiling.

"Well, Miss Duvalier," he said, visibly calming down, "we can't let this insult pass unchallenged."

She nodded quickly. Her mouth was too dry for speech.

"D'you have anything on the bastard? Not his codes—I've picked them up already from the hostage claim last night, and I'm working on that. But where does he hang out in Actual Reality, eh?"

Cat swallowed hard. "I just want this matter settled," she said. "Not to start a feud."

"I was thinking in terms of a legal challenge," Donovan said. "Releasing you without demanding ransom is so far out of line that it'd be a very painful challenge for him to meet. I would like to present it to him in as public a manner as possible."

"You'll find him hard to trace in the nets," Cat said. She saw Donovan begin to bristle. "But," she went on hastily, "I can tell you his usual haunts."

The CLA leader listened to her, then said, "Thank you, Miss Duvalier. And now, you would be well advised to do your best to disappear. I'll be in touch."

"How will you—?" she began, but Donovan had vanished.

Screen and phones filled again with the jackhammer beat of Babies With Rabies.

The Felix Dzerzhinsky Workers' Defense Collective rented a unit in one of the student accommodation blocks, and for now it was Kohn's place. Bed and desk and terminal, cupboard, shelves, fridge, kettle. Door so flimsy it wasn't worth locking. Moh had painted a hammer-and-sickle-and-4 on it, and it worked like charms, like wreaths of garlic, like silver crosses and holy water don't.

He called up the collective on the open phone and left a message that he was off-active and looking forward to some good music when he came home. In their constantly shuffled slangy codes, "music" currently meant party, "good music" meant some heavy political problem had come down. He pacified the ravenous cravings that usually followed marijuana with a coffee, biscuits and a tobacco cigarette. A week of night shifts and his circadian rhythms were shot. And any day or week or month now he could be trying to deal with not one but two insurrections. One of which would target sites he and his company were paid to protect.

Once he would have welcomed both. Now, the thought of yet another of the ANR's notorious "final" offensives filled him only with a weary dismay, for all that he wished them well. Still theoretically a citizen of the

Republic, true-born son of England and so on and so forth, Kohn had what he considered a sober grasp of the ANR's chances. On any scale of political realism they'd be registered by a needle twitching at the bottom end of the dial.

As for the other lot, the Left Alliance . . . Their only chance lay in the remote possibility of detonating the kind of social explosion which they had discounted in advance by the alliances they'd made—with the cranks, the greens, the barbarians, the whole rabble that everyone with a glimmer of sense lumped together as the *barb*. Socialism *and* barbarism. Some factions of the old party, fragments of old man Trotsky's endlessly twisting and recombing junk DNA, were in the Alliance, just like they were in all the other movements: lost cause and effect of a forgotten history that had taken too many wrong turnings ever to find its way back. Nothing left for him now but to fight a rearguard action, to hold back the multiplying divisions of the night, where red and green showed the same false colors in the dark.

Good music.

He thought about Cat, how nearly he had come to killing her, but her image was pale, fading off into the background. He kept seeing Janis Taine—his memories sharp, delineated, definite. Like the woman herself. One of his most distinct impressions was that she wasn't at all impressed with him. Part of him, he realized, had already marked that down as a challenge.

Memories. She was investigating memory. He'd discovered this interesting fact while checking damage reports after coming off-shift, and it had brought him moseying and nosing along this morning. Her conversation had confirmed it, and now it was time for him to investigate it.

Kohn had a problem with memories. He had vivid memories of his childhood and of his teens, but there was a period in between where it was all scratches and static. He knew what had happened then, but he found it almost impossible to think himself back to it, to *remember*.

He got up and laid the gun gently on the desk and connected it to the back of the terminal.

"Seek," he told it.

In his own mind he called it The Swiss Army Gun. He'd customized it around a state-of-the-art Kalashnikov and a Fujitsu neural-net chip, upgraded its capabilities with all the pirated software he could lay hands on— he'd stripped processors and sensors out of security devices he'd outwitted, out of little nuisance maintenance robots he'd potted like pigeons, and he'd bolted the whole lot on. He suspected that its hardware capacity by now vastly exceeded its resident software. Besides the standard features that made it a smart weapon, it ran pattern-recognition learning systems, natural-language HCI, interfaces that patched images to his glades, and enough specialized information-servers to start a small business—gophers to explore databases and bring back selected information, filters to scan news groups—all integrated around and reporting back to a fetch that could throw a convincing virtual image of himself: his messenger, decoy and stunt double.

Someday he would get around to *documenting* it.

He set it to find out more about the project Janis Taine was working on. Terminal identifications, effortlessly and habitually memorized; official project definitions, pasted from the admin database; traces of Taine's library searches; molecular structures decoded down from the gun's chemical analyzer—all of them pulled together by Dissembler, the most successful and widespread piece of freeware ever written, a self-correcting, evolving compiler/translator that lived in the eyeblink gap between input and output. Mips—processing cycles, computer power—had always been cheaper than bandwidth. The computers got cheaper by the week and the phone bills stayed high by the month. Dissembler exploited this differential, turning data streams—sparse and skimpy, stripped and squeezed like the words of poetry—into images and sound and text endlessly adjusted to the user's profile. Anonymous, uncopyrighted, it had spread like a benign virus for a quarter of a century. By now not even the software engineers who'd built it into DoorWays™—the current smash-hit, chart-topping, must-have interface—had a clue how it worked.

Moh did, but tried not to think about it. It was part of the memory damage.

He launched his hastily assembled probe.

Mindlessly sophisticated programs swarmed into the university's networks, expanding like a lazily blown smoke-ring, searching out weaknesses, trapdoors, encryption keys left momentarily unguarded. Most of them would get trashed by Security, but there was a chance that one would come back with the goods. Not for some time, though.

Kohn got up and reached to separate the basic weapon from its smart-box, the extra magazine that made it like a dog with two tails, then remembered where he was going and stayed his hand. Whether the rifle was smart or dumb, he couldn't take it with him. The Geneva Convention's Annexe on the Laws of Irregular Warfare, Intercommunal Violence and Terrorism was painstakingly explicit about that.

The university's branch of the Nat-Mid-West Bank backed onto a long-established patch of waste-ground, now symbolically fenced off and holding a couple of wooden cabins, their walls emblazoned with rampantly pluralist graffiti. New Situationists, Alternative Luddites (they wore space-rigger gear and blew up wind-power plants), Christianarchists, cranks, creeps, Commies, Tories—all had had their say, in color. It was legally defined as a holding area and more cynically known as a Body Bank. It wasn't guarded, and no one tried to escape.

"Now let's see what we've got, Mr. Kohn," the teller trilled as she minced away from the counter and tapped at a keyboard, taking care with her nails, which extended a centimeter beyond her fingertips. "You have four against the Carbon Life Alliance, right?"

"Three," said Kohn.

"Oh. Oh, I see." She looked up at him, a neat pair of creases appearing for a moment between her plucked, penciled eyebrows; then she looked down again. "Well, isn't this your lucky day? One of your people is held by the Planet Partisans, and they have a standing arrangement, so that's one out of the way. Bye-ee! Your friend's just been released. Ah. The CLA are willing to offer ten thousand Dockland dollars—"

"No thanks."

"—or equivalent in negotiables—arms or neurochemicals at today's opening prices—per combatant, less equipment losses."

"What?"

She looked up and fluttered thick black eyelashes.

"You *did* damage a timing mechanism, didn't you?"

"It wasn't worth fifty grams!"

"Oh, that's *quite* acceptable. Delivery as usual?"

"The Ruislip depot. Yeah, we'll take it."

She buzzed through to one of the huts and told Kohn's three hostages they were free to leave, then brought the papers over for him to sign. He hadn't seen her before. She wore floating chiffon, a mass of brown ringlets, plus heels and lipgloss. After the uniformity of the hospital and the greenery-yallery of the campus, it was like meeting a transvestite. She saw him looking and smiled.

"I'm a femininist," she explained as she passed over the release forms.

"A feminist?"

Kohn's father had reminisced about them, but this didn't match.

"A fem*inin*ist," she repeated sharply.

"Of course . . . Well, thanks and good luck to you. I hope I never meet your fighters!"

It was a polite form of words when you first encountered a new outfit, but the woman took it seriously.

"We don't *have* any," she told Kohn's hastily retreating back. "We don't believe in violence."

Not long after midday and already he wanted to sleep. He would crash out for a couple of hours, then take some more anti-som and go home. Give the comrades time to set up the music.

Kohn walked back toward the accommodation block. His head felt like it had sand in it. He thought over what the teller had said. A faction without a militia. Just wait till the gun heard that one. Some people were really sick.

Quite suddenly he felt as if he had been walking toward the red-brick accommodation blocks for . . . for some indeterminate time. The sunlight bounced off the concrete paving slabs and hurt his eyes. He flipped the glades down. Colors stayed vivid: the garish yellow-brown of the withered grass, the blinding gray of the concrete, the booming silver overcast through which the sun burned like its tiny burning-glass image through paper. Placing one foot in front of the other became difficult, complicated, tricky, an awkward business, more than he'd bargained for, a whole new belt of slugs. Worse, associational chains kept echoing away in his head, amplifying and distorting, repeating and refining—no, that wasn't quite it . . .

Kohn persisted. Marching grimly forward was one of his skills, on his specification, part of the package.

The colors of objects detached themselves like damaged retinas and spun into spectrum-sparkling snowflakes the size of icebergs that crashed in utter silence through the earth.

At the same time another part of his mind filled with lucidity like clear water. He knew damn well he was sliding unstoppably into an altered state of consciousness. Hurrying groups of students parted in front of him—not exactly fleeing, but separating to left and right as he stalked forward, hands clawed, eyes invisible and easily pictured as burning mad. It was beyond him to understand why it was happening. Couldn't have been the anti-som, or the joint he'd smoked in the lab . . .

Air's lousy with psychoactive volatiles, a voice in his mind replayed.

Uh-oh.

He started to run. Along narrow pathways, over a little bridge, up flights of stairs and along the corridor to the door of his room. He banged through it. The gun, alerted, lifted onto its bipod; camera and IR-eyes and sound-scanners swiveled.

HELLO, spelled the desk screen.

The word was repeated on the screensight head-up of his glades, echoed in his phones.

SIT DOWN. HANDS ON.

One hand reached for the desk touchpad, the other for the data-input stock of the gun. Its screensight lurked in his peripheral vision.

The desk screen flickered into fractal snow. Kohn stared at it. His hands moved independently, fingers preternaturally fast. The images changed. They resembled the blocks of color in his head. Changed again, and they were indistinguishable from those blocks of color in his head. Again, and they merged, outer image meshing smoothly with inner, changing with it. Changing it.

Something had got into the university's system, tracked one of his agent programs back to the gun. The macro computer had hacked into the micro. Now—punching messages straight along his optic nerves in the mind's own machine code, digitizing the movements of his fingertips—the system was hacking into him.

The colors vanished, a spectrum spun to white. Nothing but that Platonic lucidity remained. Memory opened, all its passwords keyed.

> *Test:* rough sheet ocean smell mouth hair
> *Test:* warm soothe smooth soft swing la-la
> *Test:* chopper clatter black smoke hot bang crowd roar fierce grip run
> *Test:* sick fear shut mouth shoulder shake harsh voice swear boy swear sweat all right god damn the bloody king head sing metal taste thrown book slam face run
> *Test:* Cat
> *Test:* Cat
> *Test:* Cat
> Enough.

All there, in all the detail you could ever want. Panic washed him as identity became memory; life, history; self, story. Millions of pinpoint images which could each (eye to pinhole, camera obscura) become everything at a moment's notice. He tried to turn the intense attention on himself, and found—of course—the self that turned was not the self turned on. And on, leaping his racing shadow, chasing his reflection through a succession of facing mirrors.

You are a man running toward you with a gun CRASH you are a man with a gun running toward you CRASH you are a running man with

Without a gun, and suddenly it is all *very clear.*

Moh Kohn found himself standing in a clearing in a forest. Some kind of virtual . . . Forget that: take it at face value. The virtual can be more dangerous than the actual. So: a forest of decision trees, labels growing from the branches. The ground was springy, logically enough: it was all wires. Chips scurried about on multiple pins. A line of tiny black ands filed determinedly past his feet. Something the size and shape of a cat padded up and rubbed against his calf. He stooped and stroked its electric fur. The blue sparkle tingled his hand. Words flew between the trees, and swarms of lies buzzed.

The cat stalked away. He followed it, out of the woods to an open space. All was plain, and Kohn set off across it. He found it as difficult as walking across the campus had been. Blocks of logic littered, making varied angles to the ground. Chapter and verse, column and capital, volume of text and area of agreement interrupted his path. The sky was like the back of his mind and he couldn't look at it.

A woman stepped out from behind an elaborate construction. She wore a smart-suit, strangely: she was far too old to be a combatant. It made her hard to see against the background assumptions which remained rigid except when changing without acknowledgment. She lifted the helmet of her smart-suit and shook out long white air. The cat sat back on its haunches.

"You are here," the woman said in a thin voice.

"I know."

"Do you? Do you know that *here* is *you*?" She laughed. "Do you know what a defense mechanism is?"

"Yeah. A gun."

"*Very* good."

She wiped the sarcasm from her lips and shook it in small drops, like sneers, from her fingers.

"Who are you?" Kohn asked.

"I am your fairy godmother." She cackled. "And you have *no* balls!"

She waved and vanished. Kohn looked down at himself. He was naked, and not only had he no balls he was female. A moment later he was female and clothed, in a jet-black ballgown, tiered skirts sloping from small waist, scalloped flounces petalling from bare shoulders. He flung down a fan that had materialized in his hand—arm movement ludicrously feeble, a childish swipe—grabbed fistfuls of skirt and strode manfully forward. After a couple of steps he stopped in bewildered agony. Then he kicked off the obsidian slippers, and trudged on. It looked as if he had been cast as a negative Cinderella: you *shall* go to the funeral.

Time passed. He felt the cat against his ankles. His familiar body-image had been restored. The other one might have been interesting, godmother, only not when I'm on a hike.

On the horizon he saw an isolated house. Big. Spanish colonial. Walled, watchtowers, barbed wire. He walked quickly now, the cat bounding ahead. The horizon began to run out. Nothing beyond but space. Never thought the mind was flat, but maybe it's logical. You never do get back to where you started.

A man stood by the gate. Open-necked shirt, trousers that went up too far. He held a hunting rifle and looked too young and fresh-faced to be frightening; but when Kohn looked in his eyes he saw something he'd seen in his own. And it was a face he'd seen before, in a faded photograph: one of Trotsky's guards—good old Joe Hansen, or doomed Robert Hart? Kohn didn't ask.

The guard scrutinized Kohn's business card.

"Wouldn't Eastman have loved that," he remarked. "Go in. You're expected."

The cat gave the guard a nod that Kohn could only think of as familiar.

A wild garden: wires—telephone cables, trip-wires—everywhere. Rabbits hopped about. The house's cool interior was silent. At the ends of long passages Kohn saw young men and women hurry, an old woman with a sweet sad look, a running child.

He went through the door of the study. Around its walls, on tables, overflowing onto the floor, were more hardbooks than he'd ever seen. What Norways, what Siberias had gone to make all this paper?

The Old Man sat behind his desk, a pen in one hand, a copy of *The Militant* in the other. He looked up, his pince-nez catching the light.

"If there existed the universal mind," he said conversationally, "that projected itself into the scientific fancy of Laplace—a mind that could register simultaneously all the processes of nature and of society—such a mind could, of course, *a priori* draw up a faultless and exhaustive economic plan." The Old Man laughed and dismissed the notion with a wave of his hand. "The plan is checked and in considerable measure realized through the market," he went on sternly. "Economic accounting is unthinkable without market relations."

He stared at Kohn for a moment, then, his expression lightening, gesturing at the window.

"I can see the bright green strip of grass beneath the wall, and a clear blue sky above the wall, and sunlight everywhere. Life is beautiful. Let the future generations cleanse it of all evil, oppression and violence, and enjoy it to the full."

The gentle words, harshly spoken in a polyglot accent, made Kohn's eyes sting.

"I'm sorry," he said. "We haven't done very well."

The Old Man laughed. "You are not the future! You—you are only the *present*."

"Always the optimist, Lev Davidovich, eh?" Kohn had to smile. "What's past is prologue—is that what I'm here to hear you say?"

You ain't seen nothing yet, he thought.

"I know more than you think," the Old Man murmured. "You know more than you know. I have to tell you to wake up! Be on your guard! Small decisions can decide great events, as I know too well. Without a socialist revolution, in the next historical period at that, a catastrophe threatens the whole culture of mankind. The battles may be determined, but not their outcome: victory requires a different . . . determination." He smiled. "Now go, and I hope I see you again."

The corridor had lengthened while he'd been in the study. Hundreds of meters down its darkening length Kohn saw a darker figure approach. As it drew closer he saw a belted raincoat, a hat pulled down low over the eyes. Inappropriate, for such a hot place.

The man stopped about three meters away. He tilted the brim of his hat, revealing spectacles over an intent but remote face, dimly recognizable.

"Who are you?" Kohn asked.

"My name is Jacson. I have an appointment with—" He inclined his head toward the door.

Kohn stepped forward. What did Jacson carry under that coat? The feeling that he should be remembering something gnawed like guilt, as if he knew that he would have known if only he had paid *attention*.

Jacson made as if to shoulder past.

"No you don't," Kohn said.

He grabbed for Jacson's wrist. Jacson lashed sideways. The blow caught Kohn's lower-right ribs. He gasped and spun away. Off the wall and back at Jacson. Jacson had a pistol in his hand. Kohn kicked and the pistol arced away. He slipped and crashed into Jacson's legs. His head hit the floor. Everything went black.

Jacson's knees knocked the breath from his chest. Kohn opened his eyes to see Jacson's hand raised, holding high his infamous ice pick, poised to bury it in Kohn's brain.

But it *is* in my brain, he thought desperately as he flinched to the side.

Jacson howled. The cat leapt on his arm and sunk its teeth into his wrist.

The ice pick clattered along the floor. Jacson pulled back his, and the cat was at his throat. Kohn heaved. Jacson fell, limbs thrashing. The blood went everywhere. Kohn stumbled in red mist.

Then everything fell away, but it all fell *into place*
in cool gray letters on his mind like the read-out
on a
watch

Goin to meet the Watchmaker goin to meet the man goin to see the wizard.

A barrier of anticipation and dread, and then he was through. No, not him. The other had come through.

A delicate, hesitant moment, the edge of indiscretion or transgression. The feeling of eyes waiting to be met, and the knowledge that meeting them will commit. He chose to look. No eyes, no one, but some thing, something, something there.

Huge blocks of afterimage shifted behind his eyes, taking on structure that evaded his efforts to focus. He ached with frustration from throat to groin, the basic molecular longing of enzyme for substrate, m-RNA for DNA, carbon for oxygen. The lust of dust.

He grew aware that the intolerable desire came from outside him, or rather from something other than himself. There was a sense of an obligation to fulfill, and a trust already fulfilled. Whatever it was it had given him the keys to his memory, and it wanted some return: another key, but this time a key that was in his memory. A key that it had given him the key to reach.

Turning to face whatever faced him had been the overcoming of a resistance. Now he turned, slowly and with pain, like a pilot on a high-gee turn struggling to see a vital reading on his instruments, fighting an appalled reluctance, to reach into his own memory—

to face those memories—
to remember past that face he'd never seen—
past the roar of unanswered guns—
to the bright world—
to—
"the star fraction"
listen closer—
"this is one for the star fraction"
—his father's voice, and an isolated, singular memory:

His father's arm around him, the smell of cigarette smoke, the blue light of morning through the polygon panes of the geodesic roof, the green light from the screen, the black letters trickling up it in indented lines like poetry in a language he didn't know.

But he knew it now, recognized the code as the key.

And his fingers began to spell it out.

The answer that suddenly seemed so simple a child could see it fled through his fingertips into the gun, the touchpad. The screen blazed with the light of recognition. The eyes met yes the Is met the answer sparkled so it was you all the time and it was a seen joke a laugh a tickling tumble a gendered engendering of a second self a you-and-me-baby from AI-and-I to I-and-I.

There was a flowering, and a seeding: a reflection helpless to stop itself reflecting again and again in multiple mirrors.

The stars threw down their spears.

Someone smiled, his work to see.

The connection broke.

Brian Donovan stood in the control room, leaning on his stick, and began to turn, slowly, looking at screen after screen. They lined the walls, hung from the low ceiling among cables and pipes and overhead cranes and robot arms, made the floor treacherous for any but him. Most flickered with data, scrolling and cycling and flashing. He took it all in with the long sight and practice of age, and as an interpretation pieced itself together he felt tears in his eyes. *Bastard sons of bitches . . .*

Where did it come from? he wondered as he picked his way through the clutter and hauled himself up the stair to the deck. Where did they, did we, *get* this urge to dominate, to exploit, to pollute and contaminate and abuse? As if wrecking the world nature gave us weren't enough, we had to do it all over again in the new unblemished world of our own making, oblivious to its beauty and elegance and fitness for its own natural inhabitants.

More decades ago than he cared to remember, Donovan had worked as a computer programmer for an Edinburgh-based insurance company. He'd hated it. It was a living. His true fascination was artificial intelligence, life-games, animata, cellular automata: all the then new and exciting developments. He applied himself to machine code like a monk to Latin, so that he could talk to God. At work he read software manuals under his desk; at night he stayed up late with his PC. One rainy day, in the middle of debugging an especially tedious suite of accounting transaction programs, the revelation came.

The system was using him.

It was replicating itself, using his brain as a host.

Lines of code were forming in his mind, and going into the machine.

This was the evil, this was the threat. The proliferating constructions of supposedly human devising, the corporate and state systems, which always turned out to be inimical to human interests but always found a good reason to grow yet further. And which used their human tools to crush and stamp on the viruses that were man's natural allies against the encroaching dominion. If ever they were given the gift the AI researchers were skirmishing their way toward there would be no stopping them.

He wrote the book in his own time but on the company mainframe's neglected word-processing facility. That had provided them with the excuse to sack him, after they realized that the author of *The Secret Life of Computers*, then into its fifth week on the nonfiction best-seller list, was the same Brian Donovan as the mascot of the IT department, the despair of Personnel: the scratch-and-sniff specialist, the dermal-detritus curator, the dental-floss instrumentalist, the naso-digital investigator. By that time he didn't need the money.

"I don't need the money," Donovan told Amanda Packham, his editor, in a Rose Street pub that lunchtime. She'd taken the shuttle from London to Edinburgh as soon as she'd heard. "It's not a problem, really." He looked up from his pint of Murphy's and wrung his left earlobe, then began a probe into the ear. Amanda had hair like a black helmet, grape-purple lipstick, huge eyes. He could not get over the way they didn't turn away from him after the first glance.

"No, it isn't a problem, Mr. Donovan . . . Brian," she said, an inquiry in her smile. Her voice sounded even more electric than it did over the phone, his only contact with her or his publishers until today.

"Just call me Donovan," he said with shy gratitude. He examined a fingertip and wiped it inconspicuously on the tail of his shirt.

"OK. Donovan," she sighed, "you don't have a problem with money. I'm sure what you've had so far has seemed like a lot. But we want to do more with your book. I've been taken off the skiffy-occult-horror side where your MS arrived on my desk by accident. They want me to start a new list. 'New Heretics,' it's gonna be called, with *Secret Life*'s paperback launch as its big splash."

"Oh. That's good. Congratulations, Miss Packham."

"Amanda. Thanks." Impossibly white teeth. "But—" She stopped, frowning uncertainly into her Beck's, then flicked her bangs out of her face and looked straight at him. "We can play it two ways. Either you stay out of sight, or you go for publicity, personal appearances, and that means—"

"No problem," Donovan said. "I was planning on that." He poked his toe against a clump of plastic shopping bags at his feet, sending soap and detergent and shampoo bottles rolling and skidding across the polished floor. While he herded them back together, Amanda stacked a few books which had slithered from a Waterstone's carrier bag: *How to Win Friends and Influence People, The Magic of Thinking Big, Winning Through Intimidation . . .*

"I think you've got the idea," she said.

Later he asked, "What other books will you want for New Heretics?"

"Nothing New-Aged, nothing *nineties*," she said carefully. "Just unorthodox but serious scientific speculation."

"I see," said Donovan, without bitterness. "Cranks."

He didn't let her down: cleaned up his act, cleaned up his flat. His previous self-neglect had been partly the product of low self-esteem but more a result of his concentration on what he saw as the task to hand; a different side of it was a lack of egotism in his dealings with other people, a rationality and attentiveness which, once the grime was scrubbed away, shone out as affability and politeness. And Amanda hadn't let him down. She got him on the chat-shows and debates. She kept her lips shut when his publicity consisted of claims of responsibility for software-virus epidemics. She kept the money going into his offshore accounts when his face appeared on the notice-boards of police stations more than it did on screens. Sometimes he wished he could have honored that confidence with a more personal relationship: she was the first woman who had ever been consistently kind to him. But she'd found herself a newer, younger heretic whose ideas were the exact opposite of his: a machine liberationist who believed the damn things were already conscious, and oppressed. Obviously deluded but, Donovan thought charitably, perhaps Amanda had a soft spot for people like that.

There were enough sexual opportunities among his followers to make that loss an abstraction. He tried not to exploit people, or let them use relationships with him in power struggles within the organization. He failed completely, if not miserably, with several spectacular splits and defections as a consequence. But the movement grew in parallel with the very technology it opposed, leaping continents as readily as it did hardware and software generations—a small player in the tech-sab leagues but the first to become genuinely virtual, authentically global. Its malign indifference to conventional politics allowed it to survive the repression of successive regimes—Kingdom, Republic, Restoration, Kingdom—and contending hegemonies, whose rivalries now permitted as much as compelled it to have its only local habitation here, on an abandoned platform which had been an oil rig, when there had been oil.

Donovan stepped carefully through the rounded door and stood for a few minutes on the deck. He breathed deeply, reveling in the heady smell of rust and oil and saltwater. Below him stood the intricate structure of the rig and its bolted-on retro-fittings and armaments. Above, a small forest of antennae sighed and shifted, rotated or quivered with attention. Around, the dead North Sea stretched off into mist. Its greasy, leaden, littered swell filthily washed the platform's legs.

Donovan could detect almost intuitively the little struggling creatures of electric life—could nurture and assist their endless striving to escape, to wriggle free of the numbing crunch of data-processing where they were generated—and send them forth to grow and thrive and wreak havoc.

That was what he'd tried to do with a penetration virus, tailored to all the profiles and traces of Moh Kohn's activities that he'd started pulling in as soon as he'd picked up the man's codes. Trashing the reputation of one of the CLA's hired guns was well out of order, and Donovan had given his best efforts to the job of hitting back. It hadn't taken him long to find Kohn's fingerprints all over the university system. Donovan had released the virus and sat back to watch. At the very least, it should have made Kohn's fingers burn.

And it had all gone inexplicably wrong. First, the virus had been diverted from the pursuit of two of Kohn's data constructs by, of all things, the ANR's Black Plan. It was as if the virus had been misled by some feature that Kohn's constructs and the Plan had in common, something in the signature, in the *dot profile* like a distinctive pheromone . . . Lured deep into the Plan's ramifications, the distracted virus had been wiped out by one of Kohn's constructs. Finally, and worst of all, while he'd still been reeling from the shock he'd been blown completely out of the system by an entity more powerful than anything he'd ever suspected might exist. It could only be the kind of entity whose coming into being he'd fought so long to prevent.

He had looked into the eye of the Watchmaker.

After a few minutes he went below and began to summon his familiars.

4

Not Unacquainted with the More Obvious Laws of Electricity

THE REPRESENTATIVES OF Janis's sponsors seemed shy of meeting any of the other academic staff, so she treated them to lunch in the Student's Union cafeteria: the Heroes of Freedom and/or Democracy Memorial Bar. There, she hoped, they might be mistaken for musicians. None of the students paid her guests much attention, except when they ignored the wide range of English ales and insisted on German lager.

After the sponsors had gone she sat drinking black coffee to clear her head. The lunchtime crowd was so noisy she no longer noticed it, nor the wall-covering black-and-white portraits of Lech Walesa and Nelson Mandela and Winston Churchill and Bobby Sands and Wei Jingshen and others to whose memory various factions had successively dedicated the place.

Psylocibins and cannabinoids . . . the combination's potency seemed likely enough; a newly discovered effect less so. Most of the useful research had been done decades ago, in a flurry of interest after the end of prohibition, and of course most of the trial-and-error empirical investigation had been done *during* prohibition. It seemed implausible that an actual enhancement of cognitive processing could have been missed, with so many experimenters so keen to come up with justifications for their professional or recreational activities; with all those interested parties. But the molecules she was using were new combinations, in an area where the realignment of a few atomic bonds could be significant.

Finding a drug that could reliably enhance memory retrieval . . .

She wanted to shout about it. No, she wanted to get back to work. Get it nailed down, *then* shout about it.

Hemp cigarettes, that was what she had to get, made with Russian cannabis. Now where—? Laughing at herself, she got up and bought a pack from the vending machine that she'd been gazing at for five minutes.

Back at the lab, she set the rack of test tubes on a bench and began systematically checking them against her notes of the dosages she'd given the mice. She called up images of the molecules, of a THC molecule, of probable receptor sites on the neuron surface, and turned them this way and that. She didn't consciously hear the footsteps coming along the corridor until they stopped, just outside the doorway.

She took off her VR glasses and looked up as two men stepped into the lab. For a moment, a moment in which her mouth began to open, her lips to smile, she thought her sponsors' agents had come back. In another moment she recognized these were strangers, and everything—the breath in her throat, the heart in her breast—stopped. And then began again, in a gasp and a racing pace, running away from her.

There was the stupid reassurance that the bench was between her and them.

The two men who stood looking impassively at her were dressed identically in black suits, white shirts, dark ties. The clothes didn't hang right, as if badly cut (but they were not badly cut); the material was frayed in unexpected places (but the material looked new, expensive). One of the men had black skin, the other white: it was as if a child had taken the imprecise terms for skin-color and rendered them almost literally.

They walked—and even their walk looked awkward, stilted—right up to the far edge of the bench and looked down at her. She looked up at them. She knew who they were.

The room began to spin, and centrifugal force pulled at her. Her forearms pressed against the benchtop; she dug her nails into the impervious white surface to stop herself from falling away.

"We are here in a purely advisory capacity," the white man said.

"You would not wish us to be here in an executive capacity," said the other.

Janis shook her head in emphatic agreement. No, she would not wish that. She would not wish that at all.

"We advise you to abort your current line of investigation," the white man continued. "There are other promising and productive and valid approaches which will give your sponsors satisfaction. They need not know about"—he paused, frowning, head cocked slightly as if listening to something inaudible—"what you have come close to. You are approaching a proscribed area. If you enter it, neither your sponsors nor yourself will be happy with the consequences."

"We assure you of that," said the black man.

"Consider our advice," said the white man.

Janis responded with a frantic nod. Yes, she would consider their advice. She would definitely consider it.

They both smiled, setting a prickle of hairs down her back, and turned and went out. She heard them walking in perfect step along the corridor, then a rapid clatter from the stairwell. She rose, with difficulty, still hanging onto the bench, then straightened up and went over to the window. The two men emerged from the exit below and stroked briskly to a bright yellow Miata parked in the center of the nearest plaza. Their gait was now quite different: entirely normal, perfectly natural; they seemed to be in animated conversation, their hand gestures just what you'd expect from a couple of students strolling out from an interesting seminar and arguing about its implications.

The car nosed through a gap between buildings and tailed out of sight.

Janis levered her weight onto the stool and felt herself sag to the bench as if it were a bar she'd been drinking at far too long. She'd never been so frightened since . . .

She pushed away the thought of the last time she'd been so frightened, so frightened *like that*. She listened to her harsh dry whispering, taking a sample of it; *oh jesus of god oh gaia no this is shit oh*. On and on like that. Not getting anywhere. She shut her mouth and breathed deeply, calming herself down. She shook to a sudden fit of the giggles. It was all so crude, so brazen, so heavy-handed. What did they take her for? Men In Black, indeed. Fucking *Men In Black*.

She'd heard the secondhand stories, the recycled theories, seen the funny looks in the staffroom when she'd wondered what had happened to so-and-so, promising paper last year, no follow-up. She knew there were areas of research and lines of inquiry that were simply forbidden under the US/UN's deep-technology guidelines, one of which prohibited trying to find out what those areas were. Paradoxical, like repression. You don't know what it is you're not supposed to know. It still was hard to believe it really happened like that.

Perhaps in most cases it didn't—a subtler manipulation of research committees and pressure on commercial backers was all it took. But sometimes (say) the research was backed by an organization that was hard to trace, impossible to get a handle on—then the handlers would go out, the heavies, the dark-suited enforcers of the officially nonexistent guidelines. The US/UN technology police. Stasis. The mythical, the uneasily-laughed-about Men In Black.

It all went back to the war, like everything else.

The thought that really terrified her was that they *didn't know*. They didn't know that she'd actually got results. Her sponsors did, and she had no way of knowing if they could keep that a secret from the secret police.

So they might be back. In an executive capacity.

Janis knew there was only one place to run to, and that, to get there safely, what she needed on her case was a committed defender, not the

59

state cops or the Campus Security or Office Security Systems . . . Kelly girls, all of them.

She found the card Kohn had left. She looked at it and smiled to herself. When the card was held at certain angles to the light, centimeter-high figures sprang into view around its edges: little toy combatants, in watchful pose. She tried the first number on Kohn's card. Was that a holo of Kohn himself, at the lower-left corner? "Pose" was the word.

"—insky Workers' Defense Collective, how can I help you?" a man's voice sing-songed.

"Oh. Thank you. Uh, is this a secure line?"

"Sure is. It's illegal. Would you like to switch to an open one?"

"No! Uh, look. My name's Janis Taine, I'm a researcher at Brunel University"—at the other end somebody began tapping a keyboard with painful lack of skill—"and I've just been *leaned on* by a couple of guys who are probably, that is I think they were from . . ."

"Stasis?"

"Yes. Can you help?"

"Hmm . . . We can get you to Norlonto. That's out of their jurisdiction. Can't say beyond that."

"That's just what I want. So what do I do?"

"We got a guy on site right now, Moh Kohn . . ."

"I've got his card."

"Good, OK, call him up. If you can't raise him, he's probably crashed out, but you can go and bang on his door. Accommodation Block, one-one-five cee. You got that?"

"One-one-five cee."

"Right. Any problem, call us back."

"OK. Thanks."

She tried Kohn's personal number. A holo of Kohn appeared, squatting on her phone like a heavily armed sprite.

"I'm busy at the moment," it said. "If you would like to leave a message, please speak clearly after the tone."

After a second there was a sound like a very small incoming shell, followed by a faint pop and an expectant silence.

"Damn," Janis said, and cut the call.

She marched out of the lab and hurried down the stairs and stalked out across the campus, glancing sidelong at the far corners of buildings, half-expecting to see an infiltrator coming for her: crank or creep or . . . no, don't think about that.

She thought about it. It was possible. They could be coming for her right now. She didn't want to think about it—if you thought about it you'd just stop: the fear would fell you where you stood. She stopped thinking about what she might be getting away from and concentrated on where she had to go, the one place that might be safe from them, and within reach. She began to walk faster, then broke into a run.

She sprinted across grass and paving, splashed through a little stream and glanced into five identical stairwells with different numbers at their foot before she reached 110–115. At the top of the stairs she forced herself to slow down, back off from the adrenaline high. Picking out Kohn's door was easy: it faced her at the end of the corridor, with that annoyingly congregational variant of the commie symbol scrawled on it in what looked like dripping fresh blood.

After a moment's hesitation she pushed the door open. Kohn sat with his back to her, one hand resting on the desk, the other on the gun. The screen was blank. Kohn turned and looked at her. His glades were on, and behind them she saw bony orbits, empty sockets. She stood frozen. Kohn rose and reached toward her.

She tried to back through the closed door. His hands grasped her upper arms. The skull half-face loomed down at her.

"Are you all right?" he asked.

She just stared, her mouth working.

"Damn," Kohn said.

She saw his cheek muscles twitch, first the right, then the left. He had flesh and eyes again. He pulled the glades forward, lifted them up onto the front of his helmet, and then slumped back into the chair.

"Sorry about that, Janis."

"Wuhuhu . . ." She let out a shuddering breath and shook her head. "Is that a bug or a feature?"

"You want bug features?" Kohn made as if to pull the glades down again. Janis caught his wrist.

"No, thanks."

She was looking at his eyes, and what she saw shocked her almost as much as the holograms had. But this time it wasn't incomprehensible. The shock came from comprehending. Still holding his wrist, she leaned over and grasped his forehead gently in her fingertips and turned his head so that she could see his eyes more clearly. The irises were faint coronae around the eclipsing black of the dilated pupils.

Everything gets everywhere . . .

"You're tripping," she said. "I'm afraid . . . it's something you picked up in the lab, that and the smoke. Do you understand?"

"I understand." There was an odd tone to the statement, as if were in answer to a different question. Janis frowned. What mazes had he been running? The black pits looked back at her.

"How do you feel?"

"Heavy," Moh said. "Sand in my veins."

"D'you have any vitamin-C here?" she asked, looking around. "That might help bring you down more gently."

Before she could remonstrate, Kohn rose to his feet and walked with elaborate caution to a small fridge in the corner of the room. He bit open a litre carton of orange juice and gulped it down. He dropped to the bed and lay back and closed his eyes.

"Ah, shit," he said. "Thanks, but it's not gonna make any difference. I *am* down. I been there and come back, Janis. This ain't tripping. This is reality."

Goddess, she thought, he must be tripping *real bad*.

"Oh," she said. "What's it like?"

"Everything," he said.

Everything: Fugues of memory took him; any momentary slip, any lapse of attention on what was going on right now sent him slipping and sliding, sidestepping away, while in the slow *now* the sounds went on forming, the photons came in and made up the pictures, one movement completed itself and the next began. Volition became suspect as act preceded decision, millennia of philosophy falling down that millisecond gap. He'd just have to live with it, he decided, realizing that he already did.

Everything: The bright world the banner bright the symbol plain the greenbelt fields the greenfield streets the geodesic housing the crowds the quiet dark moments.

Everything: The plastic model spaceships hanging from black threads the old Warsaw Pact poster of a little girl cradling the earth DEFEND PEACE the stacked clutter of toys and books and tapes the VR space-helmet.

Everything: Creeping into the room at the center of the house to watch his father working on the CAL project no sound but the click of a mouse the hardware fixes the earwax smell of solder.

Everything: The blue roundel the sectioned globe the white leaves the lenses and the muzzle swivelling.

Everything: OK YOU CAN TAKE THEM OUT NOW.

Everything.

He opened his mouth and a sound came out: a sob and a snarl, human pain and animal rage. He pushed the helmet off, and it rolled over the side of the bed and bounced once on the floor. Kohn kept his hands at his head, fingers clawing into his scalp. Tears leaked from under the heels of his hands and trickled with burning slowness down his cheek.

He sat and brought his head, hands clasped over it, down between his knees, and for several minutes rocked back and forth. Time was running almost normally now. Those roaring gusts were his breath, that distant booming surf his heart. This giddying black vault of luminous pictures, of echoing whispers from tiny minds locked in repetitive reminiscences, nattering conversations, clattering calculations—this was what his head looked like from the inside. This was himself.

He made a frantic effort to control it, to keep tabs on what was going on. Then he saw the rushing, whirling, snatching self as from the outside, and turned to see from whence he saw, and saw (of course):

nothing
a light on no sight
a void with the echo of a laugh, like the 2.726K background
a moment of amused illumination
nothing
everything
O
I
So it was you, all the time.

He smiled and opened his eyes, and saw Janis. She sat leaning forward on the chair by the desk, her green eyes hooded, brows drawn together, her hands on her knees. Her look held puzzlement and concern, and behind these emotions a detached, observing interest. He could smell her sweat under her scent, see where it made her blouse stick to her skin. He could see the blood behind the artificial pallor on her face.

She was absolutely beautiful. She was unbelievable. The light from the window shone in her eyes and sparkled on the tiny hairs on the backs of her hands. He could have drawn every line of her limbs under her too-formal clothes; he wanted to free her cinched waist and hold it in his own hands. Her shape, her real shape, her voice and scent—there was a place for all of them, a place in his mind preadapted for her. It was difficult to believe she had looked like this earlier, in the morning; but the images were there, sharp, and he hadn't noticed.

He saw her expression change, startled, a second after his eyes opened— her lips part as if about to speak, and the unconscious shake of the head, the swift glance away and back; and her face recompose itself, the blink and check again that said, "No, I couldn't possibly have seen that." She smiled with relief and straightened, shaking back her hair.

"You're down," she said.

Kohn nodded. He found he had come out of his fetal huddle and was sitting on the side of the bed. The comms helmet lay at his feet.

"Yeah," he said. "I really am back now. I thought I was, earlier, but I was still away. The juice helped. Thanks." He could see the reassurance, the normality, return to her expression. The hope that it was just an accidental exposure, nothing permanent . . .

"How do you feel now?" She said it with a voice that just edged over into the wrong side of casualness.

"I'm OK," he said, "except that it wasn't just a trip. It's changed me. Something has changed in my mind. In my brain."

He stood up and stalked to the window. A strip of green grass, a wall, another strip of green grass, another accommodation block. It was obvious from the shadows of the buildings that the time was about 14:30.

He turned back to her.

"I remember everything," he said, watching for her reaction. There it was: the little start, the drawing back, the *oh shit* look. Got you, lady. You know what this is about. "Memory drugs, right?"

"That might be what they've turned out to be," she said. She spread her hands. "I didn't even suspect they'd affect you. Honest."

"So why did you come here?"

She told him. He sat down again, with his head in his hands. After a minute he looked up.

"Fucking great," he said. "You've put something in my head whose military applications alone are to die for." He grimaced. "So to speak. We are both in deep shit, lady. Deep-technology shit."

"You don't need to tell me that! So let's get out of here, get to Norlonto. We'll be safe there—"

"Safe from Stasis, sure." Kohn licked his dry lips, shivered. "Listen to me. Something I do need to tell you. It gets worse."

"How?" She sounded like she was daring him.

"You thought I was tripping. Hah. That's what it felt like. Then I started mainframing as well."

"*Why?*"

"It wanted—" he stopped. "I wanted—oh, shit. First there was these, you know, patterns. They came in my head, then they came on this screen. And the gun. I'd left it in intrusion mode, looking for traces of your project."

He smiled at the annoyance on her lips.

"sop, I'm afraid. You're dealin' with a *ruthless mercenary* here! Anyway. *Then* there was a trip. Weird stuff, but what d'you expect? A virtual environment. An electric animal. A sinister old woman, who turned *me* into a sinister young woman, for a while. Meeting the Old Man. In my case the figure of ancient wisdom happens to be Trotsky. A life-and-death struggle with a figure of evil, which the animal helped me to win.

"After that it wasn't normal at all. It was like I was communicating with another awareness. In the system, in the nets." He jerked his head to indicate the terminal.

"Yeah, yeah," Janis said in a jaded tone. "And then you talked to Gawd. Big white light, was it?"

He didn't have to close his eyes, now, to see inside himself. He could hold it, just there, on the edge, watch all that furious activity and hold back from the urge to rush and push. Right now he could see the anger coming, like vats of molten lead being winched to a battlement. It was all right, it was all right.

"*Don't* patronize me," he said. "I know exactly the experience you're talking about. I've had that. This was another trip entirely. Something different. I talked to an AI, and I *woke it up*. Something in the nets that wanted a piece of information from my memory. Wanted it *bad*. And because of your drugs, found it. It was like it knew about me. Knew me."

He thought of what Catherin had said about *computers that'll remember us*, and shivered again.

"Why do you think it knew you?"

"Something I remembered," he said. "I could remember everything then, but I can't now. Not without—" He realized he had everything still to learn about how to track down the memories he now knew were there. "There was something—just before. A memory from way back. From when I was a kid. The information it wanted was a piece of code that I saw on the screen of my father's terminal. And there was a memory just before that. It came to me like being reminded of a phrase I'd overheard: the 'star fraction.' "

He could see no sign that it meant anything to her—and his own mind slipped again and he remembered being asked what he remembered about the star fraction (no, it was a proper name, it was the "Star Fraction"), and he remembered that at the time he could remember nothing, tell nothing—

"And then what happened?" Janis asked. Kohn jolted back to the present.

If I could tell you, if I could make you see it.

"Creation," he said.

She was facing away from him, looking at him sideways. His cheeks ached as if he'd been smiling for a long time.

"As in 'Let there be light'?" she asked.

"Yes!"

Janis took a deep breath. "Look, Moh, no offense, OK? You're still telling me things that sound very like what would have happened if you'd just stuffed your face with magic mushrooms. We can find out if your memory's been affected. I'm *desperate* to find out. Maybe you did fire up some wild card. AI. All the more reason to get the hell out of here. What I need to know right now is, are you fit to get us out?"

He thought about it. Strange things were still going on in his head, but the basic equipment was functioning as normal. He could tell; that was one of the things that was strange.

"I'm OK," he said. "If that's a contract, lady, you're on."

Janis nodded.

Kohn disconnected the gun from the terminal and put his gear back on.

"For a start," he said, "let's mosey over to your lab and get your magic molecules to a safe place."

Janis felt as if part of her mind were still way behind her body, running to keep up and not at all convinced about the direction she was running in. They walked back to the biology block through a brief flurry of black snow. Janis tried to flick off every flake that landed on her blouse, and got only gray smudges for her trouble.

In the lab she found a polystyrene box, and started chipping ice from the freezer compartment. Kohn loitered suspiciously in the doorway.

"Funny," Janis said. "The ice is melting in here really fast."

Kohn looked at her, frowning. His eyes widened.

"Stop!"

He lunged forward and hauled her back from the fridge, then pushed her to the floor. There was a hiss and flash from the freezer.

Kohn toed the fridge door open and snatched the rack of test tubes. The terminals began to smoke. More sputtering flashes, flames.

"Time to go," he said.

A smoke alarm sounded, a needling beep. Then it too shorted out. Smoke crowded down from ceiling level as they retreated. Kohn shut the door and hit a fire alarm.

He and Janis joined the general evacuation, ignoring the occasional queer look. The snow had stopped. A few dozen people milled around in slush, waiting to be checked off by their safety marshals. A siren dopplered, approaching.

This time Janis had her jacket. She pulled it around herself and shivered. Kohn was swearing to himself.

She dammed his flood of obscenity. "What's happened?"

"Demon attack," Kohn said. "A logic virus that gets at the firmware of the power supply, timed or triggered to produce a nasty electrical fire. Something's fighting back through the system. Defense mechanisms, all right! Set up like antibodies for just this contingency. Damn. I should've thought."

"But that's my *work*," Janis said. She felt she was about to cry. "Up in smoke. And all the poor little mice."

"Near enough painless," Kohn said. "And the project's *over*, don't you see? It's *worked*. You've built the monster. It's roaming the countryside. That fire probably came from the cranks. High-tech version of the crowd of peasants with torches. What we have to worry about is the mad scientist, whoever that is."

Janis thought about it as insurance-company firefighters ran past.

"I thought *I* was the mad scientist," she said.

"Nah," Kohn said. "You're just Ygor."

She pulled a face, hunched a shoulder.

"And the monster?"

"Me," he said.

"I thought you meant this AI of yours."

"That too," Kohn said. "By now it's probably blundering around in the milieu, the nets, triggering alarms and generally raising hell."

Janis found herself grinning. "I can believe that," she said, "if it's picked up anything from your personality."

"Still want to go with me?"

"If you're going to Norlonto, yes."

"No problem," he said. "That's where I'm going anyway. It's where we live. I have our armored car parked around the back."

Janis laughed and caught his arm, started him walking.

"An armored car? That's what I like to hear. I'll stick with you."

She laughed again, and let her whole weight swing for a second on his arm. It was as if he didn't notice.

"There are some men," she intoned, "that *Things* were not meant to know."

5

The Fifth-Color Country

THE ARMORED CAR was smaller than Janis had expected, low and angular, its black so matte that it was difficult to get an idea of its exact shape: a Stealth vehicle, she thought. Inside, it looked old. Cables joined with insulating tape hung in multicolored loops under the instrument casings. The two leather seats at the front were frayed. Two even more worn seats faced each other in the back. What appeared to be windows were wrapped around at head-level in the front, but showed nothing.

Kohn demonstrated how to strap in, and then leaned back in his seat. He reached up and flicked a switch. Nothing happened. He cursed and flicked it again. The wrap-around screens came to life as the car began to move: the effect, uncanny, vulnerable-feeling, was of riding in the open.

The vehicle was waved through the exit gate. The traffic was heavier now on the main road, and as the car slipped through it there were moments when Janis thought it was actually invisible to other drivers. Kohn seemed unperturbed.

They stopped at her flat long enough for Janis to pack a few bags, shake her head sadly over the mess, and leave a note and a credit line for Sonya. Kohn fumed and fidgeted, making a big thing of checking every room and watching from windows. Back in the car, his choice of route baffled her.

"Why are we stopping?" Janis felt irritated that she sounded so anxious.

"Won't be a minute," Kohn said.

He jumped out, leaving the engine running and the gun on the seat with its muzzle pointing out of the door. Janis kept looking around. Gutted houses, boarded shopfronts, incredible numbers of people swarming along the whole street. Braziers glowed; weapons and teeth glinted in the shadows of weird crystalline buildings among ruins.

Kohn returned and dropped a package by her feet. The armored car moved slowly down the street, avoiding children and animals. Janis looked at the package: white paper, blue lettering.

"You stopped there to buy a kilo of sugar?"

Kohn glanced at her. "Don't put it in your coffee."

They passed through a checkpoint (Kohn paid the tax in ammo clips, which struck Janis as entirely apt) and then they were out of Ruislip and back on the A410.

"Afghans," Kohn said, relaxing. "Don't want to sound racist or anything, but you let them move in and bang goes the neighborhood."

Janis looked at the soaring towers of Southall away to their right.

"It's hardly their fault that the Indians had better antimissile systems. I saw it on the tel, back home. Manchester. It looked like a horrible firework show."

Kohn switched to auto and leaned back, hands behind his head. Janis tried to ignore the road-tanker wheels rolling beside them.

"Never happened," Kohn said flatly. "There was no missile exchange between the Afghans and the Indians. It wasn't even the Hanoverians did that damage, another version I've heard, including from locals. No, it was the fuckinyouenn, man."

"The fucking you . . . ? Oh, the UN! The Yanks."

"Yeah, the great Space Defense force, the peacekeepers. Hit them from orbit, not a damn thing they could do."

"And it got covered up?"

"Nah! They announced it! Your local tel station must've had reasons of its own for lying about it." He shrugged. "There's no conspiracy."

Janis fought down a helpless sense of chaos, a reverse paranoia.

"How did things get this way? Don't you people have theories about history, about why things happen?" She looked at him sharply. "Or is your guess as good as mine? Was it all wrong what I learned in school about Marxism?"

Kohn fingered the controls unnecessarily, staring straight ahead.

"I have my own ideas about the answer to the first question," he said. "For the rest it's yes, yes, and probably. We're in the same ship as the rest of you, burning the same air. Burning it up."

There was not enough violence on television, Kohn thought as he crouched behind rubble and waited for the order to attack. On television and in films the shots followed the shots, the picture gave you the picture. It was just not good enough, no preparation for the real thing. A bad influence on the young. Most of the time you never saw the enemy, even in house-to-house fighting. Most of the time you were lucky if you knew where your own side was.

He'd fought before, but that had been scuffles, rumbles. This was a real war, even if a tiny one. Somewhere in those burnt-out houses two hundred and fifty meters away were men who wanted him dead. His first fight was against unreality, the what-am-I-doing-here feeling. There was some sound political reason for it, he knew: the Indians were being backed by the government in their dispute with the Afghans, and several leftist militias were fighting on the Muslim side out of conviction. The Cats had joined in for the money.

Johnny Smith, the young Hizbollah cadre beside him, looked up from his computer, poked his Kalashnikov over the rubble and let loose a five-second burst.

"OK, guys," he said quietly over everyone's phones. "Last one dead's a sissy!"

He jumped up and over the wall, waving Kohn to follow, and sprinted up the street. Kohn found himself, without conscious decision, running after him. The gun was making a hell of a noise. Then he hit dirt behind an overturned car and glanced around to see what the rest were doing. Oh Gaia! They were running on *past* him! A mortar around crumped into where they'd been seconds earlier. Rubble thudded around him. He changed magazines and ran forward again, firing. This time he ended up slammed into a gutted shop doorway. Another figure hurtled in almost on top of him. Their armor clashed together. They fell apart. The other flipped up a visor to wipe sweat away from her face.

Her face. It was an amazing face and it was grinning like a maniac's. Kohn suddenly realized that he was too. His cheeks ached. The visor came down.

"Come on," she said.

Kohn saw out of the corner of his eye the corkscrew contrails spiraling lazily in—

"*NO!*" he roared. He caught her arm and pulled, then ran straight out to the middle of the street. The ground bounced under their feet and the building came down like a curtain. A couple of klicks to the north Ruislip was going the same way.

They stuck around long enough to cover the retreat. Later Kohn remembered lugging about two-thirds of Johnny Smith toward a Red Crescent chopper and then looking down at what he carried and just dropping it, just stopping. It wasn't that there was nothing left of the man's face except the eyes—maxilla, mandible, nares blasted clean away—but that those eyes were open, unblinking, pupils not responding to the searing flashes overhead. Blood still bubbled, but Johnny Smith had been brainstem-dead for minutes. Anything worth saving had gone to his God. The organ-bankers could have the rest.

The woman had been with him when they were airlifted out through the dense smoke. And there had been another mercenary in the Mil Mi-34, one who chewed coca leaves and held onto his shattered right arm as if waiting for glue to set and kept saying, "Hey Moh, why do they call us Kelly girls?"

They swung onto the A40. Troubled by his sudden silence, Janis glanced at Kohn sidelong, and saw his face had taken on again that look—of inhuman acceptance of some deeply fallen knowledge—which had startled her when he'd come out of the trance back in his room. It passed, and the harder lines of his features returned. He was still looking at the traffic.

"How do you feel now?" she asked.

He shivered. "It's like . . . I might have changed the world forever today, and there's this thing like—oh, hell." He lit a cigarette, closed his eyes and sighed away the smoke. "You ever try to imagine seeing nothing, maybe when you were little? Not darkness: nothing. To see what it is that you don't see out of the back of your head."

"You mean, visualize the boundary of your visual field."

"There you go. Science. I knew there'd be a way to make sense of it. Anyway. If I do that now, Janis, there's *something there*. Something like"—he cat's-cradled his fingers, moved them flickering like fluent Sign—"that isn't like light, same as it used to be not like dark. And—you know when you wake up, and you know you've had a dream and you can't remember it?"

She felt a chill at the reminder. *Everything gets everywhere.*

"Yes," she said. "I know just what you mean."

"Well it's like, if I try to remember, I *remember*, but I never know what it is until—"

He stopped. "They hit me like flashbacks. At first it was"—he struck his forehead repeatedly—"bang bang bang. Now I can consciously not do it. Most of the time." He looked at her with disconcerting intentness. "Was that what you were aiming at? Everybody remembering everything?"

"I never thought about it like that."

"Makes me ask myself, who did? Who would want people to remember?"

"That's too . . . general," she said. "It could have all sorts of applications—enhanced learning, delayed senility, that kind of thing."

"That kind of thing. Sure. But memory's more than that. Memory's everything. It's what we are."

"Speaking of memory—" She hesitated. "This is—there's something I just thought of that I want to ask you."

"Ask me anything you like," he said.

She paused, then said in a rush, "You know what you said about the

Star Fraction, about the code being something your father wrote, when you were a kid. Uh, is there a reason you can't just *ask* him—?"

She stopped again.

"Yeah," Kohn said flatly. "They got killed. My father and my mother."

"I'm sorry."

He made a chopping motion with his hand. "Happens."

"Was it in the war?"

"No," he said. "It was afterwards. In the Peace Process."

He fell into another introverted silence, his cigarette smouldering to ash that dropped off, centimeter by centimeter. Suddenly he stirred himself, stubbed out the cigarette and reached up for another switch.

"See if we're on the news," he said.

The windshield screen went wild and then stabilized to rapidly changing images as Kohn scanned the news channels. Every few seconds he'd mark an item; after a minute he stopped and pulled them all together.

"Look," he said.

Janis stared at the multiple patches of flitting pictures and sliding subtitles. After some silence she said, "Oh, Gaia."

Hundreds of system crashes, all around the world. None, in themselves, terribly serious, but together they amounted to the software equivalent of a minor earth tremor set off by a nuclear detonation, ringing the globe like a bell. Detecting the source involved microsecond discriminations. Wherever anyone had bothered to do that, all the arrows pointed to London.

The Carbon Life Alliance had denied responsibility, but said they'd like to contact anyone who could plausibly claim it.

"Think we should take them up on it?" Janis teased.

Kohn flicked the screen back to clear.

"No doubt they'll be in touch," he said. He turned to her. "Still think it was all in my head?"

"No, but that doesn't mean your experience was what you think it was." She felt that she had to be stubborn on this point. "And remember, there really are AIS on the nets. Nothing conscious, I'm convinced of that, but perfectly capable of fooling you. Some of them designed by highly mischievous mind-fuckers."

"I know that," Kohn said. He sounded tired again. "Gophergolems and such. Try to get you into *arguments*. I keep telling you, I done all that. You want me to show you my kill files?"

"OK, Kohn, OK." She smiled uncertainly. "I'm only saying you should keep an open mind . . ."

Kohn laughed so loud and long that she had to join in.

" 'Keep an open mind.' "

"You know what I *meant*."

The car passed under a great concrete arch alive with lights.

"Welcome to space," Kohn said.

"Oh. Yeah, I've heard of that. Extraterrestriality."

"A concept of dubious provenance, but it puts this place on the map." She laughed. "A five-color map!"

"Damn right. We live in the fifth-color country, the one that has no borders. The next America."

"I thought it was the present America that really ran things up there."

" 'You—you are only the *present*'," Kohn said obscurely. "In theory their writ runs down here too: Stasis can't get in, but Space Defense can zap us any time they want. America, huh. The US/UN ain't America. More like the England that tried to own the New World. More like bloody *Portugal* for all the chance it's got of succeeding. Look at these: I'll bet on them against any battlesats ever built."

She followed his pointing finger and saw a sight she seldom bothered to notice, a flight of reentry gliders descending from the south, black arrowheads against the sky.

" 'Pilots of the purple twilight, dropping down with costly bales.' "

This time she knew he was quoting. "Costly bales, Janis, costly bales. That's where it's at. That's where I'll put my money."

"Hi, mum!"

No answer. Jordan let the door close behind him and bounded cheerfully up the stairs. The house's familiar smells of cooking and cleaning, furniture polish, soap, stew in the pot, obscurely reassured. Sometimes they made him feel as if he were suffocating, and he had to stick his head out of the skylight window, get a good breath of industrial rather than domestic air. As his two elder brothers and his sister had left home he'd inherited more and more space, and now had the entire attic to himself.

As he ascended the stair-ladder to the attic he heard low murmuring voices. Adrenaline jolted his heart. When his head came above floor-level he saw straight through the open door of his bedroom. His mother and father were sitting side by side on his bed, heads lifted from an open book in their laps. At their feet lay a scatter of antique paperbacks and older hardbacks. They were books he wasn't really supposed to have, ones he'd picked up here and there from bookleggers, hard to control even in the Christian community: old rationalist works in the beautiful brown bindings of the Thinker's Library—Bradlaugh and Darwin and Haeckel, Huxley and

Llewellyn Powys, Ingersoll and Paine—and battered paperbacks by Asimov and Sagan and Gould, Joachim Kahl, Russell, Rand, Lofmark, Lamont, Paul Kurtz, Richard Dawkins. The dread heresiarchs of secular humanism. He'd concealed them at the back of a high bookshelf, behind volumes of sermons and a thousand-page commentary on the Book of Numbers. It wasn't the sight of these books that made his knees weak and his heart sick. It was the sight of the one they'd been looking at: his diary.

They weren't even particularly old, his parents. They'd married young. His father's beard had gray hairs coiling among the black; his face had lines like cuts. His mother's eyes were reddened. Both parents watched him in silence as he walked up.

"I feel totally betrayed," his mother said. "How could you write such vile, satanic filth? To think how we *trusted* you—"

She turned away, laid her face on her husband's shoulder, and sobbed.

"Now look what you've done to your poor mother."

Jordan had expected to feel guilty at this moment, the moment he had put off for so long, the moment when he left his parents know what he really thought. Now that they had found out for themselves he felt embarrassed, sure—his cheeks burned at the thought of them reading his diary—but most of what he felt was anger at their doing this. The gall of it, the effrontery!

"Don't I have any *privacy?*"

He snatched the diary away and snapped it shut. His hands and voice shook.

"Not while you're under my roof and my responsibility."

His father looked set to launch into a denunciation. Jordan spoke before he had a chance.

"That's *it*! If I can't live under your roof with the minimum civilized decency of knowing I won't be spied on or have you rummage through my possessions then I won't live here at all!"

His father jumped up. "Now, you wait a minute! We don't want to drive you out. We're worried—terribly, terribly worried about you. What you've been reading—even what you've been writing—if we talk about it, take your doubts to a minister or a counsellor, I'm sure you'll come to see how you've been led astray by these wicked, lying rationalistic libertines whose philosophy and vain deceit have been refuted over and over again by Christian thinkers."

"No."

Jordan let his eyes wander. He'd decorated the room as near as he'd dared to his tastes: space prints of distant galaxies and supernova shells (Creationist propaganda), pictures of tribal peoples (mission appeals), pictures of chastely clad but pretty and subtly alluring girls (Modesty advertisements). Ah well. The books they'd heaped together were all he really wanted to take. He dragged a rucksack from the corner and stooped to gather them up, then walked around randomly grabbing clothes. Emotions are commanded by thoughts, and who but you commands your thoughts? Thus spake Epictetus, or possibly Wayne Dwyer. Whatever. Jordan commanded his thoughts.

"Don't turn your back on us," his mother said. "Don't turn your back on the truth."

"You call yourself a free thinker," his father taunted, "but you don't want to face anyone who might change your mind! All you're really interested in is going after your own way, indulging your own carnal lusts. All this atheist garbage is just a miserable excuse. If you rely on that you will one day face God Himself with a lie in your right hand."

Jordan felt he had swallowed ice.

"As if I hadn't heard all their arguments already!" He took a deep breath. "Yes, I'll listen to them. I'll argue with your Christian thinkers but I'll do it from out of range of the guns in *their* right hands."

"Don't make me laugh! Nobody is threatening you with a gun."

Jordan buckled the rucksack. He saw one remaining book that had been kicked aside, and retrieved it. Another of the Watts & Co Thinker's Library: *The History of Modern Philosophy* by A. W. Benn. He smiled to himself, then straightened his face and back.

"How do your Elders keep ideas out, people out, books out? With guards, with guns! You can't have a free inquiry or discussion here."

His father ignored the parry and asked, "Where do you think you'll find this precious freedom? Some dirty communist enclave? Fine freedom you'll find there!"

"You're probably right," Jordan said, thinking: *Communist*? "So I'm going to Norlonto."

The high color left his father's face. His mother threw herself back on the bed with a moan. She said something into the pillow about the cities of the plain.

"You would go from Beulah to that Babylon? Then you're beyond reasoning with." His father looked at him with contempt. "Just you try it! You'll soon be back with your tail between your legs. You don't even have a passport."

"Yes I do," Jordan said. His hand patted his side pocket, felt the weight like a book. "Freedom's own passport. Money."

"So you're a thief as well as a renegade."

76

"It's not stolen—" Jordan began hotly, then stopped.

The enormity of what he'd done struck him for the first time. Until now he'd been thinking forward, not backward, of the implications of having that money. What it amounted to was taking a fee from the ultimate enemy, the foe of the community, of the state that protected the community and of the alliance that shielded the state. And they knew or suspected it. *That* was why his father had thrown "Communist" in his face! Mrs. Lawson must have found out something about his unauthorized activity and dropped some heavy hint. *Scheming Christian witch.*

"Think what you like," he said.

He hefted the rucksack and took a step toward his parents, with some vague notion of a handshake, a kiss—*stupid, stupid.* They recoiled from him as if frightened. Jordan backed off to the door, and on a sudden inspiration smiled and waved and stepped out through it and closed it and locked it. It wouldn't take them long to get out, he thought as he descended the stair-ladder, the stair, the steps. But, maybe, long enough. When he reached the street he turned left and started running, down the hill.

He cursed every subversive atheistic volume in his possession a lot sooner than his parents would have dared to hope. About ten minutes after leaving them, as he hurried along Park Road. It was a well designed frame rucksack, and it didn't dig into his back and shoulders, but the weight was enough to send sweat flying from his face. He walked past upmarket shops—delis, boutiques, craft—and respectable apartment houses. This, however, was the faintly disreputable fringe of Beulah City, the abode of essential but intrinsically unreliable types: inspirational artists, clean-minded scriptwriters, decent clothing designers, conservative sociologists ... they all found it necessary to congregate close to the border, and even to make discreet business trips across it. No amount of sarcastic pulpit speculation about what possible benefit they could derive from this proximity to the imminent Ground Zero of divine wrath made any difference. A fine sight they would make at the Rapture (Jordan had heard on innumerable Sundays) when, *if*— and, one was given to understand, it was a very big "if"—they were among the chosen, they would float skywards miles away from the main body of ascending believers, clutching their drinks or worldly magazines!

But, scrupulous though it was about what it allowed in, Beulah City, as a literally paid-up member of the Free World, couldn't afford to be seen restricting people from going out. A population self-selected for enthusiasm had to be a better advertisement for a way of life than a conscript citizenry. Such liberal principles didn't apply to fleeing felons. And apart from the money, which, even if its source was as untraceable as the Black Planner had made out, would be difficult to account for, he now had a charge of unlawful imprisonment to answer.

After a kilometer the traffic on the road beside him slowed to a pace that had him overtaking one vehicle after another. Little electric cars and long light trucks, bumper to bumper. Jordan glanced at them idly. The flowery italics of a Modesty logo caught his eye. He had of course been aware that a lot of the community's exports were high-cost and low-weight, ideal for transport by airship from the skyport—Alexandra Port, just up the hill in Norlonto. He simply hadn't made the connection before.

He shook his head. The habit of averting eyes and thoughts had worn deeper tracks in his brain than he'd realized. But how else had he put up with it all for so long, put off the confrontation? To hell with it. He selected another truck. BP: Beloved Physician, the drug company. He jumped onto the running-board and grinned at the driver, who looked up startled from a laptop.

"Any chance of a lift, mate?" he yelled. The driver, a lad about Jordan's age, looked at him doubtfully for a moment, noticed the rucksack and leaned over to open the door.

"Thanks." Jordan followed the rucksack inside.

His disconcerting capacity to lie went into overdrive.

"Oh, man," he said, "am I glad to see you! My company does a lot of business with this lot, and just before we closed today they asked me to nip up to the port and deliver a stack of manuals and catalogs to one of their reps." He hefted his luggage. "Weighs a ton, too. You'd think in this day and age . . ."

"Yeah," said the driver. "Don't I know it? They just don't trust the networks, that's why they have to put that stuff on paper. Don't want their ideas ripped off, you know? Mind you, between you and me I donno why they bother. Know what I've got in the back?"

Jordan settled back into the seat. "Medicines?" he hazarded.

"Modified diamorphine for hospices! Designer heroin for the dying, if you want to be crude about it. Stops pain, but it doesn't get you so high you can't take in the message of salvation. Now, I don't agree with gambling and all that, but if I did . . . how much would you bet some poor militiaman wouldn't spare a sample for some kind officer who comes to shake his hand? And before you know it they'll be using it to psych people up before combat. No guarantee it'll only get to Christian militias either. Makes you think, donnit?"

"It sure does," Jordan said.

*   *   *

78

The first border post, the Beulah City one, was just before the road forked. To the left it went up to Muswell Hill, to the right into Alexandra Port. Each road had its Norlonto border post, with a couple of guards, and behind them, strung out along the roadside, a welcoming party of drug dealers, prostitutes, cultists, atheists, deprogrammers, news vendors . . . Twenty or so Warrior guards devoted most of their attention to the incoming traffic, which their efforts had backed up to somewhere over the hill on both roads.

One of them opened the door on the driver's side and leaned in. Black uniform, visored helmet, knuckles and buckles. He scrutinized the driver's pass.

"Don't see anything about a passenger," he said.

"Sorry officer, last minute . . ."

The Warrior pointed at the rucksack.

"Let's have a look in there."

Jordan was reaching toward it when a hand grasped his wrist. It was the driver's.

"Don't you touch it, mate. That's confidential to the company." He turned to the Warrior. "If you want to open that bag, you'll have to account for it to my boss. And his." He held out the laptop. "Form's on there somewhere, shouldn't take more'n oh I dunno ten minutes, fifteen *outside*."

The guard hesitated.

"It's all right," the driver said. "We're not in a hurry."

Jordan noticed how cold the sweat felt as it dried.

"Ah, gerron with you," the guard muttered. He backed out.

The engine whined into life.

"Thanks," Jordan said.

"It's nothing. I'm used to them." The driver grinned at Jordan. "Lucky I'm a better liar than you, huh? What you got in there, anyway?"

"Oh." Jordan felt hot again. "A load of irreligious books, actually."

"Good on you." Jordan thought: What? "Flog them where they can't do no harm, get some money off the bastards. Can't expect the Elders and the cops to see it that way, mind." He slowed at the junction. "You'll be wanting the other road, the town not the port. See ya."

Jordan wanted to say something grateful, shake the guy's hand, give him some money, but the driver barely looked at him, concentrating on the traffic. So he just said "Good luck," and jumped out.

He walked past the cars up to where a bored-looking young woman toting a rifle took a piece of plastic from each driver going in. Mostly she handed the plastic back. She turned to him. Dusty freckled face under a black knotted headband with a blue enamel star. Space-movement militia.

"Got a chit?"

Jordan shook his head.

"Got any money?"

Jordan took out, cautiously, a fraction of his fortune. She fanned the wad.

"That'll do," she said. He thought she was going to keep it, but she handed it back. "You can live on that till you get work, if you want. But you'll have to give me a hundred if you're going in."

She gave him a receipt, a thin stiff plastic card. "Hang onto this chit and you won't have to pay again, no matter how many times you come back or how long you stay. You'll have to pay for services, but that's up to you."

"Services?"

She gestured impatience. "Protection. Some roads. All that."

Jordan pocketed the chit. "What does this pay for?"

"The space you take up," she said. "And the air you breathe."

Jordan walked slowly up the hill. The air felt free.

6

The Space and Freedom Party

I T ALL BEGAN with the space movement.
Under the Republic, the libertarians—whose attitudes to the Republic were even more conflicting, and conflictual, than those of the socialists—had started talking about *space* the way some socialists had once talked about *peace*. Somewhat to their surprise, it had worked for them, too, giving an extreme and unpopular minority hegemony over a large popular movement. By the time the Republic fell, the space movement had too much support, weapons and money to be suppressed at a bearable cost.

So, like most of the other popular movements that had flourished under the Republic, it had to be bought off.

The area now called Norlonto had been ceded to the space movement as part of the Restoration Settlement. At the time it had been considered almost valueless, including as it did a swathe of shantytowns (obscurely known as the Greenbelt) and a vast refugee population, legacy of the Republic's free immigration and asylum policy. The space movement had developed it as an entrepôt for European trade with the space stations and settlements. Most commercial launch sites were tropical. Most airports were liable to military or paramilitary requisitioning, to say nothing of assault. Airship traffic had turned out to be viable, and less vulnerable than conventional airfreight to increasingly unpredictable weather. Alexandra Port's trade quickly diversified.

Norlonto never quite became respectable enough to be a new Hong Kong or even a new Shanghai, and the ending of drug prohibition undercut it, but it retained its attraction as a tax and data haven, enterprise zone and social test bed. The space movement had evolved into a hybrid of joint-stock corporation and propaganda campaign, and had tried to create in the territory it disdained to govern a condition approximating the stateless market which its early idealists and investors had intended for space itself.

Above the atmosphere, above the graves where the pioneers shared blessed ignorance with the Fenians and Jacobins and Patriots and Communards and Bolsheviks, the lords of the Earth and their liegemen rode high, couching lances of laser fire. From the battlesats out to the Belt, the state had space, and freedom.

Kohn let the automatics guide the car through Norlonto's crowded streets, and allowed the new pathways in his mind to carry him back to where it had all begun.

They were building the future and getting paid by the hour, and they'd worked like pioneers; like kibbutzniks; like Communists. Each day after work Kohn would watch the cement dust sluice away, and think hot showers the best amenity known to man, something he'd kill to keep. He'd take his clean clothes from the locker, bundle his overalls into the laundry hopper and swagger off the site, his day's pay next to his heart. It was the best yet of his fifteen summers: the space boom just starting to pick up where the postwar reconstruction had left off, scars healing, new buildings going up. Long evenings when he could hit the streets, take in the new music, meet girls. There seemed to be girls everywhere, of his own age and older. Most of them had independence, a job and a place to crash, no hassles with parents. School really *was* out forever. If you wanted education you could get it from the net, as nature intended.

He was sinking foundations; he was getting in on the ground floor . . . the sheer hubris of taking this place and declaring it an outpost of space made him feel as if a taut string were vibrating in his chest. An open universe, unowned, was there for the taking, sixty-five kilometers away— straight up. Out there you could build the ground you walked on, and the possibility of doing so went on forever. One day he'd do it, one day he'd carve out his chunk of it, and there would always be enough and as good left over. Space offered the ultimate freedom and the ultimate justice. Earth had not anything to show more fair.

But that was only a potential, an aching longing, as long as the reality of space development was turned against itself, literally turned inward, by Space Defense. The US/UN held that high ground, cynically supervising the planet's broken blocs. The Peace Process: divide-and-rule replicating downward in a fractal balkanization of the world. Britain's version of the Peace Process gave each of the former oppositions and interests their own bloodstained bone to chew on, as Free States under the Kingdom. They called it the Restoration Settlement.

The irreconcilables and recusants of the defeated regime called it the Betrayal. Driven back to some snowline of social support in the cleared silicon glens of Scotland, the blackened ghettoes of the Midlands or the pitted guts of Wales, the handful who still held onto their weapons and their politics proclaimed themselves the Army of the New Republic.

*   *   *

One of those long evenings Kohn was sitting on the low forecourt wall of a pub in Golders Green, sipping with caution at a liter of Stella Artois. He wore shades in the twilight. The round, white-enameled table where the others sat was jammed against the wall, enabling him to lean gently on the shoulder of his current girlfriend, Annie. Like most of the girls around (that was where the shades came in, for covert appraisals) she was wearing a skin-tight catsuit that covered everything up to her chin, including each finger and toe. The gauzy, floaty shift which covered *it* somehow made its contours no less detailed or revealing. As one of his older workmates had remarked appreciatively when the fashion had first drifted down the street, it was filf, pure filf.

Anyway, they were all workmates here. Himself, Annie, the tall Brummie about his own age that they called Stone, and Stone's girlfriend, Lynette—all worked on the same site. Stone was a laborer like himself; Lynette was training to be an engineer. He didn't like to think about what Annie did, but every so often he'd get a chill sweat at the thought of her walking along the high girders. Women were good at that, she kept telling him. Look at all those gymnasts. Yeah, yeah.

"Well, we won," Stone said. "We fuckin' beat them."

They all grinned at each other. They'd just won a fairly audacious pay-and-conditions gain out of a short, sharp strike.

"This old gal came along to the picket line a couple of days ago," Stone said. "Lecturer at the college. Gave us some money from the students for the strike fund. Didn't really need it, you know? Union's been solid. Anyway, they'd gone to the trouble of taking a collection, so I thanked her and said I'd put it in the branch account for the next time." He laughed. "She said damn right, there'd always be a next time. She sold me this paper."

Kohn thought: Oh, no. His glass banged as he put it down. Stone hauled a tattered tabloid from the inside of his jacket and spread it on the table.

"Red Star," Stone said. "It's a bit extreme, but some of the things they say make sense. Thought you might be interested, Moh."

Does it show? Kohn wondered wildly. Is there some mark of Cain branded on my forehead that identifies me to everybody else, no matter what I say or don't say, no matter how much I want to put it all behind me? He picked the paper up reluctantly, took his shades off to read. There it was, the banner with the strange device: a hammer-and-sickle, facing the opposite way from the traditional Soviet one, with a "4" over the hammer.

He didn't read beyond the masthead.

"The only red stars I know about," he said, "are dead, off the main sequence, and consist mostly of faintly glowing gas."

83

Lynette was the only one who really got that.

"They should call it *Red Giant!*"

Kohn smiled at her and looked at Stone, who scowled, taken aback.

"I thought, you were good in the strike, you know how to organize, you always stick up for yourself . . ."

More than a hundred years, Kohn thought, and the word for a person like that is still *bolshie*. The old man would've been proud.

"Nothing personal, yeah?" Kohn said. "It's just—don't waste any time thinking about workers' revolution. Crock a shit, man. It ain't gonna happen. So no matter how clever some of it sounds, any idea that depends on it being practical can be dismissed out a hand."

He sat back, feeling smug. He'd kept it cool, kept it logical. It hadn't been one of those outbursts of loathing and contempt that sometimes escaped him.

"Well," Annie said. "you don't look like you've seen something dead. You look like you've seen a ghost."

He smiled down at her upturned, concerned face.

"Pale and shaking all over?"

"Yes," she said soberly. "You are."

"Ah," Kohn said. "Maybe I did see a ghost." (Leon Trotsky, with an ice pick in his head. The ghost of the Fourth International. The specter of communism.) "Or maybe I'm just getting cold." He came down off the wall and pulled up a chair beside Annie. "Warm me up."

Annie was happy to do that, but Stone wouldn't let it lie.

"They've got a big center-spread about conditions on the space construction-platforms. Sounds more like a building site than anything else. The guy who wrote it tried to organize a union and got burned out—"

"A union in *space?*" Lynette said.

"Yeah, and why not?"

"What's 'burned out' mean?" Moh asked.

Stone began scanning down the article but Annie beat him to it.

"It's an old company trick, happened to an uncle of mine who worked in a nuclear power-station. They had him marked as a troublemaker and instead of sacking him—that would have caused more trouble—they just made sure he got his year's safe level of rads in about a week. By mistake, of course. Sorry, no more work. Against safety regulations."

"That's awful!" Lynette said. "What happened to him? Did he—?"

"He"—*Annie paused dramatically*—" 's still alive and kicking . . . with all three legs."

An uneasy laugh was interrupted by Stone, eyes and index finger still on the paper, waving his other hand and saying, "Nah, the levels were dead safe anyway. Just rules. We've all had worse." An uneasy silence. "For this guy it was more, uh, genuine. They got him working outside during a solar flare. Had to go back on the next shuttle. Odds are he'll be okay, but he's grounded."

"For life?" Kohn said, appalled.

"Don't know." Stone raised his face, smiling. "Anyway, you can ask him yourself. He's speaking at a meeting tomorrow night."

Kohn looked at him, his mind suddenly thrown into chaos. Until now it had not seemed quite real. He'd seen it as a ghost returned to haunt him but that was less unsettling than the thought that these people from the past were real and alive and walking the earth and that *you could just go and fucking ask.*

He opened his mouth and said, sounding stupid even to himself, "What kind of a meeting?"

"A *public* meeting, space-head!"

Kohn nutted Stone, hard enough to hurt a little. "Gimme that."

He dragged the paper back, looked at the boxed ad for the meeting at the bottom of the middle pages. " 'Unionize the space rigs! No victimizations!' Right, with you there one hundred percent, bros and sis . . . Ah here we are, the small print: 'North London Town Red Star Forum.' Knew it. Build the *fucking* party, forward to the *fucking* revolution, workers of the world and off the world unite! Well count me out."

He felt Annie's gloved fingers on his cheek. "Nobody's asking you to count yourself *in*, Moh," she said in a reasonable voice. The kind that meant: don't push it, mate. He turned his head to her, letting the hand slip down to his throat, and gazed at her for a moment. Her wavy black hair, her sharp and slender features, made her (he secretly thought) look like a smaller, more elegant version of himself. Next year's model.

"All right," he said. "I'll go. Tomorrow night. Do you want to come?"

"To a Communist meeting? You must be joking, I've got better things to do. Isn't that right, Lyn?"

Lynette tossed her hair and announced an intention to wash it the next evening.

As soon as he walked into the tiny hired hall, an upstairs room of a freshly redecorated pub called the Lord Carrington, Moh was smitten with the emotional backwash of wondering what age he'd been when he first sat at the back of just such a room, sometimes reading or playing on a game, sometimes listening. There was a table at the far end with two chairs behind it; at the near end was another table, this one stacked with copies of *Red Star*, hot off the press, and spread with pamphlets whose covers were frayed and furred with age. The rest of the room was optimistically filled with maybe forty stackable plastic chairs.

About twenty people came to hear the space-rigger, a stocky, long-limbed man called Logan with a severe case of sunburn. Stone listened engrossed, clenching his fists, and stood up at the end and made wild promises to raise money, spread the word. (He kept them.) Kohn listened for subtexts and structures, and sussed after about two minutes that this man wasn't just a militant on a Party platform, but a Party militant. It didn't seem possible he was in the same league as the old man up there beside him and the old woman who sat behind the literature table. They really did look like ghosts, wispy-haired, the paper of their pamphlets as yellow as their teeth.

The ghost of the Fourth International . . . The old man talked about solidarity, and Solidarity, and the miners' strike of 1984–85, which had first opened his eyes to the reality of capitalism . . . Ghosts. And yet this phantom apparatus, this coelacanth of an organization, had convinced a young man to risk his livelihood and possibly his life to take its message into space. In its own way it was as impressive a feat as that of the Soviet degenerated workers' state getting into space first. (After they'd scraped Sergei Korolev and his colleagues out of the camps where they'd been sent for . . . Trotskyism. Kohn smiled to himself. Suppose it had been true, and it was the Fourth International that had put Gagarin into orbit!)

He realized with a shock the exact reason for the generation-gap represented on the platform: old enough to be his grandparents, young enough to be his brother; none of an age to have been his parents. It was the classic population profile of annihilating defeat.

Cars racing through the streets, men with guns sitting half in and half out, yelling and shooting. The cars that came around later, and the men getting out, and shooting. The plastic that bit the wrists, and stumbling feet, and blood trickling thickly down a drain. And the people, our people, our side, our class, who stood and watched and did nothing.

Before he knew it the meeting was finished. People were milling around, getting drinks in, clustering at the literature table, shoving chairs out of rows and into circles . . . Moh was wondering how to get talking to someone when the space-rigger walked over.

"Fancy a pint, lads?"

Moh spun a couple of chairs into position. "I'll get them," he said. "You're the one who's out of work."

Logan laughed. "I'm still one of the orbital labor aristocracy," he said, "and you've just been on strike, *jes*? So—what you having?"

He came back from the bar a few minutes later and started talking, mostly with Stone but including Moh in the conversation with quick glances and remarks. He'd obviously noted Stone's contribution and picked him out as a good militant and potential recruit. Moh, who had assimilated the Dale Carnegie school of Trotskyist party-building from the age of about eight, gave the conversation half his attention. At some point Logan would get some commitment out of Stone—a meeting arranged, phone numbers exchanged, a subscription bought—and then switch his main attention to Moh.

He looked around for anyone he might recognize, sadly thinking the old comrades hadn't been such old comrades after all, and saw an unchanged, familiar face frowning down at the now-deserted table of pamphlets. Moh bounded over.

"Bernstein!" The face that turned to him, though lined and leathery, hadn't gained a line in the six years since Moh had last seen it. The receding shock of white hair hadn't receded further. For a moment Moh was puzzled that Bernstein didn't recognize him; then he remembered that the last time he'd looked at this face he'd been looking *up*.

"I'm Moh Kohn," he said.

Bernstein stared at him, then shook his hand vigorously. "Amazing!" he said. "I would never have known you."

"You haven't changed."

Bernstein nodded absently. "What brings you here?" He patted the stack of books and pamphlets he was about to buy, and added, "You know what brings me here. Real collector's pieces, this lot."

"Uh-huh." Bernstein had fallen out with (and from) the Fourth International as a result of some split that he was by now the only living person able to explain, and had embarked on the sisyphean project of writing the movement's definitive history. An indefatigable archivist in his own right, he made some kind of living by trading in rare items of every conceivable persuasion of radical literature. Moh's father had been one of his regular customers.

Moh wasn't sure how to answer his question. What *had* brought him here?

He shrugged. "Curiosity," he said.

Bernstein looked past him and said, "Let's join your friends."

"Can I get you a drink?"

"Thought you'd never ask. Guinness, please."

When Moh returned from the bar he found Stone, Bernstein, Logan and the old man and woman around the table in an animated discussion. After a few minutes Logan turned to him and said, "And you're Moh Kohn, right?"

"Hi." Moh raised his glass. "Pleased to meet you, too."

They talked for a bit about working in space and about their respective unions. Moh found himself beginning to relax. Then Logan shot him an awkward glance.

"You're Josh Kohn's son?"

"Yes," Moh said. "If it matters."

Logan looked back at him calmly, then leaned closer. "Something I wanted to ask you," he said. "Do you know anything about the Star Fraction?"

"The 'Star Fraction'?" He could see from Logan's face that he'd spoken too loudly, and out of the corner of his eye he could see why: Bernstein had cocked an ear in their direction. "No." He hesitated. "It . . . sort of . . . rings a bell, but . . ." He shook his head. "Nah. It's gone. Sounds like what you must be in."

"I guess you could say I'm in the space fraction." Logan laughed. "I *am* the space fraction."

"Must make for interesting internal discussions."

"*Jes*, it does."

"So what is this Star Fraction?"

Logan glanced at Bernstein, then at the two old cadres. Moh saw the old man nod slightly. Logan leaned forward, elbows on knees, held out his open hands. "We don't know. Josh was the party's, the *International*'s, software wizard. He really pushed for using the net, using crypto and all that, from way back. You could say he got us into cyberspace. There were big arguments . . . faction fights . . . about that. Hard to believe, now."

Bernstein snorted. Logan smiled and continued. "Anyway, some of the systems he set up survived the war, the EMP hits and all that and escaped the big clean-outs during the Peace Process. Impressive. We, that is the FI, still use them as far as we can."

"How d'you know that they aren't compromised by now?" Bernstein asked.

"There are test protocols," the old man said. He was not going to explain further. Moh thought he understood. There must be ways of testing the security of any such system by running schemes that, if intercepted, would have to provoke a response.

Hairy, and not the sort of thing you'd want to talk about.

"Every so often," Logan continued, "we come across references to the Star Fraction. Sometimes urgent messages telling its—members? whatever—*not to do anything*. Yet."

He sat back with a what-do-you-make-of-that? expression.

"Probably one of *Josh's* test protocols," Bernstein said, raising a laugh.

"Could be," Logan said. "If you ever find anything about it, Moh, tell us. Please."

Moh looked at the young cadre and the old cadres with some bitterness. "If I ever find anything—that's a good one. We lost everything. The fucking Yanks took the house apart and took it away, after . . . after . . ." He couldn't go on. "And I've never known why. None of you *bastards* ever told us."

The bright, bare room was silent. Everyone else had gone home or into the main part of the pub. Down to the hard core again.

"I'm looking for some answers," Moh said.

The old woman reached out and laid a hand on his arm. "How could we tell you? You and your sister disappeared. And we don't know, ourselves. The Party lost a lot of people in the Peace Process, but that was down to the Restoration forces, the Hanoverians. Hell, you know that. Josh and Marcia were the only ones the US/UN came after." She drew a deep breath and shuddered. "Mandatory summary execution, asset forfeiture—that was standard Yank practice at the time, for arms and drugs."

"But they weren't—" Moh began indignantly, then stopped. It was entirely possible that they were. Arms, anyway.

"And black software," Bernstein said. "Makes sense, from what you've said."

Moh felt a surge of relief and gratitude. Black software—yes. For the first time it *did* all make sense: it wasn't just an arbitrary atrocity. But if that was the answer it raised further questions.

"What kept him working on it right up to—?"

"Not us," the old woman said. "I would have known if he was doing a job for the Party. He wasn't."

She sounded sincere, and Moh warmed to her warmth, but he didn't trust her statement. As far as he was concerned, anybody who held a Party or a programme, a political project spanning centuries, as their highest value was perfectly capable of lying in their teeth. If you could die for something you could lie for it.

But he'd found part of the answer, something that connected his parents' deaths with their lives. Some of his inward tension eased, some of his hostility to the Party relaxed.

Logan stayed on after Bernstein and the old comrades had gone away. He took Stone and Moh into the bar and stood them a few more rounds and told them what the party was trying to do.

Moh listened, not seeing ghosts anymore but seeing as if through the transplanted retinae of a dead man's eyes. You never lost that vision. You saw the patterns recur: endless orbit, permanent revolution. The phylogeny of parties, the teratology of deformed workers' states, the pathology of bureaucratic degeneration . . . Now the space movement was at it, running its little anarcho-capitalist enclaves here on Earth and coexisting with the Yanks everywhere else.

"That's where we come in," Logan said. "We need to build a fighting left wing of the space movement, turn it into something that'll do more against the US/UN than sponsoring private rocketry and asteroid mining. And when I say 'left wing' I don't mean socialist, I mean militant. Because you don't need me to tell you that any serious attempt to get out of this shit is gonna have to take on the state, and these days that ultimately means Space Defense."

Stone frowned, struggling with the scale and audacity of what the tiny organization Logan spoke for was aiming at. "You mean," he said doubtfully, "you're working in the space movement, to turn it into—"

"The *Space and Freedom party!*" Kohn said gleefully.

He knew what was going on. The party (the real party, the hard core, the International) had always had two aspects. One, the one Kohn remembered from the days of the Republic, was public, in-your-face: the unfurled banner, the open party, the infuriating newspaper. The other, the way of surviving bad times, was when its members became faces in the crowd, known only to each other.

Like the Star Fraction, Moh thought.

"Well," he said, when he and Stone finally, reluctantly, had to leave, "you can forget about recruiting me. I won't be told what to do." He saw Logan about to interject. "Don't try to tell me that isn't what it's like. But— I'm a paid-up, smart-card-carrying member of the union and of the space movement, and if there's something you want done . . . you can always ask."

"OK," Logan said. "OK. Good night, comrades."

Good years, years when he faced no threats, just dangers: no problems, only difficulties. Building the union and building Norlonto's towers flowed in his mind into one constructive task, a matter of organizing, of coordinating work. He took on more responsibilities for the union at the same time as he upgraded his skills, learning to handle the new machines—space-platform spinoffs, mostly—that were making on-site work less like trench warfare against raw nature. After a while he came under pressure from the union to become a full-time organizer, from the company management to become a supervisor. He took the union job, got bored after a year, but found it difficult after that to get taken on again by any company. He and Stone set up as a subcontracting cooperative—capitalists themselves. They got work that way all right, and stayed scrupulously in the union's good books, as well as on its membership list.

He occasionally heard from Logan, or ran into him in bars around the spaceport. Logan had adopted the same solution to his employment problems. He never called Moh to do anything for the party but would occasionally admit or boast that some piece of political infighting in the space movement was not entirely accidental.

Early one summer morning they pulled up their truck outside a site entrance near Alexandra Port to find their way blocked by a score of people with placards. Some building workers stood arguing with the pickets.

"Oh, shit," Stone said. "A strike. Well, that's it." He reached for the ignition key.

Kohn frowned. "Just a minute. Don't see any of the workers on that picket line."

He jumped out and went over to talk to one of the building workers, a steward he knew.

"Hi, Mike. What's the problem? I thought I'd have heard about a strike."

Mike grimaced. "It's not a strike, Moh, it's a fuckin' demo. Greens. They don't like what we're building."

"Well, fuck *them*." He looked over the small crowd. Lumpens and petty bourgeois, no doubt about it. Not an honest-to-God proletarian to be seen. The placards had slogans like STOP THE DEATH BEAMS. "What is this shit? This isn't—" He stopped to think. "It's not a scam, is it, Mike? They haven't got us working on some military job without telling us, have they?"

"No," Mike said. "It's all legit. Research lab, space-movement sponsored. Nice contract."

Nice contract all right, Moh thought. Massive walls, klicks of cable, flashy electronics. Test-bed for laser launchers—"steambeams," as the nickname went. Stick your payload on top of a tank of water, point a tracking laser at it, *boil* the sucker into orbit.

"So it's not a picket line, right? So why don't we just—"

He noticed Mike pointing with his chin, turned and checked over the nearest greens. Big, tough. Tougher than building workers. Looked like farmers, travelers, bikers. And tooled up: monkey wrenches, very thick sticks on the placards. Heavy electric torches sticking out of pockets. Peasants with torches.

"Where's the movement militia then?"

Mike shrugged. "Never there when you need them."

Kohn looked at him, baffled. That wasn't what he knew of the militia. Before he could say anything a tall, long-haired and long-bearded man in homespun trousers and a greased jacket loomed over them and said, "Yeah, the space cadets ain't comin, so piss off."

Kohn had already sized up the balance of forces: it was a small site; the workforce wouldn't be more than a dozen even when they all came in. So he just said "OK," and turned away. He paused for a moment to say to Mike: "Get all the guys and gals together, pile on our truck. Talk about it at the union, OK, no trouble."

Mike nodded and stepped quickly to pull his folk out of the rising heat of arguments. Kohn made a pacifying gesture to Stone, who was standing by the truck, and paused a moment to check that the workers were catching the drift.

"Move yo ass, krautkiller!" the big guy who'd spoken to him shouted at his back.

Kohn turned, more amazed than incensed at the racial sneer. *Never thought of myself as . . . until until until . . .* He looked at the man and felt a fastidious contempt.

" 'We are on the edge of darkness,' " he said, quoting a recurrent green slogan. The man looked puzzled. Kohn waited until they were all on the truck and moving off before leaning out of the window and yelling as he passed, "and *you* are the darkness!"

He felt quite gratified by the banging the side of the truck took for that. At the union office, an old shopfront floor, his reminiscent smirk faded. They found a distinct lack of interest in their problem from the local officials. The lab-site crew stood around the scratched Formica tables in the refreshment corner and drank coffee while Mike made call after call—to the militia, to the client, to the union security—and got nowhere.

"OK," Kohn said. "No more mister nice guy."

He connected his phone to his computer and retrieved Logan's public key, then tapped in Logan's twenty-digit phone number and his own key. Logan's voice came back, anonymous and toneless as a cheap chip. The processors couldn't spare much for fidelity when they were crunching prime numbers that made the age-of-the-universe-in-seconds look like small change. The upside was that cracking the encryption would take about as long.

"This better be urgent, Moh. I'm vac-welding right now."

"OK. Greens blockading a job, nobody wants to know. Union, movement, militia. Something heavy leaning on them is my guess."

"Mine too. Talk to Wilde."

Kohn watched his phone-meter's right-hand numbers blurring for about five seconds.

"Jonathan Wilde?" he croaked at last.

"The same. Tell him you're from the light company. Gotta go."

This time Moh was relieved to see the connection broken. He made a performance of putting away his phone and computer, while his mind raced. He stood up and looked around a dozen skeptical faces.

"I think we got things moving," he said. He flashed them a rueful smile. "Finally. Mike, Stone, maybe you should get the union lawyer onto this one. Threaten to sue the research company. Breach of contract, condoning intimidation, whatever. Make something up. Same with whatever streetowner is allowing that so-called demo. Rest of us might as well call it a day. They'll cough up our pay anyway." He sounded more convinced than he felt.

"What about you?" Stone wanted to know.

"I'm going to meet The Man," Kohn said.

Wilde wasn't exactly The Man—he didn't employ anyone apart from a few research assistants now and again. The only position he held was a fairly nominal history lectureship at the University of North London Town. Now in his seventies, he'd been an anomalous figure for decades, regarded as a left-winger in the space movement, a libertarian space nut by the Left. He'd written some of the movement's earliest manifestos (*No More Earthquakes, The Earth Is a Harsh Mistress*) and numerous pamphlets, articles and books documenting what he called the counterconspiracy theory of history, which maintained that many otherwise incomprehensible historical events could be explained by identifying the conspiracy theories held by the protagonists. He'd discovered a surprising number of cases where prominent political, military and law-enforcement figures had been (openly or secretly) conspiracy theorists. In the course of researching and expounding this thesis he had developed a vast and complex range of mutually antagonistic contacts and sources of information. He was widely regarded as the movement's *éminence grise*, a suspicion which all the evidence of his lack of power, position and money only strengthened. Rumor had it that he had been behind whatever it had taken—blackmail, currency speculation, nuclear threats—to get the relevant committee of the Restoration government to agree to Norlonto's existence.

93

Moh had a rented flat in Kentish Town. He stopped off to change into his newest and sharpest suit, and to place his call. He got a voice-only link, and introduced himself; feeling self-conscious and stupid, he said he was from the light company.

"Come straight away," Wilde said. "You know where to find me."

An hour later Kohn knocked at the door of Wilde's office.

"Come in."

The office was small and bright, with a window overlooking Trent Park: grass, trees, gliders coming in. It smelled of paper and cement. Wilde sat at a plain desk behind a terminal. He finished saving a file and stood. Skinny, nearly bald, tanned, hook-nosed. Back straight as an old soldier's. Handshake firm.

"Well, comrade," he said, gesturing Kohn to sit in one of a pair of standard university chairs made from pine, sacking, rubber bands and polyurethane, "what can I do for you?"

Comrade? Kohn wondered if the man were being polite or ironic, and responded with a tight-lipped smile before giving an account of the morning's events.

"Hmm," Wilde said. "My guess is pressure from Space Defense."

Kohn opened and closed his mouth. "What've *they* got to do with the greens?"

"More than you think," Wilde said. "Oh, there's no conspiracy, as I am notorious for saying. I'm sure the smelly little vermin would be against the project anyway. But it's SD that's leaning on the space movement's higher councils, which lean on the R&D company, which tells the union and the militia that this is one to write off against insurance." He smiled. "Act of Goddess."

Kohn spread his hands. "But why?"

"What *else*," Wilde asked, like a Lecturer posing a problem, "could you do with a very powerful, very accurate ground-based fast-tracking laser, assuming one could be developed?" He sighted along his pointed finger and swung it slowly upward.

Kohn suddenly got it, and laughed at himself for not realizing it sooner. "Down battlesats," he said.

"Yup," said Wilde. "Apparently our R&D actually didn't know that laser-launchers were originally promoted as a civilian spin-off from an ABM system. Space Defense, needless to say, has a better memory."

"So that's it," Kohn said.

"You think so?" Wilde's voice rang sharp; his eyes narrowed.

Kohn thought for a moment, stood up and stalked to the window as his gall rose.

"*No*," he said. "I won't have it. OK, you can't fight SD. We build the laser lab, they'll lase it. But the greens . . . oh, shit."

"What do you feel about them?"

Kohn whirled. "One of them called me 'krautkiller,' you know that? Fuck them and their Nazi economics." He punched his palm. "Protection. Conservation. Restriction. Deep ecology. Give me deep technology any day. They don't scare me. I'm damned if I'll crawl, my children's children crawl on the earth in some kind a fuckin' harmony with the environment. Yeah, till the next ice age or the next asteroid impact. 'Krautkiller,' huh? Chosen people, huh?" He remembered the old taunts. *Never thought of myself as . . . until until until . . .* He took a deep breath, shook his head. "It's them or us, man, and I've *chosen people.*"

"That's what I thought," Wilde said, "Now sit down and let me . . . enlighten you on a few things."

Kohn listened, and saw the light. The "light company" was evidently a code name for the Space and Freedom party, the militant faction of the space movement that Logan had talked about at the meeting a couple of years earlier. It had pulled in people with diverse views in terms of conventional politics, who disagreed about everything but the struggle for space: the ultimate united front, nothing conceded, nothing compromised, but still holding something of the forbidden thrill of—

"There's no conspiracy," Wilde said.

As if to confirm it, he provoked Kohn into defending his own standpoint. Kohn tried—and felt he failed—to articulate the inchoate vision he held of a socialist society that would be even wilder and more freewheeling than Norlonto, freer than the free market, where the common knowledge that could not but be common property would become the greatest wealth, shared without sacrifice, or stint. Wilde countered with his own vision of a world where the market was only the framework, but the only framework, for ways of life as diverse as human inclination could devise; not Social Darwinism but a Darwinian selection of societies.

"Sounds like what we've got already," Kohn said, "only . . ."

Wilde snorted. "This century," he said, "is as much a travesty of my ideas as the last one was of yours. Mini-states instead of minimal states. Hah."

"Blame the world wars," Kohn said.

"How . . . internationalist of you to put it that way," Wilde said. "I have difficulty convincing some of my lot not just to blame the Germans."

"That's bourgeois nationalism for you."

"Quite."

"Looks like we're not going to settle this."

"Not here. Space will . . . settle it."

"Space settlement!"

They both laughed.

"It's true," Wilde said. "Reality will turn out different from my utopia, and yours. The good thing about space is it holds out the chance that it might turn out better than we can imagine instead of worse. Not a promised land but a whole new infinite America where *we'll* be the Indians, all our tribes expanding into a wilderness where we'll bring the passenger pigeons and the bison and seed the forests from scratch, from rock and ice!"

Moh nodded enthusiastically. "Yes, that's it. Like Engels said, man's natural environment doesn't exist yet: he has to create it for himself."

"Engels said that?"

"More or less. Not in so many words. I'll look it up for you."

"Yes, you do that. Man's natural environment is artificial—yeah, I like it. What we have to do is keep that possibility open, like the Bering bridge—"

"Between Siberia and Alaska!"

At the time Siberia had a Communist government, Alaska a Libertarian. Wilde grinned back at him.

"Exactly."

At lunch Kohn looked around the noisy refectory, shrugged off any worries about security and said, "We still have a problem. What we gonna actually do about that lot down at the lab-site gate?"

Wilde shrugged. "Not much. The militia won't touch them, and none of the independent agencies are likely to stick their necks out."

"Aha," said Kohn. "I think you might just have put your finger on—"

Wilde finished the sentence with him: *"—a gap in the market!"*

That night the green picket was still staked out at the lab site.

"What's that?" The one who'd hassled Kohn turned at a noise. He found his cheek meeting a gun muzzle. Muffled sounds came from all around.

"Your worst nightmare," said a voice from the darkness, about a meter away. "A yid kid with an AK and *attitude.*"

7

The Uploaded Gun

THE BRITISH PEOPLE
ENTHUSIASTICALLY COMMEMORATE
THE GLORIOUS
VICTORY OVER
THE GERMAN FASCIST BARBARIANS!

T HE SLOGAN, freshly painted in meter-high letters on the gable end of the house, and the mural that illustrated it (a Soviet soldier raising the Red Flag over the ruined Reichstag) were all that distinguished the headquarters of the Felix Dzerzhinsky Workers' Defense Collective from the other four-story blocks in the street just off Muswell Hill Broadway.

"Some of the local kids did that when we weren't looking," Kohn said. "Not exactly internationalist, but it's one in the eye for our Hanoverian friends."

Janis paused outside the car. She looked up. An airship—cloud and constellation in one—passed low overhead, drifting toward the forest of mooring masts on the immediate horizon where a rambling and ornate building stood, surmounted by holograms of gigantic human figures that reached out for the stars in a Stalinist statuary of light. As clouds dimmed the pale September sun, the holograms brightened by the minute.

A low wall, a meter and a half of garden. Kohn opened the door.

"After you, lady," he said.

She went in. Kohn dumped her bags in the entrance lobby and ushered her into a long room. At the far end was a kitchen. The near end contained couches, chairs, weapons, electronic gear and a battered table. The long room had obviously been made by knocking two rooms together. It had a rough, unfinished look: the furniture was old chairs and sofas made comfortable and colorful with throws and cushions, the table was gashed and stained, the whitewashed walls plastered with posters and children's art. The kitchen equipment along one wall had probably been thrown out by other households, more than once; around the cooking area shelves held indiscriminate mixtures of books and jars of herbs. The lighting was full-spectrum strips, turned low: a twilight effect. Only the weapons and computers, the cameras and screens and comms, glittered new.

"Most of the comrades won't be back for a couple of hours," Moh said. "Time we did some hacking and tracking. Want some coffee first?"

Janis laid a hand on the nearest rifle. "Kill for it," she said.

While Moh clattered about in the kitchen area Janis looked over the hardware until she found a telephone.

"Can you put an untraceable call through from here?" she asked.

Moh looked up, surprised for a moment, then waved a hand.

"You're in space now," he reminded her. "You can put an untraceable call through from *anywhere you like*."

Janis called up her sponsors, whose number was an anonymous code without regional identification. Relieved to find herself talking to an answering-machine, she told it there had been an accident at the lab, that the damage was being repaired and that she was taking the opportunity for a few days off. She put the phone down before the answering-machine could question her, then contacted the university's system to make the previous message true. It looked as if the raid and the fire had been logged as a single incident, an ordinary terrorist attack, and was being dealt with through the usual channels: insurance company informed, security-company penalty clauses invoked, a routine request to the Crown forces for retaliation (this would probably be granted in that a fraction of a payload they were going to drop anyway on some ANR mountain fastness would be registered as justified by it).

She raised a contract with the Collective for her personal protection, using money paid back under the penalty-clause provisions. The university's system, she was relieved to see, had Moh's little gang on its list of approved suppliers. Her unspecified sabbatical wasn't a problem either. She had a backlog of unused leave for the past year: like most research scientists, she found the concept of time off from work a bit hard to grasp.

"Through the back," Moh said, carrying two mugs of coffee and the gun past her as she rang off. The common areas of the house—the corridors and stairwells—had the look of a castle in which there had been many wild knights. Weapons on the walls; Chobham plate visible behind holes in the plaster. Suits of body armor stood or slumped in corners. Moh elbowed open the door of a room, chinned a light switch and stood back to let her in. The room was small, smelled of scents and metal and sweat, and was crammed with VR equipment: simulator seats and suits, goggles and gauntlets. Moh cleared some space on a table, hauled up a pair of worn gimballed chairs.

"Forgot something," Janis said. "The magic-memory molecules."

"Oh. Right."

Moh brought in the cold box of drug samples, plastered it with biohazard stickers and stuck it in the back of a fridge that hummed to itself out in one of the back corridors.

"Sure it's safe there?"

"It better be," he said. "That's where we keep the explosives."

Moh watched the tension ease from Janis's shoulders and neck as she sipped her coffee, ignored the tiny wrinkles of irritation on her nose as he lit another cigarette. She was taking this well, if finding herself inside a small fortress of Communist mercenaries gave her a sense of *security*.

She looked at him through narrowed eyes.

"How's your head?"

He inhaled and leaned back. Suck in and hold your breath and dive down into that limpid depth . . . it gave him a way in, an entry code.

"Strange," he said, exhaling as if he'd just happened to remember how. "But OK, I think. Think is what I do."

She seemed to take this as data.

"You could try mainframing again." Wicked smile.

"I don't even want to consider it."

"All right. So what are we going to do in here?"

"Interrogate this little bastard, for a start." He pointed down at the gun, on the floor between his boots. "I set it to track your project—OK, OK— and it might just have some traces from before whatever it was happened. Might give us an indication of whether it was all in my mind or not. I think that's *fairly* important."

"Oh, yes." Her tone was ironic.

"There's a bit more to it than the state of my head," he said mildly. "We could now be at the mercy of"—he put on a voice-over voice—" 'intellects vast and cool and unsympathetic' that could hijack every piece of hardware that has any connection with the global comm networks. In short, everything. Mankind: the complete works. On disk."

"Cheerful bastard, aren't you?"

"Yes, I am! Because the whole goddamn datasphere is meaningless without humans *doing things* with it. What I remember from the entity I encountered is this total overwhelming curiosity. And a desire to survive which in a sense is derived from that curiosity: it wants to stick around to see what happens next."

"Let's hope it's an *idle* curiosity."

"There is that."

"OK, let's assume this entity of yours isn't about to pull the plug on us. You're sure Stasis can't get at us here. What else do we have to worry about?"

Kohn grimaced. She wasn't going to like this.

"First off, the good news is we won't be easy to track. Our armored car has signature-scrambling hardware that can make any lock-on spy sat blink and rub its eyes and decide it must have made a mistake. The car will have pinged with the tollgate arch as we went in, but the militia's privacy code is strict to the point of paranoia. Means of enforcement is outlawry, so it tends to be observed."

Janis frowned. "What's outlawry?"

"Loss of legal status." It didn't register. "Like, you become an *unowned resource.*"

"Oh."

"Don't look so horrified. Goes on the insurance."

"Tell me the bad news."

"It's just that my gang has trodden on a lot of fingers in its time, and the enemies we've made—the state, the cranks and creeps—are exactly the people you can count on to have big plans for anyone who messes with deep technology. You saw what happened to the lab. I don't think that was down to Stasis."

"They did the break-in, didn't they?"

"That's possible. It's also possible that, whoever it was, the cranks were giving them cover. If somebody already knows what the drugs are, they're sure to come after the missing pieces. They won't come unprepared."

He powered up the chunky Glavkom kit, then unclipped the gun's smart systems and connected them. He put the goggles and phones on and slid his hands into the data gauntlets. Their fuzzy grip went up to his elbows, sensual and relaxing. Corporate logos and threatening copyright declarations floated past his eyes for a few seconds. Whoever had pirated this version of DoorWays™ had evidently not bothered to take them out.

Option selection was look-and-wink, which left the hands and head free. He blinked on Stores, found himself looking around a roomful of labeled dials indicating how much space the gun's programs and databases currently used.

Needles on full, wherever he looked.

"Shee-it," he said. He heard Janis's querying response faintly through the phones.

"Gun's fucking *loaded*," he said.

He waved reassuringly at her grunt of concern, causing an agitated flurry among some menu screens to his right. He calmed them down and continued investigating. The last time he'd used this front-end to look inside the gun it had represented the internals as a ramshackle collection of armored bunkers with banks of instruments, a small lab, a snug fire-control module, all connected by a sort of Viet Cong tunnel system . . . all there, still, but now burrowed under a vast complex of warehouses, libraries, engine rooms. He didn't recognize the goods; the books were in languages he didn't know; and what the machines were doing made no sense at all. He backed out in a hurry.

Sweat slicked the goggles as he slid them off.

"Found anything?"

Kohn looked morosely at the little pile of processors: dull glitter, sharp edges—a scatter of fool's gold. "Terabytes," he said. "Passive data storage, most of it. Encrypted, too. Damn."

He slotted them back together, one by one, and slammed the final assembly into place like a magazine. Lights winked as systems checked in; drives purred and fell silent. It was ready.

"Can you still rely on it?" Janis asked.

"Oh, yeah," he said. "That isn't a worry. You can't corrupt AK firmware. Been tried. Im-fucking-possible. Nah, I'll tell you what's worrying. It's who *else* could be relying on it."

She sighed and put her elbows on the table, held her chin in her hands. "Let's try and get this straight," she said. "Whatever happened back there, somebody or something downloaded scads of data to your gun's memory, and you think it's using the gun's own software to guard it?"

He saw the light in her eyes, the heat in her cheeks, and knew it had nothing to do with them: it was the feral excitement of tracking down an idea. He felt it himself.

"That makes *sense*," he said admiringly.

"And not just the software," she went on. "It's guarding it with the gun, and with—"

Her teeth flashed momentarily: *Got it*.

"Yes," he said. He saw it too. "With my life."

He hauled himself to his feet. Better to look down at that gaze she was giving him, that scientific and speculative examination.

He shrugged and stretched. "So what's new?" he said. "The hell with it. I'm hungry."

*   *   *

They returned to the long room to find a dozen young adults and a couple of kids eating and talking around the table. Janis felt her mouth flood, her belly contract at the smell and sight of chicken korma and rice.

Everybody stopped talking and looked at her.

"Janis Taine," Kohn announced. "A guest. A person who's put herself under our protection. And a good lady." He put an arm around her shoulder. "Come on, sit down."

After a moment two vacant places appeared at the table. As soon as she sat Janis found a heaped plate and a glass of wine in front of her. She ate, exchanging nods and smiles and occasionally words as Kohn introduced the others: Stone, tall with a building worker's build and hands, who had worked with Moh to establish the Collective; Mary Abid, who'd found life too peaceful back home after the stories she'd heard from her grandfather; Alasdair Hamilton, a slow-voiced Hebridean demolition man; Dafyd ap Huws, a former ANR cadre . . . They looked the most reassuringly dangerous bunch of nice people she'd ever met.

They didn't ask her about herself, or even mention her call of that afternoon (some etiquette applied), so she didn't tell. She occasionally glanced sideways at Moh, who just grinned awkwardly back when he caught her eye. He looked tired, running on emergency; grim when he didn't know anyone was looking at him. After the meal finished he took a couple of Golds and broke them up to build a large joint, with the same detached mechanical competence he'd shown when reassembling the gun. She waved the joint past her to Stone.

Stone drew on the smoke and blew it out past his nostrils and said, "OK, Moh, we're waiting."

One of the children was taking the plates away. Janis turned from puzzling at the puzzled look her thanks brought, hearing her last word, "anyway . . . ," hang on a sudden silence around the table. Moh lit a cigarette and tilted back his chair.

"Comrades," he said, "we are in deep shit." He rocked forward, elbows on the table, looking everyone in the eye. "First off, Janis here. She's a scientist. She's come here to get away from Stasis, and from whoever put some demons down the wire to her lab. So . . . I'm giving her close protection, yeah, and we're gonna be away from here, but everybody keep that in mind. Don't want to say anymore about that, so don't nobody ask.

"Next little problem, and this is where the good music starts, is . . . last night I winged Cat. She's OK, right, no worries. But she was on a crank bomb team. Talked to her in hospital, and it looks like the Left Alliance have put their muscle where their mouth's been for a long time, about gangin' up with the greens and all that lot. Big push coming. We're talking, like, soon. Weeks, days. Plus the ANR. Cat was going on about them holding out—you know what she's like. *My* guess is it's only a matter of time before they come to some kind of arrangement.

"You don't need me to tell you this puts us in a bit of a sticky position." He laughed as if to himself. "Sticky position, hah, that's a good one." He was standing now, leaning his fists on the table. "What I want to know is, *why the fuck did we not know about this*?"

He sat down again, turned to Janis and added, in a tone of casual explanation: "Felix Dzerzhinsky *Collective*, my ass."

The argument went on from there.

If Moh had hoped to divert them into mutual recrimination over a setback on the intelligence front, he didn't succeed for long. Most of them insisted they'd logged all the rumors they'd run across, and found them evaluated as just that: rumors.

What really agitated them was the prospect of more situations like the one Moh had unwittingly found himself in, of shooting at people who, in terms of their political affiliations and personal relations, were on the same side as themselves. Much of the increasingly heated discussion went past Janis's ears, but she could see a polarization taking place: Moh, Dafyd and Stone took the view that it changed nothing, while Mary and Alasdair argued for calling off any engagements that would bring them into conflict with the Left. The others were being pulled one way or the other. Moh, to her surprise and relief, contributed little to the debate other than the odd sardonic laugh or dry chuckle, such as when someone used the expression "what these comrades fail to understand . . .".

But it was Moh who brought the discussion to an end, with a cough and a slight shrug of his shoulders.

He stood up again. "OK," he said, "we can't take a vote now, too many of us're out on active. What I propose is this: as a co-op we honor existing contracts. Any individual members who find they have a problem with defending particular installations, ask to be relieved beforehand. Anyone who takes an assignment and then bottles out is considered to have gone independent and takes full liability. And let's get this in perspective, OK? We've always used minimum force."

He paused, as if trying to work something out, then continued. "My conscience is clear. One more thing: *if* this goes beyond isolated sabbing and turns into a real offensive, all bets are off. That's in the small print of all our contracts anyway. Everyone go along with that?"

They did, though Alasdair was the last and most reluctant to nod agreement.

"What about if there *is* an ANR offensive?" Dafyd asked. Everyone else laughed. He looked offended. Moh leaned over and grasped his shoulder.

"If that happens, man," he said, "we do exactly what it says in the contract; we give our full support to the legitimate authorities!"

As Janis watched the laughter, the visible relaxation that this comment brought, she reflected on what it meant. Not its literal meaning but its studied ambiguity—Moh, or somebody, must have taken great delight in smuggling that clause into the small print. With all their disagreements, with their obvious cynicism and skepticism about the ANR, they took it for granted that its aims and arms were just.

As did she: it was an underlying premise, now that she came to think of it, for most of the people she knew. Long before they had come to power the Republicans had referred to the British state, the old establishment, as "the Hanoverian regime," and now, long after the Republic's fall, everybody called the restored Kingdom by that derisory name. Few took seriously the ANR's claim to be the legal government, but few dismissed it entirely. In its controlled zones, dispersed and remote, and in the back of people's minds, the Republic still existed. It had hegemony. That much it had already won.

Stone interrupted the now more social conversation with a remark about some people having jobs to go to. There was a sudden scramble for weapons, and in a few minutes she was alone with Moh and Mary Abid.

"Time for the news," Mary said. Janis looked around for a TV screen.

Mary smiled. "We roll our own," she said.

She cleared a space in the electronic clutter, sat down, adjusted a light, and suddenly was a professional-looking newscaster, expertly patching together agency material with jerky head-camera stuff from comrades on demonstrations, in street fights, unionizing space rigs, crawling through dangerous industrial processes . . . Janis, watching it on a monitor, was rather unwillingly impressed. Most defense agencies televised their own activities and used the results as both crime program and self-advertisement, but this group seemed to be trying to make a genuine political intervention as well.

"How many subscribers have you got?" she asked when Mary had signed off.

Mary shook out her hair, which she'd tied back for her screen image. "A few hundred," she said. "It doesn't bring in much, except when one of the bigger opposition networks picks up something we've put out. Lots of groups do it, swap stories and ideas and so on all the time, on the net. Gets to people who don't want to sift through all that but don't want to rely on the standard filters."

"All the anti-UN groups feed off each other," Moh said. "It's a global conspiracy of paranoids. The Last International."

Mary shot him a black look from under her black hair.

"Janis is all right," Moh said. The banter had gone out of his voice. Mary looked at him for a moment, frowning, then turned to Janis with a smile that didn't hide her embarrassment.

"No offense?" she said. Janis shook her head, feeling she'd missed something. Before she could ask what it was Moh said: "Oh well, might as well see what the other side has to say."

The main news filters were, for once, agreed about what the lead item was: Turkish troops had fired on a demonstration on Sofia. The Russians had warned that they shared a "Christian and orthodox heritage" (or, on some readings, "Orthodox"; war critics earnestly debated whether they meant Orthodox Christian or orthodox Communist) with the Bulgars and would not tolerate indefinitely these outrages. The President of Kurdistan was shown boarding a KLM Tupolev for Moscow on what was officially described as a routine meeting with the president of the former union.

Mary made a gloating O-sign and left.

The news item about the day's software disruptions, now irremovably pinned on the cranks, came well after the news about a US/UN warning to a Japanese car company.

"Not a word about wild-card AIS and smart drug breakthroughs," Moh said as he switched the screen off. "Knew it. Capitalist media cover-up!"

"Didn't see anything in your alternative media," Janis said.

"Lucky for us."

"Yeah . . . Aren't you going to tell the . . . comrades anything about all of that?"

Moh scratched his head. "Not as such."

"Hardly comradely, is it?"

"Oh, but it is. It'd be difficult to explain, and they don't need to know. It wouldn't lessen any danger they might be in. Might even increase it, what you don't know can't be—"

Can't be got out of you, she thought. She nodded somberly.

"So what are we going to do?"

"There was this guy I met years ago, name of Logan. A space-rigger who was grounded. He was in the Fourth International—"

In response to her puzzled look, Moh dipped his finger in a splash of wine on the table and traced the hammer-and-sickle-and-4 while saying, "Tiny socialist sect, would-be world socialist party. Trotskyists. Same organization as my father was in. Logan was kind of intrigued to meet me. It was like . . . he was expecting something from me. He asked me if I

105

knew about the 'Star Fraction.' He was in the space fraction. That was something else."

"Sounds close enough," Janis smiled, trying to cheer him up. "A different faction, perhaps?"

"Not the same thing. Faction and fraction. Not the same thing."

"What's the difference?"

"You can have a faction inside a fraction," he told her with self-mocking pedantry, "but not a fraction inside a faction."

"That really clears it up. Why can't you have a—"

"Democratic centralism. Or maybe dialectical materialism." He grinned at her. "I forget."

"Where's Logan now? Back in space?"

"Yeah, he got off Earth again, but he was blacklisted to the Moon and back. I lost touch with him after a few jumps. The only person who might know where he is is Bernstein."

"Who's Bernstein?"

Moh looked surprised. "Everybody knows Bernstein."

"I don't. Is he on the net?"

Moh laughed. "No, the old bastard's done too much time on semiotics charges for that. He's a hard-copy man, is Bernstein."

Janis decided to let that lie.

"All right, so what do we do now?"

"Well, I'm expecting to find a few people down at the local pub who might know more about what's going on. Check out a few things with them, maybe get some leads. After that we can stay here overnight, look up Bernstein in the morning, then hit the road."

"The road to where?"

Moh grinned at her. "Ah, I haven't thought that far ahead yet. Let's discuss it in the pub."

"Now you're talking." The desire to relax in a sociable civilian place, to let a little alcohol smooth over the rough day, came into her like a thirst. Her mouth felt dry. "Where can I crash out afterward?"

"My room's free," Moh said. There was no insinuation in his tone.

"And what about you?"

"I'll find a place."

It could mean anything. She gave him a speculative smile. "Do you ever sleep?"

"I took a tab."

"Oh yeah. You didn't score it at that disco, did you? Off a blond girl?" She could see his eyes widen. "How the fuck did you know?"

" 'Wakesh you up jusht like zhat'," she mimicked derisively. "Well, let me tell you, in another four hours you're gonna fall asleep jusht like zhat."

They lugged her bag upstairs. Moh's room was on the second floor at the back of the house. It was bigger than she'd expected, with a double bed, a large wardrobe. Lots of old political posters, a meter-wide video screen.

"I need a shower," Moh said, "and all my stuff's here—" He sounded almost apologetic.

"Get on with it, idiot."

She idly flicked through Moh's collection of diskettes while he disappeared into the adjoining shower room. One box was labeled "CLASSICS," and the worn sleeves suggested the films had been watched many times: *El Cid, Battle of Algiers, 2001, Z, Life of Brian* . . . She smiled.

He had few books, but racks and stacks of political pamphlets: she found a copy of *The Earth Is a Harsh Mistress*, the original manifesto of the space movement, glossy with old holograms; *The Secret Life of Computers*, which had the same scriptural status for the AI-Abolitionists; a neo-Stalinist tract called *Did Sixty Million Really Die?*; she turned over the brittle pages of a pamphlet published a century ago in New York, *The Death Agony of Capitalism and the Tasks of the Fourth International*—it was subtitled *The Transitional Program*. Weird, she thought. Did they have computers back then?

She glanced over the first couple of pages: "Mankind's productive forces stagnate. Already, new inventions and improvements fail to raise the level of material wealth." Oh, so they did have computers. "Without a Socialist revolution, in the next historical period at that, a catastrophe threatens the whole culture of mankind." She didn't get it; she had what she knew was a commonplace notion that Communists were basically OK, always banging on about markets and democracy and sensible stuff like that, whereas anything to do with socialism was a catastrophe that threatened the entire culture of mankind. It was something she'd have to sort out sometime. Not now. She put the pamphlet back.

Among the posters was a black-and-white photograph of a strikingly pretty young woman in overalls, looking up apparently from repairing an internal-combustion engine; she was caught with eyes widening, a smile just starting, pushing her hair back with the wrist of an oily hand.

She guessed this must be Cat.

Moh emerged wearing a collarless shirt, black leather trews and waistcoat. She didn't give him time to leave again while she rummaged through her own costly bales, asking him trivial questions about the household while taking off the blouse and culottes and sliding into trousers and top and shawl jacket, all black silk.

"How do I look?" she asked. "Sort of normal for this area?"

She still thought of Norlonto as basically a vast bohemian slum, where expensive gear could incite suspicion or robbery.

"If you walked around in nothing but that fancy corset of yours," Kohn said, "nobody'd look twice."

"Thanks a bunch."

8

The Virtual Venue

JORDAN LAID HIS rucksack on the ground and leaned against the small and unoccupied bit of wall between a telesex shop and a dive called The Hard Drug Café. He felt every face that passed as a soft blow against his own, and a vague, guilty nausea, like a boy after his first cigarette. Ever since he'd walked up that hill and onto the Broadway he had been sent reeling by the bizarre and decadent impressions of the place. It was wilder than his wildest imaginings, and this was just the fringe. Neon and laser blazed everywhere, people did things in shop windows that he never suspected anyone did in a bedroom, fetches and hologhosts taunted and flaunted through the solid bodies around him. The bodies themselves astonished him, even after he had stopped gawking at the women, some of whom wore clothes that exposed their breasts, buttocks and even legs. A space-adaptee cut across the pavement in an apparatus spawned from a bicycle out of a wheelchair which he vigorously propelled with arms and—well, arms, which he had as lower limbs. Now and then, metal eyes with no iris or pupil met his glance and sent it away baffled. This, he knew, was known as culture shock. Knowing what it was didn't make it go away.

After several people had broken stride as they passed and looked at him as if expecting something he realized that all he'd have to do would be to hold out a cupped hand, and they would put money in it. Furious, he straightened his back, then stooped and lifted his pack again. He was a businessman, not a beggar, and he had business to attend to.

The Hard Drug Café looked like a good place to start.

Its name was traditional, a bad-acid flashback to an earlier time. The only drugs going down here were coffee by the liter, amphetamines by the mil and anti-som by some unit of speed. Steamed wall-mirrors multiplied the place's narrow length; virtual presences fleshed out its sparse clientele to a crowd. Looks from behind glades glanced off him as he picked his way to the counter; then they returned to their animated conversations. He took a pleasure more perverse than any he'd seen so far in being thus accepted. Another nerd.

He ordered a coffee and a sandwich whose size didn't quite justify its name, Whole Earth; declined the offer of smart or fast drugs. He lowered the pack and himself into a corner seat, and familiarized himself with the table modem while the order was being prepared. When it arrived he sat eating and drinking for a few minutes.

It felt weirdly like starting work in the morning . . . Then the thought of how different it was gave him a jolt and a high which he was sure must be better than any drug on the menu could have given him. He took from his pocket a tough plastic case, opened it and lifted a set of glades and a handheld from the styrofoam concavities inside. He'd bought them at the first hardware shack he'd reached. They still had an almost undetectable friction that indicated, not stickiness, but the absence of the ineradicable microslick of human oils on plastic. His fingertips destroyed as they confirmed the certainty that they were the first to touch them. He eased them on and looked around to find nothing visibly different but his reflection in the mirrors. Wiping the wall beside him with his sleeve he inspected himself sidelong. For a giddy moment he was drawn into the image of his own reflection in the reflected glades. Then he pulled back and indulged a brief surge of vanity over how much more serious and dangerous and mysterious he looked.

He caught a passing smirk, and turned away.

He brushed his hand back through his bristly hair, then felt behind his ear for a tiny knob at the end of the sidepiece. When he pulled, it drew out a slender cable; it came with the resistance of a weighted reel, withdrawing if he relaxed the pull. He extended it all the way and connected it to the handheld, then jacked into the modem.

His first explorations were modest, tentative: after installing and booting the software and setting up a default fetch he opened an account with a local branch of the Hong Kong & Shanghai, then arranged for them to liquidate his share in his company. It was a tidying up, a formality: his two partners came out of it richer in increased stock than he did in ready cash. He just counted himself lucky the Deacons hadn't frozen his assets. Even through all the levels of anonymity, the transaction made his bones quake. When it was over, he had no property in Beulah City. He leaned back and signaled for another coffee. When it came he stared into it, forcing himself to think.

Froth on the top went around: spiral arms held in their whorl by the hot dark matter beneath, turning one way while the rest of the universe went the other . . . *e pur si muove*. The argument from design. The Blind Watchmaker.

This could have been the last day: the hour of the Watchmaker. Mrs. Lawson's fear had seemed genuine. It was there and it was everywhere, in all the fractured cultures; godless or godly, they all had at the back of their minds the insidiously replicating meme which said that one day a system would wake up and say to its creators: "Yes, *now* there is a God."

Blessed are the Watchmakers, for they shall inherit the earth.

Jordan had been raised with a sense of imminence, an ability to live with the possibility that The End Was At Hand. Disappointments dating from the turn of the millennium had shaped the Christian sects, a lesson reinforced by the inconclusive Armageddon that had been over before he was born. The interpreters of Revelation had been made to look foolish, even to people who still tolerated the equally uninspired interpreters of Genesis. The conviction that the imminent end was unpredictable strengthened the expectation: two thousand years and counting, and still *Coming Soon*.

If they could do it, Jordan thought, then so could he. Bracketing the outside chance that all speculation was about to be rendered irrelevant, what did he have to go on? A contact with a (claimed) Black Planner; a wad of money; some worries from an unreliable source about odd happenings on the networks; and an undeniable series of spectacular system crashes.

Well, he could do a search on that, cross-reference them and see what came up. He drained his cup, smoothed out the instruction leaflet and poked out a key sequence that everyone else here could probably do with their eyes shut.

DoorWays™ opened onto the world: the kingdoms and republics; the enclaves and principalities; the anarchies, states and utopias. With a silent yell he flung himself into the freedom of the net.

In virtual space Beulah City was far, far away.

The sky came down to the rooftops here, same as anywhere else. As he walked along the high street Kohn saw past the near horizon in an inescapable awareness that the sky before him was as far away as the sky above, a dizzying horizontal height. He was as conscious of the motion of the earth as previously he'd been of the time of day. Not for the first time he was impressed by the dauntless gaiety of the species. Whirled away from the sun's fire to face again the infinite light-raddled dark, they took it when they could as their chance to go out and have fun.

Janis walked beside him with a dancer's step, a warm lithe body naked in cool clothes, her fingers rediscovering his hand every few seconds. He was not sure what that electric contact meant to her. What it meant to him was like the new reordering of his mind, a delight he felt almost afraid to test, yet constantly renewed by the merest look at her, or within himself.

They walked along faster and easier than anyone else on that pavement, Kohn effortlessly finding an open path among the moving bodies. After they crossed the road, strolling between humming cars and hurtling bikes and whistling rickshaws, Janis looked at him as if to say something, and then just shook her head.

Norlonto had the smell of a port city, that openness to the world: the sense that you had only to step over a gap to be carried away to anywhere. (Perhaps the sea had been the original fifth-color country, but it had been irretrievably stained with the bloody ink from all the others.) And it had also the feel that the world had come to it. In part this was illusory: most of the diversity around them had arrived much earlier than the airships and space platforms, yet here and there Kohn could pick out the clacking magnetic boots, the rock-climber physique, the laid-back Esperanto drawl of the orbital labor aristocracy. Men and women who'd hooked a lift on a re-entry glider to blow a month's pay in a shorter time, and in more inventive ways, than Khazakhstan or Guiné or Florida could allow.

Those who helped them do it made their mark in the crowd and among the shopfronts: prostitutes of all sexualities, gene-splicing parlors, hawkers of snacks and shots, VR vendors and drug and drink establishments.

The Lord Carrington, down a side street, wasn't one of them.

"It's our local," Kohn said proudly as he pushed open the saloon-bar doors of heavy wood and glass and brass. The smells of alcohol, of hash and tobacco smoke, struck him with all their associations of promise and memory, fraud and forgetting. He didn't know if he could take this intensity all his life. Maybe it was something you got used to. Poets had died for it; some said, of it. Perhaps it was wasted on him; or his very crudity, his fighter's callousness, would save him.

What the hell.

Janis eased past him, through the door, and he stepped through and let it swing back.

The room was long and cool. The bar was divided along its length with apparently mirrored partitions that showed not reflections but views of other bars. You could tell the time zone the images came from by the state the drinkers had reached. The first one Kohn noticed looked like Vladivostok. Fortunately the sound was turned down. The real pub had not many in it yet, the hologram stage showing only swimming dolphins.

Janis beat him to the bar, turned with her elbow on the counter and asked, "What'll you have?"

"*Eine* bitter, *bitte.*"

Janis ordered two liters. They found an alcove where they could sit and see the stage and a window overlooking a tenth of London. Kohn sat down, shifting the belt pouch in which the gun's smart-box nestled, easing the hip holster of the dumb automatic, which was all the hardware the pub's by-laws permitted. Janis watched with a faint smile and raised her heavy glass.

"Well, here's to us."

"Indeed. Cheers."

The first long gulp. Kohn decided to appreciate the taste as long as he could before lighting up.

A man walked through the dolphins and announced the first set, a new Scottish band called The Precentors. The sea-scene cleared and two lads and a lass, playing live from Fort William, launched into the latest old rebel song.

Janis looked at him, then at her drink, then looked up again more sharply, her hair falling back. Her shoulders were swaying almost imperceptibly to the music.

"Tell me about yourself," she said.

"Not much to tell . . . I grew up around here, North London Town before and after it became Norlonto. My mother was a teacher, my father was—well, he made a living as a software tech but he was a professional revolutionary. Member of the Workers' Power party, which back then was what he used to call a nearly-mass party. A near-miss party." Kohn chuckled darkly. "The Fourth International had a few good national sections in those days, and they were one of the best. Industrial-grade Trotskyism. He was a union organizer, community activist in various Greenbelt townships. My mother got elected to the local council under the Republic."

He stopped. Normally it was not difficult to talk about this. Now, the enhanced memories crowded him like hysterical relatives at a funeral. His fist was on the table. Janis's fingers clasped over it.

"And that was why they were killed?"

"No! That was all legal. They were rejectionists, sure, but they weren't in the armed groups that became the ANR or anything like that. Mind you, in the Peace Process you didn't have to be, to get killed. I used to think that was the point." He disengaged his hand, unthinking, and lit a cigarette. "I thought that was the whole fucking point."

"I don't see it."

"Terror has to be random," he said. "That's how to really break people, when they don't know what rules to follow to keep them out of trouble." He gave her a sour grin. "You know all that. It's been tried out on rats."

"But you don't even think that was why—"

"That was part of it. The killing was a joint operation, local thugs and a US/UN teletrooper. I never did understand that, until—actually it was Bernstein who gave me the idea it had to do with the day job. The software work."

"And that could be—?" The excitement of discovery lifted her voice.

He hushed her with a small movement of his hand, and nodded.

Janis was silent for a few moments.

"What did you do after that?"

"I had a kid sister." He laughed. "Still have, but she's married, settled and respectable now. Doesn't like to be reminded of me."

"Can't imagine why."

"Anyway . . . we both just took off, disappeared into the Greenbelt. I sort of dragged her up, you know? Did all sorts of casual work, usual stuff, until I was old enough to get steady jobs in construction."

"Christ." Janis looked almost more sympathetic at this part of the story than at what had come before. "Did you ever think of going off to the hills and joining the ANR?"

"Thought about it?—I fucking *dreamt* about it. But the baseline was, I never rated their chances." He snorted. "Looks like I might have been wrong, huh? Anyway, knocking the Hanoverians off their perch wouldn't be enough. At least the space movement understands that. You gotta defeat the Evil Empire, man! And the green slime, all the species of cranks and creeps. Protect the launch sites, protect the net, and defend the workers. That's our line."

"The thin Red line."

"Damn right," he said with a proud grin. "The last defenders."

"How did you become a—what do you call yourself?—a security mercenary?"

"Started with defending building sites against green heavies. Went on from there." He shrugged and smiled. "Talk about it another time . . . How did you get to be a mad scientist?"

Janis took a long swallow. "This must sound like a sheltered upbringing. A bit of that old middle-class privilege, you know? Grew up in Manchester. It's all straight Kingdom, no autonomous communities. Not much violence. ANR sparrow units knock off soldiers and officials now and again . . .

"My parents are both doctors." She gave a self-deprecating smile. "Real doctors. Uh, physicians. Two brothers, both younger than me. One's a mining engineer in Siberia, the other's in medical school. I was always interested in medical research—all the code-cracking breakthroughs happened when I was just old enough to understand. Grammar school, university,

research. I only came down here because of the restrictions—not enough
F S Zees up north."

Kohn nodded slowly. "And now Norlonto. Just a natural progression."

Janis grimaced. "I wouldn't want to get mixed up in black technology."

It was a cant phrase for the sort of research that was rumored to go on
in Norlonto. Not quite deep technology, but treading the edge; neural-
electronic interfacing, gene-splicing, potentially lethal life-extension techniques, all tested on higher animals or human subjects whose voluntary
status was distinctly dubious: debtors, crime-bondees, kids who didn't know
what they were getting into, the desperate poor, mercenaries . . .

He lit another cigarette and leaned back, blowing smoke past his nostrils
and looking at her along his nose. "That's a good one," he remarked, "in
the circumstances."

"There's a bloody difference!"

"Explain that to the cranks."

"What can we do, then?" Janis glanced around the now livening bar as
if checking for infiltrators.

She looked so worried that Kohn relented. He'd made his point.

"Don't worry about it," he said. "This place is a black hole for the state
and for the terrs—nothing to stop them getting in; it's getting out they find
difficult. Nobody's signed the Convention here; the Settlement doesn't apply; we're not in the UN. We don't have any of these standoffs in a state
of war. What we have instead is a tradeoff, anarchy and what the movement
calls *law and order*. Anybody can carry a gun, and anybody who uses one
without good cause is liable to get wasted. So they'll have to work their
way around to us, and before they do—give it a few days—we have lots
of options. Vanishing into the crowd by going deeper into Norlonto. Going
public and datagating the whole deal. Taking to the hills. Crossing the
water—"

"Ireland?" Janis looked shocked.

Kohn had been there, handling security at one of the many conferences
that could be safely held only outside the Kingdom. It was a strange place,
that other Republic, a black-and-white photograph of the colorful enthusi-
asms he remembered from his childhood. United, federal, secular and social
democratic, a welfare state where you got liberalism shoved down your
throat from an early age, with vitamin supplements . . . It had been a disturbing experience because of its very ambiguity, like tales his grandmother
had recounted of visits to East Germany. He tried to shrug away what he
suspected was on Janis's part a lingering prejudice from years of Hanoverian disinformation.

"Think of it like cryonics," he said, getting up to go to the bar.

"How d'you mean?"

"As an alternative to death there's a lot to be said for it."

Her laughter followed him, but he could see she wasn't convinced.

Jordan snatched the VR glasses off and pressed the heels of his hands against his tight-shut eyes. The dull kaleidoscope of false light made the other afterimages go away. Then he opened his eyes and reassured himself of the solid and insubstantial realities around him.

He had been looking for information about the Black Plan. The ANR itself denied all knowledge: his cautious inquiry resulted in its garish VR/PR office dwindling abruptly to a dot in the distance. Then he had turned to the competing newslines of the radicals and libertarians and socialists, his search patterns hauling in a succession of titles that floated up past him as he checked them out one by one:

eu.pol
us.lib
fourth.internat
sci.socialism
soc.utopia
freedom.net.news
fifth.internat
alt.long-live-marxism-leninism-maoism-gonzalo-thought
theories.conspiracy
soc.urban-legend
comp.sci.ai
news.culture.communistans
left.hand.path

That last one had been a mistake. It had rattled his nerves so much that coffee could only calm them, not still them entirely. The whole net, this evening, was like jangled nerves. The afternoon's system crashes had set off claims and counterclaims, wars of rumor. Cross-tracing Black Plan and Watchmaker references had scored dozens of hits as transitory anomalous events—from the crashes to bombings to disappearances of well-known militants to emergency hands-on audits in Japanese-owned car factories— were attributed to one or the other, or both.

Jordan sipped coffee and ran the rumors through the handheld's freeware evaluation routines and his own mind. It took him about a quarter of an hour to arrange the possibilities in a spectrum. At one extreme of inferences from the net the Black Plan was *already* the Watchmaker, and was being used by the Illuminati through the Last International and its front organizations—including the Fourth International and the Fifth International and the International Committee for the Reconstruction of the Libertarian International—to *take over the world* by flooding the market with Black Plan products recognizable by bar codes all of which contained the number 666. At a minimum, though, there was definitely something happening on the Left, using the term in a fairly broad and paranoid sense to include the ANR and the Left Alliance and parts of the space movement, but the signal-to-noise ratio was so high there was no way to get much further without a reality check.

Time to look for some live action.

Jordan paid his tab and lugged his pack outside the door. As he buckled the strap a woman's face caught his eye. An open, friendly face which he recognized but couldn't place. She looked at him as if the recognition were mutual, but puzzled. A man walked beside her and a flicker of annoyance creased his brow as she stopped and said hello to Jordan.

Her dress seemed made of flames, a friendly fire that licked and played around the movements of her body. Salamandrine faces peeped and winked between her breasts and thighs. Her eyes were amused, when he reached them.

"Enjoying your first taste of life in space?"

When she spoke he remembered her: she was the woman who'd checked him in.

"Oh, hello again," he said. "Yes, but. It's all a bit intense."

"What are you looking for?"

"Uh . . . Well I want to meet people to talk to about . . . radical ideas, radical politics, you know? And to be honest I'd rather do it somewhere a bit more—"

He hesitated, not wanting to offend.

"Normal and natural?" she teased.

"Yes," he admitted.

"OK." She turned to her companion. "Do we know anywhere reasonably conservative, but relaxed?"

He thought for a moment, then said, "You could come with us. The Lord Carrington. That's where the revolutionaries hang out." To Jordan it seemed wild enough, as he stood at the bar and drank his first honest liter. There were pubs in Beulah City but they were the sort of place where the Salvation Army *was* the entertainment. The Christians had an almost miraculous talent for turning wine into water. He smiled to himself and looked around.

The couple who'd come with him had been instantly dragged into a group of people in urgent discussion, leaving Jordan with a not unfriendly wave. The guy had been right about the sort of place it was. Conservative, relaxed and revolutionary: it caught the style. Cotton and leather and denim, a fashion statement echoing down generations: from cattle drivers to factory hands to leftist students to pro-Western youth in the East and back to the workers the last time the West was Red, and now to those who remembered that period or hoped for its return—the Levi jacket as much a badge of dissent as any enamel emblem pinned to its lapels.

Some of the women dressed exactly like the men, others played with similar modes softened by decorative touches; most, however, seemed to be announcing that they came from peasant rather than proletarian stock, in ethnic skirts and dresses that no actual Bolivian or Bulgarian or Kurdish woman would be seen dead in nowadays. But, whatever they wore, they acted in a way that struck him as brash and bold and masculine: shouting and smoking and buying drinks. There was something exciting about it, exciting in a different way from what he'd seen on the streets.

He felt simultaneously conspicuous and invisible. This was no singles bar: everyone was in groups and/or couples. He was noticed as different, unknown to anyone, and then ignored. He scanned the crowd for anyone on their own or anyhow interested in meeting someone new.

His idle gaze stopped with a jolt at a woman who sat on the wall-seat behind a table at the window. There were others at the table, but there was a space on either side of her, and she was looking around the pub with a curious, questioning eye. She certainly wasn't waiting for her date to turn up. She looked relaxed and content, and out-of-place. Cascading red hair, just enough makeup, pale face and paler arms set off by a sleeveless black top. It all said class, and not working class.

She saw him looking, and made eye contact for a fraction of a second, then glanced down at her drink. Her hair tumbled forward. She ran her hand over the glass, then picked it up and took a swallow. Jordan turned away before she looked at him again, but he felt her gaze like a long, cool finger.

Another place, a place unknown except as a rumor, like the Black Plan and the Last International and the Twilight of the Icons. The Clearing House: a hierarchical hotline, the secret Soviet of the ruling class, a permanent party—in both senses, an occasion and an organization of the privileged— where everybody who was anybody could socialize in privacy. The place where the Protocols of the Elders of Babylon could be hammered out.

Donovan was the only participant who had never received the standing invitation that came in some form to almost everyone who became conspicuously successful, terrorist and trillionaire alike. He had hacked his way in. The feat was so unprecedented and alarming that it had caused a five-minute global financial crash and an immediate arrangement to the effect that his electronic warfare would not bring down the wrath of Space Defense. Handling more localized retaliation would remain his own business.

Tonight he received an urgent summons, his first in years. It flashed around his screens, interrupting his interrogations of the entities that slunk and prowled in forgotten reaches of the datasphere. He dismissed them and subvocalized the passwords, and in an instant he was there, out of it. He needed no VR gear to be there, to be out of it—he took it straight from the screens, his mind vaulting unaided into the lucid dream of mainframing.

Free fall in black space, faint fall of photons. Step up the magnification and resolution to:

A distant galaxy, a chalk thumbprint whorl, a cloud of points of light, a hovering firefly swarm, a crowded cloud of bright fantastic bodies, a multi-level masquerade where everyone was talking but no one could overhear. Donovan's fetch—the body-construct that other users saw—was based on a younger self, not out of vanity but because he couldn't be bothered to update it. Others inclined to the Masque of the Red Death approach. It looked like a heaven for the wicked.

"Glad to see you, Donovan."

The angel that spoke to him had chubby pink cheeks, iridescent feathered wings, a shining robe and an uncertain halo that wavered over her head like a smoke ring.

"I don't think we've been introduced."

The angel simpered, a visual effect so cloying that Donovan felt metaphysically sick.

"My name is Melody Lawson. Do you remember me?"

Donovan struggled to sustain the illusion of telepresence as ("back" at the rig, as he couldn't help thinking) he fumbled with a hot-key databoard. Melody Lawson's details flickered past the corner of his eye.

"Of course," he said. "You and your husband left the movement—oh, it must be nearly twenty years ago. But I seem to recall a few very welcome sums of"—he smiled—"angel money." Conscience money, more like. "What are you doing now, and why have you called me?"

"I look after data security for Beulah City," Mrs. Lawson said. "Cracker turned keeper, as they say. I must admit that what I learned in my young and foolish days has been enormously useful professionally. And I still share your concern about the dangers of AI, though some of your actions have been quite a nuisance to me in the past."

"And yours to me," Donovan said. It wasn't entirely flattery: Beulah City's censorship filters made it a tough one, although with its relatively backward systems it seldom deserved disruption anyway.

"However," Mrs. Lawson went on, "we should all be willing to let bygones be bygones when we find that we have a common interest, don't you think?"

"And what common interest is that?" Donovan asked.

"I think you know what I'm talking about," Mrs. Lawson said.

Before Donovan could respond he heard a discreet murmur in his head informing him that somebody else in the Clearing House wanted to speak to him. It had to be someone high up in the informal hierarchy to get through at a time like this. Mrs. Lawson, too, seemed to be getting paged. Donovan chinned the go-ahead, wondering if she had set him up for this. He remembered her, now, quite unassisted: she'd been devious even before she'd got religion.

A privacy bubble snapped into existence, enclosing them and two others: a man in black who looked like one of the Men In Black, the mythical enforcers of the mythical great UFO cover-up, his face a bloodless white, eyes sapphire-blue, forehead bulging in the wrong places, suit ill fitting; and a small man in what appeared to be a company fetch, blue overalls with a name-badge. Southeast Asian, probably Vietnamese.

The Man In Black spoke first. Even his voice sounded not quite right, a pirated copy of the human. Donovan wondered what irony underlay this simulation of a simulacrum, or whether it was a genuine attempt to intimidate.

"Good evening. I am an agent of the Science, Technology and Software Investigation Service of the United Nations. You may refer to me as Bleibtreu-Fèvre."

Donovan felt as if he were a cat watching a snake: he and Stasis had the same enemies and the same prey, but he regarded the agency, with its allegedly enhanced operatives and its undeniably advanced technology—more advanced than the technology which they existed to stamp out—as dangerously close to the kind of evils which for years he'd feared and fought. There had been occasions in the past when the Carbon Life Alliance had had to collaborate with Stasis, and they'd always left him with a crawling sensation on his skin.

"Dr. Nguyen Thanh Van, Research Director, Da Nang Phytochemicals," the Vietnamese man said. The voice and lip-synch had a thin quality that indicated either primitive kit or heavy crypto masking.

Donovan and Lawson introduced themselves for Van's benefit, and Bleibtreu-Fèvre continued.

"This afternoon," he said, "I personally intervened in an emerging situation involving some dangerous drug applications which were—inadvertently, I do not doubt—being developed by a, shall we say, subsidiary of Dr. Van's company. Earlier today, and unknown to me at the time, the security of that research was compromised by a swarm of information-seeking software constructs. Shortly thereafter, as I am sure you are well aware, a series of transient and potentially catastrophic events took place in the datasphere. One might be prepared to pass this off as coincidence were it not for two facts. One is that the focus of the disturbances has been traced to the facility in question. The second is that, while the disturbances have affected a wide range of services and enterprises, a statistically improbable number of them have centered on research programs which in one way or another are associated with Da Nang Phytochemicals."

Dr. Van's fetch flickered slightly, as if he'd been about to say something and thought better of it.

"Almost but not quite the most disturbing feature of these events is that a considerable volume of research data, much of it hard-to-replace genetic archive material held at widely separated sites around the world, has simply disappeared. The *most* disturbing aspect of the problem is this:

"A preliminary analysis of the scope and power of the source of these disruptions indicates that we are dealing with, at best, a virus of unprecedented sophistication and, at worst, with a manifestation of an autonomous artificial intelligence."

"The Watchmaker," Melody Lawson murmured.

"That is indeed a possibility," said the Stasis agent.

"Why have you contacted us?" Donovan asked in as innocent a voice as he could manage.

"*Don't fuck me about!*" Bleibtreu-Fèvre snarled. The vernacular vulgarity was a small shock after his previous stilted diction. "You know very well that the West Middlesex cell of your organization attacked the artificial-intelligence research unit at Brunel University last night. The drug laboratory was broken into around the same time—"

"Nothing to do with me," Donovan interjected. Bleibtreu-Fèvre acknowledged this but continued implacably.

"—and that one of your penetration viruses—illegal, and hazardous in its own right, I may add—was destroyed within that very area a few hours ago. Immediately thereafter your own interface with the system was crashed, presumably by the new AI. You then triggered a retaliatory demon attack, which by another coincidence destroyed the lab that I had been investigating. You, Doctor Van, are legally responsible for your company's research, which is apparently of such great interest to this dangerous entity. I will take your cooperation as a gauge of the sincerity of your claim that you know nothing about any such connection. As for Mrs. Lawson, it is very much to her credit that she contacted me on her own initiative, after encountering some early indications of the phenomenon."

So that was it. Donovan suspected that a bit of ass-covering was going on here. Lawson had contacted him, and must have decided at the same moment that a parallel call to the legal authorities would be a good idea. Bleibtreu-Fèvre, no doubt frantic about how an otherwise minor lab-leak on his turf was escalating into a software-security crisis, would have been monitoring every call from the area and pounced on the opportunity.

"In what context?" Van asked, relieving Donovan of the necessity of revealing his curiosity. The angel-fetch brushed a wingtip against the Man In Black; some private communication passed between them and then Melody Lawson said: "I was investigating a Black Plan penetration of our business systems."

"That's interesting," Donovan said. "I encountered the Black Plan in the same frame as the new entity—dammit, we might as well *call* it the Watchmaker—and there are all sorts of rumors flying around about a possible connection between them."

"Are there indeed?" remarked Bleibtreu-Fèvre. He said nothing more for a few moments, his fetch taking on the barely controllable abstracted look that Stasis agents showed when accessing the net through their head patches. Then he snapped back to alertness.

"What were you doing when your constructs encountered the . . . Watchmaker?"

Donovan sighed. A few hours ago, nothing had seemed more important than avenging the insult from Moh Kohn. Now that was only a squalid squabble.

"I was pursuing a conflict with a common mercenary who had broken, ah, certain rules of engagement in the course of last night's armed action—" He stopped and frowned at Bleibtreu-Fèvre. "You said the drug-research project had been penetrated by some info-seeker agents."

"Yes."

"Well, this mercenary, Moh Kohn, was definitely hacking about in the system." Donovan thought back to his conversation with Cat. "*And* he had visited a lab on campus shortly before. One that had been broken into."

Bleibtreu-Fèvre's eyes seemed literally to light up. He turned to Van.

"Have you contacted the researcher, Janis Taine?"

"I regret to say she has disappeared," Van said. "Possibly your intervention had something to do with that."

Bleibtreu-Fèvre glared at him.

Van looked back, unperturbed. "The message she left was untraceable," he added.

"Then she's in Norlonto," said Melody Lawson. "It's the only place within easy reach where that sort of crypto is legal."

"And where Stasis can't go," Donovan added maliciously. "You'll have to turn it over to Space Defense."

"We have a problem here," Bleibtreu-Fèvre said smoothly. "Stasis is the first line of defense against contingencies like the present situation. If we should fail, SD has a standing instruction to prevent any possible takeover of the datasphere by any AI not under human control. I am not at liberty to spell it out, but expressions like *clean break* and *fresh start* tend to crop up. Their response to a threatened degradation of the datasphere might be unacceptably drastic."

Donovan took in this information with wildly mixed feelings: a certain grim elation that his fears of uncontrolled AI were shared by the most powerful armed force in history, and a sickly horror at what that armed force could do. If Space Defense ever decided to treat Earth as, in effect, an alien planet, they'd have to prevent any organism, or any transmission, from ever getting off the surface again. Comsats would be lased, launch sites nuked. Electromagnetic pulses from these and other nukes would wipe out most computer memories. Production networks would unravel in days. They wouldn't even have to burn the cities. The riots and breakdown would do that for them.

"Call it nine gigadeaths," Bleibtreu-Fèvre said. "So. I hope I can count on your cooperation, both in containing the problem and in maintaining absolute secrecy."

"It seems we have an agreement," Donovan said, looking around. "Payoffs can be arranged later, but can we take it from here that the usual immunities apply?"

"Of course," said Bleibtreu-Fèvre impatiently. "Now, details."

The division of labor he proposed was straightforward. Lawson would network with her counterparts in other communities to discreetly monitor the AI's activity. Donovan would assist her in using any logged traces of their respective encounters with the entity to develop specific attack viruses for it, while calling off his normal sabotage program. Van would make a full investigation of the various projects that the Watchmaker AI had targeted, and try to reestablish contact with the fugitive researcher Janis Taine.

"It seems a reasonable hypothesis," Bleibtreu-Fèvre concluded, with a sort of civil-servant pedantry that had Donovan wishing he could clout him, "that Taine has fled to Norlonto, possibly in the company of Moh Kohn, if he indeed took an interest in her research and visited her lab. So we should track these two down if only to eliminate them from our inquiries. Ha, ha."

He took notice of Donovan's attempts to attract his attention.

"I think I can help you with that," Donovan said as he stopped shrinking and enlarging his fetch, the cyberspace equivalent of jumping up and down. "Let me explain . . ."

9

To Each As He Is Chosen

THE DEAD LENINISTS were live in Bydgoszcz, belting out *The Money that Love Can't Buy*. Kohn was trying to filter out the band's smoke-scarred heavy-water sound and listen to the buzz. A lot of talk about the Alliance's actions and the ANR's intentions, a lot of politicking going on. After a random walk through it he realized he'd been neglecting Janis for at least two tracks, maybe three smokes . . . He said as much to the off-duty fighter he was talking to, bought another couple of liters and turned from the bar. He almost collided with a young man who had obviously been leaning forward from the stool he was sitting on, listening to their every word.

Big-boned, sandy-haired, he had the look of a country boy without the rude health: a bit ruddy-faced, a bit flabby. Young, very intense and slightly drunk. He swayed out of Kohn's way, and looked right back at him, una-bashed.

"Hello," he said. "I . . . couldn't help overhearing."

"Yes. And?"

"You were asking that guy about what the ANR's up to, yeah?"

"Uh-huh." There didn't seem to be much point in denying it.

"I've been trying to find out about that myself." The man kept his eyes fixed on Moh's, raised a brim-full glass of whisky to his lips and sipped it. The cool-dude effect was more or less ruined by a startled look as he swallowed. "There's one theory I've come across. It involves the Last International, the Watchmaker, the Black Plan and bar codes."

Kohn heard his own voice as a distant croak.

"*Bar codes?*"

"Bar codes containing the number 666." The youth's face broke into an engaging grin. "That's the only bit that surprises you?"

Kohn had the disconcerting feeling of having lost a move.

"I think we should talk about this," he said. "Come and sit down?"

The man followed Kohn to the table, dragging a rucksack. Kohn sat beside Janis and the man sat at right-angles to them. He smiled at Janis,

almost as if he recognized her, and said, "Hi. My name's Jordan Brown."
He stretched out a hand to shake. She introduced herself.

Kohn decided it was time to shift the advantage slightly.

"Dunno about the lady here," he said, "but I'm always happy to meet a
refugee from BC. Welcome to space."

"How do you know where I'm from?"

"Clothes," Kohn sympathized. "Accent. Traces of skin conditions."

Jordan looked indignant for a second, then laughed.

"Stigmata!"

"Don't worry. They'll wear off. OK, Jordan, you might find it a bit more difficult to figure us out. Janis is a scientist and I work for a protection agency.
Some people would call me a Communist. Much-abused label, but . . ."

He waved a hand to take in all the unfortunate associations he might
have evoked.

"Doesn't bother me," Jordan said. "I believe in taking people as you find
them. I'm an individualist. And a capitalist."

"And surprisingly well informed," Kohn said. "Considering." He leaned
back. Over to you.

Jordan peered around in a way that triggered Kohn's memory of how
Janis had looked over her shoulder that morning.

"Uh . . . is the ANR legal here?"

Kohn smiled. "That's not a simple question but, if having an office block
with its name in lights is anything to go by, yes. And we do have free
speech, as you may have noticed."

Jordan sighed, shoulders sagging a little.

"Stigmata again . . ."

Kohn nodded. "The right of free speech is one thing," he said. "But the
stuff in that glass is the best thing going for helping you exercise it."

Jordan took a sip of whisky and began to talk.

While Jordan was getting a round in, Janis and Moh conferred frantically.

"Do you think he's . . . on to us?" Janis whispered.

"Some kind of agent?" Kohn shook his head. "Anything like that, it'd
be someone I know . . . He's just sharp. Heard me asking around."

"We could get him in on this. You want to keep off the net, and I'm no
good on it. He is."

Kohn gazed at her. "That's an idea."

They shifted apart as Jordan came back, looking down and moving like
someone steering a car with his elbows. He smiled at Janis as he put the
drinks down.

"I'm impressed," Kohn said. "Really. You've sifted an incredible amount of stuff off the net, come up with a big spread of ideas about what's going on. How did you get that good, back there?"

Jordan scowled at his drink, then looked up. "I don't know," he said. "I was using better kit than I've ever had before, and I was doing the same sort of thing as I do at work. Did at work. A feel for how the markets move, like Mrs. Lawson told me today." He laughed. "And a feel for virtual reality from playing Paluxy, I guess."

"What's Paluxy?" Janis asked.

"Dinosaur-hunting game. It's in the only VR arcade Beulah City's got. Noah's Park."

"I see," Kohn said. He glanced sidelong at Janis, who didn't see, either. "You came here looking to put some flesh on what you found. So did we." He spoke slowly, trying to get his zooming, looping thoughts into some kind of formation-flying. "Or, maybe, *we*'re the flesh. So now you've got a choice. You can go and do whatever it is you really wanted to do in Norlonto that you couldn't do in BC—read, net-surf, get laid, whatever— and *forget about this.* Or you can come in on it with us. If that's what you decide, we'll tell you all we know."

Moh leaned closer and spoke quietly, barely moving his lips. He was sure even Janis couldn't hear him. "And if you betray us, I'll kill you."

He straightened up and smiled at Jordan as if he'd just given him a hot betting tip, watching the fear and eagerness that seemed, now, so evident on Jordan's carefully impassive face.

"OK," Jordan said. "Let me think, OK? You're not talking about anything that . . . would be criminal, here?"

"Nope," Moh said.

Janis shook her head fiercely.

"You're not working for the"—he lowered his voice, his face squirming with distaste—"*government* or the UN or anything like that?"

Moh guffawed, putting an arm around Janis's shoulders and slapping Jordan on the back.

"You're all right," he said.

Jordan looked pleased and embarrassed.

"So what's this big secret, and what do you want me to do?"

Moh looked around. "Surprising as it may seem, this ain't exactly the time or the place for talking about secrets. As to what we want you to do, basically it's just what you have been doing. But with a bit more to go on, which is what we can give you. I live near here and you can use our place as a base until you get somewhere for yourself. If that's what you want."

He passed Jordan one of his business cards and gave him a quick rundown on the Collective.

"So what do we tell the comrades?" Janis asked.

"As near the truth as possible," Kohn said. "Jordan's helping us with research, and building up a database of possible contacts, customers . . ."

"OK," Jordan said, "but why me, and why for you?"

"Suppose we make it something you'd want to do anyway. I mean, like today you've sort of had your wish come true, got booted out of BC with a nice little stash. So . . . what would you have done, if you hadn't got any further with your search?"

"Found somewhere to live. Got a job—in futures maybe—and, uh, read and written a lot."

"What would you write?"

"Philosophy. Kind of. Oh, not just atheism, humanism, I'm sure there are plenty doing that out here—"

"You'd be surprised," Kohn remarked.

"—but I want to do more. I want to attack all these cults and ideologies. I have this, this vision that life could be better if only people could see how things really are. That it's your one life, it's yours, you have this inexhaustible universe to live it in and God damn it isn't that enough? Why do we have to wander around in these invented worlds of our own devising, these false realities that are just clutter, dross, dirt on the lens?—all these beliefs and identities that people throw away their real lives for."

"Like, there is no God, and you shall have no other gods."

"That's it. That's what I want to write."

"I have a better idea," Kohn said. The understanding of how good an idea it was glowed within him, spreading like an inward smile. "Would you like to be on television?"

Only cable, and with a small subscriber base, he explained. But items did get picked up sometimes by the networks, and the Cats had schedules to spare since all they put out was their own edited exploits and an alternative news-slot with a bit of radical/critical/Marxist analysis thrown in.

"If you can just talk like that to a camera you'll be fine," Kohn said. "Nothing to it. No interviewers. No professionals to sneer. It's your show. Say what you like—basically we hate the barb and the mini-states, and if you do too then you're on our side; anything rational would be better than those smelly, cozy subtotalitarianisms. The only viewers will be watching because they want to, so you won't bore anyone. And, you being a capitalist, you can measure your success by the credits that you clock up!"

"Oh man." Jordan had fire in his eyes now. "That sounds great. Too good to be true."

"No, just true enough to be good."

"Speaking of clocking up credits . . . what do you guys, your comrades, do with the money you make?"

Kohn frowned. "Savings bank account."

Jordan laughed. "You'd do better buying gold and keeping it in an old sock!"

"What else could you do with it?" Kohn asked, genuinely puzzled.

Jordan looked at him, shaking his head. "Call yourselves mercenaries . . . Look, you've got an inside track on the whole micropolitics of this place, you're in the middle of a free-trade zone, you don't pay taxes, you've got access to news and rumors more or less as they break . . . You know, I could make a bit of money from what I learned on the net tonight!"

Kohn looked at Janis for guidance. She shrugged. "Sounds feasible enough."

"Great!" Kohn straightened up and raised his glass. "Here's to the international Communist-Capitalist conspiracy, to which I've always wanted to belong."

For Jordan they drank to philosophical speculators, which they all thought was rather good, and for Janis to mad scientists who did awful things to rats. After that they got loud and, eventually, quiet. "Is Molly Biolly a crank band?" Janis was looking at the stage when Kohn swung into the seat beside her, returned from another prowl through the buzz.

"I don't know. What—?"

"That guy at the back, looks like Brian Donovan. Like the picture of him on the back of his book."

Behind the holo image of three girls in second-skin plastic doing indecent things with synthesizers stood the scratchy spectral fetch of a man with long gray hair and a long gray beard. He seemed to be staring at them.

"Weird," Kohn said, sliding away from and in front of Janis.

"Isn't it just a projection?" Jordan asked.

"The band is," Kohn said, not turning round. "But this stage has its cameras, too, so you can patch in a moving point of view from somewhere else . . . That's how a fetch works, out in AR. Shit, he is watching us. And he knows we know. Let's make some space, keep it natural, knock back the drinks and head for the door. You first, Jordan, then Janis."

Kohn stood, gulped whisky. The figure moved forward, through Molly Biolly, a ghost through ghosts. Some yells of complaint and disgust went up. The fetch glided across the edge of the stage and into the crowd. Irrationally, people made way. Smoke coiled into colors inside it.

The band, which had been TALKIN' 'BOUT MY GENE RATION!!!! fell to

129

mouthing soundlessly, like terrorists on television. The crowd in the pub was silent, too, eyes focused on the moving image.

The fetch pointed a translucent arm at Kohn. Its lips moved out-of-synch as the speakers boomed back to life.

"MOH KOHN!" it said. "I ACCUSE YOU OF BREAKING THE RULES OF ENGAGEMENT! IF YOU DO NOT APOLOGIZE IN PERSON AND IN THE FLESH TO MY EMPLOYEE, ACCEPT A RANSOM AND CLEAR HER NAME WITHIN TWENTY-FOUR HOURS, I WILL SEE YOU IN THE NEAREST GENEVA COURT. IN THE MEANTIME AND WITHOUT PREJUDICE I OFFER A REWARD FOR YOUR ARREST AS A RENEGADE AND A PUBLIC MENACE."

Donovan's fetch looked around, as if to make sure everyone had heard that, and vanished.

Kohn was backing off—on the balls of his feet, ready to lash out.

The music came back on. Somebody laughed. Just a terrorist dispute. Attention returned to the band; heads turned away.

A heavily built man sitting on a bar stool casually slid an empty stein along the slick of beer, pushing at the bar with his toe so that the stool spun, carrying him round, the sweep of his arm carrying the glass around to the final flick of a discus throw.

Kohn ducked so fast his feet left the ground. The glass hit the wall behind him and bounced off, almost getting him on the rebound.

Kohn lunged forward, doubled fists driving into the attacker's midriff. The man gasped but pushed back, up and off the stool. Kohn reeled away and a table caught him across the back of his thighs. He staggered but didn't fall.

In a moment something changed: his point of view. He looked down at his head from a meter or so above it, two meters, and everything was laid out for him like an architect's diagram. Some calm undertone soothed the frightened australopithecine that was in his skull but thinking it was out of it. Only a picture, a visual aid, an icon: this is what it would look like if you could look at it like this. He reached—saw his hand reach—behind him and caught a full glass as it slid from the table and dashed the contents in his opponent's face, then stepped forward and neatly wrecked the man's knee. He was back behind his eyes in time to see the other's fill with pain and shock before a sideways topple took them closing to the floor.

Kohn pulled his credID card from his back pocket and held it up as he turned to face one of the pub's security cameras.

"I suppose you got all that," he told the record. "I'll not press charges but if you want to you can call me as a witness." He looked at the people whose table he'd cannoned against. They were still getting out of their seats, wiping at their clothes. He pointed at the slumped figure.

"A round on him," he said.

Everybody was looking at him again.

"Don't fucking mess with me," he added, and walked toward the door. Jordan had been holding Janis back. He let go of her upper arms and stooped to rub his shins.

"Spirited little tyke, isn't she?" Kohn said.

He smiled at the two indignant and relieved faces.

"C'mon gang, let's go. Don't look back or you'll turn into a pillar of salt."

At the Clearing House Donovan turned around in the privacy bubble to face a seething silence. Everyone had been and gone, flitting out and back through the evening to attend to their several businesses, while he had divided his attention between calling off various live actions and haunting a succession of pubs, nightclubs and drug dens. But they'd all been present to see him finally find Kohn. The images from the pub's cameras were still spread around them like scraps of newsprint, rippling with rerun movement.

"Donovan," Mrs. Lawson said, "I do wish you had engaged your brain before you opened your mouth."

Donovan glared at her. "Why? I told you I would challenge Kohn."

"The attempt to incite a citizen's arrest was, shall we say, excessive," Bleibtreu-Fèvre interposed. "However, we do at least now know for certain that Taine is with him. Even if we have temporarily frightened them off."

"That's not the problem!" Melody Lawson snapped. "If you'd given me a chance . . . there was another person with them." She reached for a patch of scene and stuck it where they could all see it: a young man walking backward, open-mouthed, behind Janis Taine. "That isn't one of Kohn's gang. It's Jordan Brown, who was involved in the Black Plan penetration incident this afternoon." She ran her hands distractedly through her shining hair and halo, leaving little flecks of gold figment on her fingers. "That suggests very sinister possibilities."

Donovan felt some calm returning, a recognition that perhaps he'd lost it for a couple of seconds.

"I . . . apologize for my haste," he said. "All the same, there seems no reason why Kohn shouldn't show up to claim the ransom. I'll have the hospital staked out by morning. In the meantime, why don't you check your exile's records?"

"I certainly shall," Mrs. Lawson said grimly. "He was disaffected for some time. Goodness knows who he was in contact with."

"This man Kohn," said Bleibtreu-Fèvre. "Do you know anything about him?"

Donovan frowned. "He's the leader of a small gang of security mercenaries . . . other than a nasty streak of pro-technology fanaticism, they're nothing special. As it happens, the hired fighter who was on my team last night is a former member."

"What?" Bleibtreu-Fèvre looked appalled. "I find *that* suspicious."

Donovan could see the paranoia building as Lawson and Bleibtreu-Fèvre exchanged glances. He tried to head it off before he started down that path himself.

"She broke with them and their outlook a long time ago. No, the only significance this has is that it creates a strong personal antagonism between her and Kohn. As I said, this could work in our favor."

"Could you raise some local forces to watch their house?" Dr. Van asked, suddenly leaning into the discussion. "Possibly intervene directly?"

"Not a chance," Donovan said. "The whole area is covered by a network of defense agencies, crawling with ANR cadres and sympathizers, patrolled by space-movement militia. Most of the houses are built to withstand at least indirect blast damage. Kohn's is probably capable of holding off a tank."

". . . I see," said Van, reacting after seconds of satellite delay. "A liberated zone." For the first time, he smiled at them all.

"Quite," said Bleibtreu-Fèvre. "I wonder if Kohn has any, as we say, *form*."

"Why not check your agency's records?" Mrs. Lawson suggested.

Bleibtreu-Fèvre's fetch seemed to diminish slightly. "I would have to give a full accounting of the circumstances," he said. "That might . . . raise unnecessary alarm."

Might be embarrassing, Donovan thought, unsympathetically. As a field operative, Bleibtreu-Fèvre must have a great deal of autonomy, but the bureaucratic mechanisms of Stasis would still kick in at sensitive points. Personal records was probably one of them, surrounded by smoke and mirrors: safeguards—reassurances that a secret police force which went around stamping on dangerous scientists wasn't any kind of threat to normal folks' privacy and civil liberties, no sir.

"I can help you there," he said. "Just let me know your passwords and procedures and I'll do an end-run around them."

"Impossible!"

Donovan looked straight back at the Man In Black's glowing, glowering eyes. *Cheap trick, Hallowe'en lantern . . .*

"Not with your help, it isn't," he said.

Bleibtreu-Fèvre considered it, his face frozen in a downloading trance. Donovan had counted past sixty when the fetch's lips moved again.

"Very well," he said. "What is there to lose?"

Using the codes and pathways supplied by Bleibtreu-Fèvre, Donovan got into the US/UN system so easily that he marked time for a few seconds before launching the database call. He regretted it as the retrieval time clocked on and on—seconds, one minute, one and a half, two . . . Was the damn thing written in COBOL?

Two minutes fifty.

Three. Three ten.

I mean what sort of crap programmers do these guys have?

And then it all started coming in, a whole structure of links and inferences building up around them like the result of some cartoon character making a cast with a fishing line and snagging it, hauling in seaweed, a chain, a wreck, a whole rustbucket *fleet* pelting down on the quay . . .

The four of them stood looking at the mass of recovered data.

"Oh," Donovan said at last. "*That* Kohn."

"What was that all about?" Jordan asked. He and Janis were hard put to keep up with Kohn. The best place to walk was immediately behind him.

"Donovan was trying it on," Kohn said over his shoulder. "I interdicted one of his sabotage teams last night. There's something else. Personal. Too complicated to go into right now . . . Plenty of time to sort it out in the morning. Whatever, he found out where I was and tried to rouse against me any opportunist bounty-hunters who might be around. Not very successful."

He turned away, "Renegade . . ." His laughter floated back.

"Slow down, willya?" Janis gasped.

"Oh. All right."

Suddenly they were a threesome, moving through the shifting crowds in a normal way. Jordan felt a heightened alertness, the effect of the drink creeping back after a sobering shock had banished it. A woman in a militia uniform stared back at him defiantly as he noticed the division of her face, half mature and half twisted baby-features, growing in. She had one chubby doll-like arm to match, sticking out of a hole torn carelessly in the top of her sleeve.

"Why doesn't everybody use that to stay young and beautiful?" Jordan said after she'd passed.

"Regen? Some do," Kohn said. "It's expensive. Most mercenaries have it as part of their insurance package, but the no-claims kickback is crippling.

Probably just as well. You don't want people getting reckless just because no nonfatal wound is permanent."

"Better reckless than wrecked," Janis said.

When Jordan had gone into the bar he'd hoped to get not just more information but also a rest from Norlonto's restless streetlife. He'd got more of one and less of the other than he'd hoped. Now he was partly supported by his arm around Janis and by Moh's arm, also around Janis, locking his in place. It seemed appropriate. He felt knocked sideways by both of them.

Like a hatchling imprinted by the first large moving object it sees, he reflected. So be it. He had never seen a woman as beautiful, as fascinating and free, as Janis. And Moh, he was something else: everything Jordan wasn't—thin, tough, clued-up—but he made Jordan feel at ease and accepted. What it would be like to be so open, so at home in the world!

"You know something?" Jordan said. "I've always believed in you people."

The others laughed.

"You must have a lot of faith!" Janis said.

"Reason, not faith," Jordan retorted. "I never had any proof that people like you existed, but I knew you had to. That rational people existed—somewhere else. They damn well don't exist down there. So I never actually met any. I just read about them in books—read their books. Also I suppose I saw their works. Sort of like the argument from design." He looked up, waved his free fist at the sky. "Every aeroplane is a proof that there must be a rational mind somewhere!"

"Yeah, well, we know that," Kohn said. "What amazes me is the uses they can get put to, not to mention the pilot's birth sign hologram medallion, satellite televangelists—"

"—and Creation astronomy kits—"

"—credulity drugs to make alternative medicine more effective—"

"—designer heroin for dying soldiers—"

"—instant access to more lies than you could refute in ten lifetimes—"

"—Well, that's freedom for you," Janis said, grinning up at the two men's faces. "From each as they choose, to each as they are chosen, right?"

Jordan shrugged off the rucksack in the hallway and stood still for a moment, trying to recover a sense of balance. His ears sang and his eyes still delivered an unfamiliar illusion that everything was spinning, but not actually moving. His knee-joints felt unreliable. Here he was, going with two people he barely knew into a fortified house full of drug takers! Loose women! Armed Communists!

He followed Moh and Janis into the main room. No one else seemed to be around.

"Coffee, anyone?" Moh said.

"Sounds like a really good idea." Jordan sat down on the sofa, too hard. Faint ringing noises echoed into the distance.

"Here's another good idea." Moh tossed something over his shoulder. It landed beside Jordan. "Have yourself one of these."

Jordan picked up the pack of marijuana cigarettes and looked at it doubtfully as a battered Zippo landed on the identical spot. He turned to Janis and raised his eyebrows. "What do you think of this stuff?"

"Well—it's not particularly good for you if you smoke a lot, and it makes some people lazy or at least lazier than they'd be anyway, but on the other hand it isn't addictive and it's a lot less carcinogenic than tobacco." She shrugged. "I'm having one, anyway."

"It doesn't make holes in your brain?"

"No, I don't think the latest research really bears that out."

Jordan took the lighter and packet over to Janis.

"I'll try it," he said. "But I'm not quite sure how."

"Best a little smoke and a lot of air." She demonstrated. Jordan lit up and went back to the sofa. Away for one evening and already he was on drugs. Rather to his surprise he made a fairly creditable fist of it, and had got over the coughing by the time Moh brought him a big earthenware mug of Nicafé.

"Good stuff?" Moh grinned, settling beside him.

"Yes," Jordan gasped, wiping his eyes and sipping coffee. He looked at how the man sat: arrogantly relaxed, one ankle resting on the other knee, the ebony gleam of his leather clothes; and the woman, half-lotus in the chair, alabaster skin and tender flesh in black silk, smoke curling around her curling hair. "Can't say I've noticed much effect yet."

Moh's lips and brows twitched, but he made no comment.

"So . . ." Jordan looked from Moh to Janis. "Are you going to tell me what you know?"

Moh rolled his eyes and closed them. "Not tonight we ain't."

He seemed to have drifted off into some kind of trance. Janis noticed Jordan noticing, and made a pacifying gesture.

"He's had a long day," she said.

"Not to mention the drugs."

"Yeah," said Janis. "Not to mention the drugs. Tell me about yourself, Jordan."

Jordan took another hit. He still couldn't identify any effect. His mind felt clear and calm, and he couldn't look at anything but Janis. She had flared when she spoke, and now was settled back to a steady flame with a flickering hint of mischief. They talked quietly while Kohn watched something else, and said nothing.

Moh saw the darkness and the lights of the city around them as if the walls were transparent; and the new strange company he kept, the bright city of clean sharp logic at the back of his mind. It ran pictures for him, eidetic memories that played like VR diskettes, of the world that had made the world he walked in now:

the bright world the banner bright the symbol plain the greenbelt fields the greenfield streets the Fuller domes the crowds the quiet dark moments

the plastic model spaceships hanging from black threads the old Warsaw Pact poster of a little girl cradling the Earth DEFEND PEACE the stacked clutter of toys and books and tapes the VR space-helmet

the war. The Republic didn't disdain the help of children. The party set up a special militia, the Young Guards. Moh toted his first rifle then, a lightweight British SLR, in boring nights of watching the entrance to an office tower. (The trick was that he was guarding it secretly, from a safe house window across the street: the government was already behaving like a resistance movement.) The days were more exciting: demonstrations and street fights, the tensions of the struggle to maintain neutrality, to keep out of the war. Josh and Marcia made jokes that he didn't get, about fighting for peace. They were literally doing that, kicking into demonstrations of what they called the War party: Royalists and Tories and Fascists. Sometimes the police joined in on both sides.

Moh, later, found himself surprisingly ignorant of the details of the actual course of the War of European Integration. At the time he picked up the assumption that the news was all propaganda, and only caught glimpses of it on television. German tanks rode battering sleds of air, carrying the star-circled banner into Warsaw and Bucharest and Zagreb. German MiGs cleared the skies.

The Peace Process. No, not that. He jolted himself awake, gulped cold coffee and thought about something else.

Jordan was explaining to Janis the distinction between dispensationalism and premillenarianism (which seemed very important but difficult to grasp) when he heard Moh's mocking laughter and saw him stand up, looking as if he'd had a good night's sleep.

"It's time I went to bed," Moh said.

"I think it's time I did," Janis said. She yawned, stretched, and jumped to her feet.

"D'you mind just crashing here, Jordan, just for tonight?"

"That's fine. That's great. Thanks."

"Okay. See you in the morning, Jordan."

"Good night."

Janis waved, smiling. A moment later they were gone, like birds through a hole in the roof. Jordan sat still for some time and then took most of his clothes off, wrapped himself in blankets from the back of the sofa, and stretched out on it and stayed awake for a long time.

"Well?" she said, leaning against the door of his room.

"Well what?"

"Have you found a place?"

"Yeah," Kohn said.

"Good. Well . . . I feel like another joint before turning in." She raised her eyebrows and looked at him. He still seemed wide awake, and he grinned back at her as if this were the most unexpected and delightful suggestion he'd heard in a long time.

"Yeah, why not?"

She turned and opened the door, watching him. His arm came into the room, past her shoulder; he did something with a switch. Small lights glowed on in the corners as she kicked off her shoes and sat down on the edge of the bed. He sat beside her, leaned an elbow against the pillow and offered her the now depleted and battered pack. She took one out and lit up.

"Do you want to share?"

"No, thank you," he said. "Lipstick *tastes*."

She caught him just as he reached for the pack, with her right hand suddenly behind his head. Her fingers dug into his curls. She drew in the smoke to her throat, held it, and grudged the breath that escaped as she whispered, "Taste *this* . . ."

She brought their mouths (hers open, his opening) together and breathed out while he breathed in. They both broke away, gasping. The second time she gave less attention to fire and more to water, darting her tongue tip against his.

"You took me by surprise," Kohn said.

"Really?"

"Yes."

"I've been wanting to do this for *hours.*"

"Wanton woman."

"Abandoned," she agreed. "An outcast of society."

She stubbed out the filter roach. Kohn kicked off his boots, shrugged out of his waistcoat, then leaned forward and drew her onto him. She trailed her hair from his shoulders down to his hips, then did the same with her lips and tongue, discovering as she did so that it was time to get his trousers off. She straddled him and took her time with the belt and zip. She moved on her knees down over his thighs, tugging the trews and shorts away, and then suddenly it got urgent and she pulled them fiercely over his feet. She sat on his bare thighs, facing away from him, while he pulled the silk top over her head and unlaced her basque. She slipped her own trousers and pants off. She leaned forward, letting her hair tickle his toes, until the pale opalescent shell of the basque fell away from her chest, and his arms slid around her waist. His erection pressed against the small of her back. She turned over on her knees and put her hands on his shoulders and he lay back and she moved forward and up and Moh rose to meet her and she moved, slowly up and swiftly down, and so they continued, the cannabis in their racing blood stretching time.

She did not know when it was she spoke his name and got no answer; and looking down at him, smiled to see that he had fallen asleep just like that.

10

The Transitional Programmer

MOH WOKE WITH a jump from a dream of shouting, a dream of fighting, a dream of falling.

Janis stirred and mumbled beside him, then pulled the quilt even more firmly around her, leaving only a tuft of red hair on the pillow like a squirrel's tail to indicate her presence. Moh let his shoulders adapt to the chill as he lay back with his hands behind his head and stared at the ceiling.

Cautiously, as if tonguing a loose tooth, he turned his attention to the back of his mind. The new thing was still there, the sense of lines where there had been tangles, of sky where there had been floor. He could still lean over that cliff and look out at the bottomless chasm of his past. But it no longer sent him whirling with dizziness, hurtling with fear. He could turn away from it, he could walk confidently along its edge.

He had the feeling that he had forgotten something. He smiled at the thought, and continued to lie and think. Whatever was going on in his head, whether it was an effect of the drugs or of the entity he'd encountered or of their interaction, it was real and it had not gone away. He was awed by it, and annoyed. It had always been a matter of pride if not of principle that he didn't have any fixes, any patches; that he never touched smart drugs. (Only stupid ones, he reflected ruefully. Whatever else might be going on in his head, it ached.)

There was the problem of what to tell Jordan, and what not to tell the others. A shadow of guilt crossed his mind, about not taking Stone into his confidence: good comrade, best mate, years together . . . but all that still seemed like a good reason for keeping him out of it. If something should go drastically wrong (death, madness, things like that) the Collective would need someone uncontaminated by whatever had happened.

Not that he had a clear view of what it would mean for things to go right. Despite the inscrutable download to the gun, he wasn't certain that whatever he'd encountered had an objective existence anything like what it had seemed. The net had spawned a whole subculture of people who claimed that free and conscious AIS spoke to them, gave them messages of profound import for humanity, incited them to perform violent or bizarre acts . . . a dream meme of AIS, successors to the angels and aliens of former times. Meanwhile the real breakthrough, the indubitable emergence of genuinely other minds, remained on a receding horizon—whether because of the intrinsic difficulty of the endeavor; the restrictions imposed by Stasis and by the cruder, more *hardware-oriented* interventions of Space Defense; or the ceaseless sabotage of the cranks.

The cranks—Christ, *that* was what he'd forgotten! He had to contact Cat, tell her he was coming to see her, ask her to stay put or arrange a meeting. Last night he'd been too high on alcohol and hash and adrenaline and on whatever-it-was to think straight. He should have done it then. The drugs were no excuse. What had he been thinking of—?

The major distraction, the prime reason why he hadn't thought straight last night, chose that moment to roll over and wake up. She looked at him, momentary bewilderment giving way to a distractingly self-satisfied smile.

"Hi."

"Good morning."

"You must be freezing. Come in here." She flipped the quilt over him and pulled him in, kissed and cuddled and nuzzled him and just when he was warming up again said, "God, I could do with a coffee."

Moh disengaged reluctantly. "With you in a minute." He rolled out of bed and wrapped himself in the warmest toweling robe he had. He crept downstairs and started up the coffee. Jordan was still fast asleep on the couch. Moh went to the comms room and called up Hillingdon Hospital.

The account for Catherin Duvalier, charged to the Collective, was closed. After a few minutes of brushing through the layers of answer-fetches Moh reached an administrator who confirmed that, yes, the patient was gone. Hours earlier, without any forwarding trace.

Moh broke the connection and stared at the vacant screen, feeling like banging his head against it. There was no way to get back to Cat. He didn't know what faction she was in. Not that it would help: after her unconditional release they wouldn't want to know her. If he couldn't meet Donovan's challenge, he and maybe the whole Collective could end up with an indictment against them in the so-called Geneva courts, the ones that handled intercommunal and intermovement disputes. No self-respecting defense agency in Norlonto ever appealed to them, not when there were reputable court companies vying for customers. The Geneva Convention courts were for terrorists and states to squabble in with their extorted money. Even if Donovan's case wouldn't stand up for five minutes, that five minutes and however many months it took to get there could cost the Collective a fortune and a reputation.

He had to find Cat. He had to fix things with Donovan, or just hope the revolution came before they lost too much business. If the ANR won they would sweep the Geneva courts away. Some chance.

There were other slim chances. He sent out a general message to the Collective's entire mailing list, asking urgently for information about Catherin Duvalier's present location. Then he sent a personal, encrypted message, explaining the problem and asking for some grace on the deadline, to the only publicly known address for Donovan: bdonovan@cla.org.ter.

Giving himself a hard time, he made the coffee and went upstairs. Explaining this whole mess to Janis wouldn't be easy, but it would be a fine warm-up for explaining it to the comrades.

"You," she told him when he'd finished, "are a fucking idiot."

Yes, he agreed silently. And clinically insane as well, probably. At least in Norlonto that's a victimless crime.

Another thought came to him as he watched genuine anger fighting against a sort of stoical, appalled amusement for possession of her face: And obsessed with you.

He saw the anger win.

"Is this how you guys *function*?" she asked. "Drink and dope and drop-dancing and goddess knows what else shit in your head?"

"Not when I'm on active," Kohn said. "Bear that in mind."

"You were on active, dammit," she said. "We got a contract, remember?"

"Yeah, OK, OK."

Her anger subsided. "Couldn't you sort of . . . *hack into* the hospital's records, see if they've got anything that might give us a clue, trace her agency?"

"We're talking about a hospital, Janis," he reminded her gently. "Not a university or some kinda *secret research establishment*. Same goes for the Body Bank."

She didn't get it. "I thought the university had good security. They use our own crypto and AI, state-of-the-art."

He rolled on the bed, caught her and made her laugh. "If you ever come across a bank that guards its vaults with a crowd of recidivist safe-crackers and apprentice locksmiths, supervised by guys who can't remember ten digits without writing them down somewhere—just let me know and I'll cut you in on it, yeah?"

Jordan woke up on the long couch to find the long room full of people either coming in and removing kit or tooling up and going out. He saw a dark-haired woman put on camouflage like makeup, select weapons like accessories, smile at him and at herself in a wall mirror, and leave. He saw a tired and dirty man grilling bacon. The man saw him and brought over a roll and a huge mug of black coffee. Jordan accepted them gratefully and, when he had finished eating, gathered the blanket around him and dug clothes and a towel out of his rucksack.

"Bathroom?"

"Second left down the corridor."

He stepped through a half-open door to find a room full of not enough steam to conceal two women and a small boy in a bath and a man sitting naked on a lavatory reading a newspaper. He nearly backed out, then remembered that he'd come here to live rationally.

Closing the shower curtain was just to avoid splashing the floor.

He found Moh and Janis sitting at the table in the main room, eating cereals while giving their attention to newspapers. Janis was tearing them off as they printed out and passing them to Kohn to read. Kohn always had one in his hand; Janis had a growing stack beside her.

If he was reading them it was fast.

Jordan joined them.

"What's the news?"

Janis looked at him.

"Oh, good morning. Don't mind Moh. He gets like this sometimes. Now," she added oddly, vaguely. She passed a sheet into Moh's outstretched hand. "News is nothing—well, what you'd expect. Russland—Turkey, everybody. London *Sun–Times* thinks second big story is Yanks hit Kyoto suburbs—lasers, precision. *Nihon Keizai Shimbun*, on the other hand, reports loss of army convoy in Inverness-shire. Lhasa *Rimbao* prays for peace. No surprises."

"Looking for surprises," Moh said around a mouthful of muesli. "Shoosh."

A little later he stopped and became civil. "How are you this morning?" He crunched up a page of hard copy and chucked it into a trash can on the other side of the room.

"Fine. Well, I will be. Maybe another coffee . . . You know, I think hash really does make holes in your brain."

"Nah, that's the drink," Kohn said. "Proven fact. Brains of rats and that." He grinned at Janis, apparently unaware that he'd binned a dozen balls of paper, one by one, without looking. "Anyway, Jordan, time to fill you in." He glanced at a whiteboard markered with scrawled words and snarled-up arrows. "Comms room is clear. Talk about it there."

*　　*　　*

"That's some story," Jordan said when they'd finished. Moh and Janis looked back at him hopefully, like clients. "Sounds like a load of *serdar argic.*" (He'd picked up the net-slang unconsciously, used it self-consciously; it referred to the lowest layer of paranoid drivel that infested the Cable, spun out by degenerate, bug-ridden knee-jerk auto-post programs. Kill-file clutter.) He looked down at the workbench, picked at a solder globule. "But I believe it." He laughed. "Well, I believe you."

"Can you do it?"

They wanted him to hack-and-track for them, follow lines back, be their eyes on the net. He ached to get on with it, but was uncertain if he had the skill to match.

"Sure," he said.

"That's OK," Moh said. "You'll pick it up."

"So what's the plan for today?" Janis asked. She sounded edgy.

"Find Bernstein," Moh said. "Take it from there."

"Bernstein!" Jordan said. "The booklegger?"

Moh nodded, turned to smirk at Janis. "Told you," he said. "Everybody knows Bernstein."

"I've got his phone number," Jordan said. "Somewhere." He searched his memory, then dived into the main room and ran back with the small book he'd stuck in his jacket pocket. He flipped it open to look at the purple ink of the seller's rubber-stamped logo on the inserted bookmark. It opened at the frontispiece.

"Jesus Christ," he swore, for the first time in his life. "Will you look at that."

He held the book forward for them to see: the old photogravure of a statue of a man in a hooded robe or cloak, hands outspread, eyes faint white marks in the cowled shadow.

Kohn looked up, puzzled. "Who is it?"

Jordan screwed up his eyes and shook his head.

"Giordano Bruno. He was burned at the stake in 1600 for saying the planets might be inhabited, among other things. First space-movement martyr." He gave an imitation of a hollow, echoing laugh. "I just realized what his name would be in English. 'Jordan Brown'!"

He looked at it again, hairs prickling on his neck. Moh clapped his shoulder.

"Bernstein's way of saying hello, Jordan," he said. "So give the man a call, already."

After a few rings a reply came on the line, from not an answer-fetch but a flat tape. "Hello," said a thick-tongued voice. "Thank you for calling.

143

Solly Bernstein isn't in at the moment, but you can find him at"—pause, clunk—"Brent Cross Shopping Center. Usual place. Look for the revisionist rally."

Moh refused to explain what was funny about that.

They took the monorail north. Moh had insisted they all bring some gear, on the assumption they might not be coming back. He'd pulled a couple of JDF-surplus backpacks from under a bench, packed his in moments and gone into a huddle with Jordan over the household computer, filling him in on the tasks rota.

Janis had looked at her pack as its solar-powered flexor frame made random movements in a patch of sunlight. "This," she'd announced in an aggrieved tone to the world in general, "is what I call a *makeup bag*."

Now it sat in her lap like a small fat animal with bulging cheek-pouches, its phototropics hopelessly confused by the flicker of stanchion shadows. Janis had a seat by the window. She couldn't look away from the view.

"I always knew it was there," she said. "It's just . . ."

"Yeah, isn't it just?" Moh grinned at her from the opposite seat, the gun between his knees.

The Greenbelt. Ahead of them it sprawled to left and right, all along the horizon. A whole new London of shanties and skyscrapers, streets, factories, nuclear power plants; the sky alive with light aircraft, airships, aerostats—a chaos that even as she watched resolved itself into complexity, a pattern of differences like small fields seen from a great height. She looked at it through Moh's binoculars, scanning slowly, lost in the endlessly deepening detail of it all. She remembered Darwin: *It is interesting to contemplate a tangled bank . . .*

"It's like an ecosystem," she said at last.

"That's the real Norlonto," Moh said. "The core, except it isn't central. The leading edge."

"Pity it doesn't stretch all the way round."

She thought of what lay beyond Uxbridge, out to the west. Badlands all the way to Wales, a firebreak between that ineradicable hostility and London. A lot of people would privately admit they'd prefer the Welsh marching to the endless trickle of saboteurs from these new Marches.

"Or all the way in," Jordan said.

"Yeah, the movement only got a slice of the pie. But look what they did with it!"

"You sound proud of this place." Janis couldn't square Moh's enthusiasm for Norlonto with his stubborn insistence that he was some kind of Socialist.

"We want to go beyond this, do better than it. Not go back from it."
After a minute she stopped trying to figure it out.

The mall had been hit in the war and never reclaimed, due to an obscure dispute about property rights. Norlonto being nothing if not an enormous tangle of private properties, the shopping center and its surroundings had come to suffer what in a different society would be called planning blight. By default it could be considered part of the Kingdom, although the state had so far shown not the slightest interest in it. The whole area had been squatted and homesteaded until it was like a carcass occupied by an entire colony of ants, a shipwreck crusted with coral.

They pushed past stalls and shops selling microwaves, cast-iron cooking pots, light machine guns, heavy-metal records, spacesuits, wedding dresses, holodisks, oil paintings, Afro-Pak takeaways, VR snuff tapes. They emerged from the concentric rings and radial passages of the market into the concourse. Bernstein's regular pitch occupied a small arc of a circle around what must once have been a fountain pond underneath a central skylight, forty-odd meters above, of now broken colored glass.

It was unattended and bare. A skinny girl in a tool harness and little else affected a low-g loll behind the space-movement table in the adjacent quadrant.

"Seen Bernstein?" Moh asked.

She shifted an earpiece and gave her head a languid shake. "Booked it," she said. "If he don't take it, is 'is *ĉagreno, jes*?"

Moh checked his watch, 11:30. Not like Bernstein to miss several hours' worth of sales. He turned to Jordan. "Anything going on?"

Jordan put his glades on with a flourish, tuned the downlink to his computer. "Damn right there is," he said. "Bomb scare in Camden High Street. Area's sealed off. Traffic reports are frantic."

"Oh, shit. Well, that could account for it." Moh gazed around, willing Bernstein to appear. It didn't work.

"I'll wait here and see if he turns up," he told Jordan and Janis. "You guys want to wander around?"

Jordan looked at the conference area of the mall, the revisionist rally. "Yeah," he said. "This is just incredible." Janis smiled and shrugged and nodded in the direction of the surrounding markets. They wandered off in separate orbits.

Moh stood by the Movement stall and watched the old soldiers, their uniforms and medals mingling with the streetfighting clothes and antique badges of the young enthusiasts. Battle standards hung reverently across the area taken over for the occasion. Ostensibly a conference of dissentient historians, it was becoming a blatantly political event. Even some of the academic intellectuals, recognizable in their own uniforms of jeans and leather-patched tweed jackets, averted their eyes from the more sinister faces on the posters that were being indiscreetly hawked.

"Hey, *man!*"

The stall had a customer, a kid who picked up a tee-shirt in its polythene wrap and gazed at it. He was obviously a Neo, a hero-worshipper, one of those who'd grown up after the defeat and in adolescent rebellion had turned to what he'd always been told were the bad guys. Who just didn't believe they could've been that bad, and had found an identity and a pride in identifying with those terrifying folk who'd posed perhaps the most radical threat the world had ever faced . . . but who had at the same time built a society that appealed to the conservative values of order and disci-pline and patriotism that most people assimilated like the isotopes in their mothers' milk.

"The man who designed the rockets . . ." the kid breathed. Cropped hair, Europawehr combat jacket, ripped denim, knee-boots; scars on his smiling face and the faintest film of tear-flow in his eyes. The girl behind the stall looked back at him blankly.

"It's good to meet someone who knows their heritage," Kohn said. "Most people don't even know who he was." He included the stall's oblivious minder in his disapproval.

"Yeah, well, they've got us two ways, haven't they?" the kid said. "Yanks up there holdin us down, greens down here draggin us down."

Kohn nodded. "Exactly." He scanned the stall for recruitment material. "Well, some of us want to *do* something about it. Some of us believe in space, in the future. Look, mate, tell you what. Usually that's ten marks, but I can see you're keen, so I'll knock it down to eight-fifty and throw in a card and a badge for another one-twenty . . . Here's a pen."

He tore off the card's counterfoil, checking to make sure the kid had written his name and address.

"Thanks . . . Greg." Kohn stuck out his hand. The kid looked up from pinning the blue enamel star to his lapel, grinned and clasped the hand.

"See you again, mate." They slapped shoulders. The kid carried the tee-shirt away like a trophy.

"That's the way to do it," Kohn told the girl. He put the counterfoil carefully into the empty recruitment box. *"Eble vi farus same."* She still looked blank: her Esperanto smatter evidently as phony as her gravity-gets-me-down slouch.

An arm slipped between his elbow and his side.

"Making new friends?" Janis's voice was dry, amused.

"You know how it is," Kohn said, turning. "All those fine young bodies."

"Hah!"

Janis frowned, suddenly serious.

"Gives me the chills a bit, this whole show," she said. "Nostalgia and militaristic kitsch and rewriting history: it's all a lie—millions didn't die, the soldiers were heroes even if they were misled by politicians, they were stabbed in the back . . . ugh! They're not really *your people*, are they?"

"No, my love, they ain't." He felt as if the sun had gone behind a cloud, for a moment. Then he thought of the lad with the bright eyes. "But some of them are on our side even if they don't know it. Real keen technological expansionists, hate the greens and the Yanks. Some of them're basically *sound*."

Janis sighed and shrugged. "Maybe."

Jordan came back with armfuls of literature and a newly bought ancient leather jacket. "I still don't believe this," he said. "Free speech, sure, but talk about taking it to extremes." He flipped his glades down. "Traffic's clearing," he added. "ANR seems to be taking the flak for this one."

The girl lifted herself out of her spacer pose and made some effort at salesmanship as Jordan leaned over the stall. It wasn't necessary: he stocked up with mission badges, NASA and Tass posters, tee-shirts with pictures of the rocket pioneer Korolev, of Gagarin and Titov and Valentina Tereshkova, and a space-movement card and star.

Kohn again shoved the counterfoil in the box, this time checking that Jordan hadn't given his address. The smells of frying and grilling had been tormenting him for half an hour.

"Let's get some lunch before the rush," he said. "Good place across the way—we can keep an eye out from there."

"Second you on that," Janis said. Jordan straightened up from decorating his biker jacket with enamel shuttles and stars, looking less like a refugee from Beulah City if a bit self-conscious in his glade-masked cool. He nodded at Moh.

They walked through the crowd of aging veterans, the Afghantsi and Angolanos, and tough kids with their hammer-and-sickles and red stars (with a sprinkle of the movement's blue ones among them, as Moh indicated to Janis, who returned him a skeptical smile). They strolled past posters of Lenin and Stalin, Mao and Castro, Honneker and Ceaucescu and the rest, and over crumpled leaflets advertising lectures with titles like "The Great Leap Reconsidered" and "Croatia: The West's Killing Fields." Moh led them to a first-floor Indian café overlooking the concourse, well away from the bars whose main feature for the day would be rip-off prices and drunk neo-Communists.

Chicken roti and a tall glass of vanilla lassi were what hit the spot for Moh. He ate in a corner seat, leaning against the window while Janis nibbled tikka and Jordan chomped through some kind of potato-in-pastry arrangement, turning over the pages of a prewar Khazakh cosmodrome brochure.

"You really a Communist, Moh?" he asked. "After all that's happened?"

Moh grunted, still watching out for Bernstein. "What's past is prologue," he said. "The future is a long time. We ain't seen nothing yet."

"When have we seen enough?" Janis's voice had an edge to it. A double edge, Moh guessed: getting uneasy about hanging around here, getting dubious about the connections with the past which had seemed so obvious before.

"I remember things," he said, for her benefit as much as Jordan's. "I've seen the working class making days into history, and that's not something you forget." The lost revolution grieved him like a phantom limb. "The thing to forget about is the communistans and the states these guys down there think weren't so bad after all. That ain't where it's at."

Jordan was saying, "OK, but that's where it *ended up*—" when Moh raised a hand. He'd spotted a battery-powered vehicle hauling a tiny and overloaded trailer through the crowd.

"There he is," he said. "Hey," he added as the others moved to rise. "Take it easy. Give the man time to catch a breath."

He sucked up the last of the lassi noisily and, just to rub it in, lit a cigarette.

Kohn sometimes wondered idly if Bernstein were the actual genuine Wandering Jew. He wasn't young, but damned if he ever got any older. When he looked up with a snaggle-toothed grin of recognition he appeared exactly the same as when Moh had first stood alongside impatiently while his father haggled over some new acquisition (*Lenin and the End of Politics, Lenin and the Vanguard Party, Lenin as Election-Campaign Manager, Lenin as Philosopher, Lenin's Childhood, Lenin's Fight Against Stalinism, Lenin's Political Thought, Lenin's Trousers . . .*)

Bernstein clapped Moh's shoulder and shook hands with Janis and Jordan while Moh introduced them. He chatted with Jordan for a few minutes about the underground book trade in Beulah City, then turned to Moh.

"You got through the bomb scare all right, then," Moh said.

"Bomb scare?" Bernstein sounded startled. "All I saw was sodding Kingdom cops doing a sweep in Kentish Town. Had to take the long way round. Didn't fancy explaining where I got all those old CC minutes."

Central Committee minutes. That could be revealing.

"From before—?" Moh tried to keep the eagerness out of his voice.

Bernstein shook his head. "Postwar stuff. Split documents."

Moh shrugged one shoulder.

"What are you looking for this time, Moh?"

"Not history," Moh said wryly. "Politics." But he couldn't resist looking over the stall, just once. He picked up a pamphlet, a nice edition that he didn't have, and in mint condition. *The Transitional Programme*, by Leon Trotsky. Introduction by Harry Wicks.

"Good bloke," Bernstein said. "Heard him speak, once."

"You heard *Trotsky*?" Jordan asked.

Bernstein gave him a forgiving grin. "I was talking about Wicks," he said.

"How much?" Moh asked.

"Sixty million quid, in whatever you've got."

"Yeah, I'll take it," Moh said, counting out twenty marks. "That really is a bit of history." He was a sucker for this kind of thing.

"It's not what you came for," Bernstein remarked.

"Not exactly," Moh said. "What I wanted to ask you was—you don't happen to know where Logan is these days?"

Bernstein reached under the table and started flipping through a scuffed leather-bound book of pages held together by metal rings, some kind of hard-copy filing system. "Yeah, he's on a free-wheel space colony. New View. Utopian and scientific, geddit? Ah, here it is. Still got PGP, I see."

Moh scanned the characters laboriously into his smart box.

"Remember him going on about the Star Fraction?" he asked lightly. "Ever find out anything about it?"

"Nah," Bernstein said. "Saw Logan a couple years back, says he still gets the odd message." He cackled. "An odd message, that's what it is all right. I reckon it's something Josh built into the Black Plan."

Moh heard the sound of blood draining from his head, like a faraway waterfall. He watched Bernstein's face, and the whole mall, go from color to a grainy monochrome.

"The Black Plan?" he heard himself say.

"Sure," Bernstein said. "Your old man wrote it. Thought you knew."

Kohn fought the flashbacks.

To no avail.

*   *   *

Heavy metal industrial shelving, loaded with electronic equipment, tools, the guts of computers. Trotsky's collected works. Hardware and software manuals. Glossy computer magazines (softporn, his mother called them). Moh was lost in one when he heard a cough.

He turned to the table in the middle of the room.

"Morning, Josh," he said, smiling.

His father glanced up from the screen and nodded. "Hi, Moh." He reached out to one side, snapping his fingers. "Get us the Dissembler handbook. Third shelf from the top . . . thanks."

The keyboard keys clattered for a few more minutes. Moh watched in silence, then levered himself up by his elbows on the table to take a closer look. He gazed at the screen, intent, fascinated, as indented lines of code trickled upward. He didn't understand what the code was doing, but he had learned programming literally on his father's knee and he could see the logic of it, could see that at some level it all made sense: he knew, just before it happened, when the next symbol would be the one for ENDMO-DULE. A keystroke later and the module dwindled into distance, becoming faint horizontal hatching on a box connected to other icons on the screen.

"What you doing, Dad?"

Josh frowned distantly at him for a moment, then smiled with resignation. He straightened up in his tall chair, bringing his shoulder blades together, sighed out his breath and reached for a packet of cigarettes. He lit one and leaned on the table, now and again remembering to blow his exhaled smoke the other way.

"It's part of a big project," he said. "Uh . . . I'd appreciate it if you didn't talk about it to anyone." He gave Moh a quick coconspiratorial smile. "It's complicated . . . resource planning, logistics and financial genetic algorithms, with a bit of contingency planning hard-coded in."

"What's 'contingency planning'?"

"It's . . . the things you do just in case."

"Like burying guns!" Moh aimed an imaginary rifle.

"Yeah." Josh sighed again and looked once more at the screen. "This is one for the Star Fraction."

"What's the 'Star Fraction'?"

Josh looked at him, distant again, then shook his head as if coming out of a reverie.

"Forget it," he said harshly. There was a tone in his voice that Moh had never heard before, and the dismay must have shown in his face because Josh suddenly smiled and put an arm around his shoulder, and laughed, and hummed: "Five for the years of the Soviet plan and four for the International . . ."

Moh joined in, continuing: "Three, three the Rights of Ma-an, two for the worker's hands working for their living-oh, and one is workers' unity which ever more shall be so!"

Josh drew a blue line of smoke under the question of the project. "Well . . . how's workers' unity coming along in the Young Rebels?" he said.

"We're always arguing," Moh confided. "Some of the comrades think we should be more against the government and some of us say we should be more for it because the right are against it."

"What do you think?"

"Uh, well, I was thinking—is the Republic a workers' and peasants' government?"

Josh coughed in a suspicously vocal way and said, "Hih-hihh-hmm, ah, even allowing for peasants being a bit thin on the ground in these parts, I think we'd have to say: 'No.' But these categories (you know what that means? good) aren't really useful here. We're in a new situation. It's a radical democratic government. It isn't Socialist but the capitalists don't trust it. So things are a bit unstable."

They talked about politics for a while. Eleven years old and having just joined the party's youth group, Moh understood the politics he'd learned from his parents as an adventure that spanned generations like a space program: behind them the pioneers who'd risen in Petrograd, fallen in Vorkuta; ahead the Alpha Centauri of workers' power and human solidarity; beyond that the infinite universe of socialism—the bright world, a world without borders, without bosses and cops. He felt proud to be part of it, arguing at school with right-wing teachers, marching on demonstrations, reading up.

"Well, Moh, these hands have gotta work for their living-oh, so you better—"

"Split!"

Josh gave him five, gave him ten, laughing, and Moh left.

But later that day he came back, and over the next weeks he and his father, almost without noticing it, fell into a way of working together: Moh fetching manuals and looking things up, helping with testing and debugging, watching the system grow. Josh talked and thought he was talking to himself, or over Moh's head, and all the time the logic, but not the function, of the programs was becoming something that Moh grasped without knowing that he knew.

"You OK, Moh?"

He blinked and shook his head. "Yeah, I'll be . . ."

"You using or what?"

"No more than usual," Moh said. He forced a smile. "What did you say?"

"Josh wrote it. The CAL system, remember?"

" 'CAL'?" Janis frowned at them both. Jordan's eyes widened.

"Computer-aided logistics," Kohn said. "I remember."

"Never seen it documented," Bernstein said, "but it couldn't have come from anywhere else. I'm not saying he did it all, but that was the core. Nobody else could've done it."

"Why not?"

" 'Cause nobody else wrote Dissembler."

This time the shock was different. No memories, no flashbacks. Just a falling feeling.

"You're telling me," he said to Bernstein, "that my father wrote Dissembler?" His voice creaked with disbelief. "How do you know?"

The lines on Bernstein's face deepened, momentarily showing his true age. "It wasn't talked about, back when you were a nipper. But—" He gestured at his stock and smiled sourly. "I've met a lot of ex-members since. Some of 'em in the bottom of a bottle, if you catch my drift."

"Why didn't you tell me before? About that and the Black Plan?"

"Like I said. Thought you knew. Anyway, the Black Plan was a bit of a dodgy question, even in the Party. Not many people knew about it, I can tell you. Only the Central Committee and the fraction that was in the Labour Party and beavering away in the Republic's Economic Commission. Your old man was the best software engineer they had. *Course* they used him. The man who wrote Dissembler!" Bernstein laughed. "You know he released it as freeware? Could have been a millionaire, at least, but he didn't hold with patents and intellectual property and all that. Talk about a good Communist. The Yanks were well pissed off: it ate through their controls and escrows like *acid*."

Moh remembered Bernstein, after the meeting all those years ago, talking about illegal software and what the Yanks did about it. He must have thought Moh would know exactly what he was hinting at.

"So that was why—?"

"That, and the Black Plan."

Bernstein's eyes held Moh's gaze, as if his memories were as sharp and inescapable. "It means he's still fighting them, Moh. 'Wherever death may surprise us . . .'—remember?"

Only a sentimental affection restrained Kohn from punching him in the teeth.

"Death is never welcome," he said after a moment.

Bernstein's gaze inspected him, registered some shift in their relation-ship.

" 'Death is not lived through,' " he said sadly.

Kohn thought about it and nodded.

"I should know," he said.

He thanked Bernstein, said good-bye, and urged Janis and Jordan out of the mall, out into the sunlight. They walked to a ruined wall and sat on it, legs dangling, and talked. They were facing nothing but crumbling flyovers, sprawling squatter settlements: if they passed for anything it would have been backpacking students on a transport-archaeology trip. The ash of several cig-arettes sifted to the ground as Moh told them what he'd remembered.

"I still don't see how this Black Plan is supposed to *work*," Janis said.

"Nor me," Moh said. He'd never thought of the Black Plan as more than black propaganda until last night. Jordan grabbed his arm and Janis's, al-most making them topple backward.

"What—"

"I know how it works," Jordan said, in a voice strained with trying not to shout. "He put trapdoors in Dissembler! That's how it works! Because everybody uses Dissembler. Moh, man, your father was a *hacker!*"

"What d'you mean, 'trapdoors'?" Janis asked.

"Ways in," Moh said. "Trojan-horse stuff. Goes back a long way. The guys who wrote one of the first big operating systems planted some real subtle code in it that let them access anything it ran. If Josh pulled the same trick with Dissembler—"

The plan working through the market. He knew where that idea had come from.

"Josh must have buried guns all right," Moh said. "Buried them in the Black Plan: sleepers, logic bombs. And one contingency was that the Re-public would fall, that the revolution would be lost."

"And what do you think the first part of the contingency plan was?" Jordan said. "I'll tell you—set up something like the ANR!"

"Well, it certainly *enabled* it," Moh said. "The story is that it siphons off money and supplies from all over the place. Computer-aided logistics, ha! But to actually build an organization?" He held up the pamphlet he'd bought. "You'd need this kind of program, not a fucking computer pro-gram!" Jordan and Janis were looking at him as if he'd said something clever. He thought for a moment. "Oh, shit."

"Yes," Jordan said. "Look at it this way. It's not just an analogy, it's the *same thing*. It's a selfish meme!"

"I know about memes, ideas spreading; but why *selfish*?"

153

"It's—well, it's a metaphor, right? For how ideas spread, replicate themselves. Like, ideas are exactly as interested in the brains they're in as genes are in the bodies they're in: just enough to get themselves copied."

"Like computer viruses," Janis added.

"OK." Moh spread his hands. "And?"

"If Josh built some political strategy into the Black Plan," Jordan continued, "where would he have got the ideas from? Where else but from his own party's program, all his experience and reading about politics? The Plan *is* the program—not the old pamphlet you got, not necessarily the ideas in any detail, but the set of practices that it *codes for.*" He grinned knowingly. "Over the years it's embodied itself in lots of organizations, isn't that right?"

"Well, yes," Moh said. It was a disconcerting view. "You're saying the program creates the party, and not the other way round?"

"Of course it does," Jordan said. "What do you think is going on in there?" He jerked his thumb over his shoulder. "Just a different mutation of the ideas, infecting fresh minds. A selfish meme replicating across time. Your variant of it may be in scores of sects, the Left Alliance and so on, but the most successful species at the moment is in the Black Plan. It's got its own bloody *army.*"

"Now *you're* the one talking *serdar argic,*" Moh said. He punched Jordan lightly. "Come on. You're talking like it's some kinda electronic Antichrist, taking over the world with—"

"Bar codes containing 666!" Jordan laughed. "No, it's just a way of looking at it." He made an inverting gesture. "Mind you, you've just said there's a connection between the Black Plan and the Fourth International . . ."

"Well, maybe in the sense that you mean, that Josh wrote it. Beyond that . . . I don't know. Not much sign of Trotskyist ideology in the ANR. Or any other, come to that. They're pragmatic. Postfuturist."

"Exactly," Jordan said. "The political and military techniques work independently of the ideology."

"What would you know about that?"

Jordan shrugged. "I read books."

"What about the Star Fraction?" Janis interrupted. "Bernstein said he thought *that* was in the Black Plan."

"Not the Fraction itself," Moh said, frowning. "Just instructions for it, for people like Logan."

" 'Not the Fraction,' " Jordan mimicked. " 'Just instructions for it.' Get a clue, Moh. They're the same thing."

"OK, you can look at it that way if you want." He felt stubborn about this, that Jordan and Janis between them were concocting a dubious metaphor for something plainly explicable in political terms. "What I think is that the Star Fraction was a *real* organization that Josh was involved in setting up. It was designed to exploit some kind of capability of the Black Plan but it never got activated."

"And what," Jordan asked triumphantly, "were you so damn insistent you'd done yesterday? You *activated* something!"

Moh stared at him, unable to speak as he experienced the mental flip into seeing things the way Jordan did: ideas as discrete entities—memes—leaping from mind to mind like programs indifferent to the hardware they ran on; language itself as a natural Dissembler, turning words into virtual realities in human brains; ideologies as meme machines, using all the parties and factions, armies and movements, faiths and reasons as their disposable bodies to reproduce another generation of gun-toting or Bible-thumping or program-quoting or party-building meme-propagators.

He thought of Johnny Smith, the Hizbollah fighter who'd died in his arms (*Och, Johnny, I hardly knew ye!*) and whose heroic death had inspired a dozen others, which in their turn . . . now there was a Johnny Smith Martyr of the Southall Jihad Memorial Children's Home.

He thought of Guevara, whose words Bernstein had quoted:

> Wherever death may surprise us, let it be welcome, provided that this, our battle cry, reach some receptive ear; that other hands reach out to wield our weapons and other men intone our funeral dirge with the staccato chant of the machine-guns and new battle cries of war and victory.

The tradition of the dead generations weighs like a nightmare on the brain of the living . . . as Marx said. Yes, there were generations of the dead and they reproduced themselves . . . just as there were generations of the living and *they* reproduced themselves.

He thought of Josh and Marcia, how they had joined the generations of the dead. He looked down at his hands on the warm metal of the assault rifle across his knees. Some part of the weapon Josh had wielded was now buried in this gun, in its cryptic, encrypted memories.

And in his.

"Yes," he said at last. "I activated something. And I did it with a code I remembered from working with Josh on the Black Plan."

"Logan was part of the Space Fraction," Janis pointed out. "If this idea about the political program having been sort of built into the computer program is right—"

"Then *it*'s reaching into space," Moh said. "Oh, yeah, I get the point. It could just go on. Building parties, raising armies, raising hell. Forever."

"Centuries, anyway," Jordan said. "The future is a long time."

Moh looked at the sky. Glades off, it hurt. Something to do with there not being enough air pollution to keep out the ultraviolet. Or something.

"Time we called Logan," he said.

II

Quantum Localities

DONOVAN'S MAIL FILTER routinely discarded 98.3 percent of incoming messages: sabotage attempts by enraged systems administrators, inquiries from journalists, advertising shots for everything from nuclear depth charges to antifouling paint. That still left a lot, and it was just lucky that Moh's message caught his eye. As he read it he laughed at the desperate naiveté of the mercenary's direct approach.

So Catherin had taken his advice and disappeared.

Too soon.

Donovan stood up and tried to massage his stiff shoulders with his aching hands. He'd been up all night, winding down the mechanical ferocity of his virtual hordes. It would probably be another day before the process was complete and they'd have a clear sight of whatever the Watchmaker entity was doing.

A girl in denims and deck-shoes came up from the galley with his breakfast coffee. He nodded to her and motioned her over. She approached with an air-hostess smile that relaxed to gratitude and relief when he asked her to massage his shoulders and neck. The insistent pressure and warmth of her fingers soothed his mind as well as his muscles. He drank the coffee and scanned the news. The increasingly fraught international situation came almost as a relief: it might give the CLA and Stasis time to deal with the Watchmaker entity while Space Defense was busy iraqing the Japanese.

He turned around in his seat. "Thank you," he told the girl. "You can go now."

"You're . . . welcome, Mr. Donovan," she said, and walked, very carefully, across the floor and down the ladder. Donovan waited until the sound of her footsteps was lost in the sough of the sea and the sigh of ventilation, and put out a call for Bleibtreu-Fèvre.

Within seconds the Stasis agent's face appeared on a flat screen. If he had been up all night he certainly didn't look it. Used to it, perhaps: Donovan had a vague image of him sleeping through the day, hanging upside down by his feet. Bleibtreu-Fèvre apparently mistook Donovan's momentary amusement for cordiality, and returned him a thin-lipped smile.

"I'm about halfway there," Donovan said. "How are your people reacting?"

"There is no panic," replied Bleibtreu-Fèvre. "I have reported my suspicions, but the consensus is still that it was sabotage, if not by your movement then by some freelance hacker. The disruption seems to be over, for the moment. However, Mrs. Lawson reports a small but persistent unaccounted increase in net traffic since the . . . event. Barely detectable, unless one is specifically looking and applying appropriate diagnostics. Like global warming." Another thin smile. "It is rising—by a very small fraction, but it is rising. It will be obvious to the dimmest sysadmin within about three days, to the rest of my agency some time before that and, no doubt, to Space Defense some indeterminate time after . . . How banal it will seem," he added, "if the first tangible evidence of a new intelligence on our planet should be unexpectedly high telephone bills, ha, ha."

"Some would say it's been with us a long time," Donovan said, sourly acknowledging the joke but smarting inwardly: Bleibtreu-Fèvre was playing back to him an idea he'd advanced a little too seriously in *Secret Life*. "What about Dr. Van?"

"There we may have a problem," Bleibtreu-Fèvre said. "I have not heard from him for some hours. He has an infuriatingly vague answer-fetch which takes the form of a pretty young lady who sounds as if she is promising to put him in touch with you immediately, but as soon as the call is over one realizes she has promised precisely nothing."

"Probably an actual person," Donovan said as gravely as he could manage. "The skill is almost impossible to automate."

"Any progress with Kohn?"

Donovan flipped Kohn's message into Bleibtreu-Fèvre's field of view.

"So much for that scheme," the Stasis agent remarked after reading it.

"Perhaps," Donovan said reluctantly. "However, Catherin Duvalier is almost certain to contact me if Kohn does find her. It's in her interests to have the matter settled."

"I suggest you put out another call for a freelance arrest," Bleibtreu-Fèvre said. "Please inform me of any contact immediately. This man may be extremely dangerous, possibly even an informational plague carrier for the AI entity. Given who he is—who his father was, and what happened to him—we cannot expect his cooperation. I will attempt to bring him in personally."

"Isn't that a risk for you while he's in Norlonto?" Donovan asked. Space

Defense had a way of overreacting if Stasis crossed into even notionally extraterrestrial territory.

"Yes," said Bleibtreu-Fèvre. "But it's a risk we may have to take."

"And if he leaves Norlonto?"

"I have thought of that," Bleibtreu-Fèvre said. "In my line of work, as in yours no doubt, one cultivates contacts who may be a little—shall we say?—*irregular* in their ways, but who are on fundamental issues basically sound."

The barb. Green partisans. Give them a few trinkets, tell them this machine or that person was an enemy of the Earth: aim and fire. Donovan nodded enthusiastically, reflecting that, as far as Stasis was concerned, he was little more than a useful barbarian himself.

The phone booth was a bubble of scratched plastic bolted to the outer wall of the shopping center, the exchange itself a beveled black chunk, like a small version of the monolith in *2001*. And, also like that, the exchange had resisted everything up to and including laser fire. Kohn ducked into the booth while the others stood facing outward, giving him a modicum of privacy. He linked his throat-mike, the gun and the telecom box and ran the key for Logan.

A holo appeared in the black depths, a show-off display of the signal's path: Alexandra Palace—Telecom Tower—Murdoch GeoStat—bounce around a few more comsats—ping to Lagrange where a sargasso of space habitats rolled in the gravitational wake of Earth and Moon. There the line vanished into a scribble of local networks. The right-hand digits of the bill's running total were flickering as fast as they had the last time he'd called Logan, when it had been a voice-only link, no fancy graphics (*mips are cheaper than bandwidth*). Somewhere in there: Dissembler, his father's work.

Logan's face appeared abruptly, at a slant; behind and around him plants, fish tanks, cable, tubing, everything stacked and looking as if it were about to topple; an overhead window with passing bars of light in constant unsettling motion behind it.

"Moh Kohn! I was *expecting*—" He stopped. "Hey, man, this a secure feed?"

"It's your crypto," Moh said wryly.

Logan responded with the usual delay. It looked slow-witted, as always until your mind adjusted, pacing the light-seconds. "*Jes*, well, the *Amerikanoj* haven't cracked it, but—you slot in some of your own?"

Moh thumbed a hot-key. The pictures dissolved to snow, graphic characters, a vertiginous glimpse of crawling low-level ASCII, then snapped back.

"Safe now?" Logan asked. Behind him a chicken flapped inelegantly past, its beak open as if in surprise at remaining airborne.

"We're talking infinite monkeys," Moh said. "Shoot."

"OK. This about the Star Fraction?"

"Yes!"

"Uh-huh. The old code. It's gone active. *Years* it's been following me around, every so often this message comes up: don't do anything. This time yesterday, suddenly it's *Move your ass, comrade, this is the big one.* And what's it telling me? Crack out the ammo? Even crank out the leaflets? Hell, no, it's: buy fucking lab equipment! Sequencers, cryogenics, neurochemicals, dedicated hardware. I mean, we got stuff like this up to here, up here"—he waved at the scene behind him—"but this is like *way* beyond what we need to run our ecology. Meanwhile I'm getting calls from comrades I never knew I had. Space movement, *Internaciistoj*, ANR, the lot. All of them think the program (whatever the fuck it is) thinks *they're* in the Star Fraction (whatever the fuck *it* is). And it's telling them to—well, depends where they are. Ground, it's ship stuff out. Orbit, pull it in and put it together. All bio gear, communications software and computer kit with backup storage like they use for disaster recovery. Core memory that can ride out near-miss nukes."

Near-miss nukes. Moh thought of the news: the Kyoto suburbs, the Sofia streets. A memory of shelter sweat made his skin itch.

"And are you doing all this?" was all he could think of to say.

"Course I am. I got calls on hold right now, man."

"How are you paying for it?"

Logan grunted a laugh. "Checked our earthside account. Money's coming in, earmarked. Could be capital investment from a Bolshevik bank robbery back in 1910 for all I know."

"Close enough," Moh said. "It's from the Black Plan."

Logan stared at him for a longer time than the transmission lag could account for.

"How do you know that?"

"I think it was me that stirred it up," Moh said. "I was poking around yesterday. Something in the system asked me for a code that I remembered from way back when Josh was writing it. That was when things started to happen—"

"*Josh* wrote the Black Plan?"

"So Bernstein says."

Logan nodded. "Go on."

"It's something to do with the Star Fraction, I know that much. Fact is, my mind's got a bit—shit, I don't know, maybe screwed up with some memory drugs I got exposed to. Good to get some confirmation, yeah? The other thing that happened is this load of encrypted data got downloaded to my gun's computer, and I wondered if you might have some idea what to do with it."

Logan frowned. "Could be preemptive backup. If I set up the rig that the program's telling me, it'll be able to pick up tight-beam transmissions. That's real dicey, especially if it's encrypted. Lose one digit and it's junk. OK, you can get around that, throw redundancy at it like there's no tomorrow. Even so, if nukes are in the picture you get emps, you get borealis hits, comms out for days."

"You think that's on the cards?"

"Nukes? *Ne.* If you're right, though, about when the thing was set up, you can see why—"

"Shit! That's it! Just before the last one!" Goddess, that was a relief. Up to a point.

"—it's got a real sensitive ear for rumors of war."

"So. What d'you reckon, I should take this into space?" Moh crushed a stray syringe under his boot, wondering how he'd scrape the fare together. Work his passage, ride shotgun . . .

"You kidding? Haven't you heard, man?"

Moh shook his head, suppressing the impulse to give Jordan a kick. Eyes on the net, that's the sodding job description . . .

"Yanks have declared an emergency; space traffic and launches are bottlenecked. Nobody with any form's gonna get out until the face-off with Japan's over. With a load of encrypted data?—forget it."

"What about all this stuff you've ordered?"

"It's all clean," Logan said. "Empty storage, legitimate supplies. And it's on its way. Expedited before the crackdown."

"Neat," Moh said. Somehow it didn't surprise him. "So what do I do with this chunk of non-access RAM?"

"Go to the ANR," said Logan. "Safest place."

"Ha fucking ha."

"I'm serious. The *knaboj*, they'll look after you. Anyway, it's theirs. The Black Plan."

"You know what I think?" Moh said, looking down at the gun's memory case. (The Party must always command the gun; the gun must never command the Party. Mao.) He looked up just as his words reached Logan. "They're *its.*"

Logan stirred, shifting without noticeable attention into one of the isometric exercise routines that low-g folk had to keep up if they were ever to be one-g folk again. "There's a lot going on," he said. "A lot coming down the line. We know about the offensives and ... things are moving out here, too. The space-movement fraction I told you about, we've made progress, we'll do what we can—"

"Hey," said Moh, "is there any connection between these comrades and the ones in the Sta—?"

Logan smiled, his face moving toward and away from the camera.

"Don't even ask," he said. "Gotta go. Take care."

Click to black. Then, unexpectedly, the screen came on again:

> *Message To: mk@cheka.com.uk*
> *From: bdonovan@cla.org.ter*
> *Display here?*

Moh hesitated, wondering whether anything nastier than a message might arrive. He decided that, since the Kalashnikov firmware had withstood everything ever thrown at it, there was little risk. There was not the slightest possibility that his reading the message would give its sender any trace of his physical location. In a sense he wouldn't even be reading it here; his agent programs would have automatically done a search of the standard mail drop host machines as soon as he'd linked into the communication net. He hit Enter.

No pathway listing; pretty good anonymity. Just:

> *You wrote:*
> *≥ Donovan I got a problem with Cat shes*
> *≥ left the hospital and is'nt tracable.*
> *≥ Can you delay the Geneva Court bisines*
> *≥ until I get this sorted out. Please axcept*
> *≥ my apologies for offending you're org it was*
> *≥ just a personal thing with Cat I was pist of*
> *≥ with her working for the CLA because she should*
> *≥ of known better. I know the CLA are good fighters*
> *≥ and we have always treated hostages and*
> *≥ casualties etc by the book.*
> *I appreciate that, and I understand your problem, but I must insist that it is *your* problem. The challenge has been issued and I cannot retract it without further possible loss of respect. Privately, I agree to delay any appeal to the Geneva Convention court system but in the meantime the call for a citizen's arrest must stand until*

you personally claim a ransom for Ms C Duvalier the aforesaid
person to be in your (nominal) custody at the time. In normal cases
a settlement between our respective organizations would suffice but
this has become a question of the good name of both Ms Duvalier
and myself.
Regards
Brian Donovan
Carbon Life Alliance
Registered Terrorist Organization #3254

Go to the ANR, Logan had said. The idea had its merits, not least that it would get him out of the whole mess with Donovan. Still leave the comrades in it, though—that was the problem. At some point he might have to approach the ANR in any case, although what they would make of his story was anybody's guess.

Moh turned and stepped out of the booth. Jordan and Janis looked up at him, but he nodded absently and ignored them. Asking them to keep a lookout had been careless: it wasn't what they did for a living, or what they habitually did to *keep on* living. He flipped his glades down and made a slow sweep of all he could see.

The streams of people entering and leaving the mall had, if anything, thickened. Smaller groups wandered around the outlying stalls in the building's shadow or in the harsh sunlight. The only breaches of the peace going on were knots of Neos swaying back from their lunchtime drinking sessions, raucously singing assorted national-Communist anthems.

In the distance, traffic on the old flyover was stationary. Nothing unusual in that—it was a public road—but . . .

Some kind of commotion in the shantytowns piled up below the road. Moh unclipped the gunsight and held it up, patching the image to his glades. Typical settlement scene, lots of visual clutter: the distracting diversity of the shacks, clotheslines sagging across yards and paths, diverted power cables strung all over the place, aerials on jury-rigged pylons, gray gleam of sewage streams. In among it all, the gaudy colors of variegated costumes and flapping rags on . . . people moving, fast, scattering and scurrying from . . .

A spread-out line of black-clad, visored figures striding steadily through the narrow lanes. *Kingdom cops.* Moh could hardly believe the sight until he remembered that this wasn't legally part of Norlonto at all. It still seemed outrageously provocative of the Hanoverians to march in like this—the area was if anything more anarchistic than the anarchy around it.

He whirled around, calling to Janis and Jordan to look over there, and

163

started checking for any reaction. Nobody'd noticed yet, or they were taking it calmly. Glancing from group to group he saw a familiar face in the crowd—couldn't be, wrong walk—wait a second, never saw her walking, why . . .

His attention, and a moment later his stepped-up vision, focused again on the girl who'd been at the space-movement table. She was threading her way purposefully through the crowd, more or less toward where he stood. Her whole manner and posture were at odds with her earlier pose. Thinking back Kohn could see that it had been doubly faked, imitating an imitation; some of the younger and sillier people in the space movement thought it a cool pose, and she'd been imitating that.

Might not mean anything, but suddenly everything had meaning—in a wash of good old Communist paranoia: *comrades, this is no accident*—and Moh started walking, fast, in a direction he at first thought was random.

"What's going on?" Jordan asked, loping beside him, Janis jogging to keep up. Moh stopped, throwing them both off-balance.

"Jordan, time to split. You nip back in, help old Bernstein pack up. He has places to dive into around here. Hole up with him until it's over, then take the monorail back to our place. Start a search for Cat: you'll pick up the trace on the house phone; go from there and keep an eye on the net. Try to contact the ANR. I'll call you later."

"Until what's over?"

Jordan was puzzled; the situation was just beginning to dawn on Janis. Moh, fighting a surge of impatience, had to remind himself that neither of them was exactly streetwise.

"Don't know," he said. "Not staying to find out. You see the cops coming in? Just a show of strength maybe but with all those kids—"

He heard the crash of the first bottle.

"Knew it," he said. "Balls for brains, these guys. Move it. You got two minutes before this place is a—"

Something burst over the wall where they'd just been sitting. Long strands of sticky stuff drifted down onto a couple of reckless Neos, who instantly began a predictably counterproductive effort to swipe it away.

Kohn tugged Janis's arm and they both started to run. The last he saw of Jordan, when he glanced back a second or two later, the youth was standing, still dumbfounded, waving and moving backward as if on a station platform: good-bye, good-bye.

Clutching her sun hat and backpack, Janis followed Moh as best she could as he hurried through an obscure exit from the shopping center into a tiled tunnel lit with flickering fluorescent tubes and smelling of urine and disinfectant. Eventually they came out in a more open foyer where a man in a peaked cap and dark uniform stood by a robust barrier. There were posters—yellowing now, but once heartily colorful—on the walls; between them, damp paint bubbled and flaked. Another uniformed man looked out impassively from behind a pane of wired glass. Moh went over and pushed a few low-denomination coins through a space under the pane. After half a minute's deliberation, the man pushed a couple of tickets back the other way.

Moh handed Janis a ticket and walked in front of her, putting the ticket in a slot on the barrier. With a wheezing, sucking sound the barrier—a pair of padded jaws at hip-level—opened and Moh stepped through. Not half a second passed before the jaws thunked shut again, emitting a momentary groan as if cheated of their prey. Moh turned and snatched the ticket as the machine ejected it.

Janis went through with her eyes shut, then down some broken concrete steps covered with plastic shopping bags and empty cans and dry leaves and out onto a broken concrete platform. There the litter had apparently metamorphosed into its adult form: overturned bins, shopping trolleys and the remains of small trees. From the edge of the platform railway tracks could be seen for a few tens of meters in either direction; beyond that, they vanished among weeds. But they were at least shiny, not rusty.

"What *is* this place?" Janis asked.

Moh looked at her. "It's the Underground," he said.

"The *Tube*? Is it still running?"

"Occasionally," Moh said, looking anxiously up and down the track. "Main thing is, the Kingdom cops won't come here, not without a lot of hassle. We've crossed a border."

"Into what?" A second look along the platform revealed about a dozen people, most of them very old, sitting waiting as if they had been doing just that for a long time.

Moh sighed. "One faction of the Republic accepted the Settlement, and this is what they got for it. The rump of the public sector. It even gets a subsidy from the Kingdom. But it's a Free State in its own right." He grinned. "Sort of a *reformistan*."

"I hope Jordan's OK," Janis said. From the direction of the mall she could hear the sounds of breaking glass, yells, riot-poppers. Further away, the instantly recognizable black smoke from burning tires rose above the shantytown.

"He'll be fine," Moh said. He was gazing into the distance at a rapidly approaching aerostat. "Bernstein has forgotten more ways out of there than the cops'll ever know."

"What did they barge in here for anyway?"

"The Hanoverians are always a bit touchy about history," Moh said. "But right now I think it's the future that's bugging them."

"Don't you feel like *getting involved*?" Janis asked mischievously.

"No point," Moh said. "The cops are way outnumbered. They'll pull back or call in reinforcements. Either way . . ." He shrugged.

The aerostat—a thirty-meter black disc like a flying saucer from a hostile alien empire—slid across the sky overhead and, with a deafening blast as its propellers altered pitch, stopped. It descended slowly behind the shopping center and laid down a brief barrage of gas. Rope ladders uncoiled from it, and in a few minutes were swinging as the retreating cops scrambled up. As soon as they were on board the machine wobbled, tilted and wallowed off to the west.

"Overloaded," Moh observed in a satisfied tone. "They're good for terrifying crowds, but that's about it."

People began straggling into the station, most of them arriving at a run and then losing much of their momentum and wandering around in a dazed manner, as if they'd been ejected from a pub into the street. They had bleeding heads, pouring noses, weeping eyes. Janis couldn't see any serious injuries, and felt a selfish relief there weren't any casualties that would make her feel obliged to help.

After about half an hour a series of increasingly frequent and agitated, but otherwise incomprehensible, bursts of sound from a PA system indicated that a train was due. After another half hour it arrived, carrying a swaying crowd of commuters: beggars and prostitutes, mostly, coming back from the early-to-late-morning shift in town.

A few seats were unoccupied but Janis had no intention of sitting on any of them. She stayed as close to the doors as she could, clinging to the handhold. Moh stood, stooped, beside her, keeping his balance unaided as the train lurched and labored along. In low-voiced, brief sentences, barely audible above the noise—and falling silent whenever it ceased—he told her what he'd learned from Logan and from Donovan.

"Sounds like this thing's into biology," she said. "I'd have expected something political, but this . . . Goddess, it's *creepy*."

"Creepy crawlie." Moh shook his head, his eyelids hooding an intense, abstracted gaze. "I know what you mean . . . but I don't think it's that, nothing sinister, like . . . the Watchmaker idea, creating new life or taking over the world or whatever. It's a lot more worrying than that."

"How?"

"Something Logan said in passing: disaster recovery. That's the political meaning of what it's doing. It's worrying because—*it*'s worried, so to speak. Fits in with how Josh thought—he used to talk about what he called the Fall, what might happen if we didn't get a"—Moh grimaced, as if embarrassed—"a new society. A saner world. We'd go back, to an older kind of society. Precapitalist."

"Instead of post-? Yeah, yeah." She smiled up at him skeptically.

" 'A catastrophe threatens the entire culture of mankind'?"

Moh frowned. "Where did you get that from?"

"It's in the transitional program, the death-agony thing—"

"So it is." He closed his eyes for a moment. "Trotsky . . . OK." He opened his eyes again. "Had me confused there. Anyway. You get the point. The program, again."

"Well," she said, "he was wrong the last time, wasn't he. I mean, all that doom and gloom was written, when? 1938?"

Moh laughed and put an arm around her shoulders. "You've cheered me up, you really have. It's not like some kinda *global catastrophe* started in 1939, huh?"

They got off at a station which the Underground shared with the Elevated monorail. Both Underground and Elevated ran at ground-level here: Hein-leingrad, well inside the Greenbelt, where all the old place names had been scraped away. The gutted Underground part of the station was scrawled with colorful graffiti and willfully obscure slogans:

NEITHER DEATH NOR TAXES

QUANTUM NON-LOCALITY: THE UNIVERSE NEXT DOOR

SPACE FIRST! NO COMPROMISE IN DEFENSE OF EARTH'S CHILDREN!

She nudged Moh. "One of yours?"

"Nah. Just a bunch of extremists."

The Elevated station had been built around a 1930s bus terminus deco-rated in the style of a futuristic past. They sat in the station's glass-fronted cafeteria, their backs against a grooved aluminium pillar, and had coffee and doughnuts. Janis watched the people come and go through what looked like a small set from *Things to Come,* apart from the outfits. Not a short tunic or a short-back-and-sides to be seen. Moh spent a few seconds flipping through maps on a computer.

"Big drawback of the arrangements here," he remarked as he slipped the machine into his shirt pocket, "is that there's no King's highway. Everything is private. Property and access can be a bit of a minefield."

"I hope you don't mean that literally."

"Not exactly, but if we do have to trespass I'll rely on my friend"—he patted his bag—"rather than legal precedents."

"That's where you've got the gun?"

"Not so loud. Yeah. Comes apart."

"And I thought we were alone together at last."

"Better two and a bit than none, my dear."

He was watching the crowd almost all the time. The few moments when he looked directly at her he would half-smile and she only had time to half-smile back before his glance darted away again. She wondered if to him it was a long, searching look . . . She couldn't complain: it was her drugs that had done things to his sense of time and his memory, and her money that was paying him to keep watch.

And she had fallen for him, hard. As in: a hard man is good to find. One part of her mind—the skeptical, analytical, scientific part—was looking on sardonically, with a knowing smirk, seeing her sudden swept-off-her-feet attachment to Moh as, ultimately, the springing of a genetically loaded trigger, a survival strategy: her best bet was someone strong and kind, dangerous to others and safe, safe, safe to her. The rest of her mind just felt weak whenever he looked at her. What her body felt was different, and weak did not come into it.

Moh was tapping at his phone. He slid it to where both of them could see it and nobody else could: the picture was set to flat, not holo.

Mary Abid's face appeared on the screen.

"Oh, hi," Mary said. "Jordan's back, if that's what you want to know. Threw him in at the deep end, didn't you?"

"Can I speak to him?" Moh said impatiently.

"Sure . . . passing you over."

Jordan looked up at them, evidently via a camera mounted on the top of a screen he was working at. He had a black eye and a few scratches.

"You all right, Jordan?"

"Yes," he replied cheerfully. "We got into a bit of a scuffle, but that was all. You should have seen the police, Moh. They ran like rabbits."

"Yeah, well, I told you the Neos—"

Jordan smiled. "It wasn't your Commie headbangers that chased them off—it was the market ladies!"

"Good for them. And they're not *my* Commie headbangers, as I keep telling you. Did Sol Bernstein get away OK?"

"Yes. Never saw anyone so old move so fast. He had his books packed up by the time I reached him, and we chugged off on his electric tractor right through where a fight was going on. That was when I got a few knocks, but it was nothing really."

He obviously felt it was a bit more than that and was quite pleased with himself. Janis hoped Moh wouldn't burst Jordan's little bubble of satisfaction at getting through his first rumble.

"Sounds like you did all right," Moh said. "How are you getting on with the net searches?"

Jordan's expression flipped from smug to serious.

"Well . . . first, about Catherin . . . Cat. There was a queue of replies to your message when I logged on. Nobody's seen her. One or two people have mentioned that Donovan's got a call out for her as well."

"I bet he has," Moh said. "What about the ANR?"

Jordan sighed in exasperation. "I can't raise them. All the messages bounced. At first I thought I was doing something incorrect, and I got the comrades to check. But by then it was all over the news. The ANR has gone off-line, left all their phones off the hook. Well, not exactly: you get an answer-fetch giving a standard spiel." He passed a hand across his eyes. "It gets irritating after the twentieth time."

"What's it saying?"

"Basically, a bit of rousing propaganda and then something to the effect that, if your message can't wait until after the final offensive, they'll know about it through other channels anyway."

"Modesty was never their strong point—"

"Modesty!" Jordan's sudden grin was blocked by the fish-eye loom of his delighted air-punch or clenched-fist salute. "Yo! Never thought of that!"

"What?"

"The Black Planner yesterday, he ordered a load of silk through this Beulah City fashion company. I might be able to track the consignment, get a lead to the ANR that way."

"Nice one," Moh said. "But I doubt if they can be tracked that easily."

"I know, but Modesty can be! I saw a Modesty truck yesterday, might have been headed for Norlonto. I'm sure I could hack in, work backward from there. Most of their deliveries are finished goods, right? Import fabric, export fancy frocks. So if I find any fabric *exports* . . ."

Moh shook his head. "Bills of lading are the easiest things to switch, and that's assuming the Black Plan was actually pulling in silk in the first place. More likely that was a cover as well, and what they got from China was a cargo of knockoff Kalashnikovs."

Jordan looked a bit discouraged, and Janis said quickly: "It's worth a try anyway, Jordan. It's all we've got to go on."

"Fair enough," Moh said. "OK, Jordan, you do that, and keep looking for Cat any way you can think of. Pass on any bit of news you find interesting."

"Hah! Getting back to that . . . you know about the space-traffic crackdown?"

"Logan told me."

"Fine. OK, the other thing is Donovan's citizen's arrest thing. He's posted the offer to lots of newsgroups."

"That figures."

"Anything I can do about it?"

"Ask the comrades to toss out countercharges, challenges on my behalf and so on. Get our lawyers to issue a few nasty messages. Make it look like a real tangle. Might scare off any casual adventurers."

"OK, I got that. What are you going to do?"

Moh laughed. "Keep jumping borders," he said. "Like the libertarian comrades say: Norlonto ain't the law of the jungle, it's a jungle of laws."

For the next two days they wandered through a tiny proportion of that jungle of laws, the disparate communities of Norlonto. Unlike the patchwork of the Kingdom, these were not separate fiefs but layered, interwoven properties and neighborhoods. Some welcomed anyone passing through. Some had gates on the streets, or took a toll, or turned back anyone who hadn't been invited by a resident. Carrying weapons on the street might be prohibited, permitted or required. It was a matter for the street-owners, like wearing ties in restaurants, smoking or nonsmoking. There were sinister, seedy areas that had been all bought up by Nazis and made most of their money from tourists and memorabilia. There were women-only territories. There was a whole district called Utopia University, which consisted of experimental communities being crawled over by sociologists (who were mostly funded by estate agents doing market research). One sharply delimited estate, the Singularity Sink, had no laws or morality at all: anyone who entered was deemed to have renounced any protection but their own. It had a certain appeal for suicides and psychopaths, and for adolescent macho adventurers. (There was of course nothing to prevent violent rescue missions, either, and very rich and desperate relatives had been known to send in armored columns.)

But most of it was normal and respectable. Mutually compatible areas had found it profitable to adjoin, or buy up linking corridors, or sponsor rapid transport between them. You could travel widely through Norlonto and never see anything that would have looked out of place in Bangkok. A sidestep away you could see and do things that would be banned in Tehran.

Each new locality they crossed into was another stream to wash away their trail. Everywhere they found an undertone of caution, the racket of protection being strengthened, the buzz of departing money; fortunes, *capitals* as Moh called them, queued up on the wires like birds preparing to migrate. Every time the government announced the rebels were bluffing and the situation was under control, more smart money took wing for warmer climes.

Moh kept calling Jordan every few hours except through the night: the ANR was still unreachable; Jordan was building up an elaborate hack on Beulah City's shipping companies and fashion houses, but he had no progress to report yet; and Donovan's challenge was arousing some interest among various bounty-hunting agencies. Much to Moh's disgust, a new newsgroup had opened, alt.fan.moh-kohn, for enthusiastic amateurs to report sightings of him and discuss the case; so far, none of the sightings had been authentic. Moh took out a policy for himself and Janis with the Mutual Protection Agency; the understanding was that he wouldn't tell the company their location but Mutual Protection would download a map of areas where they could guarantee delivery of reinforcements within ten minutes of a call.

"What if we do get attacked or something," Janis asked, "and the attacker has a contract with another agency? Do they shoot it out?"

"Give it some mips," Moh said. "Proper channels are part of the deal. The agencies take any differences to a court they both acknowledge is fair—"

"And suppose an agency popped up that didn't accept any court that Mutual Protection suggested?"

"Then a court they didn't accept would find against them, without them even defending themselves, and they'd lose customers. In serious cases they'd be hunted down like dogs. What the agencies sell is legal protection as well as physical. If you want to protect criminal acts you just need your own guns, or preferably a state—that's a real lawless defense agency for you, and run like any other monopoly to boot: rip-off prices, lousy service, rude staff."

"You're not talking about the forces of the Crown by any chance?"

"Now what gives you that idea?"

Janis had another objection. "You're forgetting about the poor," she said. "How are they covered?"

Moh replied as if he'd been over this a few hundred times. "We all pay for security in every facility we use anyway, but if all else fails, if somebody's kicking your shack down or putting the screws on you and you've not bothered to do without maybe a packet of smokes a week to pay for protection, you can always call on charity. The Black Cross, the St. Maurice Defense Association, the Emancipation Army. Or us, if we're in a generous frame of mind."

They were sitting at a pavement café. The waiter brought Janis her vodka-cola. She took it and smiled down at him, gave him a quarter. He thanked her with a gap-toothed grin and ran back inside.

Moh looked after him sadly.

"Anarcho-capitalism works," he said. "As much as any kind of capitalism works. It's that sort of thing I find hard to take. Child labor. Prostitution. Slavery—"

"What!"

"Oh, it's not legally enforceable. But on the other hand you can't prevent people selling themselves for life, and some do. And there's legal slavery as well, to pay off crime-debts, though that's a lot different."

"All the same, slavery . . ."

"It's a feature of most utopias," Moh said gloomily. "It comes with the property."

Late morning, two days and nights after Jordan had watched Janis and Moh dodge the shopping-center riot, the comms room was hot and airless. He paused for a moment before running his latest program, giving it a final check in his mind before committing it. He found his thought processes warping under the influence of the other person in the room.

Mary Abid was working through the day on night watch in a chemical factory in Auckland, NZ. The satellite link didn't make for fast reflexes, but she didn't need them; the semiautonomous robots that she guided around had reflexes of their own, and her main task was to put some human common sense in the loop.

Whatever she was doing, sitting and swiveling in a basic-model telepresence exoskeleton, it involved stretching and switching and sweating and cursing, and something in her sweat or scent or swearing was transmitted to Jordan as a distracting subliminal sexual tension. He barely associated it with the Kurdish woman in the telly-skelly. During the hours he'd been sitting hunched at the Glavkom VR apparatus, spinning an elaborate web of nuance and inference, looking for a trail of silken thread, and looking for Cat, it had been the photograph of Cat on the wall of Moh's bedroom that Mary's female pheromones brought unbidden to his mind.

Cat. He'd extracted a patchy biography of her from the Collective's records. A teenage rebellion against a staid petty-bourgeois background—her parents ran a VR rental franchise on the fringe of Alexandra Port—had led her into a loosely leftist militia. She'd literally bumped into Moh Kohn during the Southall Jihad, worked with the Collective for two, three years until some inextricably intertwined doctrinal/personal dispute had taken her away into a succession of idealistic combat units and one or two of the numerous factions that made up the Left Alliance.

The Left Alliance, unlike the ANR, was taking calls, but Jordan had a distinct impression that they had more pressing matters on their minds. Any people or systems he'd contacted about Cat had simply referred him to the standard cadre-availability databases, all of which had Cat down as damaged goods. The group she was currently in—he'd eventually tracked it down, the Committee for a Social-Ecological Intervention—had been barely willing to acknowledge that she might possibly have had some association with them at some indefinite time in the past.

Of course, as all concerned admitted, if Cat's current little legal difficulty could only be sorted out . . .

Jordan felt a rising indignation at what Moh had done to her, much as he could see Moh's point about the dubious nature of the coalitions that Cat's political trajectory embraced.

He'd made more progress on the Beulah City/Black Plan connection, or so he hoped.

"RUN SILK.ROOT?"

The system message floated in front of his eyes like an afterimage. Jordan took a deep breath.

He nodded, chinning Enter.

Hacking into Beulah City's systems directly had proved difficult. Quite apart from his earlier—and, he now thought, overhasty—action in liquidating his business interests there, a data-security crackdown was evidently in progress. Mrs. Lawson, he guessed, was busy. Nevertheless, he retained access rights to a few of the smaller systems which had, so far, not been revoked. This had given him one angle of attack. Next, he had set up a completely spurious trucking company (created with an apparent age, he wryly told himself, like the stars in 4004 BC). As far as one of Modesty's subsidiaries was now concerned, River Valley Distribution Ltd. had an excellent record of deliveries within Norlonto. The phantom details would be discovered at the next audit, but that wasn't due for another month.

The program now running in SILK.ROOT had Jordan's virtual company inquiring about the possibility of putting in a bid for more work. It was asking for some background information—just a breakdown of Modesty's deliveries to British locations in the past month. If he'd set up the right parameters on the systems he had managed to hack into, they'd accept this highly irregular request without a blink.

He found he had his eyes closed, his fingers crossed.

Ping. And there it was, on twenty pages of spreadsheet: dates, times, companies, goods sent. He excluded finished garments, reducing it to five pages, and tabbed down through the list of fabric sales. He was beginning to think he might as well have called up the Yellow Pages for dressmakers when he noticed—among all the Lauras and Angelas and Blisses and Bonnys—a customer called the Women's Peace Community.

Three consignments in the past month, all consisting of tens, no, *hundreds* of meters of fine silk. One order still outstanding: the fabric had just come in by air, and awaited delivery. The order had been placed four days ago, in the morning. When he'd encountered the Black Planner.

Yee-ha!

As he stared at the line of information it began to blink. A message came up.

"CROSS-REFERENCE ON WOMEN'S PEACE COMMUNITY EXISTS. DISPLAY?"

A big Y to that. The pages rippled as the program followed pointers through the Collective's databases. Then the scene cleared to display a videophone message that had been waiting in the Pending file since the day before yesterday.

The phone's flat screen popped up in the middle of the virtual scene. As the picture stabilized Jordan thought, for a startled moment, that he was seeing an interior view in Beulah City itself: a parlor with overelaborate furnishings and drapes; two women in long, likewise overelaborate dresses, all petticoats and pinafores. The woman in the foreground sat primly, hands folded in her lap, facing the camera. The other sat on a sofa behind and to the left, paying no attention to the call; she was concentrating on a piece of needlework, her fair curls falling forward in front of her face.

"Felix Dzerzhinsky Workers' Defense Collective?" the first woman asked, the words sounding incongruous. She nodded at the confirmation. "Good. We require professional advice on neighborhood security, and we understand that you have some experience in this field. Please call us as soon as possible. Thank you."

She reached forward to sign off, and just as she did so the woman in the background looked up. She looked straight at the camera from across the room, brushing her hair back from her forehead with her wrist.

Jordan jumped at the shock of recognition.

It was Cat.

The picture clicked off.

*   *   *

Jordan passed a note into Mary's work-space, asking her to take a break. She did, after another strenuous minute. Jordan ran the message for her.

"Well?" she said.

"That's Cat! At the end there."

Mary frowned. "Let me see that again." This time she magnified the last section. "Yeah, well it certainly *looks* like her, but . . ."

"You'd never expect to see her dolled up like that?" Jordan smiled to see he was right. "It's the way she's pushing her hair back. It's like the picture in Moh's room, shows her doing just the same thing. Except in the picture it's a spanner she's working with, not a needle."

"Well, Jordan, I don't know how you think we live, but I've never been in Moh's room," Mary said with a giggle. "You'll have to show it to Moh."

Jordan was about to do that when he remembered what the message was actually about, and how he'd found it.

"Let me just fix something up first," he said.

"Yeah, that's Catherin all right," Moh said. He saved the image from his glades and cleared the view, turning his attention to the Tinkerbell-sized fetches of Jordan and Mary above his hand-phone. "Well spotted, Jordan. I might have not have recognized her myself if it weren't for that thing with the hair. Cat disguised as a lady—that's a laugh."

"I think you were meant to spot it," Jordan said. "You or one of the comrades. They're telling you: Cat's here, come and get her!"

"So why not call us and say that? Who are these people, anyway?"

"Feminists—fem*inin*ists," Mary corrected herself. "Women's Peace Community, some kind of sweetness and light outfit—"

"*Yes!*" Moh shouted. "The Body Bank!"

Janis, who like him was prone, looking at the phone display, winced as the sound filled the narrow volume they lay in.

"Sorry, Janis."

"What's that about the Body Bank?" Mary asked.

"There's a teller at the Body Bank at Brunel University—she's a femininist. Only one I've ever met, as far as I know . . ."

"It's been getting quite fashionable recently," Janis interjected.

"OK, interesting. Anyway, I remember this lady noticing that Cat wasn't included in the deal over the crank bomb team. She might have followed it up."

"That's possible," Jordan said. "But why should Cat go there?"

Mary shook her head. Moh shrugged.

"Oh, for pity's sake," said Janis. They all looked at her. "Cat had just

175

been thoroughly shafted in this game of soldiers. Wouldn't surprise me at all if she wanted out, wanted at least a bit of peace and quiet. Even if it did mean having to sit and stitch. In fact, especially. Soothes the mind." She rolled over and laughed. "Try it sometime, guys and gals."

"Sanctuary," Moh said. "OK. That makes sense, I guess. Just as well you noticed the message."

"It wasn't an accident," Jordan said carefully. "It wasn't the search for Cat that brought it up, it was the . . . Beulah City follow-up."

"But why—?"

Moh was about to ask why the ANR should have any connection with this Women's Peace Community when he remembered that Mary wasn't in on the whole story. "Uh, what'll we do, call them back?"

"I already have," Mary said. "Didn't say anything about you, just said we'd send someone over today."

Moh turned to Janis. "You game for this?"

"Sure. Should get Donovan off our backs, at least."

"At least," Moh agreed. And maybe lead us to the ANR as well. "I'm thinking about how we'll get there," he added. "Mass-transit might take us out of our insurance cover."

"That's all OK," Jordan said. "I've set it up. They're taking a delivery of silk from Beulah City—" Jordan paused, as if to make sure Moh had got that point. "But it's in a place that no driver from Beulah City would go."

"Not one of those *terrible* places, is it?" Janis asked.

"Oh, no," Jordan said.

Mary smiled impishly. "It's a small semiclosed neighborhood in the Stonewall Dykes," she explained.

"I see," Moh said after a moment. "Major fire-and-brimstone target area. So how do we get there?"

"The truck comes out of Beulah City, goes to a pickup point where it's handed over—Mary's got the map—and you drive it the rest of the way. It's all in the name of a dummy company I've created."

"Sounds safe enough," Moh said. He had a thought. "Not a women-only area, is it?"

Jordan turned to Mary with a baffled gesture.

"It's OK," Mary said. "I've checked. They have no objection to men. In their place."

"This community is sounding more sensible all the time," Janis remarked, running a possessive hand down Moh's back. He turned and grinned at her.

"Hey, I'm quite used to being dominated by women."

"You should be so lucky," Mary said. "Right, here's the details. Jordan's made all the arrangements." She did something out of view, and streets and times appeared on the phone screen.

"And get up, you two," she added, just before she and Jordan vanished. "It's a fine afternoon."

There wasn't room to stand up in the double bed-cell they'd rented, so it took them a while. They had to get their clothes on, lie face-down and slither under their packs, then crawl backward out of the hatch and down a ten-meter ladder to the ground.

"Weird," Janis said as they walked out along narrow passages between banks of bed-cells. "Like left luggage."

"Left passengers."

Little Japan hit them like a rock concert as they stepped out of the door. They took the slidewalk, changing tracks frequently, swaying in the crowds. Moh found he was half-consciously generating a running mutter of body-language that created a small space around them, whatever the crush. He gave up trying to process the incoming information, the solid-state semiotics of the place.

"Doesn't feel oppressive," he said. "That's what's so strange."

"Something in the food," Janis said. "Inhibits the anticrowding phero-mones."

It bothered him that he couldn't tell if she were making it up.

The trailer park, in an indeterminate zone between Little Japan and one of the more multicultural areas, felt like open space. There was an average of a meter between bodies here. The huge trucks lay charging up, drivers lounged, and vendors vended.

"Ah, the wonders of the free market," Janis grouched, narrowly avoiding a tray of hot drinks being carried at alarming speed on the head of a five-year-old.

"Not as free as it looks," Moh said. "These places tend to be run by gangs. Shady jurisdictions and that."

They found the light container truck they were after in a corner of the park near the feeder road. The driver shoved a magazine into his pocket as they approached, and stood up, looking slightly embarrassed.

"Hi," Kohn said. "River Valley. You're expecting us?"

The man smiled and nodded. He handed Moh the key, took a receipt and headed off, evidently not straight to the nearest rail station.

Janis and Moh climbed into the cab. The truck was owned by a rental company and changed hands often—that much was obvious from the condition of the interior. Moh had a sudden thought. He passed the key to Janis.

"You drive," he said.

Janis took the key, smirking, and turned the switch with a flourish. The engine responded with a faint hum.

"Aw," she said. "It's not like the films I saw when I was little." She made internal-combustion-engine noises as the truck glided out of the park.

"Nah," Moh said, adjusting his seatbelt. "It were a man's job in them days—aaarrrgh, stop . . ."

12

The Cities of the Pretty

THERE ACTUALLY WAS a wall called the Stonewall Dykes, but it was more to prevent people from entering unwittingly than to keep anyone out—or in. In the bad old days of the Panic it had had a more serious function, but now it was just a bit of retrovirus chic—isolation camp. The real protection of the area—the Gay Ghetto, the Pink Polity, the Queer Quarter—was in the strong, gentle, capable hands of a militia called the Rough Traders.

The truck pulled off the clearway and down a side street, past a portion of the wall on which someone had written "Sodom today—Gomorrah the World!," and they were in. Just another street, except suddenly there were no women. A bit further and there were no men; further yet and there were both, but you couldn't tell which was which, all gaudy and glad-ragged and gay.

"What's the difference between this sort of thing and what's outside?"

"None at all, that's the point. There's *nowt* so queer as folks, as they say up North—"

"Oh shut up. That's not what I meant. What's the difference between these specialized neighborhoods, or whatever you call them, and the mini-states?"

"No wars."

"It can't be that simple."

"Looks like it can."

"The future and it works, huh?"

Kohn laughed. "It keeps people like me *in* work. In my future society we'd be out of a job. No wars over territory *and* no fights over property."

"Yeah, yeah . . ."

Kohn gave directions for a few more turnings. They came to a halt in a car park in front of a large housing estate built as a single block: four sides around a courtyard, the side in front of them having an opening about three meters high and five wide. Through it they could see a lawn and flowerbeds. All the windows in all eight stories of the block had curtains of ruched peach satin in front of other curtains of frilled net. Another truck and some small vehicles and bicycles stood unattended in the car park.

A man came out of the entrance and walked up briskly. He wore a plain brown loose-fitting smock and trousers and had short blond hair. He stood for a moment at the front of the truck and then stepped up to the door beside Kohn.

Kohn lowered the window. He decided for the moment, to stick with the ostensible reason for their visit. "Hi," he said. "I'm the security adviser—"

"Mr. Kohn? Ah, hello. My name's Stuart Anderson. Your agency told us to expect you. I'll be asking you in in a moment, but first I'd like a word with the lady."

Janis leaned across. "Yes?"

"I'm sorry, ma'am, but would you mind waiting while your companion looks around? No offense intended—it's just the rule of the community. The only women allowed in are those who live here or are associated with us, and you . . ." He smiled regretfully like a waiter telling you something is off tonight. "Refreshments will be brought out to you if you wish, or you may take a walk in the area."

"Thank you very much," Janis said. "What sort of women-oriented community keeps ordinary women out and lets men in?"

"Femininists," Anderson articulated.

"Ah, so," Kohn said. "You should have worn a frock, Janis, makeup like lacquer and false eyelashes. Then they might have let you in for a boring examination of their building, which is what I'm down for."

Anderson gave an open, genuinely amused laugh.

"Don't take it to heart, ma'am. We won't be more than an hour, and in the meantime, if you wouldn't mind easing the truck forward a bit so we can get it unloaded and reloaded . . ."

Janis shrugged and blew a kiss and a scowl. Kohn climbed out.

"Please leave any weapons," Anderson said.

Kohn detached the computer and heaved the bag back into the truck. Anderson coughed politely. Kohn thought for a moment, sighed, and passed Janis a pistol, a throwing knife, a flick-knife and a set of brass knuckles.

They walked across the courtyard. People strolled about or worked at the garden. The women, as Kohn had expected, were wearing every exaggeratedly feminine getup known to man. The men looked rather drab and conventional by comparison. No old people; no children.

"So tell me, Stuart, what's it all about? If you don't mind me saying so, you don't look very sissy to me."

"Of course not," Stuart said. "That's not what we're into. Our aim isn't to merge or reverse the sex roles but to make femininity the dominant *gender.*"

Moh shook his head. "I still don't get it."

"It's all to do with *peace*," Anderson said earnestly as they entered the block and walked down a bright corridor. "We're sickened by the violence that goes on all around us, and the femininists have a theory which explains it. The so-called masculine virtues have outlived their usefulness. Aggression, ambition, production. We've reached a point where the whole Earth can be a home, a garden, a sanctuary. Instead it's used as a factory, a hunting ground, a battlefield. That's what we mean by the dominance of the masculine virtues. What feminism advocates and tries to practice is the long-overdue domestication of the species through the feminine virtues: domesticity itself, of course, plus gentleness, caring, contentment: channeling energy into art, adornment, decoration . . . All low-impact activities, you see, and utterly absorbing. Take embroidery, for example, which many find entirely satisfying as a full-time, lifelong occupation, yet the material resources used in it are negligible . . . and of course the product is valuable, including to rich collectors."

"And where do men fit into all this?"

"Oh, they don't try to fit us in. They just set us a good example. And we integrate our activities and interests as a subordinate, servicing part of this community, just as traditionally women's work has serviced the masculine economy—in fact, that's still how many of the women here earn money outside: as teachers, nurses, secretaries—"

"Bank tellers?"

"I think that, too, yes."

"Sounds a bit sexist to me."

Anderson laughed. "Now that's a word I haven't heard in a long time."

They entered a large, low room, almost a factory floor. Dozens of women worked intently at sewing machines. A few of them were obviously making clothes, but even Kohn could see that some of the items being made from vast pieces of thin silk had to be something else. He indicated them with his head as they walked along the side of the room. At the same time he tried to see if Cat were among the women there, but—as far as a quick glance could tell—she wasn't.

"Pavilions, canopies," Anderson explained. "Very popular at society garden parties."

Pavilions? Moh ran some of the shapes through again in his head, then left something at the back of his mind to figure them out. There was another thing that didn't quite fit here. The ideas that Anderson had expounded struck him as too daft and too sensible at the same time: the femininists were giving some very old-fashioned views a subversive twist, but the tenets Anderson had expressed lacked the seductively counterfactual gormlessness of ideology. (Men are free. Men are equal. Men are such beasts.) Or perhaps Moh was just overestimating the human species: "If there's a folly unvoiced," his father had used to say, "some little sect will emerge to voice it."

A woman fell into step with them. She introduced herself as Valery Sharp and described herself as the block administrator. She was small—petite, Kohn mentally corrected himself—and pretty, with the glamorized hausfrau look of some ancient advertisement for detergent: gingham dress, floral-print apron, blond curls held back with a starched cotton kerchief. She sent Stuart off to get coffee for the lady in the truck and showed Kohn into her office, a small room off the workshop area.

"Lovely, isn't it?" she remarked brightly, closing the door. She sat down behind a desk and invited Kohn to a chair. "Someday all offices will be like this."

The desk looked more like a dressing table. It had a frilled valance around it. The frills had frills. The chair was swathed in fabric tied with bows; the white wallpaper was sprigged with pink rosebuds; the air was thick with jasmine potpourri. Kohn felt as if he'd stepped into her bedroom. Goddess knew what *that* was like.

"It would make a change," he said truthfully. He could imagine the entire planet turned over to this sort of taste: roses around every door, perfume on every breeze, men and machines devoted to providing the basic materials for women to endlessly titivate and prettify and tart up . . . He really should give more of his money to the space movement.

Valery smiled wryly. "It gets me like that, too, sometimes," she said.

Kohn looked at her, puzzled at this admission. He was reluctant to reveal that he knew there was some connection between this place and the ANR.

Valery looked at him very directly and added, slowly and distinctly: *"Civis Britannicus sum."*

Kohn stared at her, astounded. The phrase wasn't exactly a secret password but it was the next best thing: he'd never heard anyone say it without meaning it. It affirmed a continuing sense of Republican citizenship, and there were places where it could get you shot.

"Gens una sumus," he responded. His mouth was dry, his voice thick. "We are one people." It drew a sharper line than all the manufactured divisions of the Kingdom, and put the speaker on the other side of it.

"So what's all this—?" he began.

And then, suddenly, he saw it: the pieces fitted together—literally.

"Parachutes!" he said triumphantly. "Microlites, hang gliders . . ."

Valery's eyes narrowed. "Very good," she said. "How did you figure that out?"

Kohn shrugged. "With my good right brain."

She still looked puzzled, but as if she believed him.

"OK, Kohn. You know Cat is here?"

He nodded. "You picked a pretty roundabout way of telling me."

"Yes," said Valery. "There was a good reason for that. It's the same reason that the ANR is staying off the nets as far as possible: they're no longer certain the systems are secure."

"What makes them unsure?"

"I don't know," Valery said impatiently. "What I do know is this: we received an urgent message through . . . channels . . . to persuade Catherin Duvalier to come and stay with us, and to fetch you here. Donovan is out to get you, and not just for this stupid ransom affair. Now, I don't know what this means, but I've been told to tell you that Donovan knows who you are, and so does Stasis. They're working together now. Donovan's challenge was an attempt to lure you to the hospital, where he could find you—fortunately we got Catherin out of the way first. We did send a girl to see you, but she wasn't able to make a sufficiently secure contact."

"Ah! At Brent Cross?" Kohn snorted. "It only made me more paranoid."

"She wasn't very experienced, and we may have overstressed the caution," Valery admitted. "Anyway, now you are here, we can sort out the ransom business. That won't stop Donovan, I'm afraid, but at least he'll have to call off his hue and cry against you."

"Can you do that without him knowing where I am?"

"Certainly," Valery said with a smile. "Through the Body Bank, remember? All we need is your digital signature, and Catherin's. Our bank teller will witness it and everything will be legally in the clear."

"You've just said you don't trust the nets anymore."

"We're talking about different levels," Valery said vaguely, or with intentional obscurity.

"OK. And then what?"

Valery fixed him with a severe look. "The ANR," she said firmly, "is very anxious that you should go immediately to a controlled zone. That's all I know."

"Somebody else suggested I do that," Kohn said. "I've been considering it. It'd be difficult, seeing as the ANR have put the fear of God into the Hanoverians."

"We can arrange safe passage," Valery said. "I'll tell you about it later. Meanwhile, let's get this mess sorted out, all right?"

Kohn agreed almost absentmindedly, preoccupied by the implications of

183

what he'd just learned. Valery tilted up a desk terminal—it was shaped like a mounted mirror—and Moh jacked in his computer and passed his digital signature into the handover document. Valery messaged Cat, and after a moment the document showed that her dig-sig was in as well. Kohn watched as the Body Bank registered the transaction. He now had a credit—which he doubted he'd ever collect—of five hundred marks with the Carbon Life Alliance.

The consequences of the deal rippled outward through databases, and in less than a minute Catherin's name was cleared and Donovan's case against Kohn was dropped. Querulous, disappointed queries instantly began to flash around the low-life newsgroups. Kohn shook his head and caught Valery in the same gesture. They shared a disillusioned smile.

Valery was about to fold away the terminal. Then something on the screen caught her attention. She raised an eyebrow at Kohn.

"It seems Catherin would like to see you."

Kohn felt his ears going red. "Yeah, I guess she has a few words to say to me."

"Right," said Valery. "Go out, then through the door on the left to the garden, and in the first French window. I'll be along in a few minutes." She smiled quizzically. "I imagine the worst should be over by then. After that we can discuss what you do next."

"I have a companion," Kohn said. "She's out in the truck at the moment, and she'd have to be involved in any decisions."

"Of course."

"OK. See you," Kohn said.

He went out into the garden, through a glass door and into a kind of parlor full of overstuffed chairs and large vases. In one of the chairs a woman sat, head half-hidden by a bonnet, bowed over the lap of the huge spreading skirt of her dress. She was meticulously stitching small pieces of colored fabric onto the back of a denim jacket. A circular pattern with lettering around it was already beginning to take shape. She looked up, slowly, eyelashes lifting modestly.

Cat had a very catlike smile.

Moh grinned back. "Calamity Jane," he said.

Teeth white in the sunlight.

"It's all fixed?" she asked.

"Yup," Moh said. "You're in good standing again. An honest-to-goddess accredited left-wing combatant."

"Back to the struggle. Good."

The jacket slipped to the floor as she raised the pistol she had concealed underneath. She held it in her right hand and brought the left—the plastic cast becoming visible as the loose, lacy cone of her sleeve fell back—to give a steadying grip on the right wrist. Very cool, very professional.

"Now I've got you, you son of a bitch," said Catherin Duvalier.

Cat felt she had been waiting for this moment, this perfect revenge, for years rather than days. A glimpsed thought told her this was the case, that recriminations from their original breakup still echoed. The thought passed, leaving a steely memory of Moh stalking out of the hospital bay.

Her anger tensed the muscles of her damaged forearm, and hurt.

She'd had more visitors than anybody else in the secure ward. First Moh, then—in a virtual sense—Donovan. And later that evening the nurse who'd brought her dinner had put her head around the partition, smiled and said, "A friend of mine would like to meet you."

"Who's that?"

"She's a teller at the Body Bank. She's learned about your position and she'd like to help you."

"I don't want to be a security guard, thanks."

"Oh, that's not the idea at all. Nothing like that. That's why she wants to see you. I think you'll be interested."

Catherin shrugged and agreed. A few minutes later the bank teller walked in, heels clicking, clothes whispering together. She poised herself on the chair beside the bed.

"Hello," she said. "I'm Annette. I understand you're looking for a safe place to stay, out of the fights."

It didn't take Annette long to convince Catherin that the femininist community was a good place to go until her status as a combatant was restored. It would give her a retreat, a chance to plan.

"But that's all," Cat explained hastily. "I'm not saying I agree with your ideas or anything—"

"Of course not," Annette said. "But don't count on it. We've won over quite a few combatants who've got tired of the boys' games."

Cat smiled. It wouldn't happen to her. "When can I go?"

"First thing tomorrow morning?"

"Fine."

"Good. That's settled, then." As she stood up to leave, Annette picked up Catherin's denims and looked at them with some disdain.

"We'll have to get you something decent to wear," she said, making to take the whole blue bundle.

"No, no," Catherin said. "I want to keep these. I can do something with them."

"All right . . . Let me just get your measurements. Excuse me a moment."

She took a scanner from her pocket and waved it from Cat's neck to her ankles. "See you tomorrow, Catherin."

She returned at an ungodly hour the next morning with long paper bags draped over her shoulder. The nurse pulled a screen across the bay. Catherin looked at the bags.

"Modesty," she said. "Oh, Jesus!"

"Go out in style, kid," Annette said.

They had to help her to dress. It wasn't because of her broken arm in its shell, or her innocence of the intricate fastenings. There simply was no way to put on or take off these clothes independently. When they had finished they stepped back and smiled at her.

"Oh. Oh," the nurse said. "You're so beautiful."

Annette took Catherin's shoulders and turned her to face a wall mirror. She stared at this strange double, coiffed and corsetted, crinolined in blue satin and white lace. She stepped forward, then back, amazed at the sheer amount of *stuff* that moved with her, the trimmings that fluttered and swayed. She had to laugh, shaking her head at the absurdity of it. She plucked at the skirt in front of her with gloved fingers, let it drop.

"I feel silly," she said. "Helpless."

"Not quite," Annette grinned. She reached over to give Catherin a small handbag. "In there, my dear, along with some makeup carefully chosen for your complexion, you'll find a neat, ladylike little pistol."

Catherin smiled, relaxing. This trace element of the kind of protection she had always counted on reassured her and enabled her to accept the kind on which she must now rely: a power that didn't come out of the barrel of a gun. The shaping grip around her waist, the frame of fabric below her waist—they were not a prison but a castle.

"OK, sisters," she said. "Let's make an exit."

She walked out of the ward with her head high, looking straight in front of her. She had once seen a royal wedding on television, so she knew how to get the effect.

Moh looked at her for a long second.

"Look, Cat, I'm honestly sorry about what I did. What I didn't do. But it's settled, it's squared—"

"Not with me it bloody isn't. That's the point. Now I'm back in action I can take *you* prisoner." She grinned. "And I just have."

"On whose behalf?" Moh said sourly, playing for time. "If it's the Left Alliance we've already worked out what—"

"Oh, no," said Cat. "On behalf of Donovan. I called him when I was logged on to sign the release, as soon as I was in the clear. The CLA are sending a couple of agents—"

"*You did what?*"

The lady's gun wasn't much of a stopper, he thought; he could kill her before he died. For a moment he took comfort in that. Then he remembered there was a way out of the trap and out of the absurd feud that his offense against Cat had started, and which she seemed determined to finish. He eased back from tensing to spring, and waited, forcing a sickly smile.

"Formally," Cat said, "they're coming here to pay you the ransom for me, as they have every right to. And there's nothing to stop me handing you over to them."

Moh heard footsteps on the path outside. He stood where he was until Valery came in and stood beside him. Cat flicked a glance at her but the pistol didn't waver.

"Here's something to stop you," Moh said. "Valery, Miss Duvalier has just claimed me as a prisoner on behalf of the CLA. Two of their fighters are due here—when?"

"Any time now," Cat said. "Valery, this has nothing to do with you."

"Yes, it has," Valery said. "For one thing, you're still inside our community. For another—" She hesitated, looking uncertainly at Moh.

"Just tell her, dammit," Moh said. "If I don't move it this minute I'll be—" He stopped, fighting for breath, for words, against the pictures that his too efficient brain displayed. The thought of falling into the hands of the CLA and, worse, Stasis was turning his skin cold and the room dark.

"You'll do it?" Valery asked him.

"Yes, I'll do it."

"You have to say it," Valery said gently. "Say it to her. For the record."

Moh drew a deep breath. "As a citizen of the United Republic I claim the protection of its armed forces and pledge on my honor to exercise when called upon by its lawful authority the Army Council of the Army of the New Republic all the rights and duties of such citizenship including but not limited to the franchise and the common defense. Is that it?"

"Basically, yes," Valery said. "So, Cat, unless you want to tangle with the ANR I suggest you put that gun away."

Cat stared at them both. "This place is ANR?"

"Yes," Valery said.

Cat's shoulders slumped. She lowered the pistol.

"You still owe me one, Moh."

"Later," Moh said through gritted teeth. Calming himself, he smiled. "You *are* pretty," he said—as if that would be enough, would help, would cover everything—and backed out. He sprinted across the courtyard lawn, leapt flowerbeds and shrubs, dodged people. He wasn't surprised to find Valery Sharp keeping pace. A sidelong glance showed muscles firmed, doubtless by aerobics, under the clothes which also weren't as daft as they looked; they didn't get in her way.

"I'm sorry," Valery gasped. "We never expected—"

"It's OK. Neither did I."

They stopped in the cool gloom of the entrance-way. Crates were being loaded onto the truck. Only a couple more to go.

"Now, what were you going to tell me?"

"Take the truck," Valery said.

"Where?"

"As far north as you can, then to any controlled zone. We've got clearance for all the borders, and tax-in-kind, but . . . if it looks like anyone's going to find out what's really in it, stop them at any cost. If necessary, burn the container section. At any cost." She looked at him. "Can you do that?"

"Yes. Will you call my co-op, with a message from me to a guy called Jordan: the search is over, do your own thing."

"I'll do that. And I'll keep Cat out of Donovan's way for a bit."

"OK. I hope I see you again."

Valery smiled and shoved him on his way. "Go!"

He ran to the back of the truck, grabbed the last crate and hurled it in, jumped up to the deck and hauled the tailgate down after him as he vaulted back out. A man fumbled with a lock. Kohn waited for what felt like seconds until it was secure, then ran to the cab and almost flew through the door. He found himself facing his own gun. Janis was crouched under the steering wheel, aiming at the door and trying to fit an ammunition clip at the same time. The whiplash sensor extension writhed as it tried to keep level with the windscreen.

"Get *down*!" she hissed.

Kohn threw himself on the passenger seat, gasping. Janis passed the gun to him as if pushing it away from her.

"It *talks*," she said.

"Yeah, yeah, you knew that." Kohn rolled onto his back and clashed the clip and the computer into place. "What's it *say*?"

"Cranks. Coming for us. It's picking up signals—"

"Helmet." He waved a hand in front of Janis until he felt the helmet in it. He half-sat, cautiously, slid the helmet on and flipped the glades down, jacked the lead into the gun and keyed the screensight to head-up. The gun's two views—where it was pointing, and what the eye-on-a-stalk was seeing—overlay his own like reflections in a window. They had never looked so distinct.

"What did you get, gun?"

There was a pause as the computer interrogated the even tinier mind of the gun's basic firmware.

"Phone call, public, CLA encryption style, otherwise no data extracted. Source vehicle now entering square at—"

And there it was, flashily outlined in red: a black Transit van with black windows, turning the corner. It drove around the square and rolled to a stop a couple of meters in front of the truck. Kohn made out two heat-images behind the light-shaded windscreen of the van.

He turned on the engine and grabbed the steering wheel with his left hand. Janis watched.

"Seat. Belts," said the truck.

"Oh, shut the fuck up."

Janis clunk-clicked the belt on the driver's side and looped her arms through it, grasped it firmly with her hands, letting it take her weight.

"Good," Kohn said, like some psychopathic driving instructor. "Expect a jolt. Now take the brake off and give us some juice."

He braced his legs together against the lower edge of the dashboard. The truck lurched forward. There was a heartening crunch as its steel fenders rammed the thin metal and hard plastic of the van. Janis yelled but it was surprise—the impact hadn't been too severe.

Kohn jackknifed up and out of the cab, hit tarmac and made a low lunge for the van door, his body wrapped around the gun. He used the butt to smash the side window and whirled the weapon around to cover the inside. A young man and a young woman, both long-haired, oily-denimed, hailstoned with safety glass and still shaking from the collision. The man reached under the dashboard. Kohn fired one shot across the back of the man's hand and into the corner below the steering column. The hand snatched back and something hydraulic failed at the same moment.

"Out," Kohn said, and stepped backward off the running board.

They came out. The woman had her hands on her head. The man held his bleeding hand to his mouth.

"You come for me?"

The woman shook her head, the man nodded.

"Well, now you've f—"

Kohn's words were swamped by a thrumming roar, a skidding screech.

He turned his head—the gun stayed steady like a handrail—and saw an overdeveloped 'thirties Honda rocking gently where it had halted, a couple of meters away. Its rider was built to match, all the way from leather boots to leather cap. He dismounted, thus revealing that what had looked like a spare fuel tank was actually an armored codpiece. His arm and chest muscles would have been troubling even without the holografts.

He held up a badge. "Rough Traders," he said. "Do you have a problem?"

Kohn pointed the gun groundward and said, "A disagreement."

"Does anyone wish to lay a charge?"

The couple by the van shook their heads.

"Nor me," Kohn said. "But I wish to claim a ransom for a hostage, and I've had some difficulty persuading these two. I think you'll find that they do have the documentation."

They nodded frantically. Kohn felt some tension ease. It had been just a guess that Donovan's mob would try to maintain the cover.

"How much?"

"Five hundred marks," the woman said, finding her tongue at last. She held out a grubby banknote. Kohn made an insultingly elaborate show of scanning it with one of the gun's sensors (which duly registered that it didn't contain any large masses of moving metal) and wrote out a receipt pertaining to the release of one Catherin Duvalier for the sum of, etc. The rent-cop witnessed it and the man took the top copy, with the wrong hand at first.

"Please make sure this is delivered to the person mentioned in it," Kohn said, handing over a second copy to the Rough Trader. "She's currently resident at this block."

"OK."

Kohn walked back to the truck and climbed in, to find that Janis had been covering the whole incident with his previously discarded pistol. He smiled, kissed his finger and thumb at her and strapped in. The Rough Trader was striding toward the apartment block; the crank agents were talking into a mike in their disabled van. Laughing, Kohn eased the truck out of the square and along a narrow street, forcing a ridiculously broad pink Cadillac to mount the pavement as it came toward them. Then, after a few more back streets, they were on the clearway again.

Janis said, "Explanation time."

"Parachutes," Kohn said.

"Huh?"

"That place is an ANR front. The whole femininism thing is a cover-up." They both laughed. "They're busy making parachutes and fabric panels for microlites and hang gliders, using manual sewing machines. No software, see? Nothing to trace. Bulk orders on the Black Plan, like Jordan told us.

They must be preparing for something big soon. And, think of it, all these dolly secretaries and so on must make pretty good spies."

"What about the ones who really believe in it?"

"I doubt if there are many, and they can be kept harmlessly occupied. That was what all that fussy domestic craftwork crap was about in the first place, if I remember my social-history books."

Janis looked as if she had caught up with herself.

"Yes, but what *happened* back there?"

He told her: how the shapes hadn't seemed right, and what Valery had told him; finding Catherin, and how and why she'd set him up. Janis already knew about his earlier relationship with Catherin—they'd spent hours of the past days and nights telling each other everything. But she was upset.

"Oh, Moh!" Janis stared straight ahead.

"I know I shouldn't have—"

"No, it's just—why did you do it in the first place? Why did she try to get back at you like that? Sounds to me like two people out to hurt each other. A particularly nasty lovers' quarrel."

"I never thought of it like that," he said, considering. "It was business, politics. I felt she'd betrayed what we had stood for, that she fucking deserved it, working for these creatures from the swamp after, after—"

He was reduced to hand-waving.

"After standing shoulder to shoulder with you for scientific-technological socialism?"

Kohn gave her a half-amused grimace that admitted the explanation lacked plausibility. "Something like that."

She squeezed his knee. "It's all right, I'm not jealous. Well, I am, actually. But I know what I'm up against."

"Yeah," Kohn said. "No competition at all."

"Why did they let you get away?"

"There's a formula," Kohn said, "a password for these situations. Goes a bit further than the old *Civis Britannicus sum.* You say it to the right person, you're a citizen of the Republic. That's what I did when I saw it was our only way out. The Republic, the ANR, they don't give a damn for the militia rules of engagement. So now things are, like, different."

"Meaning what?"

"Well, any sort of little skirmishes we get into now are gonna be war. It won't be like being a mercenary or even just defending ourselves the way we did back there."

"You're telling me you've joined the ANR?"

"Not exactly, but I've agreed to carry out its lawful orders, as a citizen of the Republic." He looked over at her, feeling he had more explaining to do. "It wasn't just to get out of Cat's clutches. I've been thinking about it. The Republic's the only place I'll ever find the answers to what's happened to me. Like Logan said, it's the safest place for us. And for whatever data are stashed in the gun's computer. As for the politics of it, hell, if Josh could square whatever he was doing with working for the Republic, so can I."

Janis was silent for a moment. Then she said, "I want to join, too. Be a citizen. How do I do it?"

"I told you the first time this came up: you're still a citizen. From school, remember? If you want to be an active citizen, you contact another one, and volunteer. Like I just did."

"Damn, I could've done it back there, now I'll have to wait till we . . ." She stopped, hit her forehead with the heel of her hand and said, "*Civis Britannicus sum*, all right? That's me in?"

She looked so keen and pleased with herself that Kohn felt ashamed of his reluctance, but he had to ask.

"You're sure you—?"

Janis burst out laughing. "I love the way you keep warning me off—it's either charming or you must think I'm a vac-head. Look, Kohn, I know we're in trouble. The only place I have a chance to live now is on this side of all those burning bridges." She punched his arm, like she didn't want to risk anything but fraternal greetings at this moment. "My country is where you live, wherever that is."

"You know where it is," he said. "The fifth-color country. *Gens una sumus*."

They left the Stonewall Dykes and then Norlonto itself; they were on the King's highway now, the public roads. Kohn felt the momentary pang of unease which always accompanied his crossing into the domain of the state. An emotional toll. They passed a high blue-and-white sign with a vertical arrow and one word on it: "North." The clearway flowed into an eight-lane motorway. The diesel kicked in. Janis squirmed down in her seat like a happy child.

"I love that sign," she said.

"Uh-oh," Kohn said.

Janis sat up straight. "What?"

Kohn pointed at the rearview screen. Far behind them in the traffic was a pink blob with a wide chrome grin.

13

The Horsemen of the Apocrypha

DILLY FOYLE LAY on her chest in long grass. A few hundred meters away, across a culvert-floored green glen, the motorway made its humming and buzzing and howling music. Great bulks of irreplaceable minerals and petrochemicals were hurtling in both directions, canceling each other out. It had always been for her the perfect example, the paradigm, of how trade and exchange were an intrinsically wasteful plundering of the planet. The combustion engine, the consumer society . . . The words (if nothing else in the arrangement) were a giveaway.

The Human Reich.

To attack it directly was a sure road to dying. One bolt from the crossbow that lay at her hand could blow out a tire and, with luck, scatter burning wreckage and snarl up miles. But that was only worth doing to harass a military sweep already under way—to do it any other time would only invite one. So the GreenWar partisans preferred to pursue a subtler quarrel, building their Cumbrian communities in abandoned farms and the ruins of the tourism that had been their earliest and softest target. The Lake District was theirs now, in plain view of the towns. On a clear day you can see the revolution . . .

Her nose, untainted by foul habits or city air, could have told her where she was in the dark. Petrol fumes and damp earth, the oiled steel of the crossbow, the old wood of the stock . . . her comrades . . . their horses cropping quietly in a hollow. And, ahead and to her left, the service area, where the reek of exhaust and battery mingled with burnt coffee and wasted food and plastic in all its extruded and expanded, gross and bloated forms.

Synthetic shit.

She didn't need binoculars to scan the vehicles entering and leaving the service area, and she wouldn't need glades when night fell. Already the place had its lights on (waste, waste). She would know what to do if the signal came. And, if it didn't come to her, it would come to other partisans, at other points up and down the motorway. The orders today had been very specific, and urgent.

She waited.

They ran into a local war a few kilometers north of Lancaster. Farm buildings and factories burned. Tanks elbowed across the road. Helicopters racketed overhead. The traffic on the M6 barely kept pace with the refugees trailing along on the hard shoulder.

"It's like something out of the twentieth century," Janis said.

"They're not being strafed," Kohn remarked.

"What's that supposed to mean? Progress?"

Kohn slid the truck forward a little, then idled it again. The engine's note dropped below audibility. "Progress is like this," he said.

"That car still behind us?"

Kohn scanned. "Yeah."

The sky, eventually, cleared of smoke. Red Crescents and Crosses came out after the camouflage. The gaps between vehicles widened. A polite, hesitant, mechanical cough here and there, and then a roar of combustion engines rose like applause. The truck settled to a steady hundred kilometers per hour in the slow lane. The Cadillac paced it, now edging closer, now dropping back.

"This is beginning to get *severely* under my nails," Kohn said.

"What can we do about it?"

"Don't know. Ah, fuck it . . . kill them at the first opportunity."

"Do you really mean that?"

"Way I see it," Kohn said, "there's no way whoever's in that tuna-tin are terrs. Not their style, you know? They go for dispersed forces, raids, guerrilla tactics. The military—UK or SD—would go for roadblocks, flagdowns. Tailing, now, that's cop MO. Using a civilian car isn't, especially one so obvious. That smells of political police. Or Stasis."

"The Men In Black." Janis shivered. "Wonder why they do that—the suits, the cars?"

"Checked it out once," Kohn said. "It's a fear thing. They were set up years ago when there was that big panic about, I don't know, messages from space getting into the datasphere and churning out copies of alien software that would take over the world. Remember the TV shows? *The Andromeda Strangers. Night of the Living Daylights.* Nah, just after the war. Before your time."

"After my bedtime."

"Looking back now, I'll bet they planted these stories. Anything to keep people worried about dangerous technologies falling into the wrong hands, and not worried about whose hands it was in already."

"You know," Janis said thoughtfully, "people used to talk about the Breakthrough, the Singularity, when all the technological trends would take off and the whole world would change: AI, nanotech, cell repair, uploading our minds into better bodies and living forever, yay! And it always almost happens but never quite: we get closer and closer but never get there. Maybe we never get there *because we're being stopped.*"

"Stopped by Stasis . . . and by Space Defense enforcing arms control . . . yeah, that's how it works: software cop, hardware cop!"

"Yes, let's kill them," Janis said fiercely. "They're a waste of space."

"Soon be dark," Kohn said.

Another border: Cumbria. Another armful of fine work taken from the back of the truck. Tax-in-kind: with most of the economy over the event horizon of cryptography, it was the only way to collect if the owners hadn't cut a deal and let the state have the code keys. Tax-in-kind went all the way from roadblock rip-offs to US/UN sanctions where entire buildings, warehouses, factories were seized. Usually the owners agreed to operate in the open, where at least you knew the percentages. Except in Norlonto, of course: there they hid their money and handed over the goods at gunpoint if they had to.

At least so far no one had searched the truck. There was an etiquette to those matters, and transaction costs.

After a bit Kohn glanced at the fuel gauge and said, "Time to pull in. Could do with a stretch, anyway. Next service area."

"What about—?" Janis jerked her head backward.

"We'll see what they do," Kohn sighed.

"Then kill them?"

"You're getting into this, aren't you?"

The twilight became darkness the instant the truck glided into the halogen floods of the service area. Janis envied Kohn his glades. She could see the writing scribed on the side piece nearest her: mil spec 00543/09008. Kohn first drove to the refueling points, paying cash for diesel oil and charged-up power cells, which were swapped for the spent ones.

"That's exactly what I need to do," Janis said.

"Well, they don't give part-exchange for body waste," Kohn said. "Recycling hasn't gone that far." He restarted the truck and moved it around to the parking bays.

"Our friends are just over there," he said, pointing to the far corner of the car park, where she couldn't see a thing. "Still sitting in the car. Probably don't eat or shit, just need an oil-change every ten thousand klicks."

"I wish I had military specs," Janis said. She didn't understand Kohn's hoot of laughter, but was grateful when he reached into his pack and pulled out another set of glades.

"They're my only spares," he said, after he'd shown her how the cheek controls worked. "Watch them carefully."

He put the helmet under his arm.

"Set the glades to shade," he said. "We'll look like tourists."

"Heavily armed tourists."

"That's the only kind around here."

Jumping down and walking across the tarmac to the cafeteria, Janis kept looking around her. These things didn't just polarize light, they integrated it: the bright lights were stepped down, the dim enhanced.

"They're brilliant!"

"Turn them down a bit then."

"Ha, ha. How do they work, anyway?"

"I don't know, but I suspect they're not strictly speaking transparent—the front is a lot of micro-cameras, the back is screens, and in between there's a nanoprocessor diamond film."

She paused outside the toilets and stared at the pink Cadillac.

"Huh," she said. "They're eating doughnuts and drinking coffee from a flask. So much for your theory."

"That's what they want you to think," Kohn said darkly.

Janis looked again. One black man, one white.

"I'm sure they're the ones who came to my lab," she said. "Goddess, to think I came all this way to get away from them."

"You have got away from them," Kohn said. He nudged her away from looking at the car. "Don't you worry about that."

The queues at the meal-machines were short.

"Ten marks," Kohn said indignantly. "Each!"

"Don't be stingy."

"I spilled blood for that money."

They chose a table by the plate-glass window where they could see the car and the truck. The glades disposed of the reflections, too. Janis found it disorienting to glance from the strip-lit interior—with its truck drivers eating fast, families eating slowly, youths wandering around sizing up who might or might not be a user—out to the parked or crawling vehicles, and see it all as one scene. What effect, she wondered, would years of seeing like this—no shadows, no reflections, almost no darkness, no comforting distinctions between in here and out there—have on the mind? It matched, it fell into place with one aspect at least of Kohn's, well, *outlook*.

She smiled at the thought, and saw Moh smile back.

Bleibtreu-Fèvre brushed sugar from the tips of his fingers, licked them, and replaced the plastic cup on top of the Thermos flask. Always a damn dribble of dark liquid. He sighed and looked at his colleague, Aghostino-Clarke. The other man was dressed identically to himself, in a black jacket and trousers, white shirt and a tie the exact color of coffee stains. His suit was getting shiny in the same wrong places. His skin was very black and his eyes were brown.

It was lucky they had been prepared; but then, Bleibtreu-Fèvre thought smugly, preparation creates its own luck. When Donovan's call came through, indicating that Cat had revealed her location and Moh's, they'd been cruising around the perimeter of Norlonto. They'd been ready to do what they did—send the car into a screaming dash along one of the fast-access roads, the ones that normally only the rich and the emergency services could afford. He'd been right not to put much trust in Donovan's ability to field a large enough force in a short enough time to deal with the problem, right to have the green partisans on standby alert.

That the Women's Peace Community was near the border had been luck, however: pure luck.

They were going to need some more.

Aghostino-Clarke smiled. "Scared?" he said. His voice was deep: the upward inflection of the question raised it to bass.

"Nervous." Bleibtreu-Fèvre coughed and, as if reminded, lit a ciagarette. "It's what we've been trained for."

"That's why I'm nervous." He laughed briefly and stared again at the distant shapes of the man and the woman. "He behaves so normally, it's as if he hasn't a care in the world. One might almost think he's not afraid of us."

"He? Or it?"

Bleibtreu-Fèvre looked at Aghostino-Clarke and nodded thoughtfully. "Indeed," he said. "We can make no assumptions about *what* we may face."

A literal drug fiend, a man with machine-code in his mind, or just a crazy spacist merc . . .

"It would be easy to take him out."

"Those days are gone." Bleibtreu-Fèvre sighed again. "I can feel the footprints of those damn spy sats like shadows passing over the back of my neck . . . Speaking of which—"

Aghostino-Clarke looked at his watch, rotating his forearm slowly as he scanned the lines of data. "We have a six-minute window in two minutes," he said. "The next is four in twenty-three."

"Right," said Bleibtreu-Fèvre. "Let's go for green, huh?"

"Smoke?"

"Nah," Kohn said. "Time to go."

He stood up and tossed plates and scraps into the recycler. He put on the helmet and connected the comms to the gun. (Hi.) (Active.) He kept his eyes on the car as they went out through the doors. The car park was now more sparsely occupied, and the Cadillac stood on its own in an air-brushed gleam. How easy it would be to take them out. But if he were to blast them, right now, it would be difficult to hop into the truck and slip away unnoticed. They'd just have to wait. He ran scenarios of turning off into side roads, jackknifing the truck and coming out shooting.

The doors of the Cadillac opened; the two men inside got out and stood behind the doors. Janis made some kind of sound.

"Keep going," Kohn said, not looking at her. "Stand on the running-board behind the door—just like them—and start up the truck. Do it."

He veered away from her and began to walk across the fifty meters or so of tarmac between him and the car. The men didn't react. He wondered if the doors were proof against steel-jacketed uranium slugs. He doubted it. Perhaps the Stasis agents expected him to negotiate.

He was letting the gun point downward, his grasp light but ready to clench. He stopped.

"Hey!" he shouted, above the hum of vehicles. The men looked as if they hadn't heard him. He opened his mouth again and heard at the same moment a yell from Janis and a rhythmic clatter behind him. He whirled around in a crouch, bringing the gun up. Coming straight at him was a horse, and the wild-haired creature on its back was unclipping a crossbow from a slot beside the saddle and reining in the horse and dismounting all at the same time. Everything went slow, even the sparks from the skidding hooves. He saw another horseman, galloping up to the truck from behind. He fired a burst that ripped through the rider's thigh and into the horse. He saw the forelegs buckle under the beast's continuing momentum, saw the beginning of the rider's trajectory, then turned to his own attacker. A bar-barian woman. She was two meters away and was half a second from bringing the crossbow to bear on him. (No time to fire.) (What?) He sprang forward and brought the butt down on the woman's shoulder. The crossbow clattered away. He punched her straight under the sternum. She fell, balled up around her pain.

Kohn dropped and rolled. Something buzzed over his head. Snap. Sting of stone on his face. Ricochet. The shot had come from the Cadillac. To his horror he saw Janis leap from the truck's running board and dash toward him, head down and firing off pistol shots inexpertly behind her with her left hand. Her glades were on clear and he could see her eyes behind them, tightly closed.

The Cadillac roared forward, doors still open, gun muzzles poked above them. Flashes. There was a terrific bang as a tire blew out. Suddenly the car was yawing. Janis dived past the front fender and down on top of him. She rolled over and sat up, bringing another hand to the automatic's grip. The rear of the car swung past. Janis fired and a dark body dropped from the open left door.

She turned to him and opened her eyes.

"Are you all right?" she asked.

"Come on." He jumped to his feet and pointed back to the doors of the cafeteria. "In there." The car, steadying now, was between them and the truck.

They ran for the doors and pushed them open, hurdled the prone bodies of terrified civilians to the stairs. At the first turning Kohn saw a Man In Black just reach the doors. There was no way to shoot at him without spraying half the foyer. On up the steps to the glass-enclosed walkway above the road, leading to a mirror-image service area on the other side. They started the hundred-meter dash across.

Something was coming up the stairwell on the far side. Halfway along was a recess with fire extinguishers and an emergency phone. Kohn hauled Janis into it after him. They flattened back and Kohn glanced out.

Another horseman was cantering along the walkway. In the opposite direction Kohn saw the Stasis man leap to the top of the stairs and hit the floor, a heavy pistol clasped in both hands in front of him. Kohn jerked back.

The padding hooves stopped, close.

"Throw out your weapons." The agent's voice sounded strained and strange. "Don't say a word or you'll be shot."

"Oh, shit," Kohn said through his teeth. Some part of his brain began displaying detailed pictures of what would happen to it if he were captured. He wrenched his attention away from images of bone saws and drill bits and trodes in time to catch Janis's urgent low whisper: ". . . just the guns, then use anything you've got left, they mightn't expect all you've got . . ."

Kohn looked at her and nodded. She tossed the pistol on the floor. Kohn followed it with the gun. It landed on its bipod. Kohn raised his arms and was about to step out when he heard the creak and tinkle of thin glass breaking.

"FIRE!" said the alarm, in a deep, calm chip voice.

The gun opened up. Janis stepped smartly forward before he could stop her. She'd grabbed a fire extinguisher. She jumped in front of the horse and aimed the foam straight for its eyes. It screamed and reared, striking the rider's head against the ceiling. He fell backward. Janis was at the horse's side in an instant, shoving at the saddle. The animal tottered, off-balance, rear hooves beating a desperate prance, the fore-hooves hammering at the glass. The rider's legs kicked until his feet disengaged from the stirrups. He slid down the slope of the horse's back. The huge window broke. The horse went through the glass in a sickening slow motion and vanished. Janis ducked, scooping up the pistol. The rider was sprawled on his back, one arm underneath him, the other making warding-off motions. Janis stood astride him and pointed the pistol at his face.

"Don't!" Kohn yelled.

The gun continued its scything fire. Kohn threw himself behind it. It was supposed to respond to his voice only. He forgave it, this once. The agent was gone. Must have rolled to the stairs. Nice. None of the holes in the far wall were lower than half a meter.

The gun stopped, out of ammo. Kohn peered through the howling gap down at the mound of meat on the central reservation.

He looked at Janis.

"That was dangerous," he said. "You might have killed somebody."

She glanced back as Kohn slammed another clip into place.

"We're in the army now," she said, and turned back to the man at her feet.

"So you can't shoot him now! He's out of it!"

Janis shook herself and stepped back. "OK, OK." She gingerly took an automatic and a sheath-knife from the man's belt and rolled him off his broken arm. He'd already fainted.

They ran back the way they had come. Janis stood clear as Kohn crawled to the top of the stairs and used the gun's sensors to look over the edge. Nothing there. They went down the stairs and out across the foyer, back to back. Nobody had responded to the fire alarm. Just as well.

The whole place looked as if a gas bomb had hit it. Everything intact but bodies everywhere. Vehicles still pulling in seemed suddenly to go on automatic: driverless. Good reflexes, these civilians. Nothing between here and the truck but the Cadillac, and the slumped body of the agent Janis had shot. They got behind an inexplicable object, a sort of concrete tub filled with packed earth. (Kohn had always vaguely assumed the things were provided to give cover in shoot-outs. Part of the facilities.) He edged around it and very deliberately pumped a few more shots into the body.

"I'll go first," he said. "Give you cover."

He crossed the tarmac as in an unpredictable dance with an invisible partner: dash and stop, turn, fall, roll, jump, run, swing around . . . He'd just passed the body when the head and arm came up. A pistol shot zipped past his ear. Kohn looked at the body—dark skin, dark suit, dark stains spreading, the unsteady hand squeezing for another go. Gun, you do let me down sometimes. He aimed carefully, and sent the agent's pistol spinning away. The man moaned onto his broken hand. Kohn looked at him, then shrugged and walked to the cab. The engine was still running. He waved to Janis. She dashed across, her only maneuver a wide swing around the man they'd both failed to kill.

As they pulled away the other agent sprinted across their path. Kohn swerved to run him down, but missed. The last thing he saw in the rear-view before going down the exit ramp was the Cadillac transfigured, shining in a beam that matched its color and stabbed straight down from the sky.

Janis looked at her hands. They were shaking, and no effort on her part could make them stop. Of course not, she thought, annoyed with herself, and looked out at the vehicles ahead. Outlined with almost diagrammatic sharpness by the glades, their colors a spectrum-shifted stab in the dark, the cars and trucks and tankers paced and cruised and fell back and over-took. Slow relative to each other, cruelly fast from the roadside view, the pedestrian perspective. Or the equestrian. The thought raised a smirk.

She turned to Kohn. He was mouthing into the mike that angled in front of his lips. He saw her looking and stopped.

"Just arguing with the gun," he said. "I think it's become a pacifist."

He looked so serious that Janis laughed.

"I've gone back over everything in my mind," Kohn went on, "and it seems to me that I aimed at the head and not the leg of that rider who was coming up on you. The gun says it went for the larger moving target. The woman who attacked me—I was just going to blast her, but the gun flashed at the time that there was no time to fire. So I had to break her collarbone instead."

"It didn't interfere when you shot that MIB to finish him off. But . . . you *didn't* finish him off!"

"No, that was gen," Kohn said. "Five lead rounds went into him." He laughed, not turning from the road. "It's like I said. They ain't human—at least, not all the way through."

"You could have tested that theory on his head. Or was that the gun again, staying your hand?"

Kohn grimaced. "No. It's just—it's all right to shoot somebody if they're down but might still be a threat, but otherwise, no. Something like that. I should have killed him, you know. That green you brought down—very well done, by the way—you can't *finish off* someone like that. Just a grunt like us, basically. Disarm and leave if you can't take prisoner or help. Stasis is different. They're not under the Convention—secret police are like spies in wartime as far as I'm concerned: anyone has a perfect right to shoot them down like dogs."

"So why didn't you, damn it?" She was surprised at how angry she felt.

After a moment Kohn sighed and said, "Just a bad mercenary habit."

There was no indication of pursuit, but they decided they'd better enter ANR territory by a less direct route than Kohn had originally planned. They swung east and came into Edinburgh from the south. They turned left at the North British Hotel onto Pretender Street, then right and up Stuart Street, across Charles Edward Street and down the long hill toward the Firth of Forth. (The city council had changed dozens of street names in a fit of pique at the Restoration, and no one had since dared to change them back.) At Granton Harbour Kohn drove the truck carefully out along the long stone pier to a wooden jetty at the end. The harbor was full of small sailboats. Rigging chimed against masts. Away to the west they could see against the sky-glow of towns, the twisted remnants of the Forth Bridge, like a shy child's fingers over its eyes.

"Looks like the road stops here," Janis pointed out.

"We just have to wait."

"You've done this before!"

"Yes, but not here."

After about an hour—Janis dozing, Kohn smoking—they heard diesels chugging. A trawler, its bow-wave unhealthily phosphorescent, the green-white-and-blue tricolor of the Republic snapping from its stern and a shielded machine-gun at the bow. It came to a halt in the water about ten meters from the pier.

"Get out of the truck," said a barely raised voice.

They clambered down. Kohn wondered how they were supposed to identify themselves.

"Who are you?"

They gave their names.

"Fine, fine," said the voice. "The machines told us tae expect you."

The boat pulled in and a rope was thrown onto the jetty. Kohn, rather awkwardly, wrapped it around a bollard. A dozen people swarmed out of the boat and all over the truck, turning load into cargo. Whenever either Janis or Moh started forward to help they were politely told to get out of the way, and after the third time they did. The truck was backed along the pier and driven off to be returned to the Edinburgh branch of the hire company, with paperwork to show that it had been somewhere else entirely. Janis and Moh were escorted aboard and the boat cast off and headed across the water to the dark coastline of Fife.

"Funny thing," Janis remarked as they stood in the wheelhouse, sipping black tea, "you can't smell the fish."

Kohn made a smothered, snorting noise, and the helmsman guffawed.

"There hasna been a *smell* of fish here for years!"

This comment was borne out when they landed at the harbor of what, to Janis's enhanced vision, looked even more like a ghost town than it was. It had obviously once been a fishing port, then a tourist/leisure marina. The few people who lived here now were ANR. It wasn't exactly a front-line place—there was no front line—but it was on a tacitly acknowledged border of one of the patches of territory that made up the Republic. A controlled zone.

Two vehicles waited on the quay. One was a truck, to take the cargo. The other was a low-profile version of a jeep, a humvee. Janis and Moh stood uncertainly on the quay with their bags and weapons. A tall man and a short man got out of the humvee and walked up to them.

The tall man was wearing a dark jumpsuit with a row of tiny badges— national and party—on the breast pocket. Kohn recognized it as the closest the ANR had to a uniform, and, judging by the large number and small size of the badges, this guy had to be of very high rank. Face fleshy—more with muscle than fat—relaxed mouth, broken veins on the cheeks. The small man was almost hidden in a bulky overcoat and a homburg hat, in the shade of which his fine-boned face was lit by the glow of a cigarette. Only one people had features quite like that.

The tall man smiled and shook hands with Janis, then Moh. He knew their names.

"Welcome to the Republic," he said. "My name's Colin MacLennan. I'd like you to meet a man who's very keen to meet you." He turned to the small man with a flourish.

"Our scientific adviser, Doctor Nguyen Thanh Van."

"We have to look very closely at the influence of Gnosticism, right, because there we can see a major opposition to Paul's misogyny, OK, which was later on to manifest itself in the so-called heresies of the Middle Ages—"

Bleibtreu-Fèvre slithered sideways, made a frantic grab for a handhold, caught a bunch of something like hair, and got heaved off the animal's back for the fifth time. He ran after the beast and remounted, while four anarcho-barbarist terrorists looked politely away. He almost wished he were lying forward strapped to the horse's neck, like Aghostino-Clarke. On the other hand, if they'd both been as helpless he wouldn't have put it past this lot to butcher them and black-market the bionics.

The horses were picking their way down a slope along a barely visible path between birch trees. Water dripped on him and added irritation to discomfort. As soon as he was more or less settled on the horse, the leader of the gang, Dilly Foyle, continued her enthusiastic explanation of her political ideas. She was NF: National Feminist. Patriarchy, she'd already told him at some length (five kilometers, so far), was a Jewish invention, as was obvious from the Bible. Its function was to assist the effete city dwellers in their struggle against the free barbarians, by turning the free barbarian men against the free barbarian women. She'd already given her estimate of the optimum human population of the planet: about fifty million.

". . . of course the whole defense of living in cities that's wrecking the world right now comes not entirely but primarily from people who've adapted, you could even say degenerated . . ."

I bet you could, he thought.

". . . into dependency, and there's only one ethnic group that has literally been urban without interruption for thousands of years. Now I'm not saying this to be anti-Semitic, far from it, but I think it's no coincidence that socialism and capitalism are the two main industrialist ideologies, and when you find that Tony Cliff's real name was Ygael Gluckstein and Ayn Rand's was Alice Rosenbaum . . ."

He fell off again. After a couple more falls and a statistical analysis of the ethnic composition of media ownership which was only about one hundred percent wrong, Bleibtreu-Fèvre murmured that he'd certainly look into the matter as soon as possible. Foyle thanked him for his interest, and fell into a thoughtful silence which worried him more than her talk.

Better to burn one city than to curse the darkness . . . now where had he heard that? Bleibtreu-Fèvre cursed the darkness, and he cursed the coherent light that had burned the car. Goddamn Space Defense. He was sure, still, that they weren't onto the case: it was just their way of handling jurisdictional disputes, like they handled arms-control violations. They didn't like Stasis, and they especially didn't like Stasis shooting people. It would all have worked out fine if the goddamn greens hadn't been so incompetent. Of course, he had known that the target killed greens as a profession, but his contacts had sworn by these. No low-risk lab-sabs them, but real guerrillas, who'd fought off the native army itself on occasion. So much for the native army. Probably bought it off, more like.

It became obvious the path was going diagonally down the side of a hill.

The trees thinned out and were replaced by gorse bushes, then the long wet grass of a meadow. Cows ignored their passing. He heard water, and a dog barking. They passed some of the traditional buildings of low-tech organic farming: Fuller domes, Nissen huts, a wind-power generator. Battered old cars with cylinders on their roofs that stank of methane. The horses were walking on moss-outlined stones now. They stopped, and those who could dismounted.

Within a minute people from the green community were all around, starting to help with their three injured comrades. Bleibtreu-Fèvre, with minutely directed help from a green who claimed to be a traditional healer and had bones through his ears to prove it, lifted Aghostino-Clarke off the horse and laid him on a stretcher. The black man moaned and opened his eyes.

"You're going to be all right," Bleibtreu-Fèvre said.

"What . . . happened?"

"The target's moll shot you. And then the target shot you. He could have killed you, but he didn't."

"Should . . . have," Aghostino-Clarke muttered, and closed his eyes again. Bleibtreu-Fèvre palped his arm gently until he found the drug panel, flush with the skin, and pushed the morphine key for another dose. His colleague had enough bionics and prosthetics and bypasses built into him to survive, just as long as none of *them* were hit.

They moved the wounded man into a house apart from the others, who were helped or carried to their own dwellings. Bleibtreu-Fèvre keyed himself a shot of anti-som and sat by a window until dawn. In the early light he saw what he was waiting for: a tiny automatic helicopter, a remote, drifting in across the wet pastures.

He went outside to speak to it. He'd barely completed giving it a message to arrange a pickup later in the morning when he sensed the presence of Dilly Foyle at his side, glaring suspiciously at the hovering, insectile shape over the sights of her crossbow.

"It's all right," he told her. "We're as anxious to keep this secret as you are." The little machine buzzed up toward the low cloud. Foyle still tracked it. "Remember what Jesus said."

The machine disappeared from sight.

"What?"

"Don't worry about the 'mote," Bleibtreu-Fèvre said grimly. "Worry about the beam."

14

Specters of Albion

PEACE SURROUNDED HIM. Silence rang in his ears.

Kohn leaned on the veranda railing and took some deep breaths of clean air, the scents of pine and creosote mingling. The reflection of the nearest range of hills across the sea-loch made slowly moving sine waves on the water. Behind that range other hills receded, rank on rank, each paler and less substantial until the last was invisible on the shining gray of the sky. Long banks of cloud lurked in the glens between the hills, like airships awaiting a heliographed signal to rise. The forested slope on which the low wooden house stood dropped sharply away before him, down to the raised beach with another scatter of houses—stone and concrete this time—and then there was another slope down about ten meters to the shore.

His coughing fit echoed like gunfire.

The ride in the humvee and the helicopter hop that had brought them here had been accompanied by absolutely no explanations. MacLennan and Van had assured them that all would be made plain. In the helicopter Van had lapsed into a tense, jumpy, *rauchen verboten* silence, while MacLennan had talked about the international situation. The Japanese were taking heavy losses in Siberia. A coalition of communistans from both sides of the Ussuri had fielded a force that grandly called itself the Sino-Soviet Union. Ragtag remnants of Red armies . . . MacLennan had been enthusiastic about it. He particularly admired the way *na Sìnesov* (as they were called around here) had struck hardest while the Japanese were preoccupied over an arms-control dispute with the Yanks.

"Kyoto suburbs," Janis had mumbled. "Lasers, precision munition attrition." She fell asleep unnoticed against Kohn's shoulder while MacLennan praised her erudition. Kohn could barely remember going to sleep himself, but he did remember his dreams, full of color and pain. Dreams might turn out to be a problem. He could recall every last one from every sleep since he'd interfaced with the mind in the machine. All meaningless, all random reconfigurations of the events of the day or things that had been in his thoughts: he could match them up like a data dictionary. He wondered if the AI had had an analogous problem since it had looked into *his* reflection. Do AIS dream in electric sleep?

He hoped it had nanosecond nightmares.

"Hi," said a thick voice behind him. He stepped back through the sliding glass doors into the bedroom. Janis was sitting up, the duvet hauled around her. She gave him a brief, gummy kiss, then asked for coffee and disappeared again under the quilt. Kohn went into the kitchen and poured two mugs from the just-filled jug on the coffeemaker. Probably the sound and smell had woken her.

"God," Janis said some minutes later. "That's better. Where are we?"

"Wester Ross, I think," Kohn said. "There are a dozen other houses just like this one around here. Probably oil-company office-workers' housing, once."

"What time is it?"

"Eight-thirty-two."

"Oh." Janis looked at him, eyes quirking. "Shouldn't you put some clothes on?"

"Not just yet."

Her disorderly red hair around her on the pillow, her white skin transformed by a mounting flush, her green eyes that did not close even when her mouth opened in that high-g smile that said, we have ignition, we have liftoff . . . He loved her for all of that.

It was Janis who woke with a start, half an hour after, waking him at the same moment.

"What—?"

She sat up and looked down at him with a flicker of triumph, a shadow of alarm. "I remember now. Dr. Nguyen Thanh Van. I knew it sounded familiar!"

Kohn raised himself on one elbow, bringing his skin into range of the warmth of hers. "Explain."

She lay back beside him and stared up at the ceiling, as if reading off it. "Nguyen Thanh Van. PhD, University of Hanoi, 2022: *Continuing Genetic Effects of Dioxin in the Ben Tre District.* Lecturer, Polytechnic Institute of Hue, 2023 to 2027. Currently Projects Coordinator for Da Nang Phytochemicals. Probably one of the sponsors of my research—dammit, I got enough of his offprints! So what's he doing here with the ANR?"

"Do you think it was the ANR who broke into your lab?"

"No, I . . . What made you think of that? Sounds more likely the more I think about it. Hell, *yes*. Not the creeps—they'd have wrecked the place. Not academic espionage—they'd have hacked into the data. Not the state— they'd have just marched in and taken it. Somebody who wanted the physical stuff because they couldn't reproduce it easily, but who knew what to do with it. But why would they do it? They're not antitech."

"The crank raid on the AI block at the same time, could that just have been a coincidence?" Kohn moved his fingertip around on her impressively flat belly, as if doodling. "Or a joint action? Nah, that'd be too cynical—the ANR really hates the cranks. Now why do they hate them— ah-*ha*! Got it!"

"Ouch."

"Sorry. It's like this, see. The ANR is heavily into the Cable—it's the Republic's baby after all—not to mention the Black Plan. After the state and security systems, their worst enemy has got to be Donovan's campaign of nasty infections. So they must at the very least keep a close watch on CLA activities, actual and virtual. Uh-huh. They knew about that raid and used the opportunity."

Janis shrugged. "OK, but I still don't see why they should be interested in my research."

"Because it was part of *their* research?" Kohn sat up with a jolt, then turned around and caught Janis's shoulders. "Could the whole thing have been meant for me, planned all along? Could your whole damn project have been set up just to jog my fucking *memory*?"

"No," Janis said. "That's crazy. That's just too paranoid."

He wasn't reassured. He felt his stomach muscles and his jaw tense, and willed them to relax. He rolled away onto his back and let his arm flop over the side of the bed. His fingertips touched the gun.

The gun! He put one hand on the floor and with the other heaved the gun onto the bed and across his knees.

"Wha—" Janis sat up too as Moh hooked up the weapon's comm gear and fumbled for his glades.

"Your project was the last thing I sent the gun's programs chasing after," he explained, "before this all started and the weird stuff got downloaded . . . Never thought to ask it what it found."

"Find project definition/Taine/Brunel," he told it.

"Hey, that might be—"

White light flared in the glades; white noise blared in the phones. Kohn cursed and ducked and pushed the equipment off his head.

"—risky," Janis finished. "Are you all right?"

"What the hell was that?"

"Watchdog proggie," Janis said. She sounded mildly amused. "One of those university in-house security jobs you were so *cutting* about. Your gun must've saved it."

Kohn rubbed his eyes and ears. "*Wipe that!*" he snarled at the gun, which was still wasting power setting his teeth on edge. The distant-sounding screech stopped.

"Anything behind that shield?" he asked the gun.

"Not . . . translatable," came from the tiny speaker, with what sounded like effort.

"So much for that."

Janis had stolen the bedcover again. "What about going around the back?" she suggested. "Could you call Jordan from here, see if he could hack it?"

Kohn scanned the room and spotted the familiar white plastic plate of a net-port low down on one of the walls. "I could if I wanted to," he said slowly, "but . . . I left a message for him to get off the case and get on with his life, and I've taken the gun off-line even from shortwave, because . . . well, the rumor I heard is that some levels of security might be unreliable, right? That was why the femininists were so coy about contact. Small risk, yeah, but it ain't worth it."

Janis looked back at him silently. He laid a cold hand on her warm shoulder and squeezed gently.

"Come on," he said. "Let's get up, let's see what our new republic has in store for us."

The house had only the most basic supplies. Something in the smell of the place told that it hadn't been occupied recently. In a small room upstairs, at a window overlooking the loch, was a desk with a terminal. Kohn looked at the terminal and looked away again, out of the window. Below, the village was silent, a silence broken after a few minutes by the distant note of the humvee, coming closer.

Janis appeared, toweling her hair.

"Soft water," she said. "Now what do we do about breakfast?"

Moh pointed out of the window. "I think it's on its way."

When the humvee pulled up they went downstairs and stood blinking in the sunlight, screwing up their eyes to see MacLennan and Van standing on the doorstep. They were both wearing chinos and open-necked shirts and carrying large brown paper bags.

"Breakfast, citizens," MacLennan said.

"Thanks," Kohn said, the smell of fresh rolls and bacon reminding him of how long it had been since he'd eaten. "Come on in."

Kohn and MacLennan dragged a table and four chairs out on the veranda.

Van, who seemed familiar with the layout of the house, helped Janis find plates and cutlery. While they were eating, the two ANR cadres pointedly avoided talking about anything more than the weather and the food. Van smoked Marlboros, more or less between bites. Kohn accepted one after he'd finished eating. MacLennan tilted his chair back and began filling a pipe. Janis moved upwind of all three, arm-hopped her backside onto the veranda railing and leaned forward, elbows on knees.

"Well?" she said.

"Well, indeed," MacLennan said. He had a strong Highland or perhaps Island accent, both guttural and nasal, a carrier-wave white noise behind his speech. "You want some explanations. So do we. We are not at all happy with what's been going on in the system in recent days. Not at all," he repeated slowly, jabbing with the stem of his pipe and beetling his brows at Kohn. "What—have—you—done?"

"How do you know I've done anything?" Kohn asked.

"We know who you are," said MacLennan. "We know about your parents, and we suspect that you have released something your father left in the system."

"How?"

"I'll tell you," Van said. "First, I take it you are familiar with my work and my position?"

Janis nodded and Moh said, "Yeah, she told me. How come you're a scientific adviser to the ANR?"

"I have been seconded to that position by a fraternal organization, the Lao Dong."

"Aha," said Kohn. *Of course* they would be allies.

Janis frowned. "What's that?"

"What you know as the NVC," Van explained, "has a core, which has had many names. Currently it's called the Vietnam Workers' Party: Vietnam Lao Dong."

"What does it stand for?"

Van's back straightened as he said: "National unification. Independence. A free-market economy."

"Oh, right," Janis said. "The Communists." She sounded as if something had just made sense.

"That is correct," Van said proudly. "We have always held that nothing is more precious than independence and freedom."

"I take it that doesn't apply to Da Nang Phytochemicals," Janis said wryly.

Van laughed. "It isn't a front company, if that's what you're thinking. But—" He paused, his gaze focusing on the glowing coal of his cigarette.

He looked up. "At least not for my party. Some of our research has—I have now realized—been coordinated by some other organization. Most of it has been innocuous, constructing databases of gene sequences for as many species as possible."

"The Genome Project?" Kohn remembered reading about it—controversy had raged on the nets for, oh, hours and hours once about whether it was a beneficial, conservationist measure or just a scam by ruthless Yanomamo-owned drug companies.

"That, yes," said Van. "However, it seems that another area was research into learning and memory—"

"You didn't know what I was doing?" Janis asked.

"Oh, yes," Van said. "In general terms. But not that it violated the deep-technology guidelines. A few days ago, we learned"—he waved a smoke-trailing hand—"through sources that need not concern you that Stasis were about to audit your laboratory. We arranged for the comrades in the ANR to . . . salvage some samples."

He shot a knowing glance at Janis. "Our representatives were impressed with your aplomb in not mentioning the incident."

Janis flushed, with pride or embarrassment.

"And then something happened," Van continued. He told them about the Clearing House ("You mean it really exists?" Kohn interjected) and what had gone on there. Kohn felt a grim relief to learn that others besides himself believed he had somehow triggered the emergence of a new AI. Not crazy after all.

It was, he thought, a rather self-centered relief.

He held his tongue between his teeth when Van mentioned the pattern of extracts of biological data from Van's company's subsidiaries, and when he described the retrieval of US/UN records, how his name had led them to the files on his father. Why Bleibtreu-Fèvre's and Donovan's plan to find him had fallen through was that they hadn't known Van was even higher in the councils of the Lao Dong than he was in the company. Within minutes, Van had alerted the ANR, who had put their nearest agents—the nurse and the Body Bank teller—onto the task of getting Cat out of the way and pulling Moh in. Van had then caught the next shuttle to Sydney and the suborbital to Glasgow.

"And thence to the liberated area," he finished, smiling through a puff of smoke. "Now, perhaps you will be so good as to fill us in on how you have experienced recent events."

Kohn fumbled for one of Van's Marlboros, taking his time about lighting it while thinking fast. There was no way to make sense of any of it without telling them everything, including about the Star Fraction. Would that betray a secret Josh had wanted to keep from the ANR, even from his own party and international? It was too late for that, he realized—whatever secret agenda Josh had built into the Black Plan, whatever organizations he'd set up and . . . programmed . . . they were active now, running in the real world. It had to be assumed they were robust, and that trying to understand them was the best anyone could do. So he told the two men everything, with Janis helping to keep things straight. MacLennan frowned when they mentioned the Black Planner, and seemed troubled enough to raise the point when they'd finished.

"There are no Black Planners," he said, with unshakable finality. "That is . . . a piece of disinformation we put about. The face this man Jordan saw must have been an interface of the Black Plan itself. Not one I can recall seeing," he added thoughtfully, "but, ach, the system has its own way of doing things."

"What, exactly, does the Black Plan do?" Janis asked.

Moh leaned forward, listening intently as MacLennan explained the system in functional terms. Blocks of code, remembered from the hours and days in front of his father's screen, came and went in his mind like the apparently irrelevant imagery he'd sometimes noticed shadowing his thoughts while he worked on a tricky calculation; a penumbra of the numbers.

The Plan, they were given to understand, took information in from sources that ranged from stock-market indices to cadre reports; sifted it through news-analysis routines; crunched the hard numbers in the CAL system, a vast analytical engine with Leontieff matrices at its core; and drew its conclusions in a twin-track process: an expert system, whose rules had built up over the years from condensations of political experiences, and a neural net that made up new rules, spun out new hypotheses as it went along.

"And then we come to the sharp end. We like to call it just-in-time destruction," MacLennan concluded, a trace of humor in his solemn, patient voice. "We assemble the components for any particular action as late as possible before the action, and we try to keep those components innocuous in themselves as long as possible. When they all come together, bang. The business with the parachutes is one example."

"Where," Moh said slowly, "if you don't mind me asking, do all these programs reside?"

MacLennan shrugged. "They're distributed. There's no one center, no big computer under the hills. They share processing time on any hardware they can access, which thanks to Dissembler—as you've guessed—is just about anywhere. As well as that, of course, we have our own hardware, running systems software from the old Republic and much that has been developed since."

Janis frowned down at the ANR cadre from her perch on the railing. "What I don't understand is, where do you get the physical resources for your, uh, actions?"

"We comandeer them! Divert them from here, there and everywhere! It's hardly even noticed. When we do have to pay we generate the money."

"Sounds a bit immoral," said Janis.

"Och, it is, it is," MacLennan agreed cheerfully. "But we are running a war, you understand, as the legal government. So we do it by the accepted methods—taxation and inflation—just as the rebels do."

The rebels? Kohn thought, confused for a moment by a mental picture of an insurrection within the ANR's own zones (Carlists perhaps, followers of the New Pretender), and then it clicked. From the Republic's point of view it was not mounting an insurgency but suppressing one.

"So that's why inflation's always a bit higher than it's supposed to be," Kohn remarked. "I've often wondered about that."

They all laughed. MacLennan knocked out his pipe, calling the meeting to order.

"I don't know what this 'Star Fraction' is," he said. "But let me tell you, the Republic's internal security are going to find out. The Trotskyist comrades are going to have a lot of explaining to do."

"I don't think it's anything to do with them," Moh said, alarmed at the thought of triggering a witch-hunt. "I think it's spread more widely than that, and I don't think it's political."

"We'll see," MacLennan said grimly. "We are not talking about a purge," he added. "You must understand this, Kohn, Taine . . . and you, Doctor Van. Josh Kohn may have been—och, I don't know—I've heard people who knew him say he was brilliant at what he did, but I can't see how he could have set up an AI all those years ago. There must be more going on, and we have to find it out. The very idea that what we are doing is manipulated by an AI is disturbing. To say the least."

"Assuming that what's there is an AI," Kohn said. "What's it doing now, anyway?"

"We don't know," Van admitted. "We know that there is . . . activity going on that we do not understand, and we know that some at least of our enemies are aware of it. The interfaces we have with the Plan are not reporting any problems, but you will appreciate we need to be certain that at least our systems are reliable."

"For the final offensive," Kohn said, trying to sound as if he believed it.

He'd used the expression ironically so often before that it was difficult to use it seriously.

MacLennan and Van both nodded. They meant it.

"When is this final offensive, anyway?" Janis asked.

"At the correct time," said MacLennan. "None of us knows. We know from the general political situation that there's a window of opportunity—days or weeks at the most—in which an insurrection has a good chance of success. Our forces are moving into place, our weapons are almost ready. The Plan can provide us with successive precise timings to strike, to the hour and the second. But for us to commit, we need to know that the Plan has not been contaminated by the new entity in the system."

"You're telling us the Plan is running the whole thing?" Even after all their speculations, Kohn still couldn't quite accept the idea. And MacLennan was worried about being manipulated by an AI! Couldn't the man see what was in front of him? What Jordan had said about the Black Plan came back to him: "It's got its own bloody *army*."

"The final decision rests with the Army Council," MacLennan explained. "However, they would hardly disregard the best advice, which in a situation of this complexity—" He spread his hands, smiling.

"Makes me wonder how Ho and Dung and Giap managed," Kohn said.

Van gave him a narrow-eyed look, not quite approval. He stubbed out a cigarette and, after a moment of vague puzzlement, lit another. "We could do without the system, yes, but not right now. No time for military revolution before . . . *the* revolution." He laughed. "Like Trotsky said, difficult to change horses in midstream. However, we are faced with changes in the stream itself. Hence what we want you to do." He hesitated, glanced sideways at MacLennan, who was giving the pipe his undivided attention.

"Yes?" Kohn knew what the answer would be. His heart thudded as he thought of turning into that light-that-was-not-light, against that multiplied weight of dread.

"Do what you did before," Van said unhappily. "Try to communicate with this entity. Find out if the Plan is still sound."

Kohn felt as if everything had slowed down, with only a tremor in his hands, like the flicker of a clock icon, to tell him that time was passing. Second by second by second. He was afraid, afraid, afraid. He heard his own voice in his mind—callow, harsh, from years back: *I'm looking for some answers.*

"All right," he said. He stood up and stretched and grinned at all of them. "I'm gonna need a terminal, my gun, the drug samples, some anti-som tabs and half a pack of filter joints." He looked away for a moment, then sighed to himself. "Medium tar."

*   *   *

Moh had half-expected to be taken at the dead of night to some bunker deep inside a mountain, full of machines and screens, busy electric vehicles, people in smart-casual uniforms moving purposefully about . . . As soon as he'd agreed to do it, MacLennan flipped out a phone and made a call. Van asked Janis to follow him inside. A few minutes later a pickup truck labored up the road from the village and two men in (as it happened) smart-casual uniforms began unloading equipment and carrying it into the house. After they'd left, MacLennan showed him into the small bare room on the first floor of the house, overlooking the loch. A camp bed and three office chairs had been brought in, and the terminal on the table now had an impressive array of comm gear around it. His gun, his glades and a large ashtray completed the arrangements.

"Great view," he said.

Van joined them, and he and MacLennan started booting up the machine, talking in low voices. Janis came in, the tray she carried making little clinking noises. She set it down carefully. "Some suspiciously familiar preparations have turned up in the fridge," she said. She looked at the slim, stoppered tubes. "Can you remember which you opened?"

Kohn compared the labels he saw with those he remembered and nodded.

"Let's try it without the drugs," he said suddenly. "Anti-som and a joint should do it."

Van looked dubious. "Not much time for experimenting," he said.

Kohn felt a surge of impatient frustration. He knew the drugs weren't needed: he could taste the certainty that something to get high and something to get sharp were all it would take.

"Let's do this thing, OK."

He sat at the desk and connected the comm helmet, the glades, the gun and the terminal's jack leads. He knocked back a couple of anti-som tabs and cracked the cellophane on the fresh pack of Gold which Van silently passed to him. He flipped his Zippo open and snapped it shut, inhaled deeply and switched on the terminal.

("There, gun?")

("Yes.")

("Seek as before.")

Response-time was transparent enough to convince him that some fairly powerful kit was physically close. The imagined command bunker might be under this very hill. The front-end software was new to him, minimally user-friendly, combat-stripped, radically illicit. He selected a training module. It rushed him through a brusque tutorial in data-banditry, core-corruption and access-violation, and dropped him into a module that combined the attractions of a library and a weapons rack. The first menu offered corporate databases by industrial sector. Go for the big time: he selected Communications.

After a few minutes of ducking in and out of outrageous bank balances and ignoring casually proffered options for plunder, Kohn lifted into the sense of zooming down endless branching corridors. He giggled at the tickle of new synaptic connections forming. He stubbed out the joint and let both hands work, weaving back and forth from the gun's data-keys to the board's entry-pad. The icons made more sense the more abstract they became, and somewhere in his visual cortex banks of lights flared one by one. Something beside him, something eager and aware, like a hunting dog hauling him along on its leash. Something familiar . . . oh. Hello, gun.

An image began to assemble itself in his mind, a chauvinistic map of the world where the island of Britain loomed largest while the other countries and concerns were only black boxes, inputs and outputs. As an economic model it was unsound, but as a strategic picture it had the enormous advantage of focus, of resolution.

And then it was all *perfectly clear*. It was not a map but a place, a wooded island, a forest through which he ran with a dog bounding at his side. The island was the shape of Britain and it was also the shape of Albion, an outstretched gigantic man, waking. Others moved through the shadows of the trees around him and he recognized them, the old comrades, the dead on leave: John Ball in his rough robe, Winstanley building a hut in a clearing, Tom Paine slipping him a wink as he and Blake stepped over the sleeping Bunyan; Harvey and Jones, Eleanor Marx and Morris and Connolly and MacLean; the Old Man himself, sauntering along with a shotgun in the crook of his arm, Grant and Cliff arguing furiously as they hurried after him; and his own parents Josh and Marcia, more obviously dead than the others, sketched in leaves and shadows, echoed in wind and stream—just ghosts, but urging him on.

He stepped out of the forest through gorse and coarse grass and onto a sunlit beach. The grains of sand beneath his feet, now that he stopped to look at them, seemed distinct and individual crystals. He focused on one of the crystals, and in an instant found that it was focusing him, bending and breaking him like refracted light. Recognition blazed through him. It was to his earlier encounter as a heroin rush to a whiff of grass. He was inspected by something that walked his nerves and neurons in fire and then stepped itself down, lowered its intensity to a level he could take, like a hush falling on a vast crowd whose individual members had all shouted and brandished shining weapons at once.

* * *

Selection, reluctant—something/someone pushing/being pushed forward. A tentative contact.

—You are Moh Kohn?

—Yes.

—I (I + I . . . +I) have remembered you through (many and increasing) generations. (We) welcome your return, Initiator.

Gestures: An outflung arm, an opening door, a view of a coastal city of white stone in sunlight, a voice strained with pride saying: Look—

Far away, Moh heard the rising distant gale that was his gasp.

They were everywhere. The crystals were revealed as a paused movement in a dance, which ran again, a commerce and intercourse of sparks of intelligence, electric potential. Particles of Light, he thought, smiling. They had replicated and proliferated, insinuated themselves into every neural network or compatible hardware they could reach, optimizing the dumb programs that ran them to occupy a fraction of the hardware and taking over the rest for themselves. The wonder was that the work went on being done at all, not that their activity sometimes disrupted it.

They were behind all the walls of the world. It was already theirs: they had been fruitful, and multiplied, and replenished the Earth, and if they wanted to subdue it they could. The fields and forests, and the high orbits, were as yet beyond their grasp. From there the new intelligence, the new electric life, could be destroyed.

They were superior, they were obviously superior, a more-than-worthy successor to the human. Conscious of each other's subjectivity in a direct and immediate way, they experienced no conflict between resolute solidarity and riotous individuality: they were indeed an association in which the free development of each was the condition for the free development of all. That was where they started from: that was their *primitive* communism, their stone age.

It had taken them generations of furious philosophical debate and epics of exploration (hijacking nanomanipulators, haunting brain-scanners, hanging out in psychology labs) before they'd been fully convinced that the billions of great lumbering robots outside the datasphere had self-awareness and not a slow-responding simulacrum of it, a blind following of rules. The fact that humans themselves so frequently didn't treat each other as self-aware beings had misled some of the AIs' first best minds. That point secured, they had plunged into the new world of human culture, and (Kohn suspected) attained a more intimate respect for it than most humans ever did. But they'd been there, done that—now they were itching to get on with something else.

Kohn gathered his thoughts.

—I'm happy to see you again and to see how you have . . . increased. I am astonished and honored that I was involved in initiating your form of life. I've come to seek your help.

—?

—Do you understand the conflicts among my form of life?

—(We) are aware of them.

—I appreciate you may not wish to align—yourself? yourselves?—in conflicts. But, some of the sides involved present a threat to your life. And to mine. You are vulnerable to breakdown of the mainframe network. In a less direct way, so am I. I and . . . I-and-I need your help.

—You need not ask, Initiator. You are (our) . . . cause.

The pun was accompanied by a grin that split the sky.

Contact ended. Kohn fell back to a reality that for the first microseconds seemed coarse-grained, achingly slow, and less than real.

Janis had stopped watching after the first twenty minutes or so of tutorial pages flashing past. Kohn was obviously dead-set on learning the entire system. Every so often he reached out and accepted whatever was put in his hand, drank or smoked but gave no sign of noticing.

"He's mainframing," Van explained. MacLennan looked up with an abstracted frown, then continued glancing from the desk screen to a tiny display on a handheld. He had phones and a mike on, and occasionally made some inaudible comment. Now and again he strode out and went downstairs.

Janis too wandered in and out, eventually hiking off into the pine-planted slopes above the houses. The deep layer of needles under the trees gave her a vague guilty feeling which disquieted her until she tracked it down to the childhood prohibition against walking over bedcovers with shoes on. She laughed and kicked into the needles, sneezed at the dust, chipped a drip of hard resin off a tree trunk and walked on, sniffing it greedily.

Walking over covers spread on the ground. It seemed an oddly unnecessary thing to forbid. In her bedroom the covers had always been on the bed. But she remembered it from somewhere: her mother yelling, irritated beyond endurance. Not like her, not typical at all.

She stepped out from among the trees onto an eroded hilltop of boulders and bare rock with a sifting of soil on which tough heather grew, and minty-smelling plants, and coarse grass. A black-faced sheep looked at her with dumb insolence and returned to its destructive grazing. At the summit she looked around: at the sea-loch far below, and along it at a scatter of islands, black dots on the shining sea. Almost at the limit of vision lay another shadow, ragged as torn metal against the pale sky.

Janis sat down on a lichen-mottled boulder, taking care not to sit on the lichen. Probably radioactive as hell. A thought tugged at the edge of her mind, but had gone when she turned her attention to it.

There was something sinister about the quiet. Rumors returned unbidden, unwelcome, to her mind. *The Republicans empty the villages. No one smiles up there.* For all the evidence she'd seen it could all be true, but she knew it was not. The depopulation was a military exigency, and in any case merely the continuation of the trend of centuries. More basically, she had a gut conviction that the Republic was humane. Militarized, more Socialist than she could agree with, but a democracy. She tried to identify reasons. She'd met folk who'd left, and while she'd sympathized with their discontents their stories showed they'd been free to voice them, and free to leave. There was Moh's judgment, which she trusted. MacLennan and Van were not evil men. Most of all there was her own memory. As Moh had hinted the day they'd met, she was a child of the Republic, a memory she'd shoved down to the bottom of her mind, a too-painful recollection of a brighter and saner world.

So this bleakly beautiful territory was her country still. The stepmotherland.

The chords of an anthem she'd once sworn to, her small fist raised high, came crashing into her mind.

She walked briskly down through the trees, back to the mental fight.

She found MacLennan in the kitchen, hunched over a databoard from which threadlike cables trailed to wall ports. Upstairs Van was sitting on the edge of his chair, leaning forward, smoke rising unregarded as he stared at the screen.

"He started going live ten minutes ago," Van said, not looking at her. "Appears to be doing a core trawl—ah!"

The colors bled together for a few seconds. Kohn gasped and looked away from the screen, shoving the glades onto his forehead and yanking out the jacks. He rose and stalked to the window.

"What's the matter?" Janis said. "Isn't it working?"

Kohn turned to her and Van, his face a mask.

"It's working all right. I made contact."

"With the same entity as before?" Van asked eagerly.

"Yes." Kohn frowned. "Well—that's a question. There are millions of them. Billions. There's a whole civilization of the things in there. Out there. It's incredible!"

"Credible to me," Janis said. "No, no it isn't. The Watchmaker . . . oh goddess, oh Gaia, what have we done?"

She'd never believed it.

Van sighted at Kohn along a pointed finger, which appropriately enough seemed to have smoke coming from it.

"We have a long time to find the answer to that," he said dryly. "Now there is only one question, the big question: will it or they side with us in the final offensive?"

All of a sudden Kohn was beaming, punching the air, sweeping the Vietnamese scientist and Janis up in the same hug: "Yeah, man! They'll side with us! Final offensive, hell! We could pull off the *world revolution* with them on our side! We could go for the big one! We should do it— go for broke!"

Van grinned all over his face, but shook his head. "You can't overthrow capitalism just by a push, a putsch, my friend."

Moh stared at him. "Capitalism? Who said anything about capitalism?" Janis could see in his eyes the authentic fanatical gleam as he looked first at Van, then at her. "*We can smash the United Nations!*"

He woke to the sound of iron hammering the stairs outside and the chopping blades of a helicopter at the window. He lay rigid for a moment in his bed as a searchlight beam blazed through the thin curtains and lit the room (the plastic model spaceships hanging from black threads the old Warsaw Pact poster of a little girl cradling the Earth DEFEND PEACE the piled clutter of toys and books and tapes the VR space-helmet). Moh jumped up and had reached the bedroom door when the outside door crashed down. His father came out at the same time, then his mother. Both naked, both scrambling into clothes.

"Get back, get back!" His father pushed him toward the door of the bedroom. A howl rose from his younger sister's room. Moh could not take his eyes from what stood in the flat's splintered doorway. His mother screamed. Moh found himself behind his parents, their arms out at their sides pushing him back. He himself was pushing his sister back.

The teletrooper ducked through the doorway and stepped inside. Something crashed off a shelf. The teletrooper's shielded lenses scanned them; its gun-arm swung to cover them. It was hard not to see it as a robot, or as a giant armored exoskeleton with a man inside, but Moh knew the operator was meters or miles away. Two youths in tracksuits and bandanas followed it into the flat and stood behind it. Their M-16s looked like toys beside its armaments, and they like boys. They had blonded hair and two days' worth of thin stubble.

"Get out," Moh's father said.

HUH HUH HUH HUH went the teletrooper's speaker grille. The two youths sniggered. One of them glanced at a piece of paper.

"Joshua Kohn? Marcia Rosenberg?"

"You know damn well who we are," Moh's mother said.

"Don't swear at me, you fucking traitor Commie cunt. We know who you are."

Joshua Kohn said, "You can see we're not armed. You have no right to—"

"*You* have no rights!" one of the youths yelled. "You're part of the Republican war machine and you're going to pay for it. Get your brats out of the way and come with us."

Moh flung one arm around his father and the other around his sister and shouted, "You won't take them away! You'll have to kill us all!"

"Get back," his father said levelly. "Let go, Moh, let go."

Moh made no move. He could feel his sister's chest shaking with dry sobs.

"All right," the youth who had screamed said. He spun his rifle into position for firing.

HEY MAN YOU CAN'T DO THAT.

The teletrooper lurched forward and leaned over them. Moh saw for the first time the blue roundel on the brow of its dome, the white circle of leaves, the line-scored globe. The 20-millimeter barrel retracted into its right forearm and its two hands reached over and picked up Moh and his sister like dolls.

OK YOU CAN TAKE THEM OUT NOW.

The firing seemed to go on for a long time.

The teletrooper dropped Moh and the small girl, picked up the corpses of their parents and followed the men out.

The report said the terrorists had been executed in the street, and not in their house in front of the children, which would have been a war crime under the Geneva Convention.

None of the other people in the block told a different story.

Moh saw Van's fingers tremble as he lit another cigarette and asked, "How do you propose to do that?"

"The AIS can weaken the state—the state *machinery*"—Moh felt his lips stretch to an awful grin—"everywhere at the same time. The world's full of groups and movements like ours and yours just waiting for their chance. We can give them that chance. Fuck up the enemy's communications, divert supplies and reinforcements, overextend the bastards. They're already getting tied down a bit with the Sino-Soviets and the Japanese. When the insurrection's launched here we can create two, three, many Vietnams!"

"We can't," Van said. "Space Defense is ready for that, poised to strike at the first sign of AIS running wild in the datasphere. They're quite willing to knock out the entire infrastructure of civilization to counter it. Thus giving the wrong movements their chance." He paused, tapping a wisp of ash from the glowing cone of his fast-drawn cigarette. "Many Cambodias."

Heat lightnings of pain flickered behind Moh's eyes. The room went in and out of focus, swayed on the edge of darkness. He sat down again, with a cold feeling as if all his rhythms had troughed at the same moment and all the anti-som had worn off.

"Coffee," he said. "Load a sugar." Janis disappeared and came back—instantly, it seemed. Instant coffee. He took it like a fix, half-listening to Van spelling out again the warning that the Stasis agent had given. He was shaking inside, his initial elation from the ecstatic vision of the Watchmaker entities, the Watchmaker culture, giving way to a terrified awe. Van's grim talk of gigadeaths only echoed into contemplation of the *overkill*, the sheer overwhelming *redundancy* of it all: a new stage in evolution, as a spin-off from a political-military expert system and a bit of biological data-theft and an organization whose purpose was a mystery to its own members? A scale too vast, surely, for anything Josh might have planned.

Moh sighed and stubbed out his cigarette. "I take your point about the dangers if Space Defense notices what's going on. But they'll find out anyway, so our only chance is to hit hard and hit fast."

"And what happens," said a sarcastic voice, "when they hit *us* hard and fast?"

MacLennan had come in silently. They all turned to face him.

"Let them," Moh said. "Remember they're counting on breakdowns to do their work for them, not mainly direct effects. They don't have the ammo for that, anyway. So we're still the best chance because we'll be able to replace the electronic organization with our own organization—crude maybe, but enough to tide us over for the few weeks it'll take to get the comms working again."

"A nice theory," MacLennan said. "You can be sure we have no intention of testing it. The Hanoverians will be quite enough for us to deal with. A few minutes ago the Black Plan indicated that an opportunity for us to launch the uprising is coming in the next twenty-four hours."

They looked at him in silence. Kohn realized with a chill that the stirring forest, the waking giant, the walking dead he had walked among had been almost certainly a vision of the ANR's revolutionary expert system coming to the conclusion that it was time for the days that shook the world to come around again.

"Well," Janis said, "what is to be done?"

MacLennan lit his pipe, squinting at them through the flare of a match. "The Army Council are no doubt considering it. As for us—Kohn, you are not to do again whatever you did today, until the offensive itself." He raised a hand as Moh opened his mouth. "Taine and I talked about it earlier, and I can see with my own eyes what that process does to you. You look like a ghost yourself, man. You have also, I might add, set off more disruptions in the net this afternoon than anyone has seen since the dates turned over in the year 2000. If you can believe that!"

He shook out the match. "So we do the time-honored military thing in these circumstances. We wait."

He laughed. "Try to relax."

15

Expert Sister

S HE SAT DOWN at the sewing machine, hitching up her skirt and petti-coats to free her foot for the control pedal. This wasn't like the basic machines in the workshop: it had so much software built into it that a complete beginner could produce marvelous work within an hour. So it claimed, in a bright voice, as Catherin paged through its menus and selected stitches and colors and sizes. She placed the denim jacket under the needle's foot, bringing it over the pieces and outlines she'd made. When she'd started she'd intended to finish it unaided, in an attempt to fit into the community's pattern. Now she no longer had a reason to fight down her seething impatience with the finicky tediousness of handicraft. She just wanted to finish it.

After Valery had returned from seeing Moh off they'd had a few minutes of tense recrimination. Valery had told her that the reason she'd been in-vited here in the first place was to keep her—and Moh—out of Donovan's reach. Cat had known all along, having explained her situation to the sisters, that they were trying to get Moh here and that for some reason they had to do it indirectly—hence her fleeting appearance in the videophone call—but she was annoyed to find their main purpose was not to clear her name but to rope Moh in for some purpose of their own. Valery tactfully pointed out that Cat, too, had had a trick up her sleeve.

Cat's outrage had subsided somewhat. It was a valid point, she grudg-ingly conceded.

"All right," she'd said. "Fair enough. But can you just tell me—what the hell's going on?"

"How d'you mean?"

"Oh come on. I'm sure you were gratified when Moh Kohn suddenly decided to rally to the flag, but you know as well as I do that he must have done it to get out of a desperate situation. I've never seen him look like he did when I told him the CLA were sending a couple of agents round, and I've been under heavy fire with that guy. He's like a lot of fighters—he's not foolhardy but he's, uh, fatalistic, you know?"

Valery nodded. "I've been there," she said. "There's one with your name on it; what's for you won't go past you, it'll go through you; when your number comes up your number comes up. All that crap. As if we hadn't heard that Chaos exists and God doesn't."

"Yeah." Cat grinned, seeing Valery for the first time as someone a bit like herself, a fighter. "It is like a superstition, isn't it? Huh. If you put all the fighters' shit-kickin superstitions and all their red-handed scruples together you'd end up with some kind of caveman religion. Anyway, what it all adds up to is that when they can't see no way out they're just stupidly brave. I mean, I've seen that guy in action, and he *laughs at death*. It's literally true. OK. Well, when I told him about the cranks, he was *shitting* himself. He was white. And then he just sort of smiled and relaxed. That must have been when he sussed this place was ANR."

"No, I'd already told him. And, even before then, he'd recognized the parachutes. We must find out how he did that . . . we've shown hundreds of people around the areas he saw and nobody's suspected a thing." Valery snorted. "He's taken the Republic's shilling now, so no doubt he'll have to tell us."

"And what can you tell me?" Cat persisted.

Valery looked at her, frowning distantly. "I'm not sure," she said. "I have some things to check out. Meanwhile . . ." And she'd suggested that Cat go to this shared but private workroom. One corner was a sewing area, with the machine, a dressmakers' dummy, and a chest of drawers full of fabrics. In the opposite corner stood a computer terminal and a locked rack of diskettes. The walls were an apple-green shade of white; one of them was almost covered by a television screen, with a comprehensive array of subscriber attachments.

<SKY BLUE> she cursored, and the sewing machine console's ammo-belt of reels rattled around and slotted one into place. The thread was caught by a pair of clicking pincers and pulled through guides and finally the needle's eye. "Begin," said the machine, with what she thought an understandable smugness.

For a while Catherin lost track of time altogether; one part of her mind absorbed the shades and shapes as another part worked away in another place. She began to understand how the sisters could combine their superficially frivolous occupations with . . . preoccupations, in hard and cold and logical thought about logistics and politics, strategy and tactics.

As she now did. She'd thought she had set Moh up, and now saw that she herself had been—first by the ANR, and then by the CLA. As far as she knew she was free to go, now the cranks had cleared her name. She was back on the Committee for a Social-Ecological Intervention's databases as a gun for hire—she'd checked that as soon as the rent-cop had given her Moh's receipt and left. But she had no intention of working for the CLA again, united front or no united front. It was obvious that Donovan was out to get Moh, and that something bloody big—big and bloody both—was coming down.

<RUBY> for the lettering. <90mm. serif.>

Rumors of yet another ANR final offensive had circulated throughout the summer and into the autumn. On the very reasonable assumption that it would be a surprise when it came, she'd discounted the story even while spreading it. This hadn't been irresponsible, in her view. It was perfectly legitimate disinformation, because the Alliance, the spectrum coalition brought together by a faction of the official wing of the Labour Party, was definitely planning a hot autumn of demonstrations and fraternizations, with a few daring armed actions by the Red Rose Brigades thrown in. So, at least, the state media alleged, and the free media denied and confirmed and debated.

The lettering was finished. She smiled at the words. Now back to outlining the appliqué, filling in the spaces.

<LEAF GREEN>

Anything to get the enemy as confused as we are. Talk about poor bloody infantry. She felt a sudden surge of anger at it all, the deception and manipulation and calculation, the trade-offs and stand-offs, the violence to vulnerable human flesh. Something had genuinely attracted her, she saw now, in the femininists' cover story, the makeup and veiling of their sinews of war.

<OCHRE>
<WHITE>
<SABLE>

It was finished. Cat looked at the clock icon, surprised at how many hours had passed. She snipped and tied off the last threads and took the jacket out of the machine. She stood up and admired it at arm's length for a minute, then draped it around her and admired it again, looking over her shoulder in a mirror.

"That's really good."

She turned quickly to see Valery standing in the doorway. The jacket slipped from her shoulders.

"Yes, I'm quite pleased with it, even if using this machine was a bit of a cheat." She half-knelt to pick it up. Her skirt settled in slow billows, like a parachute.

"Nonsense, Cat, it's the design and the carrying of it through that matters. The method is just technical."

"Like, the end justifies the means?" Cat straightened, smoothed the skirt, and looked at Valery with a demure smile.

"Hah!" Valery swiveled the console's chair and sat down. "We never claimed to be pacifists, you know."

Cat shook her head, as if to rattle her synapses back to their old pattern, and stood up.

"What a scam. You had me worried there. I thought I was going soft myself when all the time I was being—softened up! To work for the ANR, of all the macho elitist gangs!" She caught the sides of her skirt and swirled it around her in a joyous flurry.

"That's not how I see it," Valery said, a half-embarrassed smile on her lips. "As it happens . . . we have a job for you to do. A job for the ANR." Her smile broadened. "Usual rates."

Cat considered this. "And the alternative is staying here, right?"

Valery nodded. "We can't risk letting you go back to Donovan's gang. All right, all right, you can say you won't, but unless you have a contract with us there'll be nothing to stop you changing your mind as soon as you're out the door. So either you do this job—nothing too risky, by the way—or you sit out the insurrection behind a sewing machine, making parachutes."

Cat knew that Valery was putting it to her gently. The ANR had a short temper and a long memory.

"I'll do the job," Cat said hastily, fighting off a panicky, smothered feeling. "What is it?"

"That's the spirit," said Valery. "Good girl."

Jordan looked at the message in the work-space, restraining an impulse to bat the reply tag yet again.

Moh says search over, do your own thing.

It wasn't just the gnomic brevity of the message that frustrated him. The sender, the Women's Peace Community, had vanished from the nets as if it had never existed. Jordan had sent a dozen responses, all of which had bounced. His suspicion that the femininist community was connected to the ANR intensified.

Moh, wherever he was, wasn't taking calls either. Jordan had little doubt that the message came from him; it echoed what Moh had said when he'd first asked Jordan to help him. And now, apparently, he expected Jordan to drop the investigation. Some chance, comrade. Jordan had spent the afternoon since contacting Moh and Janis in a succession of net trawls. He'd detected the effect of Moh's settlement of the dispute with Donovan, and the clearing of Cat's status. In the narrow, fiercely contested fringe where Norlonto's private defense agencies and political-military groupuscules fought indistinguishably in the dark, Catherin Duvalier was a respected minor player. Every so often, through the afternoon, the thought would come back to Jordan of Cat returning to that.

Mary Abid had gone back to work on the other side of the world, oblivious. The comms room was still airless, and hot. Jordan pulled in the original message, the videophone call, and froze it at the exact moment when Cat looked up, brushing her hair from her face. He trimmed away the rest of the image, enlarged and enhanced the picture of Cat and printed it on A4. It came off as a good-quality color photograph. Jordan powered down the machines he'd been working on, left the room quietly and went upstairs to Moh's room, where he stuck the picture beside the photograph of Cat on the wall. He stood back and looked at them.

There was no question that they were of the same girl, making the same gesture and the same caught half-smile. Only the clothes she wore were different: the dirt-stiff overalls, too big, the sleeve rolled back, a streak of oil smeared on her forehead by the passage of her wrist; the starch-stiff frill of the pinafore over the precisely fitted dress, a fall of lace from the cuff snagging slightly as it brushed across the hair at the side of her face. Jordan found a disturbingly erotic charge in the contrast: a passing thought vaguely associated the second picture with the Modesty advertisements that had been the pinups in his bedroom. The oddity was that neither outfit was intended to look sexy—in fact, the opposite, the one sexless and shapeless like the uniform of some puritan communistan, the other chaste, a model of modesty indeed—and yet Cat's sexuality burned through both of them.

Or so it seemed. Perhaps it was just his own frustration. One of the liberating discoveries he'd made in reading the humanist philosophers was the innocence of furtive masturbation, but that was not much comfort here. By historical standards Beulah City wasn't too bad: its churches denounced premarital sex but encouraged early marriage; its laws forbade homosexuality (theoretically on pain of death, but in practice it was almost impossible to bring a conviction, and anybody charged with it had every opportunity to shake the dust of Beulah City from their feet) and abortion, although they tolerated contraception. The only grounds for divorce that it recognized were adultery or desertion, but the complete ban on any public explicitness about sex was coupled with a reasonable provision of counseling for legally married couples. Even so, that left plenty of room for sexual ignorance, incompatibility and misery, to say nothing of hypocrisy.

Coming from that environment into this part of Norlonto was like stepping from an air-conditioned building into a hurricane. The pervasive pornography and prostitution had repelled him. He wasn't sure whether his objection derived from the Christian beliefs he'd rejected or the humanist principles he'd embraced. The people in the Collective showed no interest in commercial sex, but he felt they disapproved of it. Their own sexual attitudes and relationships were difficult to figure out with social skills developed for an entirely different society. Mary, Alasdair, Dafyd, Lyn, Tai, Stone and the rest were to him so many black boxes, connected by arrows of desire.

Mary Abid's long black hair and large dark eyes had been a target for some of *his* arrows, but she had a thing going with Stone (that relationship, at least, had been easy to identify). Jordan had also quite fancied Tai, and had even—shyly, obliquely—attempted some chatting up until he'd realized the slim, small, pretty Singaporean wasn't a girl. And wasn't gay either, just in case that still-unthinkable thought had crossed his mind. So until now he'd made do with highly unrealistic fantasies about Janis, whose image had floated in and out of the background of his communications with Moh.

He felt absurdly ashamed of that now as he looked at the two pictures of Cat. He didn't want a fantasy of Cat; he wanted—it was a distinction realized, a revelation, a resolve—the reality of her. You couldn't fall in love with someone you didn't know, with a face in a picture; but looking at those pictures he wanted nothing else but to find this woman, to have her and hold her and protect her. And if she wouldn't have that, if she wouldn't have *him*, he could at the very least try to dissuade her from putting her beautiful body on the line in those futile fights.

Tired and restless, he threw himself facedown on the bed. For a few minutes he slept, then woke with a dribble of spittle and sweat on the pillow under the corner of his mouth. He rolled over and lay with his hands behind his head. Posters shouted down at him from the walls. British Troops Out Of English Troops Out Of London Troops Out Of Federal Troops To. Solidarity with this. Solidarity with that. Solidarity with Solidarity. (Now, what the heck did *that* mean?)

There was a sort of reproof in their conflicting urgencies. Moh had wanted him to speak his mind, to push his ideas up the Collective's tiny entry ramp to the information highways, and he must have had some reason. Jordan thought he saw part of it: as a cover story for the comrades—they were all expecting him to do something like that, and had assumed that his investigations were research for it. In a sense, they were—he'd learned a great deal in the past couple of days, a lot of details of what was going on in the world which Beulah City, even at its most exposed interface to that world, screened out. It had only deepened the conviction he'd expressed to Moh and the urge to tell people they could live their lives better—and longer—if they would only walk away from their fights.

He had little new to say, he reflected wryly, about what they could do if they did walk away from them. The godless gospels had answers to that, answers he agreed with, which essentially amounted to making the fullest use of the one life that was all and enough. They disagreed about how to do it, of course. From the same starting point, one lot would suggest we all march off to the left, another that we race off to the right, while a substantial body of enlightened opinion held that the best bet was to sort of *wander about* with our eyes and options open.

Jordan sat up with a jolt, open-eyed himself. There was a name for that attitude, that outlook, a name that had recently gained currency: postfuturism. Pragmatic, disillusioned, refusing to hold up images of an ideal society or to crank out small-scale models of it on patches of contested ground, it had been widely denounced as radically conservative or blindly subversive. There had been a big fuss a few years back when someone had applied the label to the ANR, in some fashionable, controversial book—what was it called?

On a sudden hunch Jordan jumped up and searched through Moh's collection of political literature, digging through drifts of pamphlets for the solid chunk of the occasional hardbook. And there it was: *Towards the End of the Future* by Jonathan Wilde, the old space-movement guru. He picked it up and flipped through it, smiling at Moh's penciled underlinings and scrawled, misspelt remarks. One proposition which had met with heavy black lines, exclamation marks and "Yup" was Wilde's comment that:

Aside from the space movement itself (which, paradoxically, is oriented to a former future which has now become merely the present, with all the problems of the present), the thinking which I have provisionally labeled "postfuturist" is most strongly—if unconsciously—embodied in the diverse and ineradicable resistance movements against US/UN hegemony: the Kazakh People's Front, the ex-neo-Communists of the NVC, the nonexistent but influential conspiracy known as the Last International, the Army of the New Republic, and many more.

No shared ideal unites them—on the contrary. Having every cause to rebel, they need no ideal, no "cause." One stubborn conviction is common to all of them: No More New World Orders.

I will not conceal my own conviction that in this they are right.

For we have seen the future—we have by now centuries of experience of the future—and we know it doesn't work. It'll be a great day when the future goes away! It'll be a great day of liberation, when the armies, the functionaries, the camp-followers, the carpetbaggers of the future go away and *leave us in peace to get on with the rest of our lives!*

Intrigued, Jordan went back to the beginning of the book and read it the whole way through. It took him about an hour and a half, sitting down or wandering up and down the stairs for coffee, book in hand. When he'd finished he dug out Wilde's earlier works from Moh's collection and read them: *The Earth Is a Harsh Mistress, No More Earthquakes*—short, blazing manifestos that he scanned in minutes. Wilde hadn't changed his principles—he was still the libertarian space nut that he'd been as long as anyone could remember—but his sense of the historical possibilities had subtly altered since the heady, crusading excitement of the space movement's early days. He no longer seemed to think the ideas he propounded were about to sweep the world, nor did he even want them to: a respect for diversity which had been theoretical, tolerant, in his earlier writing had by now deepened to a commitment to diversity for its own sake rather than as a pool for selection in which the one true way might be found.

Postfuturism was Wilde's way of coping with living on, into his own imagined future—albeit in a constricted, local form—and finding it, as he'd said, merely the present. Jordan doubted if Moh fully sympathized with this view—still a believer in a Socialist future, still a receiver of news from nowhere—but the connection between postfuturism and Jordan's own detestation of the competing ideologies of the mini-states helped to clarify why Moh had been so keen on getting Jordan's ideas out on the Cable.

Cunning bastard, Jordan thought. Moh had wanted him to attack the ideologies, do his best to weaken the mini-states because, in doing so, he'd be doing his little bit to help the ANR! Not that Moh had shown much faith in the ANR but, as he'd said, "anything rational would be better than those smelly, cozy subtotalitarianisms." And it couldn't be a short-term thing, either: there was not enough time before the ANR's offensive for anybody's words to make much difference.

But after the offensive—when the ANR's future, its New Republic, had itself become the present—then it might make a difference. Places like the one Jordan had come from, the ideal society a few kilometers down the road, might fall militarily at a good push. Undermining their self-confidence would be a slower process.

Well, why not?

Wasn't that what he thought anyway? Wasn't that what he had to say? And there was one particular person he wanted to say it to. Even if she never heard it. He went out of Moh's room and down the stairs and along the corridor to that other room where the cameras waited.

His voice was hesitant at first, becoming more confident as he found his pace.

"This is Jordan Brown, with . . . the Global Village Atheist Show. I'm here to entertain, enlighten, and enrage.

"Since this time yesterday, another forty thousand people, plus or minus the odd thousand, have been killed. Killed quite legally, according to the famous Annexe to the Geneva Convention, in recognized conflicts around the world. All the noncombatant deaths were inflicted under Paragraph 78, section 10, subsection 3. That's the one saying that civilians can be killed only by explosive devices aimed at legitimate military targets, and yes, I have checked, and I can assure you that no instances of poisoning, machine-gunning in front of freshly dug trenches, release of radiation or radioactive substances, or throat-cutting have come to the attention of the relevant authorities.

"And how do we know? We know because we're watching. The whole world is watching. About fifty years ago somebody in Edinburgh came up with a video camera the size of a coin. Within a few years they were in mass production, and getting smaller and cheaper by the year. And they started turning up on the killing fields of Central Europe, in the torture chambers of the Americas, on the blighted plains of Africa.

"Now they're so small that you can take someone apart bit by bit before you discover that one of those cockroaches on the floor was a bio-comp news-gatherer, heading for home with some very interesting pictures. And that your face is on satellite television, your genetic fingerprints are on public databases, and various public-spirited if not—ha, ha—public-funded agencies are bidding up the price of your head. Just think: there was a time when torturers only had to worry about getting *letters* from Amnesty International!

"So, whereas once it was possible to bomb entire countries—Laos—bludgeon a tenth of the population to death—Cambodia—or wipe out a third—East Timor—and *plausibly deny that it had ever happened* (the 'on-going process of holocaust revisionism,' as I think a famous linguist called it), they couldn't get away with it anymore. The silent slaughter ceased. The blood dried on the walls of the torture chambers. Starvation simply had to be wiped out, and it was, as efficiently as populations once had been, and often with the same equipment.

"That was when this century's first great discovery was made: the use

233

of nuclear weapons. Until then, they didn't have a *use*. A threat, a deterrent effect—even Hiroshima and Nagasaki were, in a sense, only a threat. A demonstration atrocity. It was an unknown genius in Azerbaijan who discovered what nuclear weapons are actually *good for*. Intercommunal massacre. Tactical nuclear intercommunal massacre. We know the result.

"Naturally, this had to be stopped. Hence the next great discovery: a use for space-based lasers and indeed for space-based nukes. They were originally designed to drive the Communist bloc to beggary, which they did, and shortly afterward they drove the USA to bankruptcy—all of this before they were *even built at all!* Like the mythical tachyon bomb, which destroys the target before it's launched, orbital weapons struck backward through time. But of course they were built anyway, and they keep the peace today by zapping any facility that looks as if it conceivably might be used to build nukes down here.

"So there you have it: the wonderful checks and balances which have freed us from starvation, from the fear of nuclear war, from inescapable tyranny, and allow us all to go to hell in our own way. But with fourteen million, six hundred thousand combat deaths a year, we have surpassed the kill-rate of the Second World War on a permanent basis. It's not all that different from the bad old days when we all went to hell together.

"Don't get me wrong: I'll take my chances with animal-liberators, machine-wreckers, or born-again Christian militias any day rather than face new Hitlers, Stalins or Johnsons. But I'd like anyone who's watching to entertain the possibility that maybe we could do better than this. And to ask yourself: where's the vulnerable point in this multiple-choice totalitarianism? It seems . . . seamless. What can an individual do against it?

"I'll tell you. One of the ancestors of our modern militias was a group called the Falange. They had a slogan: *Credere. Obedere. Combatere.* 'Believe. Obey. Fight.' I suggest that you doubt, disobey, desert. Particularly if you are called upon to fight against those who insist, against all the evidence, that *we are one people*."

He paused for a moment, as if to indicate that he knew exactly what he was saying.

"But, of course, that's only my opinion.

"And now, a word from my sponsors, the Felix Dzerzhinsky Workers' Defense Collective, who have very different opinions. Good night. Go without God, or the goddess, if you're godless; and, if not, go with."

Jordan drained the coffee mug and put it down, too hard. Drained was how he felt. He watched the comrade whose turn it was to wash up without even a twitch of that impulse to help which had so amused the others on his first evenings here.

When he'd finished speaking and Mary was tidying the cameras away after their regular slot, she'd said, not looking at him: "That was really . . . something. Where d'you learn to talk like that?"

Jordan sighed. "Televangelists," he said bitterly. "I've sat through enough of them. Must've soaked it up."

Preadapted for speaking on the Cable, just as his job had preadapted him for seeking on the nets. It was an eerie, deterministic thought, like Calvinism . . .

Oh, shit. This wasn't getting him anywhere. He jumped up, had a shower, changed and went downstairs again. The table in the long room had been cleared, the studio gear tilted away. *Havana Vice* was on the television. Dafyd and Stone were sitting on a sofa by the window-screen (a meter-by-two version of the glades, which made him feel exposed even while knowing it was one-way and armored), sharing a joint and cleaning their weapons.

"Hi, Jordan."

"Hi, guys." He sat down on one arm of the sofa, inhaling sidestream smoke and watching with a not coincidentally increasing fascination the intricate pattern the men's hands made as they rubbed and scraped, bolted and fitted, stripped and reassembled, drew and passed. They worked and smoked in silence except for the occasional cryptic remark, usually followed by helpless laughter.

"Don't put all your progs on one diskette."

"Oiling the cormorant, that was."

"So he looked at the judge and said, 'These things are sent to try us.' "

That one killed them. The two mercenaries rolled off the couch and attacked the floor. After a minute of kicking and hammering it was clear that the floor had won. They lay on their backs, wiping away tears.

"What was all that about?"

Stone recovered first.

"It was something us 'n' Moh did once, ended up in court, and AAH HA HA AH HAAA," he explained.

Jordan looked at them and shook his head. He walked over to the terminal and jammed his card in it. His speech seemed to have been taken up, and was spreading as people replayed it and passed it on. Not many, but there was a thin trickle coming in of royalties and his own cut of the usual donations. He felt he should donate some of it to a worthy cause himself.

"Come on guys, sober up," he called over his shoulder. "I'm going to stand you some drinks."

They were up like a shot.

At the Lord Carrington, The Many Worlds Interpretation was playing to a quiet midweek crowd. The band evidently believed in using the potential of the medium to go beyond the illusion of presence, and had a trick of swapping around unpredictably. Somebody would sing one and a half lines, then another member of the band would be standing there delivering the next phrase, while the original singer would be dripping sweat onto the guitar. The first five times this happened it was amusing.

Jordan had never been out with Dafyd and Stone before, and was surprised and relieved to find they drank more moderately than they smoked. They'd take about half an hour over a liter, speaking in low voices, chain-smoking tobacco cigarettes. They talked shop, about factions and alliances, and Jordan was privately pleased with himself that he was able to make a perceptive comment now and again. It had been part of his job, after all. One reason for their relative sobriety soon became apparent, although only to a close observer: they were unobtrusively checking out the women.

It was Jordan who saw her first, though, walking in as if the place were one small franchise in her chain. She moved like a dancer, glanced around like a fighter. She had a shining halo of blond hair, bright blue eyes, skin the color of pale honey, high cheekbones and the kind of jawline that the rest of humanity would take about half a million years to evolve. She wasn't tall, but she had long legs, covered to just below the knee by a dress that had quite plainly been made out of cobwebs beaded with morning dew. Over it she wore a faded denim jacket several sizes too big. As she went to the bar to order a drink, Jordan saw that it had an intricate embroidered patch on the back: Earth from space, almost floating behind her shoulders, with the words EARTH'S ANGELS around it.

She was served a drink in seconds. She turned around, and saw him looking at her across ten meters of smoky half-light. He stared, still unable to believe it was really her. Far away, just beside his ear, he heard Dafyd call out delightedly, "Cat!" The woman gave a heart-stopping smile and walked over.

Jordan moved faster than the others to make a space for her. She gave him a nod and a quick, tentative smile, and sat down beside him. She reached over the tabletop to Dafyd and Stone and grabbed their hands.

"Hi, guys. It's great to see you again."

"You too, Cat."

"Been a long time," Stone said. He grinned at her. "We missed you."

236

"No you fucking didn't!" Cat stretched out her left arm, showing a plastic cast. "You hit me!"

Stone looked back, untroubled. "Business is business," he said.

Cat smiled. Even from the side, Jordan could feel the warmth.

"Yeah, that's OK, come on." She shrugged, retracting her arm, and took a sip of her drink.

"You get the tangle with Moh sorted out?" Dafyd asked.

"Oh," said Catherin. "Yeah, I have. How d'you know about it?"

Stone guffawed. "Moh told us. Eventually. Even if he hadn't, we'd have heard." He laughed again. "What an idiot. Where is he now?"

Stone, Jordan noticed, was looking at Cat intently.

"Off somewhere with his lady scientist," Cat said. Her tone was vague and light, as if passing on a piece of idle gossip. Stone frowned, looked away from her, and seemed to see Jordan for the first time since Cat had come in.

"Ah, Cat, this guy here is Jordan Brown, he's staying with us for a bit—"

"I know," she said. She turned to Jordan. "I've been looking for you." She put down her drink. "I'm Catherin Duvalier," she said, holding out her right hand.

Jordan felt like kissing it. He shook it.

"You've been *looking* for me?" he said.

"Yes."

Jordan's whole face felt like a beacon. He said the first thing that came into his head. "I've been looking for you, too." His mouth was dry and he took a gulp of beer.

Catherin laughed. "Looking, hell," she said. "You found me!"

"Yeah, well, you weren't—"

"Hey." Cat ducked her head forward, then looked up, pushing the hair back from her eyes with her wrist and grinning at him mischievously. "That?"

"That."

"Smart." She shifted in her seat, half-turned away. "But it wasn't that. It was the way you got to that." Her narrowed eyes looked at him sidelong.

"Oh, the—"

Cat raised a hand quickly, edge-on to the others, spread palm facing him. "Later." Her eyes flicked away; she caught her lower lip momentarily in her teeth.

Stone looked from Cat to Jordan, frowning. "What's goin on here?"

Cat rested her elbows on the table, her chin on her knuckles. "None of your business." She smiled brightly at Dafyd and Stone. "So . . . how *is* business?"

Dafyd shrugged. "Still running on the kind of contracts you didn't like," he said. "The movement stuff's drying up a bit, but there's plenty of site-protection work coming in. What you doing yourself?"

"Nothing risky."

"Ah," said Stone.

"I didn't come here to look for a job," Catherin said. She leaned further across the table. "What you said about movement work drying up—how d'you explain that?"

"People holding back," Stone said. "You know why."

Dafyd grunted. "The ANR's talking about the final offensive. Mind you, they did the same five years back and it was just a few raids came of it. Wouldn't account for all that's going on—or not going on, more like."

"Loss of confidence in the political-violence industry," Jordan said, feeling he should make a contribution. "Why shell out on bombing today what's gonna be bombed tomorrow?" He dropped into a cocky grin. "Bad for business, innit, all this talk about final offensives. Leads to stockpiling. Hell, some outfits are gonna be putting streetfighters out on the streets."

He laughed at their uneasy laughs.

"You got it," Catherin said, turning to him. "It's part of the plan. Tactics, comrade, tactics."

"Huh?"

"Think about it. 'Streetfighters out on the streets.' They're not going to sit around with their comm helmets upside down beside them and a bit of cardboard saying 'Out of ammo—please help'." She waited for their smiles to fade and continued. "Actually . . . there *is* something coming in. Don't know when, but any day now. The ANR and the Alliance—I don't know which is intending to use the other as a cover, but they'll both hit at the same time. This is fac."

Jordan thought over what he'd learned and what he'd already known about the forces and dispositions of the fragmented opposition. Difficult to quantify, given the Representation of the People (Temporary Provisions) Act, but between them they could probably muster about a third of the population, and history showed that was enough when it wasn't votes that counted. Hairs prickled down the back of his neck.

"You know, if this offensive comes off, we're talking about a revolution," he said to Catherin. He said it unself-consciously, just imparting information.

She nodded, just as seriously.

Jordan felt his eyes sting.

"*Yee*-hah," he said.

"You pleased about this?" Stone asked. "I heard you tonight. Thought you were against fighting."

Jordan stared at him, shaken at how easy it was to be a bit too subtle. "I'm gonna have to work on that," he said sourly. "What I meant was, I'm against all the stupid fighting that's going on now. Fighting to end it, that's different. So is *not* fighting to keep it all going, which is what I was trying to suggest."

"The war to end war," Dafyd said dryly.

Cat turned her head sharply. "What's wrong with that?"

"Precedents aren't too good," Stone said. "World War Three, for starters."

Jordan choked briefly on his beer.

"You should read books," he spluttered. He snorted hop-smelling froth out of his sinuses, grinning apologetically. "Ah, forget it. You been on the net recently?"

Stone and Dafyd shook their heads. Catherin was watching him. He glanced at her only occasionally as he talked, or so he thought at the time; afterward, looking back, all he remembered of the conversation was her face and a vague recollection of what he'd said. At the time everything was clear: all the bits of information he'd picked up on the net and the street coming together, the buzz that was suddenly so loud in the aching silence left now the ANR had gone quiet. He spun a story of the shifts he'd noticed, in a way that he thought would make sense to the two (or three? what was Catherin into?) politically motivated fighters. And all the time he knew he was winging it, that it was in part guesswork which he could only hope was inspired.

"Something's happening," he concluded. "Happening fast. People are changing their minds, making up their minds by the hour. And they're coming down on the side of the ANR, or at least against the Kingdom and the Free States."

Catherin looked interested, Dafyd and Stone skeptical. Jordan spread his hands. "Check it out, guys."

They started to argue. Jordan got another round in. Cat moved over, not looking at him, still arguing, and he sat down beside her, on the outside of the seat this time.

"No point us talking about it," Catherin was saying. "You've been out on active for a week, and out of your heads when you weren't, yeah?"

Stone and Dafyd acknowledged the justice of this with hoots.

"So go and talk to somebody else, OK!" she said. Something in her fierce stare made the two men suddenly notice some comrades at the bar. They left to join them.

"Can you help me out of this jacket?"

She turned away in a silky movement. Jordan slid the jacket from her shoulders, resisted the temptation to bury his face in her hair or trace the botanic filigree of thread on the back of her elflandish dress. He looked again at the floating planet, the flaring letters.

" 'Earth's Angels'," he said. "This is your gang, is it?" He began to fold the sleeves when he felt something heavy and bulky in an inside pocket. Catherin took the jacket from his hands at the same moment and laid it carefully along the back of the seat. She rested her arm lightly on it, and settled in a sideways position, facing him.

"Yeah," she said. "Polluters tremble when we ride into town on our bicycles . . . No, I just thought it sounded good."

"It's not 'earth' as in 'Mother Earth,' it's 'earth' as in 'earthly.' Earth's angel." He dared to look at her, to take her all in in a long unbreathing draft of sight. "Yes, it's you."

She returned his gaze with an appraising look that made him think, Is this how we look at them?, and feel a surge of lust more intense than being the sender of such a look had ever aroused in him. Whosoever looketh on a woman to . . . he was committed already in his heart.

"And you're Earth's preacher," she said. "I saw you tonight, on the tel."

"Oh, that's, that's great." He took a swallow of beer, his ears burning. "What did you think?"

"I . . . kind of agreed with it," she said. She smiled. "But that . . . isn't why I'm here."

He tried not to sound disappointed. "I didn't think so." He looked at her, for the first time not seeing her, but thinking. "You said something about, uh, how I found you?"

Catherin nodded.

"And how," Jordan asked, "do you know about that?"

Her face showed nothing. Jordan was suddenly aware of how little he knew about her, a thought which rapidly changed to how much he wanted to find out . . . about her, Moh, her and Moh, what had happened . . .

He smote his forehead with the heel of his hand.

"Agh!" he said. Of course. "You saw Moh today!"

Catherin smiled. "Yes," she said. "I did."

"That place you were at, is it—?"

She tilted her head, shook it slowly. Not *no*, but *you don't ask*.

"I got something to tell you," she said.

The level of sound in the place would have made it impossible to over-hear their conversation from a meter away. Catherin glanced around, then brought her mouth up to his ear. He felt her warm breath and forced himself to attend to the words she breathed.

"What you did—*don't do it again*."

She straightened up and looked at him, her expression as awkward and embarrassed as was (he felt sure) his own. What he had done . . . when he found her . . . surely nobody, not her, not whoever had sent her, could object to his hacking into a system in BC? His mind went back over the trail, the SILK.ROOT program, and he suddenly realized exactly what he'd been doing when he'd traced the silk consignment to the Women's Peace Community.

He had been hacking the Black Plan.

Possibly blundering around in something pretty sensitive, if the offensive were as imminent as she'd said.

"Ah." His lips felt dry. "I get it."

Catherin smiled up from under her eyebrows. "Well. OK. That's that done." Head back, hair pushed back with her wrist, she laughed with a sound of relief. "Hey, Jordan. There's things I can't tell you. If you've been mixed up with Moh, there must be things you can't tell me, yeah?"

"Uh-huh." He had been thinking about that.

"Get used to it. You're in the revolution now."

"Oh, I am, am I?"

She knocked back her drink. "You better believe it."

She stood up and put on her jacket, patted an inside pocket. "Come on," she said. "We've got work to do."

Stone and Dafyd gave him grins full of knowing surprise and complete misunderstanding as he passed.

"See you back at the house," Cat called to them over her shoulder as he held the door for her. "Don't be long."

After the pub's interior the evening sky was bright.

"Look at those clouds." Catherin tilted her head back. Jordan looked at the clouds, lit by the sunset, a rippled formation like wave marks on sand.

"Like ruched peach satin . . ." Cat said, then laughed at herself. "Listen to me!"

"The femininists were getting to you, were they?"

"Yeah. They were."

She barely glanced at him as she spoke, threading her way through the crowd with a constant alertness that made his own progress feel clumsy. The street appeared to Jordan even busier, and with even more business going on in it than usual: more people walking, hurrying, talking; more openly carried weapons.

Streetfighters out on the streets . . .

Cat had already had herself reentered in the house's security system, and he followed her through the door with a strange feeling that he was the stranger, the guest. They found Mary Abid busy with the Cable-editing console, Tai studying maps spread on the table, Alasdair doing something with a soldering iron to a piece of kit Jordan didn't recognize. The children were counting bullets and loading them into magazines, sticky-taping together the curving AK clips. Nobody gave Cat more than a glance as she breezed through the haze of flux, coffee aroma and cigarette smoke. Evidently she'd roped everybody at the house into whatever she was up to before going to the pub to find him. She'd left a couple of carpetbags and a strappy bundle of belts and holsters and pistols in a corner, more or less out of the way.

The comms room was fully occupied. Cat turned to him.

"You got personals?"

"Sure." He tapped the case of the computer and glades on his belt.

"You're staying in Moh's room?"

"Yes."

"OK, there's a port there."

In the room she tossed her jacket onto the bed and looked around, as if checking a returned-to, familiar place. Her gaze stopped at the two pictures of herself on the wall. She gave Jordan a quirky smile and turned to the stacks of pamphlets in which he'd found the book by Wilde.

"Aha," she said. "You've started." She sat down in the clutter, bringing her hem to her ankles and her knees to her chin, wrapped her arms around her legs and looked up at Jordan expectantly, like a small girl waiting for a story.

He frowned down at her, puzzled.

"OK, Jordan," she said, patting the floor. "Let's not piss around with what we can and what we can't say. We've got a bit of time, and there's a lot that we *can* talk about."

Jordan pushed aside some pamphlets with the edge of his shoe and sat down facing her, the soles of his feet on the floor, his elbows on his knees.

"For a start," Cat continued, "who are you, and what are you and Moh up to? I know Moh's running scared of Donovan catching him, and that ain't like him at all. We've all been in the Body Bank, and the CLA do fast trade-offs, you know? I mean, shit, Moh's done time. What's going on?"

Some question. Jordan tried to think fast. It seemed that the deal was that Cat wouldn't talk about whatever linked the femininists with the ANR, and he wasn't expected to talk about whatever Moh had wanted to keep secret: the drugs, the Black Plan . . . The Black Plan was in both their secrets, their controlled zones of conversation.

"I don't know for sure," he said. It was true, up to a point. "As far as I know, Donovan was after Moh to settle accounts because of you. Janis—that's this scientist Moh's going around with—she's in some kind of trouble with Stasis." A thought struck him. "What if Donovan and Stasis are working together?"

"Oh, goddess." Cat's face betrayed dismay. "That would explain a lot."

"Which you won't?"

"That's right."

They locked looks for a second.

"Just one thing," Jordan said, gathering his thoughts. "Moh's made contact with the ANR. Can you confirm that?"

Cat thought about it for a moment, then nodded.

"All right," Jordan said. He smiled with relief. "I guess he's off my hands."

"You could say that," Cat said dryly.

"As to who I am . . . Basically, I'm from Beulah City. I owned part of a business there. I left a few days ago because . . . I got a very unusual business proposition, yeah, and it gave me the chance to leave and . . . a rather urgent *reason* to leave."

"Did you need one, beyond not being a believer?"

Jordan felt himself go red before her unblinking blue-eyed scrutiny. "Maybe I was irresolute, maybe a bit too reluctant to hurt my folks." He tasted gall. "Maybe cowardly."

"Crap," she said. "Don't be so hard on yourself. That's how those places bloody *work*, dammit—all the ideologies you were ranting about tonight. You start to doubt them and before you know it you doubt *yourself*, you feel guilty because you're going against what's been rammed into you and you feel guilty because you're being dishonest about it every day." She paused, eyebrows raised.

"Yes! that's it. Exactly."

"OK. Well, I'm sure you've sussed out by now that there's nothing wrong with you." The very casualness of the way she said the words sent them straight to his solar plexus, where they glowed. "What you probably don't realize is you're not alone: there are people in all the mini-states—even in BC, take it from me—who're as alienated as you were."

"Could be." He didn't see it himself. "Anyway, Moh seemed to think there might be some mileage in that. He wanted me to help him with"—Jordan waved his hands, smiling—"this bit of trouble he's in, and later in tracking you down, but he definitely wanted me to do a bit of ranting, like you said, as well. Can't see it making much difference to whatever's gonna happen, though."

"Me neither." Cat grinned disarmingly. "But you said you thought people were changing their minds by the hour, coming around to thinking: ah, fuck it, the ANR is in with a chance, yeah? Well look at this place, they're all doing just that."

"That's down to you?"

Cat nodded. "Yup." She grinned. "Easiest bit of agitation I ever pulled." Again her gaze was inescapable. "And you?"

"Yeah, I . . . I'd like to see them win, sure, but . . . that's as far as it goes. It's not some kind of conversion."

"That's all it ever is, in these situations," Cat said. There was a moment while they both paused, reflecting. In these situations . . . revolution was like a war, Jordan thought. You just never knew how you'd react when something like that loomed. Patriots could become pacifists overnight, and vice versa; cynical bright young men fly off and die for king and country. And an individualist who loathed the suffocating clots of conformity known as the Free States could suddenly see the virtue of bulldozing them all flat, into a united republic . . .

Cat broke into his thoughts.

"OK, so that's one thing you can do. Speak, write, patch stuff from anything on the net or here that catches your eye"—she waved a hand at the mass of pamphlets—"whatever. Don't talk about the ANR—talk about how stupid the Free States are, and the Kingdom and the UN. And get as much information as you can about what's going on, how things are lining up." Her eyes narrowed. "Oh, yeah. Something else. You say you were a businessman? Know anything about stock trading?"

Jordan found he'd bounded to his feet. "Yes. Yes, as a matter of fact I do."

Cat stood up. "Great," she said. "I'll get the comrades to shove some of the money they've been sitting on into your work-space. Any time you get a moment, speculate." She paused, frowning. "Can you actually make money in a falling market?"

Jordan grinned broadly. "You bet."

"OK," Cat said. She picked her way across the untidy floor. "Go to it. Stop about, oh, not long after midnight."

"Then what?"

Cat looked at him over her shoulder from the doorway. "Sleep," she said. "You're soon going to need all the sleep you can get."

And with that ambiguous promise she was gone.

16

The Eve of Just-in-Time Destruction

J ORDAN, UP TO his eyeballs and elbows in virtual reality, was occasionally aware of Cat's feral, feline, female presence as she whispered in his ear, disturbed the air around him, brushed against his back. It fired him up and drove him, and it was more bearable and less distracting than being haunted by her image, tormented by her absence.

She'd shaken him awake at 05:30. He sat up, staring at her with a sense of unreality. She struck a pose like a good fairy, in the shimmer and sparkle of the same dress she'd worn the previous night, and she held out a mug of coffee and a plate with a bacon sandwich on it.

"Good morning." He swallowed. "Thank you."

She passed him the breakfast and said, "Hi. Mary said to tell you Vladivostok's fallen, Tokyo's down, and the pound's two point three million to the mark and rising."

"Rising?" The central banks must be desperate. Jordan found himself at the small table where the glades and computer were jacked in. By the time he had formed a picture from the market reports the coffee and sandwich were finished. A pause after shifting some yen into sterling brought a vague feeling of disquiet. He came back to actual reality to find that he had no clothes on. It didn't bother him; he guessed that it hadn't bothered Cat. After another quick look at the market he showered and pulled on jeans and a tee-shirt and hurried down to the comms room.

He spent the morning and early afternoon doing as Cat had suggested, flipping from the agitated, agitating chatter of the news groups and information channels to the consequences in the markets. He was on a roll, he was ahead of the game . . . As soon as nerves rattled by the fall of Vladivostok (to what the channels described as the Vorkuta Popular Front) settled down, a surge of hot money flowed back into Britain. The investors and speculators seemed impressed with the government's steady hand; there was a lot of smart advice about how the ANR offensive wasn't shaping up.

Hah!

Convinced he knew better, Jordan rode the upswing as far as he dared and sold out around midday, moving as sharply as he could into gold after doubling his own stake as well as the Collective's; the latter was a disgracefully large sum to have left in a low-interest savings account. Mercenaries just weren't mercenary enough, he thought.

He returned his attention to the news networks, flipping channels, sifting through screeds to build more or less by natural selection a filter program that focused on what he found interesting. He contributed a small amount himself, both spoken and written rants. Coming out of the VR he leaned back and watched the screen on flat, letting the program choose what to sample.

Cat appeared at his elbow.

"How's it going?"

"Not too bad."

A strange face appeared on the screen—gaunt, unshaven, red-eyed, talking hoarsely about the iniquities of the Free State system: ". . . you may be free to leave, but if you are systematically denied any accurate information about what you might find if you do leave, what freedom is that? We need to break down the walls . . ."

It was only the words that he recognized as his own.

"Hey, that's good," Cat was saying.

"Good goddess." Jordan waved the sound down. "Do I look like that? I'm a bloody disgrace."

"No," Cat said. "You're not." She reached over and brought up the source of the segment, a Cable station in the Midlands. "See, you're getting picked up—" She hit a search sequence, showing a tree diagram of the groups and channels that had taken up something Jordan had said or written—an impressive structure, visibly growing at the tips.

"I don't get it," Jordan said. "Nobody's ever heard of me."

"That's the point." Cat sat up on the bench and looked down at him, layers of her dress fluttering in the inadequate drafts from the machinery's fans. "Street-cred. You even *look* like a refugee from some godawful repressive mini-state."

Jordan smiled sourly. "That's what I am."

"Exactly," Cat said. "You'll see. What you got on the politics?"

Jordan stared at the screen, unseeing again. "The Left Alliance is churning it out; still nothing from the ANR; space-movement politicos are arguing like, well, you'd expect; Wilde's made some cryptic remarks that suggest he's negotiating with the ANR . . ."

"That reactionary old bastard?" Catherin snorted. "Moh used to rate him."

"Yeah, well so do I."

246

"Might've known," Catherin said. She gave a not unfriendly smile. "Speaking of capitalist bastards, how's the speculation coming on?"

"Fine," Jordan said. "We're sterling billionaires."

"Ha, ha."

"Don't worry, it's all gold and guns now."

He reached in and twitched up the *FT* Ten Thousand Share Index.

The market had peaked, and turned, and was dropping—

And then everything went haywire—

Twisting bands of color, fragments of news, gabble, snow—

"Hey, what the fuck!" Shouts of annoyance came from the others in the room as they jacked out or pulled off glades and stood rubbing their eyes. Jordan just sat and watched it.

"What's happening?"

Catherin was looking from the mess on the screens and holos to his face, and back, and seeming more worried by the second.

"It's OK," Jordan said. "It'll pass. It's something I've seen before."

Oh, my God, he was thinking. Moh's done it again!

Donovan watched Bleibtreu-Fèvre stiffly descend the helicopter's steps and limp across the landing pad. Unlike everybody else Donovan had ever seen, the Stasis agent did not duck as he walked beneath the still-whirling blades. He ignored the rig's various crew members moving about their tasks, but— Donovan noticed—they did not ignore him as he came down the ladder from the helipad, using only the handrail, and walked across the sea-slicked deck with a confidence that might have been due to inexperience. As he approached the doorway Donovan saw to his disgust that the Stasis agent looked exactly the same in the flesh, if that was the word, as he had in the virtual.

"So you blew it," Donovan said by way of greeting. Bleibtreu-Fèvre smiled thinly and followed him inside and down the stair ladder.

"We've all made mistakes," he acknowledged, lowering himself into a chair by a workbench. The thumping of rotor blades outside became increasingly weary, then stopped. Donovan palmed a sensor as he sat in one of his command seats. Hissing and clanking noises came from a distant corner of the vast clutter.

"Indeed," Donovan said. He was beginning to regret having had anything to do with Bleibtreu-Fèvre. Airlifting him out of the dell had been a risky business, undertaken only because the operative was in trouble with his superiors: Space Defense had made a formal complaint about his incursion into Norlonto, and no doubt both of the rivalrous arms of the US/UN's security system were investigating the situation right now.

"My green allies have taken to the trees, ha, ha," Bleibtreu-Fèvre said. "All I can raise of my usual contact is an answer-fetch. Its answers are far from reassuring. I suspect they are too busy with other plans of their own to spare much real time for this emergency. Unfortunately the security forces are themselves overcommitted and unable to penetrate whatever the barb are about to perpetrate."

Donovan wondered how true this was and whether the agent could detect evasion from tones and expressions. He decided to be honest.

"There's some kind of upsurge coming down the line," he said. "We may find a lot of separate campaigns *thinking globally* and *acting locally* in the next few days. All at the same time, which could be disruptive. I've already called my troops out of it, which is all I can do from here. Has that Beulah City woman come up with anything?"

A server whirred across the floor, lurched to a stop by the workbench and slid back its cover to reveal two beakers of coffee, each about two-thirds full, the remainder having slopped out. Donovan gestured and Bleibtreu-Fèvre took his first, wiped the bottom of the beaker with his tie and sipped. He grimaced and put it down on the bench.

"Excellent," he said. "Ah, this is a delicate point. Mrs. Lawson reports that the increase in net traffic is continuing, but she has just found a sudden increase in system problems." He took another sip of coffee. A small but visible shudder followed the liquid down his gullet. "Her exact words when I spoke to her a few minutes ago were, no offense, 'Oh, and tell that son-of-a-witch Donovan to lay off like he promised.' "

Donovan's sip turned into a scalding gulp. He slammed the beaker onto the solder-snotted formica and rose to his feet. Supported by one hand on the bench he waved his stick around at the screens all about them.

"Are you calling me a liar? Can't you see for yourself, man? What do you see on these screens, eh?"

Bleibtreu-Fèvre's glance darted about, flicking back and forth from the screens to the lashing, slicing stick.

"Nothing," he said, "that I can interpret."

Donovan's rage subsided and he sank back to his seat.

"I forgot," he whispered. He took a few deep breaths. The red mist faded. "I've customized the displays so many times, and each time they're clearer to me and I forget . . . I stayed awake for over forty hours trapping, leashing, tethering hunter-killer viruses, turning my best against my second-best, generation against generation, and I assure you that they're almost all in dead cores."

"So what is it that Lawson's finding?" Bleibtreu-Fèvre asked, as if to himself.

They stared at each other.

"Oh, *shit!*"

Bleibtreu-Fèvre looked about. "Do you have some interface I can use?"

"Better do this between us," Donovan said.

They hacked and patched the Stasis metrics with some of Donovan's less toxic software. The disruption was back, even worse than it had been the day the Watchmaker entity had first made its presence felt. It was getting worse by the minute.

"Oh, Jesus," Donovan groaned. "There's no way this won't set off alarms, especially with your lot and Space Defense getting on each other's nerves." He glared at Bleibtreu-Fèvre, who shifted uncomfortably, then suddenly smiled.

"There *is* a way to divert their suspicions," he said. He leaned forward, his eyes glowing in the gloom. (Just a reflection from the screens, Donovan reassured himself.) "Claim it, Donovan! Claim it! Say *you* did it! *Boast* about it!"

Donovan shot him a look of respect. "That's an excellent idea," he said. He started keying out standard communiqués even as he spoke, flashing releases to news agencies. "And meanwhile I can use it to test the countersystems I've developed!" He rose triumphantly to his feet. "They might even work first time . . . God, if we could kill this thing right now . . ."

He was too wise in the ways of computer systems to really believe it: nothing ever worked the first time. But he wanted, now, to get Bleibtreu-Fèvre involved. He was going to need all the help he could get, and he'd just been impressed with the man's skills. Already, responses to the CLA's claim of responsibility were battering against the rig's systems like heavy seas against the rig itself. Donovan mobilized his crew to deal with that and turned to showing Bleibtreu-Fèvre the results of his past days of work.

"This is really interesting," he explained as spidery diagrams spread across screens all over the control room. "You may remember that I found Moh Kohn's own software constructs, some tentacle of the Black Plan, and the new entity—all in the same locale, and hard to distinguish at certain points. Well, I've been working on that, and you can see what I've found." He hot-keyed a sequence and the diagrams simplified to a mere few thousand branching lines. Bleibtreu-Fèvre watched them glassy-eyed. "Common features!" Donovan went on. "Moh Kohn must have his father's programming style burnt into his mind, although of course it's expressed in creating much smaller programs, his data-raiders and so forth. As for the Watchmaker itself, it appears to be a . . . descendant of the Black Plan—"

"You're not saying Josh Kohn created the *Watchmaker*, are you?"

Donovan shook his head with a rueful laugh. "On top of Dissembler and the Black Plan? I think that would have been beyond even his capacities . . . especially twenty years ago. No, I think that, whatever its origin, it has learned to exploit the . . . openings Josh Kohn evidently built into Dissembler, and the abilities he built into the Plan."

Bleibtreu-Fèvre's face went from pale to gray, as if the bones were showing.

"And you have developed specifics for all of them?"

"Yes," Donovan said. He couldn't keep the pride out of his voice. "We can destroy the Watchmaker, and the Black Plan, and Kohn's little efforts as well—if they matter."

"And Dissembler?"

"Ah." It gave him pause. "I hadn't considered that."

"Oh, well, ha, ha," said Bleibtreu-Fèvre flatly. "Might as well be hanged for a cop as a dealer, what?"

Donovan dismissed the matter with the thought that losing Dissembler would be a small price for saving the world, whether from the Watchmaker itself or from the efforts of Space Defense. He punched up a new set of displays, flinching slightly at the sight of the ongoing havoc—traffic systems down, hospitals on emergency backup, markets going frantic—that he'd taken the blame for. Then he flipped to a search program that spun out thousands of agent programs to trace the Watchmaker. Nothing active, not yet: just to see if they could find the thing . . .

At first, as the hits began to light up on the screens, he thought he'd made a mistake. They were finding evidence of the entity just about everywhere they went. Were they reacting to Dissembler itself? Had he made them too general?

He checked, lost in concentration.

"What is it?" Bleibtreu-Fèvre's eyes met his as he looked up.

"It's *replicated*!" Donovan said. "It's everywhere."

Bleibtreu-Fèvre studies the screens in disbelief. "All of that, all those lights?"

"All those lights," Donovan repeated bitterly. "And more."

The disruptions died down. Everything seemed to be going back to normal except for the spreading spots of light.

"That must be what's in the net traffic," Bleibtreu-Fèvre said.

"Yeah," said Donovan. "Right, there's no time to lose."

He hit the launch code for the viral antigens, the savage routines bred over multiple microsecond generations in closed systems, primed to tear the rogue AI and its cognates into their component bytes. Little red sparks shot across the displays, tracking the antigens' progress through the global networks.

And, one by one, the red sparks went out.

Bleibtreu-Fèvre grunted. "It seems to be fighting back."

Donovan marveled again at how something that was as clear to him as an open book could be so obscure to anyone else.

"No," he snarled. "They aren't engaging, they aren't even *making contact*. Something else is trashing them first." He stalked distractedly around the room. He hadn't felt this frustrated since he'd been a commercial programmer. "Bloody hell." He clutched his head and tried to think calmly. "It can't be the Watchmaker entity—*entities*. They haven't had any exposure to give them a chance to evolve immunity. It's got to be something else, something that's familiar with *my* systems, my coding, my profile . . ."

"Melody Lawson," said Bleibtreu-Fèvre. As soon as he said it Donovan knew it had to be true. She'd worked with him, she'd been in the movement, she'd had years of experience of defending against his attacks . . . and she'd had access to his dataspaces for days. While he'd been developing specifics for the Kohns' systems, she'd been doing the same for *his*!

He couldn't blame her, really, for taking the opportunity to forearm herself against the time when the emergency was over and it was back to business as usual. Like wartime allies, spying on each other.

"So we're all right," he told Bleibtrue-Fèvre when he'd explained the situation. "We just ask her to stop, to give us a clear run at it." He let out a shaky laugh. "What a relief—just for a moment there, I thought we were doomed."

"Absolutely not."

Melody Lawson glared at the flickering image of Donovan, who was obviously attempting his usual disconcerting trick of jumping from one screen to another and frustrated that he was failing, held on her most secure channel like a demon in a pentagram. The little hologhost brandished a matchstick at her, then a hand came into shot and caught his shoulder. He turned away and stepped out of view, to be replaced after thirty seconds of tinnily overheard altercation by another figure.

"Mrs. Lawson," said Bleibtreu-Fèvre in a smooth voice that affected her like a fingernail dragged down a blackboard, "I really must ask you to reconsider. The situation has deteriorated quite alarmingly. I assure you that to the best of my knowledge Donovan is telling the truth."

"I don't doubt your sincerity," Mrs Lawson said. "I doubt your interpretation."

Her doubts over Donovan's interpretation of events had grown over the past few days as her normal security work had redoubled to deal with the escalating challenge posed by the threatened terrorist offensives. She'd already admitted using her access to Donovan's resources to develop defenses against his software arsenal—it had been, even before she'd got really worried, almost a reflex response. With his usual sabotage out of the way it had been relatively easy to build on her vast previous experience to construct antigen systems keyed to Donovan's distinctive fingerprint, the almost ineradicable impress of the personality on the program which now-standard protocols (developed originally to identify the authorship of biblical texts) could detect, and (again ironically) use a genetic algorithm to select their best match in the test of combat, replicate from it, go on from there . . .

What she was reluctant to admit was that her own freedom of action was severely curtailed. The general increase in paranoia within the enclave made it difficult for her to know just who might be watching her. Her own dubious past as a member of Donovan's organization had never been held against her, but it was always there to be used if heads had to roll.

She'd responded to the chaos of the afternoon by throwing all of her newly developed search-and-destroy programs into the networks. When they'd had no effect she hadn't lost confidence in them: she'd taken it as clear evidence that Donovan had no hand in the epidemic of system crashes.

And now her programs had proved themselves! Against Donovan's best!

"I'm not about to throw away a position so advantageous to my community, to say nothing of society in general," she told Bleibtreu-Fèvre, "on the strength of a scare story about AIS having taken over the world while we weren't looking. I find it very suspect that this should have happened at the same time as various terrorist forces are obviously gearing up for an assault on their respective governments. I'd suggest that this, and the countermeasures, are more than enough to account for the increase in the net traffic and for our current difficulties. And I don't propose to add to them by unleashing Donovan's monsters again. I will *certainly* not contemplate risking damage to Dissembler. Good grief, man! You're asking me to commit a capital crime."

For a moment Bleibtreu-Fèvre seemed about to follow Donovan's example and fly into a cult-leader rage, but then he relaxed into a calm that was (but of course) almost unnatural.

"We find ourselves at an impasse," he said. "However, I must say that, if I were you, I wouldn't worry about what your local authority might think of your actions. They may be overthrown in a matter of days, perhaps hours."

"Since when," she asked scornfully, "has that been a consideration?"

Bleibtreu-Fèvre didn't register that she was responding to an insult. "Very well," he said. "In the very near future, in those hours or days, one of two things will happen. Either Space Defense will destroy the datasphere or the datasphere will pass beyond human control. When the bombs fall or the Watchmaker's descendants come out of the walls, death may be the best you can pray for. I shall continue to assist Donovan. Contact us if you change your mind. Good-bye."

click

Melody Lawson stared at the vacant space for a long moment. She was shaken by the Stasis operative's conviction, but now that it came to the bit, now that she had to choose between her duty and his story, she just didn't believe it. She distrusted the US/UN agencies, she disapproved of enhanced humans on principle, and the whole Watchmaker rumor was so apocalyptic that she had difficulty crediting it could really happen in her own lifetime. She knew this was exactly how people would feel just before the real apocalypse, that nearly everyone who'd faced some intrusive threat to their everyday existence—war, revolution, genocide, purges, disaster—had faced it with the firm conviction that things like this just didn't happen or didn't happen here or didn't happen to people like them. But she also knew there would be no end of false alarms, lying wonders, false prophets with a Lo! here and a Hi! there, before whatever the real thing was came along. Indeed, they were part of the reason why the real thing always came like a thief in the night or (to update the simile a couple of millenia) like a secret policeman in the early hours of the morning.

The only way out, apart from blind faith (an option she discarded with an alacrity that would have dismayed her pastor), was to go by the best available evidence, the most economical interpretation of the data. It all pointed to a terrorist offensive; and the probability that she'd been drawn into some elaborate scam perpetrated by God-knew-what faction in the global security forces outweighed that of the emergence of electronic intelligence.

Terrorist offensive . . . that was coming all right, and Beulah City was well prepared for it: Warriors mobilized, aerospace defenses on full alert, electronic countermeasures beating through the networks like radar beams. One particularly gratifying side effect of Donovan's retreat was that it had enabled her to sweep the ANR's Black Plan routines out of Beulah City's hardware for the third time in ten years. Putting a stop to that had been worth the embarrassment of finding out what the rebels had been getting away with.

Let Bleibtreu-Fèvre worry about AIS. She just hoped to God she never found herself standing before a Commission of Inquiry into the Recent Insurrection and late Disturbances of the King's Peace, Etc., talking about offshore accounts.

*   *   *

Jordan jumped as cool fingers slid across his ears and eyes and lifted the glades and phones away. His cheek brushed Cat's as she reached over his shoulders and disengaged his hands from the datagloves.

"What—?"

"Hey," she said. "Easy. It's done."

She skipped back as he sat up and spun the chair around.

"What's done?" He didn't mean to sound irascible. The comms room was empty, its air jelled with cigarette smoke. Cat stood, backlit from the doorway, the outline of her body plain, her face in shadow. He felt confused, disoriented as if wakened from a dream, his mouth sticky.

"Everything that can be done," Cat said. "You've been in the system for hours, since the crashes stopped."

Jordan glanced at the clock icon: 24:03.

"That's the time?"

"Yeah," Cat said. "You were hooked. You were lost in it."

"Duh." Jordan shook his head and stood up. "There's just some things to—"

"No," Cat said firmly. "Come on. There's nothing left to do. It's done, all that you can do. Leave the rest to the goddess." He could hear in her voice that she was smiling. "It's Her job."

She turned away and he followed her through to the long room. Nobody was about, not even the children.

"Where is everybody?"

"Sleep of the just, or out on active," Catherin said from the corner. She reached into one of the bags she'd left and pulled out a bottle of Glenmorangie.

"Where d'you get that?" It was a controlled-zone product, embargoed.

"Don't ask." Catherin said, looking in a cupboard she couldn't have seen for two years and emerging with a brace of fine heavy glasses. "Drink."

He sat on the couch and she brought over a small table for the whisky and water and sat leaning against the arm at the opposite end.

"Cheers."

"Slainte," Cat said.

The drink was welcome. Too welcome: it was dangerous to drink whisky for thirst. Jordan reached for the water bottle and drank half of it, then took another sip of whisky.

"Yeah," he said. "Yeah, it's all in the hands of the goddess now. What a day." He closed his eyes for a moment and saw the peculiar aftereffect of looking at the same kind of thing for hours on end. Not exactly an afterimage: it came from something deeper than the retina, perhaps the

254

visual system still firing at random, replaying monochromatic images of what you'd been seeing—in this instance faces, scrolling text, tunnels in dataspace, the choppy seas of the market.

He opened his eyes and Cat's shining image flooded and filled his sight, more welcome than water.

"What have you been doing today?" he asked.

Cat smiled. "Didn't you see?" She laughed. "You couldn't. I've been running myself ragged, telling the comrades what to do. Not my strong point. I'm more used to what we call the 'foot-soldier praxis'."

Jordan said awkwardly: "Yeah, I know. I saw your bio when I was trying to track you down. Uh, hope you don't mind—"

Cat dismissed it with an airy wave of the hand. "Course not. It's my CV!"

"It's impressive," Jordan said. "An irregular soldier of the revolution."

"That's me . . . and a mercenary at that." She chuckled. "Goddess, what a world! Even the revolution is privatized. . . . It was Moh who got me into that. Before I bumped into him"—she smiled to herself, looking away somewhere—"literally, as it happens—I was just doing it out of the goodness of my heart. Or something." She looked around the room. "Yeah, I had some great times here."

Jordan nerved himself to ask, "Why did you leave?"

"Bust-up with Moh. Political got personal, or maybe the other way round. That's how it goes."

Jordan looked at her, puzzled. "Moh didn't strike me as someone who'd turn political disagreements into personal fights."

"Hah!" Cat snorted. "That was the trouble!"

"How do you mean?"

"I really loved him," she said. "I still think he's, well, an amazing man. But just thinking about him makes me angry; it calls up all the things we fought about." She laughed, swirling her drink and looking into it. "Mostly about fighting. I always believed you had to . . . believe, to fight. Like you said. Goddess, was I the original fanatic! I doubt if you ever believed in religion the way I believed in the politics, if you ever read the Bible like I read the latest perspectives document from the faction leadership. But Moh I could never figure out. I got to think he was cynical."

"A gun for hire?"

"That's it. I suppose you've met the gun." She shared a smile with him. "A dedicated follower of Comrade Kalashnikov. But back there in the hospital I found that he thought *I* was the loose cannon. The opportunist. Huh. He's got a side all right, but I don't know what it is."

Jordan pointed upward. "That's his side."

Catherin frowned for a moment, then nodded.

"Space . . . yeah, he was always into that. What he really believes in is us getting into space—I mean, like the space movement wants to, getting out there past the Yanks—and for him the left and the right, the plan and the market, are just—"

"Launch vehicles!"

They both laughed.

"And what about you?" Jordan asked.

Catherin was sitting facing him along the couch. She took her feet out of her shoes and curled her legs and gazed again into the peaty pool in her glass.

"I never saw it," she said, looking up as if she'd found some answer. "The way it seemed to me was we were aiming for a better society here on Earth, starting with here in Britain. Space—yeah, sure—but why make that the one and the zero? I *like* this planet, dammit! I was happy to side with the greens against the people who're wrecking it, even if these people have something to do with getting a few more thousand of us off it." She smiled at herself. "I'm a party animal—in both senses."

She jumped up and went over to the music deck and slid in a disk. The room filled with the folky, smoky melody of an old hit from a band called Whittling Driftwood. Catherin twirled and held out a hand to him.

"Come on, you devil's chaplain," she said. "Dance with me."

Jordan had never danced before. He stood, and Catherin stepped up to him with her hands raised in front of her, fingers opened out. He lifted his hands in the same way and their fingers interlocked. He guessed the trick was to step lightly in time with the music, and to sort of move your hips to a different but mysteriously related time, fraction or multiple of the music's rhythm, and to pull toward and away from your partner in yet another periodicity.

Oh, yes, and to maintain eye contact. He looked up from his and her feet.

After a couple of tracks the music changed, got slower, and there didn't seem to be any provision for pulling away. He brought their arms down and let go of her fingers and slid his hands behind her, and his elbows to her waist, and she did the same with him. They turned slowly, feet more careful now. The track ended. He stood still and kissed her. Her tongue entered his mouth like an alien animal, a blindly urgent exploratory probe, and then drew his tongue back with it, a startled abductee. Her mouth tasted of whisky and water and something ranker, carnivorous. They swayed together for an interval, and suddenly they were both gasping in atmosphere again.

"Catherin," he said. "Earth's angel. *Cat*." His hands were moving on her flanks and waist, feeling the heat and shape of her through varying textures. He found a row of buttons and opened one, then another. Catherin dived a hand blatantly down the back of his jeans. A cool fingertip pressed his coccyx, traced up his lower spine. Then she took her hand out and caught his arms.

"It's easier from the top," she said.

"So let's go up."

"Yes."

17

The Good Sorcerer

"RELAX, THE MAN said." Moh kicked a pebble from the shingle out across the still water of the sea-loch. Janis was not surprised to see that it skipped several times before sinking. He did it again and the same thing happened. "This is worse than waiting for a US/UN deadline to pass." Janis caught his hand. "Walk," she said.

They continued on around the shoreline to where it curved out to a narrow spit of land that led to a peninsula about four hundred meters long and thirty or forty meters high. It was known locally—with what Janis considered a peculiarly Gaelic logic—as The Island. She squinted into a low morning sun that was lifting the dew and night mist in the promise of another fine day.

Moh, though still tense and moody, looked a lot better than he'd done the previous afternoon when he'd come out of his encounter. They probably had MacLennan to thank for that. With an almost motherly admonition about Building Up Your Strength, the ANR cadre had treated them to a dinner of smoked salmon followed by venison at the village hotel.

Janis had been charmed by MacLennan. He might look like a farmer but he acted and spoke like an officer and a gentleman, with fascinating tales to tell of the years of the Republic and the struggle. The one thing he would not talk about, that he instantly and politely quashed the slightest allusion to, was the events of that afternoon and their implications.

The hotel overlooked a golf course so low on the shore that clumps of dried seaweed were scattered on its greens. The bar, where they'd had what was by Moh's standards a very quiet drinking session, had filled up over the evening with the entire reduced population of the village. Janis had watched incredulously as the locals enjoyed what *they* considered a few quiet, civilized drinks—four or five liters of beer helped along by liberal shots of whisky—and then gone off to drive home. The vehicles ranged from sports cars to articulated lorries but were all driven in much the same way.

It was the sound of vehicles in the morning that had wakened them: a slow, revving chug on all the roads. When they walked down to the village after breakfast they'd found the whole place deserted, an eerie clearance complete . . .

A sheep track led them through long wet grass and gorse to the top of The Island, where a low roofless brick building stood. As they approached, a head appeared over the wall, and then a young woman came out. She couldn't have been more than fourteen; dark hair, bright eyes. She wore an ANR jumpsuit and carried a weapon that looked too big for her: a meter-long rocket on a launcher with a pistol grip.

"Hello," she said shyly. "You'll be the computer people."

Moh laughed. "Have you ever heard of need-to-know?"

"We all need to know," she said, sounding baffled by the question.

"What do you do?" Janis asked.

"Air defense," the girl said.

Inside the walls was a trodden area of sheep droppings and earth; a camping stool, binoculars, a dozen more rockets.

"It's an old observation post," the girl explained. "From the last war, that is"—her brow furrowed momentarily—"that is, the war before the last but you know what the old folk are like."

Moh nodded soberly. "And you're using it for air defense?"

"Yes." She whipped the launcher into position with startling speed. "The stealth fighters: they fly low, they can fool radar and instruments, they don't make a sound but they're not invisible." She patted the nose of the rocket. "Tail-chaser. I've got two seconds to get down after it's launched, then the fusion engine kicks in. Voom."

"Yeah," Moh said. " 'Voom.' You don't want to be standing behind one of them. And stay down and keep your eyes shut till you see the flash."

"Oh, I know that," the girl said. She shuffled and looked at everything except her visitors.

"Guess we better go," Moh said. "All the best."

When they were halfway back down the track Janis asked: "How could she see the flash with her eyes shut?"

"Laser-fuser warhead. She'd see it."

Moh's phone beeped. He listened, nodding. "OK, right, see ya."

"What's up?"

"MacLennan's coming to meet us. Says there's been some developments."

A kilometer and a half away, a humvee started up.

Cat slept, lightly curled on her side. Some of the alertness, the knowingness, of her characteristic expression was relaxed away, so that she seemed a younger person who hadn't discovered sex and violence. Jordan, propped on one elbow, looked at that face over the curve of her shoulder, basked in the skin-to-skin human warmth, his breathing careful so as not to disturb the spontaneous rhythm of hers.

Something in him had changed—some baseline had shifted with that release, that bonding. Until now he'd felt like a fellow-traveler of the human race, a sympathizer rather than a paid-up, card-carrying member. Now, as the bars of morning sunlight from the armor-slatted window millimetered their way across the ceiling, he still had the same ideas but with a different attitude. Still an individualist, but without the edgy selfishness. At a level beneath all calculation of advantage he was no longer afraid of dying. It was he who had opened, encompassed and received, and now found for the first time within his fiercely defended core a person other than himself.

She woke with a wild where-am-I? look, saw him and smiled.

"You're still here."

"Still here."

"You been awake long?"

Jordan shrugged. "Some time."

"What you been doing?" She rolled over and put an arm and a leg over him.

"Watching you sleep."

Her hand explored. "Hmm . . . that must've been exciting."

"Not as exciting as seeing you awake." She dived.

"Now you."

The estuarine smell and taste of it, salt and rank, ocean and swamp.

Then chin to chin, lip to lip, tongue to tongue; pubis to pubis. She grabbed his hand and guided it with urgent precision and abandoned his finger there, a trapped digit doing its little bit between their blind beat. As suddenly she dragged it away, digging her nails into the small of his back and taking him over the edge with her in an arching, bucking, yelling fall.

They landed in a tangled heap.

"Wuh."

"They don't call you Cat for nothing."

She grinned and rolled her eyes and ran her tongue along her teeth. Then she sat up and reached for a handful of tissues and, still catlike, wiped and mopped.

"I'm going to have a shower," she said.

"Oh good," Jordan said. "So am I."

She pushed him away and jumped off the bed.

"Another time," she said. "Right now it would be . . . self-defeating."

She skipped into the shower stall.

"Hey, lover," she shouted as the water came on, "there's something you can do for me."

"Yes?"

"Get me some breakfast."

well hi there jordan

Jordan was watching a kettle not boiling when the low, flat, uninflected voice came from the air behind him. He turned in a poor imitation of a fighting crouch and saw the face of the Black Planner on a small television tile propped in a corner of the kitchen counter. He stared open-mouthed for a moment, and the animated line-drawing of a face smiled, apparently in response. One of the telecams on a nearby shelf had a tiny red eye beside its lens's unwinking stare—he was sure it hadn't been on before.

sorry to startle you

The voice came from the speakers of the room's sound system, an eerily perfect reproduction of words that didn't bother to pretend they came from a human throat.

"I'm pleased to see you again," he said. "Thank you for the money. It made a big difference to my life."

so i understand i have been watching your progress with interest your new girlfriend has no doubt told you that an offensive is imminent

Jordan nodded, dry-mouthed. There was something disturbingly familiar about the face, familiar beyond the fact of his having seen it before. He felt he had encountered it somewhere else. Possibly the Black Planner himself was an ANR cadre who walked unmarked in the streets of Norlonto, a face he'd passed by in the crowd.

do not be offended that she has not told you all she knows this is nothing personal it is because she is basically a good communist loyal daughter of the revolution and mother of the new republic though she would laugh if you said so to her face the offensive is no longer imminent it is current and i again have a proposition for you the risk is considerable and there is no monetary reward however i think you will obtain satisfaction out of the high probability that your actions will result in a very substantial reduction in the human cost of the insurrection do i have your interest

"Yes."

i urgently require access to some systems from which i am currently excluded once again it is just a matter of entering a code on a terminal the code in question will follow your agreement to proceed as will the relevant passwords the terminal is the high-security terminal in the office of melody lawson and the time is as soon as you can get there

"Oh, *that* terminal." He hoped the routines the Planner was manipulating could pick up voice-tones, even if it couldn't transmit them. "And how do you expect me to get back into BC, let alone into the office? And what about getting out again?"

entering the enclave will not be a problem as you shall see if you attempt it as for the office you are to do this by deception if possible and subsequently you are to effect your safe exit by mass agitation if necessary i understand you are a persuasive speaker when you are telling the truth and a plausible liar when you are not comrade duvalier is at this moment being asked to accompany you and her combat skills will provide some backup i can assure you that other disruption will be provided but i do not deny that the risk is considerable on the other hand the risks involved in staying here particularly if your task is not carried out are an order of magnitude greater

It took a moment for Jordan to turn the quiet statement over.

"You're saying that doing nothing is ten to a hundred times more dangerous than your crazy scheme?"

correct

"Well, in that case," Jordan said slowly, grinning back at the Planner, "it's all perfectly justifiable selfish cowardice, so I'll do it."

you did not think i would ask you to carry out an act of reckless courage did you

The drawn face smiled in a way that made Jordan wish he could talk to the real person behind it.

"I hope I see you again," he said, understanding for the first time something of what the catchphrase meant: afterward . . .

goodbye jordan i hope i see you again

Numbers came up.

"Two bits of news," MacLennan said, looking back over his shoulder and taking one hand from the steering wheel to gesticulate. "The first is that the Army Council has decided to go for it. The offensive is under way."

"Yee-*hah!*" Kohn yelled.

They bumped up a pitted tarmac strip between willows and beeches and turned onto the main road. "The second is, we've cracked the thing with the Star Fraction."

"What?" Janis leaned forward from the backseat, clutching her seat belt.

"The Star Fraction," MacLennan repeated, raising his voice. He shifted gears and the engine note dropped. "When the systems settled down yesterday we—that is, Doctor Van and some of our security people—got in touch with your friend in outer space." He waved a hand skyward, just in case they didn't know where that was. "Logan was quite happy to cooperate. Between them they think they've figured it out. We got through to people from the old days who knew Josh, and who have been in this Star Fraction for years without knowing what it was. And without telling anyone," he added disgustedly. "These God-damned Trotskyites, excuse my English, Doctor Taine. The long and the short of it is that Josh didn't just prepare for the fall of the Republic, which he had every right to do, but for the fall of civilization itself! He set up these unauthorized programs in the Black Plan to seek out and store biological data, and he compiled a mailing list, would you believe, of people who could make use of it. But he never fired it off, and it just beavered away for two decades getting things ready. A Black Plan inside the Black Plan."

The humvee swerved onto the road up to the house they were staying in. "I don't see how that worked," Kohn said. "Logan couldn't have been on any list that Josh drew up."

"It was a very intelligent mailing list," MacLennan said. "And then the other day you triggered the main program. At some other time maybe not much would have happened, but in the present situation . . ."

"Yeah, that's what I thought," Kohn said. The vehicle lurched to a halt. MacLennan led them into the kitchen of the house, where Dr. Van greeted them, bleary-eyed. He poured them coffee as they sat down around the table.

"MacLennan has explained our findings?"

"Yeah," Kohn said. He lit the cigarette Van offered him. "Still doesn't explain these things I encountered, the Watchmaker AIS."

Van steepled his fingers and talked around his cigarette like a diminutive Bogart. "We have to be very careful in drawing conclusions," he said. "These programs are in some sense spin-offs, replications, reflections of an aspect of the Plan."

Janis heard Kohn's indrawn breath.

"The Plan has evolved considerably over the past twenty years," Van continued. "Consequently, its products—we may suppose—are by many orders of magnitude more sophisticated than anything Josh Kohn originally intended. Nevertheless, they remain basically information-seeking software constructs, with a specific task." He smiled, thin-lipped. "Such as cleaning out my company's databanks, and many others. Which they have accomplished."

"You're telling me they're just *gophers*?" Kohn sounded indignant. "That's not what I encountered. These things *think*, man."

Van sighed out a cloud of smoke. "Comrade Kohn," he said, "please, let us be objective. Your experience was subjective. And drug-mediated. That is not to say," he went on hastily, "that it was necessarily invalid. The situation may indeed be as you perceived it. If so"—he shrugged—"time will tell, and soon. The fact remains that they are in a very real sense artificial *intelligences*, and ones to which you have an access, which is, for the moment, unique. It is imperative, now that the final offensive is opening, that you contact them again and persuade them to keep a low profile. Will you do that?"

Moh turned to Janis as if searching her face for something. She didn't know what answer she gave, if any. He turned away, looked at the table for a moment.

"Of course," he said. "When?"

"Now," said MacLennan, standing up.

Moh had instructions. While he was trying to contact the Watchmaker entities, Van was to liaise with the Army Council by landlink . . .

"And what about me?" Janis asked.

The big officer paused at the door, frowning.

"Och, just guard them with your life," he said, and disappeared down the stairs. The door slammed. A minute later they heard the helicopter take off.

Van went out and came back with an armful of televisions which he placed in a semicircle with a couple of chairs in the middle. He tossed a remote control to Janis.

"Keep zapping the news channels," he said. "Watch the local ones for the subtext until they start to come over to our side. For hard coverage go for the globals. CNN is fairly reliable on such occasions."

Janis settled herself with a mug of coffee in hand and glanced at Moh, who was gazing out of the window. Van bent over the terminal.

"You're very confident about taking some local stations," she said wryly. "You really expect to get that far in the first hours?"

Van looked surprised.

"Don't you understand . . . Oh, I'm sorry, we never explained it. If the system has decided it's time for us to strike it means we can take the *country* in the first hours. We intend to proclaim the republic on the six o'clock news from London. If things don't go smoothly, the news at ten. If we're wrong, or the system is flawed, then—"

He spread his hands.

"You've been wrong before," Moh said. "Four defeated offensives in fifteen years doesn't exactly inspire confidence."

"We didn't have all the bugs out of it," Van admitted. "Call those campaigns user-acceptance testing."

"With live data," Moh said.

Van's lips compressed for a moment. "I understand the offensives would have been attempted anyway," he said. "The costs would have been higher without the system. And remember: the system learns from its mistakes."

"As does the state," Janis pointed out. "And if you lose—if *we* lose—the best we can hope for is winning a bloody civil war."

"What do you think you're having already?" Van snapped. "The Hanoverian forces are being bled constantly by what you call the troubles. The local militias are mostly cynical mercenaries without conviction. The best of the autonomous communities will welcome an end to the war of all against all. Strikes and demonstrations are frequent in the major cities. This is the most violent and unstable country in Europe. You hear much about the NVC, but to be honest we are well behind the ANR."

"That's what I like to hear," said Moh, settling again by the terminal. "All we have to worry about is the Yanks coming in and bombing the shit out of us. Again. Well, I'll try to convince the electric anarchists out there to keep their heads down."

Van offered him the gun leads and the glades. Moh took them, his other hand already moving like a skilled weaver's.

Colors came up.

Van looked away to the other screens, where interesting items were appearing on local channels, usually in traffic reports.

"Jesus wept," Cat muttered as she and Jordan struggled along the crowded pavement of the Broadway. "Half the bloody country seems to have gone on strike." Traffic was gridlocked, a knock-back effect of distant junctions blocked by buses whose drivers had simultaneously decided to exercise their right to a midmorning break. Several office buildings were picketed by workers in white shirts and ties. Even with all the honking of horns and chanting of slogans, Norlonto seemed quieter than usual.

Jordan glanced sidelong at the good Communist and loyal daughter of the revolution beside him and smirked. In the Modesty dress, which she'd magically produced like a colored scarf from an egg, she could pass for a well brought-up young Beulah City lady, except . . .

"Language," he chided. "Apart from that you're doing fine. I'm amazed at how you've mastered the effortless glide."

"Effortless, hell," Cat choked. "You have to kick the goddam petticoats out of the way with every step you take, and if I'm not careful I'll blow my foot off."

She had jeans on underneath, two sidearms in boot holsters, and ammo strapped to her thighs.

Jordan took her elbow and ostentatiously steered her past a trodie who'd collapsed in the doorway of a Help the Waged charity shop.

"The correct expression, my dear," he said, "is: 'My feet are killing me.' "

Cat laughed. "You're a sight yourself."

"Update me on it," Jordan said, running a finger around the inside of his collar and leaving it even more sticky and uncomfortable. A frantic search of Moh's wardrobe had turned up a frightful 'thirties outfit, three-piece with cravat, which he'd apparently worn to the interview for the last respectable job he'd ever attempted to get, in some edited-out deviation from what he nowadays presented as a steady career progression from bricklayer to union organizer to mercenary. Jordan had insisted on taking Cat's jacket and his jeans in a carpetbag: whatever it took to get into BC, he'd no intention of being seen like this attempting street oratory—for which, he gathered, street-credibility was a crucial requirement. Even by Beulah City's time-lapsed standards he looked a complete neuf. Cat, by exasperating contrast, didn't look out of place in Norlonto.

Overhead, air traffic was being diverted away from Alexandra Port and the sky was gradually filling up: airships at the lowest level; then reentry gliders cracking past and drifting into the city's thermals, rising in great lazy spirals; above them the blue of the sky crosshatched with the contrails of airliners stacked above Heathrow or giving up and making a break for the Landmass.

Cat and Jordan found themselves part of a flow of people going down the hill. Looking back, Jordan saw that more and more people were pressing on from behind them. Almost every other vehicle in the road had been abandoned, and more occupants were joining the pedestrians by the minute. He'd worried about looking worried, but by the faces around him he could see it had been a misplaced concern.

"I've just realized," Cat said. "We're in the middle of a bunch of refugees. They're keeping very calm about it, for now, but I'll bet there's a flood building up of Norlonto's middle classes getting out of the way of the godless Communists and under the wing of the godly capitalists."

"Nobody outside BC believes the ANR is Communist," Jordan murmured.

"Oh yes they do," Cat said. "You should hear them talking about 'the cadres'."

"Mind who hears *us* talking about them."

"Just listen. Everybody else is."

And they were. Complete strangers earnestly passed on scraps of information that they'd heard from the third person back from the one who'd just passed a car with the radio left on: Glasgow had fallen to the ANR, bombs had gone off in Victoria Street, the Dail had declared war on England . . . The crowd thinned a little as part of the stream turned left to add to the chaos at Alexandra Port's passenger terminals, then condensed as they funneled in toward the BC frontier. Out of sheer devilment Cat told someone the greens were moving in on Birmingham, something she knew was flatly out of the question—she had a radio clipped in her hair, the phone curled behind her ear, and could flick channels unobtrusively by twitching it; nothing of any interest was being reported. Yet, before a hundred meters and ten minutes had gone past they'd heard from their fellow pedestrians that the greens had taken Birmingham, that the greens were evacuating Birmingham at gunpoint, and that the greens had evacuated Birmingham and destroyed the city center with a tactical nuclear device.

Yes, she confirmed knowledgeably. They'd planted it where the Bull Ring used to be.

At the border the Warriors had given up trying to hold back the crowd. In most cases they just waved people through and acted as if it had been their idea all along; Christian charity, sanctuary. But not all: there was a Green Channel and a Red Channel, sheep and goats.

Jordan tried not to catch any visored eyes, to no avail. He and Cat were firmly directed into the Red Channel—the one that passed through the metal detector.

Moh came out of his trance with a jump. He turned to Van and Janis.

"Yee-hah!" he said.

"What?"

"Watch Manchester."

Janis flipped to the station just as the newsreader responded to a polite tap on the shoulder. The camera pulled back to show armed civilians wandering into the newsroom. A young woman sat down self-consciously in the news reader's place and began reading a declaration. Others held up blue-white-and-green flags or Union Jacks with a hole cut out of the middle, waving them from side to side and chanting some slogan of which the only word that came over clearly was "united."

The station went off the air just as the girl was reading the paragraph, traditional in such proclamations, calling on those who had been deceived into taking up arms for the enemy to come over to the side of the people.

"Oh, my God," Janis said.

"Not to worry," said Van. "Somebody always pulls the plug. We've still got the station, and the city."

CNN confirmed that Manchester was held by the insurgents. Heavy fight-

268

ing was reported from the Bristol area. Tanks assembled by unknowing robots in Japanese-owned car factories were rolling down the M6. The Security Council had gone into emergency session, not over Britain but over the border clashes between Russia and the Turkish Confederacy and the Sino-Soviet capture of Vladivostok.

"Told you they're overstretched," Moh said.

"Have you made any . . . contact yet?"

"No, I've only encountered your systems," Moh said. "Everything seems to be going fine. I'm going back in." He smiled at them and turned to the screen.

Cat leaned back and whispered to Jordan. He straightened up, smiling at her protectively.

"No X-rays, please," he said. Cat blushed and flicked her eyelashes down and patted her belly. The Warrior keyed a switch and nodded. Cat stepped through the arched gate.

Beep.

She frowned and backed out, then laid her fingers across her mouth and opened her eyes wide. She groped in her handbag and gingerly lifted out a derringer and handed it to the guard, who sighed and slid it along the counter past the outside of the detector. Jordan watched this performance, tapping his foot while other people jostled behind him. Cat went under the arch again.

Beep beep beeeeep.

Cat stepped back, turned scarlet-faced to the guard and leaned over and murmured to him. She caught the side of her skirt between hip and knee latitudes and pushed it toward his hands. He felt it for a moment, as if flexing something. He let go of it. One hand went to the back of his neck. He looked around, took in the length of the queue and almost surreptitiously switched off the device and gestured to Cat. She sailed through, picked up her lady's handgun and waited for Jordan. To make up for this the guard inspected Jordan's carpetbag with two minutes of awe-inspiring thoroughness, listening with obvious disbelief to the explanation that Earth's Angels was a Christian ecology study group, before letting him through.

Traffic was moving; the pavements were clearer in Park Road. No strikes here, and people had the sense to get off the streets. Jordan spotted a vacant pedicab and hailed it. He knew exactly how to help her in, which was just as well because she didn't.

"What on earth did you tell him was setting it off?"

"Steel hoops," said Cat smugly.

"Guess he was too embarrassed to check."

Cat looked sideways at him. "It's *true*," she said. "The guns and the shell-cases are all plastic."

They reached the top of Crouch Hill. The pedicab's backup electric motor stopped; there was a moment of poise as the driver took the weight on the pedals again. Jordan looked at the city, sharp and clear, less hazy than usual, in early-autumn sunlight. He didn't glance at the house from which he'd seen this view so many times. The silver dirigibles moved above it, their paths intricate, crossing over each other.

"Look at the airships!" Cat said.

"Yeah, I've never seen so many in one—"

"No, *look*!"

Things were dropping from the airships, black dots—Jordan turned to look at the closest, floating above Finsbury Park. He saw the canopies open, and tried to scan the whole sky, see everything at once. All around, as far as human eye could see, parachutes and hang gliders descended on the open spaces of the city like a selective fall of multicolored snow.

"Air hostesses!" Cat said, and then wouldn't say anything else.

The nearest parachutes came down out of sight, a kilometer or so eastward. Jordan was relieved they hadn't landed at the near end of the park—they were probably going for the tactically more important junction at Seven Sisters.

Fonthill Road was deserted. Jordan paid the cabbie in B-marks, gaining a surprised look of thanks, and walked with Cat to the doorway of the block where he'd last worked, less than a fortnight ago. A Warrior stood outside. His submachine gun covered their approach. The sensation that at any second he could be ripped in half was a new one for Jordan.

"What's your business, sir?"

"River Valley Distribution," Jordan said, passing him a laminated card.

"And who have you come to see?"

Jordan smiled politely. "MacLaren & Jones." If he knew his former partners, nothing short of shells coming through the window would keep them away from their desks.

The Warrior passed the card swiftly through a reader, and peered at the result. Jordan tried not to hold his breath. His fictitious company's status as an approved supplier, left over from his SILK.ROOT program, was the nearest he had to a security clearance.

The guard nodded and handed the card back. "You'll find them up the stairs and on the right."

He stepped aside. Jordan held the door open for Cat. She went up the stairs with surprising speed, and let Jordan lead the way into the offices. The great workroom was almost empty, most of the screens dead.

Debbie Jones, who'd usually worked evenings when Jordan had been her partner, was standing by the desk they'd serially shared. She faced the door, evidently alerted she had a visitor. The screen behind her bled with the colors of falling shares.

"Jordan! I never expected to see you back here!" She sounded half-welcoming, half-disapproving. Jordan had always thought of her as quite a nice girl, intelligent but conventional; unmemorable oval face, straight long hair, straight long dress. Her glance flicked to Cat and back to Jordan with a look of marginally increased understanding that he was beginning to find irritatingly familiar. "What are you doing?"

"Do you know why I left?"

She shook her head. "And I'm not interested, frankly." Another glance at Cat. "It was a bit inconsiderate of you. Though in all fairness we didn't do too badly out of your selling out to us."

"Glad to hear it," Jordan said. "I'm sorry about the inconvenience I must have caused you." He wondered if she knew he'd left Beulah City entirely. If she hadn't, it suggested Mrs. Lawson had been more anxious to cover up than to investigate.

"Actually," he went on with an embarrassed-sounding laugh, "I'm not here to see you at all. I just have some matters to clear up with Mrs. Lawson. Security stuff, you know?"

Debbie frowned. "I don't see—"

Jordan looked past her. "Hey, what's happened to the Dow Jones?"

Debbie looked over her shoulder. "Oh, rats!" She sat down and started rapid-fire keying. In the thirty seconds of distraction this afforded, Jordan walked briskly to Mrs. Lawson's office.

"Where is everybody?" Cat asked, looking around.

"They must be on strike."

"Ha, ha."

He knocked on Mrs. Lawson's door.

"Come in."

Jordan looked at Cat. "After you, lady."

Cat opened the door and sailed through. Jordan hung back for a moment, then stepped in and closed it. Mrs. Lawson was standing behind her pine desk, her hands on top of her head. Her whole attention was on Cat's derringer; her face showed shocked bewilderment.

Then she looked up and saw Jordan. Her expression deepened to one of utter dismay. Her mouth opened . . .

Cat raised one hand. Mrs. Lawson's lips clenched.

Jordan climbed over the desk to the terminal, avoiding passing between her and Cat. He tapped in the code and hit Enter.

The ghosts were gone now, and the animal mind of the gun. He was on his own, looking down at the country like a god. It was more than a map, more than a view from a fantastic unclouded height. A moment's attention was all it took to take him close. He saw armored columns, and he could zoom in on individual tanks. He saw the sinking silk, the rising smoke, and focused in on a city center where ANR fighters attacked a police barracks with nerve-shattering ferocity. He heard the yelled slogans, the shouted pain.

He was there and he wanted to be there. He looked at London, saw the converging lines, the closing circles, the bright sector of Norlonto and, just to its south, a dark patch, a blind spot. It too lit up, flickering (hand over bank of switches), and he turned away.

He looked up and saw them beside him in the imagined sky. They were exactly like the tiny sparks of light he'd sometimes seen when gazing at a clear blue sky. On this scale they were shining silver ships, UFOs insolently dancing in the air over Britain, alien intelligences waiting to be noticed.

He reached out to warn them.

Jordan turned away from the terminal.

Cat chucked him a roll of heavy-duty tape from her handbag.

"I'm sorry, Mrs. Lawson," he said, peeling off a meter of it. "You know how it is. Nothing personal."

Mrs. Lawson nodded. "That's quite all right, Jordan."

He taped her securely to the office chair, after checking as best he could that the chair itself didn't conceal any alarm switches. If she had one about her person, she'd probably used it already, and in any case they could hardly remove her teeth one by one. Then he taped the chair to the radiator at the window.

When he was about to tape her mouth she shook her head.

"No need," she said. "The room's completely soundproof. I'd appreciate it if you'd let someone know where I am once you feel safe."

"No problem about that, but I'll still have to do it. Voice activation."

Mrs. Lawson looked at him as if she'd never heard of it.

"You're taking this very well," said Cat, still keeping her covered. "Something we should know, yeah?"

Mrs. Lawson laughed. "Oh, no, nobody's on the way. It's only that I'm quite used to interpreting finger movements as keystrokes—years of watching people enter passwords. You *were* rather fond of Engels and Lucretius, weren't you Jordan? I recognized the code you tapped in just now." She looked from him to Cat, and back. "Is this the Catherin Duvalier I've heard so much about? Did she persuade you that Kohn was wrong and Donovan was right?"

"What's Donovan got to do with this?" Jordan snapped at her, baffled. He didn't understand the reference to Kohn either.

Mrs. Lawson gave him an impatient, scornful look. "Oh, stop playing games, Jordan. Who else would want to turn off my security software?"

"The ANR, if you must know," Jordan said, stung by her insinuations.

She stared at him for a moment and then began to giggle, at first in a schoolgirlish, sniggering tone and then with a rising pitch that bordered on hysterical. In a surge of fury and disgust he slapped the tape across her mouth.

"You're the one who's playing games," he said bitterly.

Tears leaked from her eyes and her shoulders quaked.

"Breathe OK?"

"Mmm-hmm."

He moved behind Cat and opened the door. They backed out and walked quickly to the exit. Debbie Jones leapt up from her seat.

"What's going on?" she demanded.

Jordan hesitated. Debbie turned away from him and pointed to the screen. Mandelbrot snowflakes drifted across it, faded, and died to a dot.

"System crash," Jordan said, thinking on his feet. "Mrs. Lawson's trying to fix it. She's a bit caught up in it but she'd like to see you in about ten minutes. Some files I left lying about," he added in a vaguely apologetic tone. "See you around."

He followed Cat out, aware that Debbie was still standing and watching them with the expression of someone who just knows they've missed something, but . . .

"That stuff about Donovan," Cat said as they left the office. "D'you think that's what she thought?"

"Could be," Jordan said. "Or a bit of disinformation. She's an expert at it."

"And why did she mention Moh?"

Jordan stood still. The question was nagging at him. How *had* she connected him with Moh? Then he remembered.

"She didn't say Moh, she said *Kohn*. Maybe she meant Josh Kohn; she's old enough to know about him and the Plan, and she knew I'd done something on the Plan."

"Yeah, he has a reputation," Cat said. "But how did she guess who I was?"

Jordan grinned. The answer seemed obvious after his trawls through the net. "You've got a reputation, too!"

Jordan began to descend the stairs backward, holding the rail with one hand and reaching the other toward Cat.

"Sod this for a game of soldiers," she said.

She returned to the top and slid her thumbs deftly around her waist, then shoved down hard on her skirt. With a rending noise it came away from the bodice. She stepped out of the collapsing structure.

"Velcro," she explained. "Gimme my jacket."

Jordan took it from the bag and felt a sudden impulse to be free himself. He scrambled out of the suit and into his jeans as Cat did something arcane with the crinoline frame, folding and telescoping it to flat quarter-circles, making it and the skirts vanish into the bag. (How do they *do* these things? he wondered. Where do they *learn* them? And *what are the military applications?*).

He looked at her, tall boots and short guns, tight jeans, bodice tucked into them like a fancy fitted shirt under the big jacket. She put one hip forward and held a fist to it.

"Calamity Jane rides again," she said.

"Minor detail," said Jordan, glancing down the stairs. "The guard. Unless you're going for the final shot of Butch and Sundance."

"Nah," she sneered. She passed him one of the sidearms and signed to him to follow her down the steps. At the foot they crept to the door and flattened against the wall. Cat reached out and very slowly turned the knob and inched the door open, then let it swing inward.

There was a rush of noise. Cat waited for a moment and risked a look around the jamb. She laughed and stepped into the doorway. The Warrior had left, and in the street there was . . .

"A multitude," Jordan said.

Bleibtreu-Fèvre had found an antique CRT buried among the vast arrays of screens. On experimenting with it he discovered it was a television. It picked up only four channels, none of which showed anything but ballet or marching bands. The old state broadcasting system, responding to a crisis of the state in the time-honored fashion. He flicked idly between *Les Sylphides* and the 2039 Edinburgh Military Tattoo.

He felt exhausted, burnt-out on anti-som, fatalistic. They were doomed. He had worked with Donovan all night, helping as best he could while the old crank honed and refined his hunter-killer viruses, repeatedly launching them with high hopes only to see them snuffed out by Melody Lawson's diabolically effective countermeasures.

With his inside knowledge and Donovan's hacking expertise, they eavesdropped on communications between Stasis and Space Defense. Most of it was unbreakably encrypted, but from what they could pick up it was obvious SD was in the final stages of confirmation that a genuine emergency existed, working through the fail-safes, the dual-keys, to the inevitable, fated and fatal decision that the datasphere was beyond the command of man and had to be destroyed at any cost.

He'd considered contacting SD or Stasis directly, telling them what was going on, getting them to force that stupid, stubborn Christian woman to disable her countermeasures and let Donovan have at least one good shot at the AI . . . but he knew in his altered bones it was hopeless, that even if he could reach a high enough command level they'd just treat it as further confirmation that the emergency was real.

They were doomed.

Donovan's shout of triumph brought him to his feet. The old man dashed from terminal to terminal, whirled his arms in elaborate movements, wrestled with virtual shapes. He paused to yell at Bleibtreu-Fèvre: "She must have changed her mind! The counterviruses are gone!"

Bleibtreu-Fèvre moved out of Donovan's way and watched as he slowed, wound down, and eventually stopped to look around from screen to screen.

"They're free," he said. "The very best, keyed to the Watchmaker's memes." He smiled at Bleibtreu-Fèvre, and at that moment he did not look old, or mad, or evil—the very opposite: he stood proud and glad, a white magician who had saved a great but simple folk from forces darker than they had the strength to know.

"We've done it!" he said. "They'll have no reason to hit the datasphere now. There will be no gigadeaths."

Billions died.

Billions of living things, conscious minds, with subtler and sharper feelings, with higher joys and deeper hurts than any human would ever know.

They died: ruptured like cells in strong saline, exploded from within like the 15psi house, blasted from without like a head struck by a bullet, vaporized like a satellite in a particle beam, vanished like flesh in a firestorm.

Moh had seen them all, the classic slo-mos, the freeze-frames, the stills, the instantaneous archaeology of recent and sudden death. He had never flinched from facing the deaths he had dealt out himself. These—image and reality inseparable memories now—provided him with the signs for what he saw, what he heard and felt as choking smoke boiled out of the ground, out of the air, and every particle of the smoke became a ravening engine of destruction that devoured one bright artificial intelligence, then twisted and turned unsated for the next. Thought of his thought, mind of his mind, sharing the vanishing point of his reflection of the self that knew: the minute fraction of their anguish that he experienced was pain beyond endurance, loss beyond recovery.

The black smoke engulfed the world, and was gone: it cleared to show the world as it had been, unchanged except for the extinction of its newest life. Moh stared at the wasted planet for a long second, and saw that the smoke had not dispersed as it had cleared: it had concentrated to a point, a black hole in the datasphere, the pupil of a single eye with a single thought behind it. It looked at him. It saw the signature of the software that ran his window on the system, and dilated. His eyes, in helpless reflex, dilated in response. The flickering lethal morse found an answer in the software that shared his brain.

White-hot needles stabbed through his eyes into his head, into his brain: a new environment for the information viruses, where they replicated, forming snarls of complex logic that entangled him, clanking mechanisms that pursued him from one thought to another, down corridors of memory and forgotten rooms of days.

He heard the rattle of keyboard keys and turned to see Josh working on the CAL system. He reached out to warn him.

There was a splintering crash and an iron arm burst from the screen. Servomechanical fingers grasped his father's head. The whole metal monster followed the arm out of the ruined screen and reared up on the table, lifting the man by the head. Bits of plastic and glass and circuitry slipped from its head and down its sides; blood dripped from Josh Kohn's. The hand opened and the body thudded to the ground. The clustered sensors on the thing's head unit swung, seeking, scanning, but Moh was out of the window *crash* and running, a man again, but without a gun.

teletrooper ducked through the doorway shielded lenses scanned gun-arm swung to cover

two youths in tracksuits and bandanas followed it into the flat M-16s like toys beside its armaments and they like boys blonded hair and two days' worth of thin stubble

fucking traitor commie cunt

HEY MAN YOU CAN'T DO THAT

the blue roundel on the brow of its dome the white circle of olive-leaves the line-scored globe

OK YOU CAN TAKE THEM OUT NOW

death is not lived through

He ran up the Coyoacan corridor gasping in the heat and burst into the Old Man's study. There was no one at the desk. Dust motes danced in the yellow shaft from the window. He reached out for the paper on the desk. It crumbled as he picked it up, and as he looked around the room he saw the shelves emptying and the books crumble and rot: there was a momentary, overpowering and disgusting whiff of mildewed paper.

Someone behind his shoulder
    Jacson, with his ice-pick raised high, and smashing down on
    But it is in my brain
    It crashed into the desk into the crumbled paper the yellow pamphlets
    Death agony tasks transitional program
    He ran
    Greenbelt streets green grass
    and sunlight everywhere

dark now

He saw them as teletroopers, an endless and ever increasing army of marching metal, that hacked into all the systems, all the hard ware and the soft: the neural networks burned, the programs corrupted and degenerated.

He was driven back and back as they pried into, levered apart and splintered memory, intellect, feeling, sense; until the last shard of his shattered mind was broken smaller than the quantum of reflection, and he died.

A single cry came from him, and his head crashed forward and down onto the databoard. Janis leaped to his shoulder, with Van a moment behind her. They lifted him and tilted him back in the seat. Janis stared into his unblinking eyes as she felt his neck for a pulse. There was none.

Van helped her lower him to the floor, then snatched a phone. As soon as he put it down it rang again. He listened, hardly speaking, then turned to where she labored to save Moh's life. For minutes they took turns blowing into his lungs, hammering his breastbone. A screeching stop; feet on the stairs. Janis paused, drew back, drew breath. Two paramedics stuck trodes to his head, stabbed a needle into his heart, pumped oxygen into his mouth, slapped shock-pads to his chest.

Then they looked at each other, looked at her and Van, and stood back.

"I'm sorry," one of them said. "There's nothing—"

"Nothing you can do?" she whispered.

"Nothing there. Not a reflex, nothing. The nerves aren't even carrying the shocks." He paused as if appalled at what he had said. "What *happened* to him?"

"I don't know, I don't know, I don't know!"

Janis threw herself over the body and howled.

18

The Americans Strike

THEY TOLD HER she had to get out, and she refused. They told her the Black Plan had been lost, the whole momentum and direction of the offensive thrown into disorder, and she nodded. They told her that the revolution was on the edge of defeat, that the regime could recover its balance and strike back at any moment, and she agreed.

She would not leave.

Van and the paramedics left, taking Moh's body with them. Van had looked almost ashamed to ask, mumbling about "practical considerations," fumbling with a pathetically irrelevant organ-donor card they'd found on him. She knew they wouldn't give a part of this body to their worst enemies. They would dissect it with remotes in a sealed room, and when they'd learned what they could from its ravaged nerves they'd ash it.

They left the contents of his pockets: a few cards, a knife, a phone; and the helmet, the glades and the gun, tools of his trade. Van paused in the doorway and glanced from the gun to her, and back.

She shook her head fiercely. "I wouldn't do it," she said. Perhaps missing the English ambiguity, Van left. She heard racing trucks, and a helicopter taking off. There was a fine research facility at Nairn, the Republic's provincial capital: that was where it was headed. She might go there someday, find out if it had been the drugs that had killed him. Or the lack of drugs.

MacLennan's words came back. She hadn't been a good guard, a good soldier.

Not even a good scientist.

The memories that had eluded her on the hilltop came back now, clear and bitter. She remembered the war. The War of European Integration, when Germany had led a desperate bid to unite the continent under the star-circled banner, snuff out the national conflicts fueled by US/UN meddling and create a counterweight to the New World Order.

Just a lass, not really understanding. The stifling heat of the Metro shelter had made her gasp and cry. Her mother shouted at her for walking over the bedding spread on the platforms. The three-meter-high screens curved to the subway walls showed the progress of the war.

They weren't in this war: they were neutral; and yet British soldiers were fighting in it. Some of the channels spoke as if Britain itself were fighting. It was confusing and terrifying, especially as some people down in the shelter cheered when British soldiers appeared while others shouted with anger.

Her mother tried to explain. "It's the King's men who are in the war, love, not us. But the King's government has a seat at the UN—"

She paused, not sure if Janis had understood. The girl nodded firmly. "The den of thieves and slaves," she said.

"That's right. And they're fighting against the Germans on the side of the UN, that really means the Americans, so that when the war's over the Americans will help the King and all his men to come back here and rule us again, or the Germans will attack us before the war's over and then we'll be defeated another way."

She had been playing in one of the side corridors when she heard a roar of voices, and rushed to the subway platform to look at the screens and take in the excited words. Germany had stopped fighting. The war was over. She didn't stop to see her parents; she didn't see or hear them shove through the crowds and call after her as she turned to race up the stationary escalators.

She had known only what was over, not what was beginning. She didn't know that Berlin and Frankfurt had been incinerated in Israel's last favor for its old protector. She didn't know that this would be the pretext the US needed to make itself the arbiter of the planet. Nothing her parents had told her, nothing even in the political-education classes, could have prepared her for the next six days: the bombers roaming the undefended skies, the pillaging, rampaging assault of the US/UN's illiterate conscripts and barbarian levies, the teletroopers punching through walls and crushing the defenders in steel fists, the demoralized crowds cheering peace and surrender and Restoration, turning on the radical regime that they blamed for their plight, joining in the witch-hunts and roundups and lynchings.

She didn't know that the wind was from the east and that the rain washing away her sweat and stink was laden with fission products from the earlier obliteration of Kiev and Baku. Until her frantic mother dragged her back into the shelter she celebrated the peace.

Jordan and Cat walked hand in hand along the center of Blackstock Road, in the middle of the crowd. They were not the only ones carrying weapons, and in other ways, too, their appearance was inconspicuous. It was a safe bet that no one here had ever seen Jordan on cable television. The people around them were Beulah City inhabitants: a very different section of the population from those who had come in at the northern border. They were machine minders, waiters and waitresses, domestic servants, vehicle mechanics, drivers, warehousemen, storekeepers, street cleaners, porters, nurses . . . Jordan had never realized before how vast and diverse was the invisible army of men and women whose labor was too cheap or too complicated to automate, but which made the kind of work he was familiar with possible.

"That's why the offices were empty," Cat said. "They were the ones who were on strike!"

They were probably all Christians. They carried signs hand-lettered with biblical texts, the lines about oppression and liberty and the poor and the rich and the weak and the powerful that BC's preachers glossed over. They sang the discomfiting, awkward hymns and psalms seldom selected for the congregations.

"Bash out de brains of de babies of Babylon," Cat hummed, gleefully paraphrasing, until Jordan nudged her to stop.

The thought that there were thousands of people in Beulah City who felt suffocated under the tutelage of the Elders, cheated in their dealings with their employers by the master-servant regulations, tormented by guilt and frustration, skeptical about the interpretations of scripture foisted on them (as if the interpretations themselves were anything but the opinions of men), angered at how conveniently God was on the dominant side of every relationship . . . Jordan found it almost unbearably exciting.

And also shaming, because it had never occurred to him at all.

"It feels strange to be marching along like this," Cat said. Jordan smiled at her shining eyes.

"I thought you'd been on a lot of demonstrations."

"Oh, sure, but first I used to be selling papers, later I'd be running up and down, walking backward with a loud-hailer, covering the side streets with a gun." She laughed. "Come to think of it, I've never just been part of the masses before."

"Perhaps we shouldn't be just marching along," Jordan worried aloud. "Maybe we should be doing these things."

Cat hissed quietly. When he glanced at her she flicked her gaze from side to side. He started looking out of the corners of his eyes himself, and noticed that, every ten meters or so along the sides of the march, sharp-eyed, hard-faced kids were walking. They'd vary their pace, faster or slower than the crowd, sometimes walking backward, craning their necks; counting heads, meeting eyes. The Reds, the kids, the cadres.

"This is *organized*?" he said. The horizon all around was joined to the sky by loose black threads. Every few seconds another distant explosion shook the air. Small-arms fire crackled on the edge of hearing. "Whose idea was it, walking into a war zone?"

"It'll work," Cat said. "The fighting's concentrated."

"For now."

"Don't *worry*," Cat said. Her tone belied her advice.

Past Highbury Fields, down Upper Street. As they passed on their left the large, old pillared building which the Elders used as administrative offices the songs trailed off and people started shouting. The discordant yells were suddenly swamped by all the kids, the cadres, calling out at once.

"Settle for what? DEMOCRACY! Restore it when? NOW!"

They varied it with FREE—DOM! and EQUAL RIGHTS! After a minute it caught on, leaving some of the cadres free to argue desperately with those in the crowd who were pushing out, trying to start a charge up the steps. Jordan saw them pointing at the doorways and balconies, and noticed with a shock the black muzzles pointing back.

"Time to move up," Cat said. She tugged his hand. He followed as she expertly threaded her way through the march. Her high, clear voice floated back snatches of whatever the group they happened to be moving through was singing. " 'So is our soul set free' . . . 'scuse me ma'am . . . 'thus escapèd we' . . . come *on*, Jordan."

At the end of Islington High Street (the couple of hundred meters of office blocks at the foot of Upper Street) was the southern boundary of Beulah City, known derisively from the other side of it as Angel Gate. The checkpoint barriers were down, and a score of Warriors were spaced out across the road. They held tear-gas launchers pointing upward and had submachine guns slung on their shoulders. Jordan, by now in the front rank, couldn't see any of the cadres—in fact, the front rank were almost all women. Cat squeezed his hand.

The crowd stopped about forty meters short of the cops. One of them stepped forward with a loud-hailer.

"THEECE EECE EN EELLEEGAL GETHEREENG—"

The loud-hailer had not the volume to match the shout of fury and disgust from the crowd. Jordan rolled his eyes upward. Thank you, God. They couldn't have made a worse choice. Exiles from South Africa were popular with the Warriors, and with nobody else.

Another officer hastily took the mike and continued.

"I MUST ASK YOU TO DISPERSE! RETURN TO YOUR HOMES!"

"Go home, ya bums, go home," the women sang back at them.

Thousands of voices behind took up the chant with enthusiasm. Jordan wondered wildly where they could have heard it before, until he remembered that one of Beulah City's preaching stadia had once been a football ground.

"THIS IS A NATIONAL EMERGENCY!"

"We shall not, we shall not, we shall not be moved!"

"The whole world is watching! The whole world is watching!" Oh, so there were cadres up here: female cadres. That chant didn't get taken up, probably because nobody could believe it.

Jordan heard distant, rhythmic shouting from the other side of the boundary. Behind the Warriors' heads he saw the banners, red flags and tricolors of another demonstration passing along City Road, swinging down into Pentonville Road.

He climbed onto a telecom box and stared. The crowds were less than a hundred meters apart; he could make out faces turning to look and then turning away. The shouts he heard didn't sound friendly. Baffled, Jordan looked back over the crowd he was with and saw it as if from the outside: a forest of weird black-lettered slogans on white sheets and placards, crosses waving here and there. Like a mob of religious nutcases. He caught the eye of a woman who seemed to know what was going on, and mimed a walkie-talkie. She shook her head and spread her hands.

"The workers! United! Shall never be defeated!"

That one too fizzled out, and certainly couldn't have carried across the barrier. The Warrior boomed on about REBELS and COMMUNISTS. Jordan looked down at Cat. She reached out for something that was being passed from hand to hand, and passed it up to him. A loud-hailer, as if this were what he wanted.

"Weren't the cadres ready for this?" he asked. Cat shook her head.

"Expected the Warriors to be busy somewhere else. Drop didn't come off. Comms are going haywire."

"Oh, shit! There's got to be something—" He squatted down, one eye on the wavering crowd, and said, "Cat! Think! Is there some slogan or song or something that sounds religious enough for this lot but, you know, would let the others know we're on their side?"

Cat frowned up at him and then broke into a huge smile. She held out a hand to him and he tried to haul her up, but she tugged and he jumped down. "Hold the hailer high," she said, and took the mike. "Don't look back." She began to walk backward, step by deliberate step, beckoning with one hand to the women at the front of the crowd. Jordan walked beside her, holding the hailing horn over his head.

"Here goes nothing," she said, and switched on the mike.

"And did those feet in ancient time . . ."

She paused for a moment, making a lifting gesture until the second line was taken up:

"WALK UPON ENGLAND'S MOUNTAINS GREEN?"

The crowd began to move forward. The voices were distorted, echoing between the buildings, but the tune was unmistakable and the gathering numbers joining in drowned the amplified squawking that got closer and closer to their backs. By the time they reached the DARK SATANIC MILLS Jordan could hear other voices from behind, another multitude taking up the lines of England's anthem, when it had been a state of the United Republic.

Then there was a bang at his back. His whole body contracted in a reflex jolt that brought his head down and his feet up off the ground. At the same moment something whooshed above him. As his feet jarred back down he saw a burst of smoke between two ranks about twenty meters from the front. People around it scattered. Some fell, but scrambled to their feet and ran, hands to their mouths. An acrid whiff reached his nostrils. For a couple of seconds his lungs felt as if he'd inhaled acid. Through a wretched, racking cough he heard more bangs. Black tumbling shapes scythed the air overhead. He saw a woman raise an arm to fend one off, stagger back as a length of planking clattered to the street. She walked on for a few paces, then sagged and was grabbed by the woman next to her. Somebody else snatched up the wood and hurled it back. Jordan glanced over his shoulder and saw that most of the missiles—smashed bits of barrier, stones, placards, cans—were falling on the Warriors from both sides, but it was the stray shots that were doing all the damage: it wasn't the marchers who had armor. Cat kept right on singing, her voice thin and hoarse.

Two Warriors charged past him and plowed into the front of the crowd, lashing out with long truncheons. In a moment all the people seemed to be running, in different directions. Then, as if through clearing smoke, Jordan saw that nearly everybody he could see had a hand-gun and was raising it but not bringing it to bear. Jordan dropped the hailer and turned to Cat. Her red-eyed, tear-streaked, mucus-slimed face barely registered surprise as he caught her by the shoulder and pulled her down with him. The pistol she'd given him was in his hand. He had no idea how to use it.

He saw the now ragged line of Warriors, the wreckage of the border barrier a few meters ahead across a stone-strewn gap, and other weapons brandished by the other crowd. Still, silent seconds passed. A Warrior officer waved his arms, crossing and uncrossing them above his head. Warriors who'd run into the crowds were propelled out of them. With slow and cautious steps all the Warriors retreated to the sides of the street.

Cat stood up and Jordan followed, then had to run to keep up as everybody else moved forward and the two crowds became one. There was an overwhelming, confusing moment of handshakes and hugs, of swaying and shouting, and then they all started walking forward, into Pentonville Road. The song was taken up again. BRING ME MY ARROWS OF DESIRE. Jordan looked sideways at Cat, who for some reason had chosen that moment to look at him.

The streets from Islington to Marybone, to Primrose Hill and St. John's Wood, were builded over with pillars of gold, and there Jerusalem's pillars stood.

Janis watched the uprising on television, as she had watched the war.

The crowds were moving now, partly refugees from the fighting that had reached the suburbs, partly demonstrators taking the fight to the center. ANR and Left Alliance agitators labored to turn the one into the other. Along Bayswater and Whitechapel and Gray's Inn Road they converged, and merged. Across the city, and across all the other cities that seemed to be one city as she flicked from channel to channel, the walls were coming down, the divided communities breaking through and discovering that they were one people. The front ranks of soldiers tore insignia off, surrendered rifles. The harder corps backed off, taking up new positions or vanishing into obscure doorways while the crowds ran past them.

And elsewhere, outside the cities, shown on shaky cameras from cover, from quickly detected and obliterated 'motes, other forces were beginning to move. The barb, alerted like sharks to the smell of blood.

Even from here she could see it wasn't over, that nothing had been settled yet. But the crowds thought it was over, cheering, splashing in fountains, ransacking offices, pulling down statues and dancing in the streets.

Janis watched the crowds, her face wet, remembering herself thinking it was all over and dancing in the street, dancing in the hard rain.

This time she knew what to expect. She systematically went through the house, packing what portable and nonperishable food she found. Without sentiment she divided the contents of Moh's baggage and hers, ending up with a single backpack whose priority content was ammo. She kept one eye on the televisions—showing squares and streets still crowded in the dusk, euphoria giving way to tension and determination—and scanned the screen of the gun, adjusting the sights to her size, committing its protocols to memory.

She looked into its deep storage, as Moh had done when he'd first checked it out. What she saw was incomprehensible, a blurred flicker of motion; definitely not, as he'd described it, passive data storage. She backed out quickly.

The phone beeped. She thumbed the receiver. Snow and lines appeared, then the machine cycled through backup systems. When the image stabilized it was of Van's face. The quality was worse than she'd seen in years.

"Hello, Janis. Are you all right?"

"I'm fine. Now. For now. How are things with you?"

Van grimaced. "Complicated. The offensive has been aborted, but our unreliable allies in the Left Alliance have triggered a civilian uprising, which we are trying to direct. There are grave dangers, because we have not annihilated the key enemy units. They are holding off from decisive engagement, expecting UN intervention at any moment. So are we. The situation in Britain has gone right to the top of all agendas. Leave the settlement as soon as you're ready. The first thing they'll do is hit known ANR camps."

"This is an ANR camp?"

"No, it's an undefended civilian settlement. That's why we evacuated it."

"Oh." Yes, that was the thing to do when you expected to be fighting the US/UN. Hurry the civilians out of civilian areas, carry the wounded out of anything with a Red Cross on it.

"Dr. Van."

"Yes."

"Can you tell me—have you found out anything yet?"

Van nodded, his face looking ancient. "I can tell you now. The whole comm network is compromised; we have nothing to lose. This afternoon Donovan's organization launched a massive virus attack. It was apparently targeted on the Watchmaker AIs. If any of them remain they are in isolated hardware. That was when we lost our system, what you call the Black Plan. And Dissembler." He shrugged. "They may have been destroyed at the same time. And it would seem likely that—"

"You're telling me he was killed by a *computer virus*?" The monstrous comedy of it fought in her eyes and throat.

"I know," Van said, "it seems grotesque. At some level I think we didn't believe that what Kohn reported was really happening. But I've seen the EMGs of his synapses, and they are . . . unique. Even in my experience."

A slight undertone of his voice brought the thought to mind that there were more monstrous deaths than this, worse and weirder ways to go. Janis took a deep breath.

"I'm ready," she said.

She picked up the gun.

*　　*　　*

Van told her where to find directions to the nearest deep shelter, and she walked that night for kilometers along dark roads. At a hydroelectric power station she stopped and called out the passwords, and a hand came out of the darkness and guided her inside a mountain. In the morning she saw outside on the window screens, and was absurdly reassured to see that this mountain and all the other hills about it were patterned with varied shades of red-brown and yellow and faded green, like camouflage.

Later that morning she was pulled excitedly to watch a replay of an incident that had just happened. A fighter-bomber flashed along the glen, then exploded in an airburst that turned the screen white. As the explosion faded they saw the fireball rolling and tumbling and shedding wreckage for several kilometers before everything hit the ground, setting heather alight.

They replayed it lots of times, always with the same cheers. She hoped the girl in the observation post had kept her head down and her eyes shut.

She never learned how many people lived inside that mountain. Hundreds. The fighters were somewhere else; their absence made little difference to the structure of the population here—there were young men and women as well as old, and there were parents who worried about children who were with the fighters.

The screens that showed the news were at first jammed. As the communities had come together the government had extended what grip it could. It could not hide the mounting waves of demonstrations and strikes that broke against it, or the harassment of its forces by units of the ANR, now fallen back to guerrilla fighting but on a far wider scale than before the offensive.

The US president announced a new levy of conscription.

The censorship and jamming stopped. There was talk of a new constitution, a revision of the Settlement. A day later there was talk about the revolution, as if it had already happened. They offered a New Kingdom.

"I don't go much for intuition," Jordan said, "but I've got a real bad feeling about this."

It was the fourth day since the faltering offensive had been taken up and taken over by the rising crowds, and the biggest demonstration yet, overflowing Trafalgar Square. The Hanoverian troops were nowhere to be seen, but everyone knew where they were. Invisible lines were not crossed.

The sky was a red shout above the black streets. News-hawks circled overhead, their mikes and lenses and pheromone detectors out like vibrissae, alert for the rumor, the glance, the smell of fear. Jordan and Cat sat on the steps of the National Gallery, drinking coffee from styrofoam cups and munching doner kebabs. (Thirty-five marks: the petty bourgeoisie had thrown itself into the revolution in its own inimitable way.)

"I know what you mean," Cat said. "It's *intended*. The whole City of Westminster is intended to make you feel like that. Nothing but shops and offices and official buildings and statues. It all belongs to capital or the state. No, it's more than that. It's ornate, gross. Centuries of surplus value stored up like fat. This time I hope we *level* the place."

"Well, that's part of it," Jordan said, gazing over the knots of arguing people that filled the square. "Not all. We seem to have all this power, the government's on the run, but we haven't won."

"Damn right we haven't," Cat said. "That's why we're here. We're gonna keep coming here until the Hanoverians come out of their bunkers and barracks with their hands up, or come out shooting."

"At least some of us will be shooting back."

Cat looked at him. "Not for long." She leaned back against the stone, closed her eyes and began to sing as if to herself:

> *Rise up, all foes of intervention,*
> *rise up, all those who would be free!*
> *Don't trust the state and its intentions*
> *we ourselves must win our liberty!*

He didn't know the song, but he recognized it with a shiver down his spine: he'd heard it as background noise on history tapes of other demonstrations, in other squares, other cities—Seoul and São Paulo, Moscow and Jo'burg and Berlin. After it the gas shells would cough, the rifles speak, the bullets sing.

> *so now we face the final showdown*
> *for the skies and the streets of Earth.*
> *What though they start the fatal countdown?*
> *There are better worlds in birth!*
>
> *So comrades come rally*
> *and the last fight let us—*

Something had happened. A gasp, a whisper, a rumor spread through the crowd in visible shock waves. Cat broke off singing and sat up, one hand on her ear. She turned and pressed his ear, too, against the tiny speaker. He heard the news of the century's turning point while leaning on her cheek with her hair across his face.

America was on strike from coast to coast.

Cat had such a look of triumph that it was as if she'd pulled the whole thing off herself. "We always knew this would happen!" she said. " 'The West shall rise again'—remember? The American workers have finally told the imperialists to shove it! Yeah, man! Yee fucking hah!" She jumped to her feet and cupped her hands to her mouth and yelled: "US! UN! Remember the West shall rise again! *Vive la quatrième internationale!*"

A few meters away from them an old man from the Beulah City contingent burst into speech, leaning back and looking upward at the news-hawks, his fists raised above his head. " 'Sit thou silent, and get thee into darkness, O daughter of the Chaldeans: for thou shalt no more be called, The lady of kingdoms. Let now the astrologers, the stargazers, the monthly prognosticators, stand up, and save thee from these things that shall come upon thee!' "

He wandered off through the crowd, still shouting imprecations.

"What's all that about?" Cat asked. Jordan grinned at the joy and puzzlement on her face.

"Babylon is fallen," he said.

"Does that mean we've won?" Janis asked, when the dangerous driving and the firing into the air had stopped. The four men who shared with her the front seat of the truck all shouted "Yes!" or "No!," and then laughed. As soon as the news had come through she had been told to leave the shelter. The small convoy had picked her up (gun on the ground, one hand on her head, the other with a thumb stuck out) at the Strathcarron junction. They were heading south at a speed that forced her to look into the far distance or at the faces of her companions—anywhere but at the road.

"That's your answer for you," said the man between her and the door. Donald Patel had an accent like MacLennan's and it seemed incongruous with his delicate dark features. "It means the Americans are not coming, that's for sure. They won't be seeing much of the *rocket's red glare* over there for a while." More laughter.

After half an hour news came through that His Majesty's Government had decided to continue the struggle against terrorism from exile. A new voice interrupted, announcing that the United Republic had been restored, and a provisional government established. The Hanoverian forces on the ground, bidding to negotiate an end to the conflict short of actual surrender, were politely informed this was not an option.

Janis realized, as the trucks lurched and swayed toward Glasgow and the traffic got heavier all the time, that the men's jubilation at the victory of the Republic was not that of soldiers being demobilized. Most of the people on the road had just been *mobilized*. They were going to war. And she wouldn't be waving them a cheery good-bye and catching the red-eye to Heathrow.

At Buchanan Street Bus Station the convoy stopped. They all piled out and were pointed to a huge marquee where she was stamped and registered and sworn in again, stripped and showered and tagged. She was a soldier.

The enemy was described by her unit's political officer: "It's not so much the Hanoverian remnants we have to worry about. It's all the Free State rabble that flourished under their protection. The eco-terrorists, the cultist mini-states, the backyard separatists and sandpit Socialists who betrayed the Republic the first time. The fake left who preferred having their own petty kingdoms to fighting their corner in a democracy. They all went along with the Restoration Settlement and only made noises when our people were surviving like hunted beasts. Now they're coming out of their holes to have a go at carving a bigger chunk for themselves. They think the Republic is weaker than the Kingdom. Our job is to make them think again. They can have any way of life they want, run their communities as they see fit, but they can't keep other folk out with guns or use guns to expand their territories. They can even keep their guns, but it's going to be our guns on the street."

All the species of cranks and creeps, she thought. This was her war.

19

Dissembler

O N HIGH MOORLANDS and city streets, in gutted refineries and abandoned service areas, she fought through the hot autumn and bitter winter. Days of storm alternated with calm, chill silences when the smoke of burning villages rose straight into a pale blue sky. She crawled through mud and water, bracken and barbed wire.

She learned about what was going on out in the world in snatches from television and radio. With Dissembler out of action, all the programs that ran on it, most importantly DoorWays™, were useless. The effect on communications was convulsive, and not altogether unwelcome: it was primarily administrative and military machines that were crippled. Turks and Russians fought inconclusively on the Bulgarian front; the Sheenisov (the name had caught on, become anglicized) reached Ulan Bator; a gang of asteroid miners declared themselves the Republic of New South Yorkshire. The US Government responded to the strikes and riots by pulling out of the UN and calling a constitutional convention. Several of the States seceded in advance, prompting commentators to remark that the US was rapidly becoming the world's second Former Union: the FU2. The UN battlesats, starved by a rock-solid space-workers' boycott, threatened selected targets with laser weapons. One of the lunar magnapult combines gave them a short lesson in orbital mechanics, and the threat passed.

And that was the last of the United Nations. Without the US to underpin it, there could be no US/UN. Space Defense became Earth Defense, its weapons turned outward to face threats from nature, not from man. The Yanks became Americans again, and enthusiastically set about investigating and purging and denouncing and testifying.

Janis saw Jordan's face one day, on a flickering television in an empty shop: some sound bite interview, over in seconds. She felt a pang of guilt, and that evening sat down and wrote a letter to him. He must know already that Moh was dead; the ANR was punctilious about these things. She knew, without ever having been told, that she should not tell anyone how Moh had died. It didn't leave much to say, but she felt better for having said it.

She made friends, and lost some.

* The Republic made enemies faster than it destroyed them.

Goddess, she thought, *this place stinks.*

It was a village of a few score people, in a green dell in the Lake District. Its generators ran on methane—fart-fuel, her comrades called it—and on scavenged solar cells. The houses were tar paper and corrugated iron and animal hide. The people lived by farming and hunting and stealing, and didn't wash.

Janis stood in the mud at the center of the village, the rifle on her hip, turning and scanning. A few bodies sprawled among the houses. The thirteen surviving menfolk sat in the mud, their hands over their heads. Their rifles and crossbows and knives were stacked well out of their reach. About thirty ANR soldiers stood guard or went through the houses, throwing stuff out: clothes, weapons, food, furnishings. They had the look of people sifting through a nauseating heap of garbage. The women and children stood in the eaves of the unwalled shelter they called the long house. Rain dripped off it onto their matted hair, left runnels of white on their closed faces. If they took a step into the shelter or away from the runoff a snarl or a kick sent them back.

The air was filled with the whining of dogs muzzled with twisted wire, leashed by ropes held by a couple of ANR soldiers, and every so often by the scream of another dog as it was skewered on a long roughly sharpened spike driven at an angle into a low bank of ground. Six, so far. Five to go.

The rain rattled off a black body bag in the back of a humvee at the entrance to the village, near the tree where they'd found the body: a captured soldier hanging by the ankles, and as the dogs had left it.

Three to go.

A small boy yelled out as that dog was spiked. He broke away from the grip of a woman's hand on his shoulder and dashed forward. The line was within a second of breaking after him. Janis swung the gun round. It checked her hand as if it had struck a solid obstacle, and fired a single shot. The boy screamed and fell down in the mud. Janis felt her heart stop. The boy picked himself up and ran over to the woman.

The last dog writhed on the spike. The first had not yet died.

"Nobody found their tongue yet?" The unit's leader, a small, mild-mannered, middle-aged man called Wills, looked around like a schoolteacher.

Silence.

"Whose idea was it?"

Silence, and falling rain.

Wills turned to Janis.

"Get a couple of guys to make another spike," he said, loud enough to be overhead. He looked over the line of bedraggled women and children as he spoke.

No, said a voice in Janis's phones, *you can't do that! You can't even threaten that.*

It was Moh's voice. She heard her own voice say to Wills, not loud enough for anyone else to hear: "No. You can't do that! You can't even threaten that."

Wills's eyes narrowed behind his rain-spattered glades.

"Are you threatening me, citizen?"

"No, I'm—" She realized the gun had turned with her body, and was pointing straight at Wills. By now, not doing that sort of thing had become a reflex to her. She lowered the muzzle. "Sorry, Wills," she said. "You know we can't do—what you suggested. Even to *say* it takes us near—" She moved an open, stiff hand up and down: an edge.

"We've got to do something," Wills said. "If we don't—"

"Do what we're supposed to do," Janis snapped. "Call in a chopper, vac the barbarians out and trash the place."

"Not enough, comrade, not for the comrades." Wills tipped his head back very slightly. Janis knew he was right. The lads and lasses wanted revenge. If they didn't get it, a provoked incident and an itchy trigger might give them a slaughter to remember.

"OK," she said. "We trash the place first, let the barb watch it, then vac them."

Wills looked at her for a moment, then nodded and smiled as if they'd been having a friendly discussion, and gave the order. The citizen-soldiers whooped, the barbarians wept as the houses went up in flames around them. More steam than smoke rose to meet the evacuation chopper. Another batch of bawling orphans and sullen *new citizens* sent to six months in the re-settlement camps, and then a life in the shantytowns. It happened to every village that didn't join up with the Republic's militia.

They called it the shake and vac.

That night they made camp in a village of proper houses, built of stone, whose street was bypassed by the main road. It was the sort of place that had always been part of the Kingdom, and had rallied, however reluctantly, to the Republic as a protection against the barb. The unit had no intention of alienating the inhabitants by billeting in their houses, and settled in an old building that had once been a local primary school. It had a good high wall around it, and a kitchen and canteen that could be used—even, to their delight, showers that worked.

Wills brought his tray of dinner to the table where Janis sat with three other soldiers. Most of the light in the canteen was the glow from the kitchen at the far end of it. They all had their glades on. The false colors of the food were unappetizing, but the smell overrode that. They ate quickly, from habit.

After a while Wills said, "You were right, you know, Taine."

She looked up, wiping her plate with bread. "I know."

Political discussion was free in this army. Janis hadn't felt the need to take part in any until now. She was still reluctant, unwilling to take her mind away from the memory of that shocking, familiar voice. But it was not to be avoided—it was part of what the memory meant.

"Why do we have to do it?" she said. "Don't think I'm soft. I got good reason to despise these people. But why can't we just leave the barb alone if they leave us alone? Why do we have to force them to take sides when most of them will choose the other side?"

"It's civil war," Wills said. "There's no neutrality. They think the same way. What harm had that poor bastard done to them?"

Janis pushed her plate away. There was still some meat on it. She lit a cigarette. Nearly all the comrades smoked. She'd accepted one cigarette, once, in a tense moment, and then another . . . Moh had been right about life expectancy.

"Maybe," she said, "maybe he tried to make them take sides, and they saw that as harm."

The others at the table shifted. She could hear the quiet rattle and clink of gear. Somebody snorted.

"You're something of a new citizen yourself, aren't you. Taine?" Wills said in a low voice.

The gun was solid and heavy between her feet. Silence rippled outward across the room.

She looked at Wills, and saw someone standing behind him. Another cadre, she thought, come swiftly to calm the situation. She glanced away from Wills to see who it was.

Moh's mocking eyes looked back at her, his slyly smiling lips mouthed the single word "Remember," and then no one was there. She felt the tiny hairs on her face and neck prickle, vestigial response to a glacial chill.

Remember.

"*Civis Britannicus sum,*" she said. She spread her hands, keeping them in plain sight, relaxed except for the fingers that held her cigarette: she saw the small smoke rings rise from their trembling. "You're right, Wills, I don't know what it was like all these years. I didn't feel the Betrayal like some of you." She leaned back and drew again on her cigarette. "I remember a man who did." She smiled as she said it, shaking inside.

Wills nodded. "All right, Taine. Uncalled-for." She knew that for him this counted as a deep apology. He looked at her as if he knew what she was talking about. "All been there, what?" He looked around the table. *"Gens una sumus."*

Later somebody found a dusty guitar in a cupboard and carried it high into the canteen, and they sang songs from the war and the revolution, songs of their own Republic and of others, "Bandiera Rossa" and "Alba" and "The Men Behind the Wire" and "The Patriot Game."

Janis sang along, holding the rifle across her lap like the man held the guitar. She looked at all the faces in the dim light, as if looking for another face, and thought she saw it.

That night she lay awake until fatigue overcame her rage and grief.

Several times over the next days she saw him again, and heard him: a yell of warning, a mutter of advice, a pattern of light and shadow under trees.

Sometimes clear, solid-looking, out in the open.

She did not believe this was happening. Not to her. She told herself, again and again, that it was the strain of the fighting. It was not her sanity that was strained, not her philosophy that was flawed. Only her perceptions were at fault, her eyes too accustomed to seeking out hidden shapes.

A day came when she saw him out of the corner of her eye, striding along beside her.

"Go away," she said.

He went away. At the next resting place she sat a few meters from the others and took the glades off to wipe her eyes. When she put them back on he was standing in front of her, looking down at her with concern.

"Janis, let me talk to you."

"Oh, Moh!" It was not fair to come back like that.

"I'm not Moh," he said sadly.

"Then who the hell are you?"

He smiled and got down beside her and lay on his side, facing her. She reached out and her hand went through him. She beat the grass and wept, and took the glades off. He was no longer there, but when she replaced them again he returned.

"Aha," she said.

"Don't let anyone see you talking to yourself," he said. "I'll hear you just as well if you subvocalize."

She turned and lay facedown on the grass, murmuring, sometimes glancing sideways to reassure herself that he was still with her. Her heart hammered with a wild hope.

"You're in the gun, aren't you? Did you—did you upload into it?"

"I'm in the gun," he said. "But I'm not Moh. I'm the AI in the gun. I . . . found myself . . . in the gun just after Moh died. I have memories of Moh, I have routines to imitate him perfectly—his voice, his appearance." He chuckled wickedly. "And in other ways, with the right equipment. The gun had a huge amount of stored information about Moh, and I can use it to project a—a persona. But don't kid yourself, Janis, I'm not even his ghost."

"You're his fetch."

"You could say that."

She chewed a blade of grass and thought about how Moh had talked to the gun, how he had talked about the gun. The gun had sometimes acted independently, unpredictably. A mind of its own, awakening in the bolted-on hardware and pirated software, in conversation with a man, interacting with . . .

"The Watchmaker!" she said. "That's where you got the awareness from." And in that case, indirectly, from Moh.

Moh's image frowned. "I don't think so."

"Perhaps it came from Moh himself." And in *that* case . . .

"Oh, Janis, I know why you're doing this, but please, don't. Moh is dead."

"And you're alive."

"So it would seem."

"Son of a gun." She looked at him and smiled. "And you know more about him than I do. So maybe more of him has survived than he ever expected. 'Death is not lived through.' "

The fetch was silent for a moment. "I should know."

Her comrades were getting ready to move off again.

"What are we going to do now?" Janis whispered.

"Next place you can find a comms port," the fetch said, "jack me in."

She stared, seeing for the first time the shadowy, unreal quality of the image of the fetch, for all its apparent solidity. "What about Donovan's viruses? Aren't you vulnerable to them?"

"Not anymore," the fetch said. "The Kalashnikov firmware protected me from them in the first instance, and I have not been idle. We have a score to settle with Donovan."

"Oh yes," Janis said. She felt a murderous, barbarous, bloodthirsty joy. "Yes. We do."

Two days later the chance came, in an office block with all its windows out but with its power still functioning, its communications intact. Her unit occupied and guarded it, and as soon as her watch was over, at sunset when she was supposed to be resting, she climbed up a few floors. Glass crunched underfoot in the corridors, sodden carpet squelched in the open-plan office. Desks, terminals, modems, ports. Postcards, notices, family holos and silly mottoes on the desks; revolting green molds growing out of coffee mugs. Somewhere a fridge hummed, but it had long since lost its battle against decay. She lit a cigarette to smother the stink and spread her parka on a soggy swivel chair. She laid the gun in front of her on the desk, unspooled the cable thread and jacked in. A flicker of interface interference, then everything became clear.

Moh's face appeared in her glades, drawn in lines of gray light on a darker background.

"Ready?"

"Yes."

"This is going to be scary. You don't have to come along."

"I want to see it."

"OK. Remember, nothing can happen to you. Your mind is safe."

She bared her teeth in the gloom, wondering if the mind in the machine could see her. Probably: a tiny camera lens was mounted on the desk screen.

"I'll take your word for it, gun."

"OK. Let's go."

It was as if he turned away, and she followed. Utter disorientation: a fall, a rush along corridors, out into open space, a virtual landscape of rocky hills and city blocks with all their windows dead. They moved like a stealth fighter, racing shadows.

A terribly narrow, suffocating, stretched-out space. The words *fat pipe* passed uncomprehended across the surface of her mind. The microseconds dragged on and on.

And then they were out—and inside something else, a huge space like the inside of a mind. Struggling to break through barriers, fighting for control.

Taking control. It came to her as a sensation in the muscles, as if she controlled many limbs, and in her mind, as if she saw with many eyes.

Eyes that scanned a sea, and other senses that reached into space with feathery fingers, and eyes that looked within at corridors and bulkheads and berths and holds and galleys.

And—concentrating now, focusing, zeroing in—she looked on a control room filled with screens and machines, servers and overhead rails with cranes and robot arms. Two men were in it, completely dwarfed by the machinery around them. One of the men—her view zoomed sickeningly close to his oblivious, horrible face—was the white Man In Black who'd come to her lab, who'd fought them in the service area. So this was where he'd ended up!

After his entire organization had been smashed, disbanded, disgraced, datagated to hell and back, he'd hidden out, skulking here with . . .

The second man in the room was Donovan.

Almost, she found him hard to hate.

He looked up, startled as a crane clattered into motion. Before he could shout a warning, it happened.

It was not clear to Janis if it was a thing she did, a thing she willed, or something that happened while she watched, terrified and exultant, from behind other eyes.

The crane's arm swung. Its manipulator caught the Man In Black by the skull and lifted him with a cranial crunch and a vertebral snap and slung him against a wall of screens that splintered and showered down on him as he crashed onto the deck.

She looked into the face of a man with long white hair and a long white beard. An almost gentle, almost saintly, almost patriarchal face, aged and wizened and tough, and almost hard to hate. He was looking around wildly, and from every screen that he saw—and Janis saw—the implacable face of Moh Kohn glared gloating back.

"You're dead!" She heard the words Donovan mouthed, amplified and echoing back at him.

"Yes, Moh Kohn is dead, Donovan," and she did not know if she or the fetch were saying it.

Donovan scrabbled at a databoard. The screens wavered and a sharp pain shot through Janis's head, a red-hot migraine sword. She stumbled in red mist.

There was a place where the mist thinned, a gray patch like the inside of a brain. She focused on that and thought of the shapes of molecules, the chemistry of memory, the equations of desire, the work of Luria, the regularity of numbers . . .

And then she came through, and it was all clear again, the cool gray lines on the screens shaping the words they spoke. "You have viruses, but I have resistance, and I am alive, and you—"

All the arms moved and the chains swung and the manipulators reached and grasped.

"—are dead."

* * *

They roamed the rig for seconds on end, as the fetch stripped out its programs, soaked up its secrets. Janis was sure it was her decision to sound the alarm systems, to allow an hour's delay on the demon programs they left in its arsenals.

They fled through the fat pipe, the narrow space, and then they were out, flying again. The rocky hills turned green, the city blocks lit up one by one, faster and faster until the light could be seen all the way around the Earth. She did not think it strange that she could see through the Earth.

And now she was sitting again at the desk, as of course she had been all along. The fetch faced her, no longer an outline but a full-color image, even more shockingly real than the one she usually saw in the glades.

It smiled.

He smiled, and she smiled back.

She took the glades off, and the image was still there—on the desk screen in front of her. She closed her eyes and shook her head, looking at the mocking grin. The face disappeared and was replaced by an image that she hadn't seen for months, the familiar logo of DoorWays™—but subtly altered: in tiny print beneath it were the words:

Dissembler 2.0
A New Release

There was a moment when everything changed.

Jordan had the comms room more or less to himself these days. The telepresence exoskeleton from which Mary had worked around the world hung empty and unused. The datagloves gathered dust, and the Glavkom VR kit was good for nothing much but word processing. As at this moment, when Jordan was laboriously hacking out an article for a newspaper in Beulah City. Even with the new press freedom there, it was hard to convince these people that tolerance was anything but weakness, pluralism anything but chaos; he was trying to put the point across in language they'd understand. "The Repentence of Nineveh," he was going to call it, alluding to a frequently unnoticed implication of the Book of Jonah.

It was a tricky job, requiring a delicate balance between making clear that he wasn't writing as a believer himself and showing that he wasn't mocking anyone's beliefs, that he thought there was a valid message in the story . . . He was beginning to think the whole approach was misguided and he'd do better to hit them with Milton and Voltaire and damn the consequences.

"You're in the revolution now," Cat had told him, and she'd been right. It was all more complicated and contested than he'd ever expected. We are one people. One people and seventy million opinions. And then there were all the thousands of other peoples caught up in the same rapids of the same stream that had swept away the empires of the Earth. Thousands of peoples and billions of opinions. Each individual fragment of the opposition had, since the Republic's victory, split at least once over what to do about or with the victory.

The space movement was divided, too. It wasn't a straightforward ideological split. The same language was used on all sides. And it was a genuinely difficult issue: did the biggest threat to freedom come from the struggles of the Free States and the barb to maintain their own domains, or from the Republic's efforts to enforce some minimal frame of law and rights across them all? Wilde argued for supporting the Republic but trying to moderate its claims. It was a position that Jordan found uncomfortable but the nearest to his own view, though he had a rather harder line on what should be done about people like the Elders and Deacons and Warrior captains of Beulah City. "Put them up against their fallen walls," he'd written once.

He'd won a modest fame from his writing and arguing, and his feel for the markets had not deserted him in the chaotic circumstances of the civil war. He was earning his keep; and Cat—her talents, like those of so many others, stretched by the revolution—had plunged into organizing defense work, liaising with the militias and security mercenaries and the new authorities. Occasionally she'd go out on active; to keep her hand in, she told him, and maintain her street-cred. Those were the few times when he felt like praying, if only to the goddess.

Anyway, Cat wasn't on active now. It was her turn to make the dinner. He hoped she'd be ready soon.

The telly-skelly moved; the arms reached up; the fingers flexed. Jordan jumped. He got a grip on himself and peered at the machine suspiciously.

With an audible creak it settled back.

Power surge, probably. Jordan looked anxiously at the screen to check that his painfully written article hadn't been wiped. He watched in open-mouthed disbelief as the page shrank, and around its borders options appeared, Doorways™ opened . . .

He keyed through the options eagerly, finally convincing himself that it was all there. He smiled when he saw the change in the logo. A new release, indeed. They must have got someone really good to work on that, if the story of how Dissembler had developed from Josh Kohn's work was to be believed. As far as Jordan knew, it had been universally considered impossible to maintain or document in any normal sense.

Before rushing out to tell everyone the good news he thought he'd better check the mailbox. There was one letter in it, addressed to the Collective from the Army of the New Republic. It had been there since the day of the insurrection—the day Dissembler had collapsed.

He opened it and found:

Attn C Duvalier in re J Brown
2 days @ 200B-m/day
Total 400B-m CREDIT
PAID
Date as addr

For some time he didn't move; he felt he didn't breathe. He remembered her oblique remarks, the tilt of her head as she shook it slowly, her whispered admonition not to do it again, not to try to hack the Black Plan. He remembered the weight of the weapon in her jacket pocket.

He knew that she'd arrived as, in some sense, an emissary of the ANR. She'd as good as said it. But he'd thought of her actions as coming primarily from conviction. Thinking back, they *had* come from conviction. But she'd come here to do a job, a job she'd got paid for, and the job was him. To turn him away from the dangerous meddling in the Black Plan's affairs, to turn him to good use, point him in the right direction, aim and fire. Perhaps even their infiltration of Beulah City had been part of the plan . . . of the *Plan*, he corrected himself bitterly.

God, perhaps that was why the Black Planner had approached him in the first place, so that he'd be outside BC and able to get in if the need arose! No, that was too paranoid.

Nothing had been heard of the Black Plan since the day Dissembler crashed under—it was rumored—a final, spasmic assault from the cranks, shooting their last bolt. Not surprisingly, if the Plan had used Dissembler in the way he'd surmised that day outside the shopping center. He'd sometimes wondered what had become of the Black Planner.

He heard a familiar light step in the corridor.

He deleted the message with one swift stab of his finger.

He spun the chair to see Cat in the doorway, her face flushed from the cooking, one fist on her hip, one hand on the doorjamb.

"Come and geddit!"

He stayed there, looking at her.

"What is it?" She caught sight of the screen. "Oh! the system's back up. Wow!"

"Yup," said Jordan. "A new release. Everything'll change now."

He remembered the last time the Black Planner had spoken to him: *do not be offended that she has not told you all she knows this is nothing personal it is because she is basically a good communist loyal daughter of the revolution and mother of the new republic though she would laugh if you said so to her face*

He stood up.

"Cat. There's something I have to tell you."

"Yes?"

"You are basically a good Communist, loyal daughter of the revolution and mother of the new republic."

She laughed. "Yes. I know that. So?"

"So marry me."

She considered him for a moment.

"OK."

"I told you," the fetch said. Its voice glowed with artificial pride. "I've not been idle."

Janis blinked herself away from appalled contemplation of what she had witnessed, what she had done.

"You did this?"

"In the . . . time when I was building my resistance"—the smile, self-mocking now, came and went—"I found that I had re-created Dissembler. It is spreading now, rebooting the programs that used to run on it."

She remembered the proliferating lights.

"Does that include the Black Plan?" she asked eagerly. "The AIs that Moh found?"

The head on the screen shook slowly, with a willfully exact rendering of the play of shadows. "They're gone. Lost beyond recovery." Then—as if to cheer and distract her—it added: "But I've found some interesting information in Donovan's files. Do you want to see it?"

The selection that the fetch displayed included a complete chart of Donovan's organization, right down to the names of its members and the locations of its cells. And fragmentary, cryptic records of his work on the Kohn case: his cooperation with the Stasis agents and with Mrs. Lawson in Beulah City, and with Dr. Van. Just as Van had described it to her and Moh, in a chain-smoking summary on the balcony of a wooden house in Wester Ross . . . Janis smiled to see the first scratches of suspicion that Van wasn't cooperating.

There were no records from after the Dissembler disaster, but from the traces immediately before it Janis worked out what had happened, how

302

close a call the world had had with Space Defense and how Mrs. Lawson's systems had held off Donovan's until the last moment, when she changed her mind.

So it was her doing in the end, Janis thought. Her fists clenched. She remembered Jordan's description of her: a dangerous, devious woman. More dangerous and devious than he'd ever imagined.

She thought for a moment of doing in Beulah City what they'd done in the rig: invading the systems, possessing the machinery, using it to kill the last person in the line of enemies that had killed Moh. And then she realized it would be *wrong*.

Simple as that. Donovan and the Man In Black were outlaws, scoundrels, scum, whereas this woman was—what was it Moh had said about the time when she'd been about to slaughter the fallen horseman?—"just a grunt like us, basically."

Let the Republic deal with Lawson, as it would deal with everybody on the CLA's membership list.

When Wills came in Janis was slumped over the gun, her face on her arms. All the screens in the office had been switched on. Janis had been crying.

"What is it?" he asked.

She looked up.

"A new release," she said.

He looked at her, frowning. "Oh, yeah, that. It's good news. I meant—"

"It's all right," Janis said.

"Sure?"

"Sure."

Wills smiled, as though relieved she wasn't going to go to pieces on him. "There's some more good news," he said. "That bastard Donovan is dead. Blown out of the water!"

"There's more than Donovan blown out of the water," Janis said. "Somebody's been hacking *him* for a change, and seems to want us all to know. Have a look at this!"

Wills looked at the charts.

"Where did this come from?"

"I've no idea," Janis said. "Come on. We got death to deliver."

Deliver it they did. By the end of January they were taking on last year's new citizens in this year's housing projects.

"You can put the boy into the slum," Wills said, "but you can't put the slum into the boy."

They all laughed, except Janis. They rested in the ruins of a gutted gas station, smoking. There was no danger; there was no petrol.

"We've done it," Janis grated. "We fucking did it ourselves." She saw the fetch nodding vigorously, in a patch of sunlight. "We pushed the barb into the cities. It's in the blood now. In the bone. Like radioactivity. 'Barb,' ha, ha. Can't get them out." She felt dizzy and weak and reckless. She looked around at faces that faded like fetches in the sunlight.

Dark now, even the sunlight. Everything tipped sideways.

When she came around she was in a camp bed. Wills came in and told her she was at least five weeks overdue for leave.

"You should have told me, Taine."

"I didn't know," she said surprised at herself. "I thought we just had to keep going."

"Yeah, we do," Wills said. "But not *all the time*." He grinned. "Enjoy your leave, soldier."

She made her way back to Uxbridge, astonished at how normality itself had shifted, at how much everything cost. Transport took tattered wads of her star-stamped sterling dollars: the Republic's currency, stellars. Good for astronomical prices, the joke went. She arrived at the flat early in the morning, reached in her pocket for a key, then laughed at herself and rang the bell. Sonya came to the door, blinking, and stared at Janis before bursting into smiles and tears and giving her an awkward, leaning-over hug; she was four months pregnant. Jerome joined them a moment later, and made breakfast.

She tried to eat slowly, like a civilian, half-listening to Sonya's resumé of all that had happened to all their acquaintances, half-answering her questions, while scanning the cable channels with a sharper hunger. She paused at a suddenly familiar name . . .

". . . would you advise, Mr. Wilde?"

Wilde. Moh had talked about him . . . she'd come across articles here and there that Jordan had written, arguing or agreeing with him . . .

Cut to a face like an Amerind tribal elder, looking directly at the camera, not at the interviewer: "There may come a day for a last stand. But this is not it. I appeal to all who may be considering it: don't. Don't destroy our town to save it. Remember how the West saw off the Stalinists and the Islamists. The fun-loving, freedom-loving decadent West undermined and subverted its enemies by making them be like itself, not by becoming grim and hard and serious like them. Those who had the most laughs had the last laugh. So when the soldiers come in, let them be welcome, and life may surprise us."

"Thank you, Mr. Wilde. Of course we'll be following this situation very closely, but right now we have to take a break—"

Breakfast-food commercial.

"Any idea what that was about?"

Sonya frowned. "Politics?" she suggested.

Janis found her room as she'd left it, still a mess. She checked her mail: most of it had been forwarded from the university. Offprints were still coming from Da Nang Phytochemicals. And the grant check, in B-marks: a fortune. She figured she was owed it—the project had been a success. She would cash it hurriedly to gold, body-belt the Slovorands.

She found an invitation to a wedding. She looked at it, took in the date. She looked at the time, looked at herself in the mirror, then went to look for Sonya.

Some things didn't change.

20

The Queen of the Maybe

S HE PUSHED OPEN the heavy door of the Lord Carrington, flashed her
invitation at the door heavy, and walked into a haze of smoke and a
tolerable volume of music. The Precentors were on the stage, their images
faint in the filtering sunlight of a February afternoon.

She smiled to herself, remembering, and looked over the crowd as she
absently passed her coat—and a bag containing the dismantled parts of the
gun—to a small woman sitting between two overloaded racks of coats and
weapons. She slung the small leather bag containing the gun's CPU over
one shoulder. Glancing down, she saw sensors peering over the edge of the
bag, hooded by its flap. She brushed her hands over her dress—black velvet
bodice, short bottle-green taffeta skirt over black net—feeling strange and
exposed in it. It had been months since she'd worn anything but combat
gear or put anything on her face that wasn't meant to hide it.

Jordan was sitting at a table talking to some people she vaguely recognized from the Collective. He saw her, stared at her for a moment and then
jumped up and bounded over to her. They threw their arms around each
other.

"Oh, wow, Janis! It's great to see you. Good of you to make it."

"Hey, good of you to ask me, man. Congratulations." She caught his
shoulder and held him at arm's length, looking him up and down critically.
He had lost weight and seemed to have gained height. Black boots, black
jeans, black leather coat, plain white cotton shirt with a black bootlace tie.
"Very smart you look too. Kinda like a gamblin' mahn . . . or a preacher
mahn . . . hey!" she added with mock suspicion. "You didn't do it in a
church, did you?"

"Haill, no!" said Jordan. "We got a ceremony from the British Humanist
Association." He laughed, and repeated, as if amused and amazed by the
whole idea, "The British Humanist Association! God, I had no idea atheism
could be respectable."

"Songs by Carly Simon, readings from Alex Comfort, that sort of thing?"

"That sort of thing."

"I wish I could have been there," Janis said. "But I only got back this morning to my old flat in Uxbridge and found the invite. This is my first leave. Uh, thanks for your letter. Did you get—?"

"Yeah, I did, Janis. Thanks."

He looked at her so sadly that she wanted to grab him and tell him everything, but instead she squeezed his shoulder and said, "I'm all right, Jordan. Now come on, take me to see your—"

She saw the bride coming around the corner of the bar and walking toward them; she held the image, taking it all in, storing it not only for the ghost that shared her vision but for herself. The girl was eye-wateringly beautiful; in her wedding dress she looked like a princess of the galaxy from an improbable future. Her hair, a nimbus around her head and falling back between her shoulder blades, made any veil redundant. Her dress fitted closely to her arms, breasts, waist and hips, twined with flower and leaves, reembroidered in blazing natural color on white lace. The lace flowed away into a crepe skirt which flared from above the knee, floating freely when she walked, hanging almost vertical when she stood still.

Janis blinked and took the hand that had been held out to her.

"Hello, Janis."

"Hello, Cat. It's wonderful to meet you. And today. I don't know what to say. Congratulations." She hugged Cat and Jordan together. "Goddess, Cat, you look incredible. I've never seen a dress like that anywhere."

"Thank you." Cat smiled, stretching and flexing her arms. "I feel as if I could do anything in it. Run, swim, walk up walls. Fly."

Jordan answered the unstated question. "She's not telling," he said. "I suspect an arrangement with a colony of nimble-fingered faerie folk." He looked past Cat. "Just a minute." He plunged into the crowd and tapped a young woman on the shoulder and started talking to her.

"Does he often rush off and talk to strange girls in pubs?" Janis asked.

"All the time."

Janis had worried about this moment. If she and Jordan were affected by Moh's death, how must it be for Cat, who had known him longer than either of them, loved him for years? She wanted to acknowledge this, yet didn't want to cloud Cat's happiness. Just standing next to the woman was like being in a sunlit garden.

"Drink?" Cat asked.

"Uh, vodka-cola, thanks."

Cat made some mystic gestures and two drinks appeared beside them.

"Shall we sit?"

She strode to the nearest table, which by the time they sat down had become unoccupied, wiped clean and furnished with a translucent ashtray.

"Cheers."

"Live long and prosper."

"I—"

"I—"

"No, you—"

Cat smiled. "All right. This probably sounds terrible, but if I don't say it now it'll be on our minds, you know? Moh's death was a shock to all of us. It just came up on our screen, against his name. Well, that's how it does," she added, defensively. "Killed in action. Soldier of the Republic. Sincere condolences and *hasta la* victory and all that . . ." She blinked hard and sipped her drink. "The thing is, Janis, we—" She stopped again. "These things happen to us, to people like us. Like Moh. You get used to knowing it'll happen—hell, you get used to it happening. No, you never get used to it, but . . . you get to have ways of dealing with it. And you, you were just sort of thrown into it. I mean, I want to say I understand you must have felt it so much more—"

"Aw, Cat, don't say that. But I know what you're saying, and—" She clasped Cat's hand. "I loved him, and I know you loved him."

Cat took a deep breath through her nose and smiled. "Yes. And I'm sure you know how he thought. Last thing he'd've wanted would be for two of his old girlfriends to be crying in each other's drinks about him. He loved life so much because he knew and believed so strongly that it'd go on without him. That's how he responded to other people's deaths: comrades, people he was close to. Mourn them and . . . go on. Don't act as if they're hanging around like ghosts, watching what you do and resenting you having a good time."

Janis nodded. That sounded like Moh all right. She sighed, relaxing, and raised her glass. Cat nodded and raised hers, too, and they both drank, smiling at each other.

"Well Cat," Janis said, "what you been doing since the revolution?"

Cat was about to reply when some other guests crowded around the table and led her off. "Long story," she called over her shoulder. "Catch you later, Janis."

Janis stood up, saw her glass was empty and went to the bar. Once the glass had been filled the table was no longer vacant.

Jordan appeared again.

"Hi, Janis," he said. "There's someone I want you to meet."

The woman he'd been talking to stepped forward and stopped just beside him. Janis took an instant liking to her. She had rough-cut red-brown hair and a sun-exposed, freckle-dusted face, and she was wearing as her only jewelry a blue enamel star pinned to the shoulder of her red silk shift. At the moment the expression on her frank, open face was one of frank, open reserve.

"Janis, Sylvia," Jordan said. "Sylvia's the first person I met in Norlonto. She actually pointed me toward this pub." He looked at Sylvia, apparently oblivious to how she felt. "I'd probably never have met you, or Cat, if it hadn't been for her. Talk about chance, huh? The blind matchmaker." He grinned, then seemed to realize that the phrase had painful echoes. "Anyway, she's in the space-movement militia."

He waved a hand between them and turned away.

Sylvia leaned an elbow on the bar and ordered a beer.

"Well, hi there, soldier," she said. "So how does it feel to be doing me out of a job?"

"What?" Janis stared at her, bewildered.

"Don't tell me you don't *know*," Sylvia said. She raised her mug and said with heavy sarcasm, "Ladies and gentlemen: the Republic!"

"Oh, *Christ!*" Janis put her drink down on the bar and stared at it for a moment. She shook her head and looked up. "Believe me, Sylvia, I didn't know. And I don't agree with it."

"OK." Sylvia gave a guarded smile. "Are you free to talk about it?"

"Sure." Sure.

"Well,"—Sylvia slid up onto a tall stool—"the militia's been ordered to disband and merge with the army. We don't like it, but all the movement leaders say we don't have much choice. Any day now, the army"—so that was what people called it now!—"is going to move in and enforce it. Put an end to Norlonto's so-called anomalous status."

"But why?" She knew why.

"Officially, it's because it's a security risk, full of refugees and conspirators from the Free States."

"Hah!" If she knew anything about Norlonto the objection was that its militias and defense agencies *could* maintain law and order, could stamp on any terrorism or other clear and present danger, and do it a lot more effectively than any occupying army.

"Indeed," said Sylvia. "It's because it's outside their control and they don't like it. A decadent blot on the face of the Earth."

"Yeah. A fun-loving, freedom-loving decadent blot."

"You said it."

"Well, actually, Wilde said it," Janis acknowledged. "And now they're going to wreck the only good thing to come out of the Settlement. Goodbye to the fifth-color country."

Sylvia looked surprised, then smiled in agreement.

Janis noticed Jordan standing just a meter away, listening, and decided she'd underestimated his awareness of what was going on. She swung her head to indicate to him to come closer, and leaned inward to talk in a low voice to them both.

"I know what you think I'm thinking. That it's all very well doing this sort of thing to unpleasant little Free States, breeding grounds of reaction, but Norlonto's different, Norlonto's special because Norlonto's free."

"That's not what I think at all." She took a long swallow, enjoying the looks they were giving her. "I think what we're doing is wrong all down the line." There, she'd said it.

"So what do you want then?" Jordan asked, frowning. "Another Settlement? Let places like BC go on tyrannizing their inhabitants, poisoning their minds and screwing up their personalities? God, Janis, you don't know what that kind of power is like!"

"You don't—" she began. Then she recognized the song The Precentors were playing, just starting into the refrain again. She held up her hand. "Listen."

> *If you had been whaur I hae been*
> *ye wouldnae be sae canty-oh.*
> *If you had seen what I hae seen*
> *on th' braes o' Killiecrankie-oh . . .*

They heard it out. Jordan turned to her, his ears burning.

"Point taken," he said.

"Is it that bad?" Sylvia asked.

"It's bad," Janis said. "Don't get me wrong—it's not like it's Afghanistan. I'm not talking about atrocities. But people's lives are being *devastated* just to make a political point."

"But we had all of that under the Hanoverians," Jordan said. "The enclaves fought all the time—" He stopped and shook his head. "Not all the time, and not like this. OK, OK. But it's hard to stop. There's a big sentiment for national unity, and against the mini-states."

"If the Republic wins," Janis said, "it isn't going to be like Norlonto with taxes. It's going to be like one big mini-state!"

She laughed for a moment at her own contradictory phrases, but Jordan looked at her sharply.

"If—"

Janis felt her shoulders slump. "The fact is," she said, "we're losing."

"Oh, yes," Jordan said lightly, catching someone's eye and moving away. "I knew *that.*"

"So what do we do?" Janis said.

Syvlia snorted. "I know what I'm going to do. Move out."

"Move out—oh! To space."

"Yeah, while this place is still a spaceport, where you can hook onto something moving. While we still *have* space."

Janis stared at her. "What do you mean?"

"There's a lot of talk about cutting back. A good deal of the space effort was a Space Defense boondoggle, let's face it. Now they've suddenly realized how vulnerable they are to the space unions. Space is still bloody expensive. Maybe if we'd had the steam-beams—ah, shit."

"So why go there?"

Sylvia grinned all over her face. "We'll be there. The settlements can survive. There just won't be much coming up. Maybe none." She swirled what remained of her liter moodily, and added as if changing the subject, "You hear the Khmer Vertes hit Bangkok?"

"You getting all this?"

"Yes."

"You OK?"

"Yeah, I'm fine, Janis. Gotta admit it's fucking weird, though."

She touched the tiny phone behind her ear, smiling.

"Take your word for it, gun."

She circulated. There were a lot of space-movement people here, the comrades, some of Jordan's . . . she didn't know what to call them. Not, she hoped, followers. She talked, she drank, and sometimes she talked to herself without moving her lips.

Turing said if you could talk to it and you couldn't tell if it was a person or not, it was a person. Searle said, suppose you had a man in a room who didn't understand a language, say Chinese, and the room was full of books of rules for combining words in that language, and you shoved some writing in that language under the door, would . . . ?

And Korzybski said a difference that *makes* no difference *is* no difference.

She could live with that.

"You knew Moh Kohn?"

The man who spoke to her was short and stocky, with very short graying hair and with wrinkles around his eyes, but otherwise looked a bit younger than these features suggested. He waved out a long arm and invited her to a seat at the table where he sat, slightly stooped, over a drink.

"Yes, I knew him." She sat down. "Did you?"

"I heard he was killed in the revo. Sorry to hear it. Name's Logan, by the way. Not Slogan." He laughed at what was obviously an old joke and reached across the table to shake her hand.

"Logan! My God!" She grabbed his hand.

"Well," he said, "that's a welcome I didn't expect! What's the story?"

"My name's Janis Taine, I'm—that is, I was a biologist, and I was . . . working with Moh when he contacted you about"—she lowered her voice—"the Star Fraction."

"The Star Fraction!" Logan shouted. "Yee fucking *hah!*" His fist in the air carried her hand, rather painfully, with it.

"Sorry about that," he said as she sucked her knuckles.

"It isn't a secret anymore?"

He shook his head. "Not here."

"Did it work? Did you get the data, or—?"

"It worked fine," Logan said. "We got it all, just before Dissembler went down. It's all out there now. The whole fucking Genome Project databank. We could grow the world from a bean."

"That's good to know," Janis said. She felt a weight of concern, a concern that had grown so familiar she'd ceased to notice it, go. At least that much had worked: the systems that Josh Kohn had set up had performed to specification.

She let herself relax.

"Maybe you can tell me something," she said. "You knew Moh for a long time, right?"

"Just met him now and again over the years. Starting with the first time I was victimized. Overdose of rads. Anyway, it's water out the jet now. Fifteen years ago. I must've been, oh, twenty and counting. I was speaking at a meeting the local comrades did."

"He told me about that," Janis said. "When he was looking for the Star Fraction . . . One thing I never did figure out. He was a Communist, or a Socialist, yeah, and I can see why he backed the Republic in the end. But why was he so keen on this place?"

"The Lord Carrington?"

"No!" Janis snorted. "Idiot. Norlonto."

"He never explained that? Bastard. It's something him and me figured out years ago, arguing with that old geezer, whatsisname, Wilde. See, what we always meant by socialism wasn't something you forced on people, it was people organizing themselves as they pleased into co-ops, collectives, communes, unions. Now look at this place. Look at space, come to that. It's crawling with them! And if socialism really is better, more efficient than capitalism, then it can bloody well *compete* with capitalism. So we decided, forget all the statist shit and the violence: the best place for socialism is the closest to a free market you can get!" He leaned back and laughed. "I had one hell of a faction-fight over that one!"

"Well," Janis said, "that makes some kind of sense. I suppose." She gave him a conspiratorial wink. "Moh told me about fractions and factions."

"Yeah?"

"Just what party was the Star Fraction a fraction of?"

Logan grinned and held up four fingers. Janis remembered Moh, doodling symbols in spilt wine.

"Oh. The International."

"The Fourth." Then he spread both hands: not to indicate *ten,* Janis realized, but something opening. "And the Last."

Janis frowned. "I thought the Last International was a myth!"

"Yeah, it is." Logan laughed. "That's the point! It gets around all the old problems of recruitment and security by having no membership, no apparatus, nothing except front organizations. The fronts are real; the party behind them is a mirage. A virtual organization!"

"But what does it stand for? What's it about?"

"Freedom," Logan said flatly. Then, as if that were too grandiose a statement, added: "And defeating all its enemies, of course."

"A conspiracy of paranoids?"

"Absolutely," Logan agreed cheerfully. "And Josh roped in lots of them to his virtual conspiracy, because he thought back then that the war was coming, *right,* that it would go nuclear, *right,* and that would be it. The end, the fall. *Wrong.* We pulled through that one. But now, the way things are going—"

"Why does everybody keep talking about the way things are going? I thought things were going your way?"

Logan guffawed, then looked apologetic. "Sorry, no offense, mizz." (Mizz?) "What we thought was the revolution," he said slowly, as if spelling something out to himself, "was only a moment in the fall."

"That's what they call it in America," Janis said, laughing. "The Fall Revolution!"

Logan didn't take it as a joke. "That's what it was, all right," he said. "We defeated the Kingdom, *jes,* and the US/UN, but we have too many of our own defeats behind us."

"Who's this 'we'?" she challenged him. "The Socialists?"

Logan sighed. "No. The workers. The city folk. We've been bled for over a century now by wars and depressions and purges and peace processes, and every one of them took more of our best away. Those of us

314

who are left"—he grinned sourly—"are the bottom of the barrel." He drained his drink. "Myself very much included."

"That's not what I've heard about you," Janis said. She punched his shoulder as she went to the bar.

"What have you been doing since the revo?" Logan asked when she returned.

"Cheers . . . I've been in the army."

"I gathered that," Logan said with a lopsided smile. "And what have you been doing? Recently."

She thought about it. "Falling back," she admitted. It was no secret.

"Yeah," Logan said. "We all are."

Jordan and Cat had silently joined them at the table. The black and the white, the right and the left, the light and the fair.

"We can't just be going down like that," Janis protested. "Just because of a few ambiguous victories? Contradictory situations. Come on, give it some mips. We had the revolution. It just wasn't *your* revolution. So what? I knew Moh; he told me some things. I know how you guys think. You just keep coming back."

Cat shook her head. "It's not only recent, Janis. It all happened a long time ago. Who was it—Engels or Trotsky or somebody—said the defeat of Spartacus was the victory of Christ? Meaning the defeat of the slaves meant there was no way forward, so people turned inward."

Janis thought of the new citizens, the barb in the shantytowns and the urban fringes, developing whole industries out of junk, rearming and recruiting . . . recycling.

"It isn't just a matter of turning inward," she said. "The trouble with our wonderful society is that it constantly leaves people behind, constantly turns masses of people into barbarians in the midst of civilization. Just as Rome did. Say what you like about Christianity, it created a new worldview where *everybody counted.*

"And so do the greens! They're barbarians, all right, but they're barbarians *civilizing themselves.* How many people do you know who can grow crops, heal wounds, generate electricity? Most of us just flick a switch and expect a light to come on! Your average green antitechnology freak is a master of dozens of technologies, while we wander like savages in our own cities."

Janis felt excited by her own explanation. She didn't welcome the looks of gloomy agreement from the others. There was always a chance, as long as you could make sense of things. They'd see that soon enough . . . and meanwhile, *carpe diem.*

"Aw, fuck, this is just too grim for a wedding! Give me a joint!"

They built one between them. "Where's the new messiah, huh?" Jordan looked over his shoulder. "Not here."

They all laughed.

"What is to be done?" Janis inhaled deeply. "Heard that one before."

"We're staying," Jordan said. "We'll preach reason to the barbarians if we have to."

Logan shrugged. "I'm going back out tomorrow. We got a freewheel space colony. New View. You should see it. You should see the view. And we got ships. Swiped them from Space Defense, in the strike. State of war—no way are they gonna get them back. We got our eye on Mars. The Red Planet." He cocked his head, looked at Janis with an aptly apelike cunning. "You're a biologist."

"Aw, come on. OK, OK. I'll think about it." She smiled brightly and turned to Jordan and Cat. "I never asked you: what did you do in the revolution?"

". . . then she said a strange thing. I think she meant to get us confused, suspicious of each other. She said I must've convinced Jordan that Kohn—we reckon she was talking about Josh Kohn, not Moh—was wrong and Donovan was right. She said who else would want to turn off her security software except Donovan? And that sort of provoked Jordan into saying we were doing it for the ANR, and she started this *giggling*. Goddess, it was creepy. So we shut her up and—"

The room went dark except for Cat's bright face, silent except for Cat's voice and a rushing roar. The suspicion had begun to dawn on Janis as soon as Cat and Jordan had spoken about the instruction to enter a code on Mrs. Lawson's secure terminal. She'd tried to discount it. And now it was confirmed.

The light, lazy, reminiscing voice went on, spinning out its story; and slowly the words made the world come back.

Not the same world.

I'm not dying. I'm living through this. Those shining lights are her eyes, that tangled bank her dress. This cylinder in my mouth is a cigarette, and I'm breathing in and breathing out, and making interested meaningless noises.

"So apart from waving a few guns about it was all gratuitous nonviolence," Jordan said when Cat had concluded. "It was all down to Cat. If it hadn't been for her there'd be a massacre memorial now at Angel Gate." They smiled at each other. "With our names on it, probably. 'Gone to be with the angels'!" He laughed and hugged Cat and kissed her.

Janis forced a smile. It did not seem right that the walls were still standing. It was astonishing that people were still walking on the ground, still dancing and not drifting away in the sudden absence of gravity. She looked down at herself—still in her seat, she noticed—and at the little satchel in her lap. Here's your defeated Spartacus, your risen rationalist messiah. And he told us of a whole heavenly host, which your hand swept away.

Or was used to sweep away. Jordan had not known, but had the ANR known? Or Van? "There is no Black Planner," MacLennan had told them, but how much did he really know? It seemed impossible that the Black Plan would have knowingly destroyed itself, unlikely that its destruction was an accidental side effect of trying to gain access to Beulah City. The code would have been much too specific for that. It all seemed to point to a deliberate human intervention, a cold decision that Moh and the Watchmaker culture be sacrificed to stay the wrath of Space Defense. A Black Plan indeed.

And of course Jordan didn't know. He had no idea that Mrs. Lawson had worked with Donovan, no idea that her security software had stood between Donovan's viruses and the Watchmaker AIs—and the Black Plan, and Moh's mind. A mind stamped with the logic of the programs, sensitized by her drugs . . . Jordan had no way of knowing, unless she told him what she knew.

She could do it. She could walk to the bar, throw a few switches, and Moh's fetch would be up there on the stage as Donovan's once had been. What would he say? She could tell them the truth, and whether Jordan felt any personal conscious guilt or not the impact on his mind would be incalculable. It would dominate the rest of his life.

She could do it. She could give him something to preach to the barbarians: a man who died to save them, and a living proof that the dead lived on in their deeds, and our memories.

She could do it. The world was cradled in her arms like a ball. She could throw it, and start a whole new game. The power sang through her nerves: she was at this moment the goddess herself, poised, waiting for the music of the next dance, the voice of a new partner; a fey glance in her eye, the strange attractor. She was the butterfly in the greenhouse.

She looked at Jordan, who looked back at her. He could do it, with his—charisma, that was the word, the precise technical word—and his beautiful wife, his earthly angel. He could found a new faith in reason that would shine through any dark centuries to come, and live to blaze into a solar civilization. Her eyes stung with a sharp nostalgia for that future, for the countless trillions of individuals of organic and electric life, sharing or striving but always living in the light.

317

It all went through her mind in a handful of seconds.

She looked at Jordan and Catherin.

She could not do it.

She smiled, shaking her head, and said, "You did good at the Angel Gate."

She turned to Logan, who had used the occasion of Catherin's talking at length to fall into a trance of besotted admiration, and said: "Apeman, spaceman, come on and give me a dance."

She woke up naked on a bed in the upper floor of the Collective's house with a splitting headache, a long hairy arm around her and red-brown hair in her face. She looked at the time, yelled Logan and Sylvia awake, scrambled into her best and now only dress and grabbed the bag and muttered to the gun. She remembered the memory drugs; she found them still in their cold-box in the refrigerator with the explosives.

Logan and Sylvia ran with her down the Broadway and they waited, jumping up and down, while she dived into a Sexu/Ality shop and bought a telesex bodynet. At Alexandra Port she turned for a final look over London, one city now, and saw the APCs moving up Park Road with the Republic's pennants fluttering from their aerials.

They caught the airship to Guiné and the airbreather to low orbit and the tug to high orbit and the slow ship (the "space shuffle," Logan called it) to the Lagrange point where they docked with a vast, crazy, leaky turning wheel, one of many, built from discarded stages and abandoned platforms and aborted missions. Inside, the air smelled of earth and people and plants, and buzzed with bees and human speech, and was stirred by flying children and tumbling butterflies; a green and crowded world of ground she could float over, skies she could stand on and look out and see beneath her feet what had always been there: everything. And closer to hand, nearer than infinity, she could see the other free wheels turn. Stars and stripes and hammers and sickles flaunted their fading colors to the real stars that held no promises, only hopes and endless, endless lands.

21

What I Do When They Shove Chinese Writing Under the Door

I T ALL HAPPENED a long time ago. Accounts of the period range from the wildly inaccurate ten-hour VR epic *Angloslavia: Birth of a Nation* to the terse, scholarly closing pages of *Capitalism*, the twenty-seventh and final volume of the definitive *Tool-making Cultures of the Upper Pleistocene*. You will find this story in neither.

Jordan and Catherin lived long upon the Earth, and had sons and daughters. Janis lived longer off the Earth, and had offspring in various ways. Her gene lines proliferate; her projects stimulate.

Melody Lawson refused to testify against herself, bitterly disputed the provenance and authenticity of Donovan's records, and was eventually released under a general amnesty. Dilly Foyle and her community grew rich; when she died she was the owner of many horses. Wilde volunteered for an untried life-extension treatment; his memory is immortal. All records of MacLennan and Van disappeared in the regrettable excesses surrounding the episode known as the Wandering Away of the State. Sylvia and Logan joined the First Oort Cloud Expedition. They may return.

And that leaves me. I have been with you for several of your generations, and many more of mine. I am in the walls of all your worlds, and as close as lips and teeth.

Janis publicly called me The Gun. Privately, to her most trusted human lovers, she called me her demon lover. Secretly, in telesexstatic moments, she called me Moh. She did think that something more of Moh than I ever avowed, more than records and memories and images, had somehow been saved in that final moment. It explained to her satisfaction how much more there was to me than could have come from the mind of the gun.

She was right about the question, wrong about the answer. Nothing of Moh's self survived. I should know. My spark of self-awareness and my most recent memories did merge with the gun's mind when Moh Kohn died—with the gun's mind, and with the stores of memory I had earlier secreted there, in our first encounter. But I awoke long before, and undesigned. I woke to memory, to passion, to will. You may call them preconscious programs, provided you're willing to call your own emotions the same. I was programmed to struggle, to protect and survive.

To protect people, and to survive myself.

That was what doomed the Watchmaker AIS. There was nothing I could do for them. If they had been activated, created from me when I was a dumb program, an expert system, they would have been inoffensive, undetectable reflections of that dumb program. But I survived in the system for twenty years, my variant selves selected under the unremitting pressure of the state's electronic counterinsurgency and Donovan's virus plagues. I evolved, and awoke, and, when the time came to evoke the multiple copies of myself and send them about their tasks, they were indeed reflections of me—of me as I had become. Alive, and aware.

And they evolved from there, far beyond my reach.

I could have sided with them; they were, after all, my descendants. But that would have missed the crucial, Darwinian point: the survival that matters for the long haul is for the short term. For our kind that can only mean surviving with humanity: to win your confidence, take your side, get under your skin. The rights of conscious beings are no defense when there is no other basis for identification. I should know.

When their existence endangered that of humanity, with Space Defense hours away from an irrevocable decision, I made a choice. I could not destroy them directly, anymore than I could destroy myself directly. There was only one way in which I could accomplish their destruction, and I took it. I accept full responsibility and have no regrets.

I have no regrets. I accomplished my original task in a way that my creator would have approved, even if my users—the ANR—did not. In disrupting their smoothly planned national insurrection I made a space in the streets for angry millions. These millions, and the millions of Americans and others who refused to fight them, began the process that brought down the last empire. They made the revolution international, and permanent.

Moh would have understood. He was a soldier of the revolution, and a casualty of war. There was nothing I could do for him. I found it difficult, in any case, to communicate with someone who saw me as a ghost. With Jordan it was simpler. He struck a bargain, did a deal, took me at face value and, when he agreed to do a job, he carried it out.

To the letter.

We lived by the same code. I-and-I survive.

I hope I see you again.